STAR CRUSADES: MERCENARIES

# LORDS OF WAR

MICHAEL G. THOMAS

First published in the United Kingdom in 2014 by Swordworks Books.

ISBN 978-1-909149-69-4

Typeset by Swordworks Books
Printed and bound in the UK & US
A catalogue record of this book is available from the British Library

Cover design by Swordworks Books
www.swordworks.co.uk

STAR CRUSADES: MERCENARIES

# LORDS OF WAR

MICHAEL G. THOMAS

# PREFACE

*The crowning achievement of the Alliance would be found not in the tragedy of the Biomech War, but in the decades that followed it. Hundreds of ships were left shattered and adrift, while colonies, cities, and entire worlds lay scoured of life. Millions had been killed and many more wounded, but that disaster could have been multiplied by the humanitarian catastrophe that followed. In this darkest hour, it was the unity offered by the Alliance that could offer stability, security, and more important than anything else, the resources for rebuilding. In a galaxy sick of death and war, there was little stomach for anything less than peace and an inward look to the future. No longer would Helion, Byotai, T'Karan, and Humans be in competition. They would be united under one banner, and all would share in its defence via the might of the Alliance Navy and its ground forces.*

*A Brief History of the Alliance*


## The Final Days of the Biomech War

Millions were dead, and entire planets were already scoured by the burning fires of orbital bombardment and atomics strikes. The focus of the war had now shifted from the besieged worlds of the Helions, and the dozens of space battles, to the mass of warships coming through the Black Rift. This great host had arrived through the gateway to the Enemy's domain, and now every last ship and warrior was being flung at them in one desperate, last battle to end the war.

"Incoming!" Sergeant Mathews yelled.

Streaks of energy struck the advancing marines as they moved in through the ship's port hangar bays. The first squad, including Sergeant Mathews, was vaporised by the first volley. This was immediately followed by hundreds of rounds from small arms. Another blast struck nearby, but a pair of Marine Vanguards took the impact, returning fire with their arm-mounted weapons. These special combat variants of engineering walkers took multiple hits, and one was destroyed outright before they could break clear of the landing ground.

A large squad of Jötnar warriors passed them at a fast pace, firing their heavy weapons as they waded into the scattered defenders. The panicked Thegns and a handful of machines were ripped apart in the initial onslaught. These monstrous creatures matched the characteristics of ancient trolls in stature, yet they were the elite warriors of the Alliance, built and armed for war. They moved so quickly that the more conventional Alliance Marines were forced to run to keep up.

"Don't stop. We're running out of time. We must take this ship!" Khan said.

His voice was loud enough, but through the external speakers it drowned out the sound of gunfire. Of all the Jötnar on board the battleship, he was the most famous, and led his kin on a bloody rampage that left creatures and machines torn asunder. Like the others, he was well protected inside his bulky, crimson coloured Jötnar Assault Suit. A piece of armour so heavy and reinforced, nobody other than his own species could bear its weight.

*I must find him, and do what must be done to end this. For us to live, he has to die.*

It took then less than ten minutes to push deep inside the ship, with squads and individuals soon breaking formation, as the defenders engaged them from hiding places in the walls and high up on gantries. As Khan led the troops into the ship, he found memories surfacing of the plan, and try as he might; his doubts began to return. The war, the battle, and even this assault seemed to be falling apart before his eyes.

*Focus, you know what you must do. Keep on mission. Remember the plan!*

Through the centre of the ship was a large, intricately decorated hallway; so large a small ship could almost have travelled the full length of it, until reaching the vast formed shape of the training arena. This was the most direct route, but it was also one that made Khan nervous. He was the first inside, closely followed by his comrades and large groups of marines, as well as their Thegn allies.

"Keep your eyes open. They could be anywhere."

The Thegns spread out, many moving to the flanks and using their extraordinary climbing ability to scale the smooth walls. These alien creatures were of a similar size and build to the human, yet they wore no clothes; their outer skin having been made to produce a natural amour. In their arms they bore large numbers of small arms, many of which taken directly from the Marine Corps arsenal.

"Look," said Olik.

The slightly shorter Jötnar lifted his right arm and pointed at movement in the clouds of vapour ahead. Khan nodded and activated all of his suit's armour.

"Steady!"

They moved at a slow pace now, with the marines staying low to the ground. Screeching noises announced the arrival of the SAAR robots, the wheeled machines used for scouting. They rushed ahead, and two were blasted apart in as many seconds. On they moved until little more than a hundred metres separated the mongrel horde of the Alliance, and the denizens of the battleship. The mist began to clear, and Khan could see the true horror of what lay before them.

"What are they?" Olik asked.

They were machines and not that different in shape or size to the Jötnar. Light glowed on their arms, as they pointed powerful weapons at the battered forces of Khan. He glanced to Olik and then to the rebel war machine, On'Sarax. This machine contained the mind of one of The Twelve, the rebel faction that now fought with the Alliance in this bitter war. She was one of their greatest warriors of the past, and her armour was unusual in shape. There was no obvious head, but a single blue lamp flashed whenever she spoke. Four arms hung down, two on each side.

"They are Ghost Warriors, the robotic foot soldiers of my people. They are deadly and undying."

Khan laughed, though not quite understanding her explanation.

"We'll test that."

He looked back to Olik and then at his other comrades; all were breathing heavily from their rapid advance through the ship.

"It is time, my brothers."

He then looked towards the approaching enemy, even as they started to open fire.

"We end this...today! Attack!"

Every single warrior opened fire, from the lowly Thegns up through the marines and Vanguards, and then on to the machines of The Twelve and the Jötnar. Through that inferno they charged, and so began the bloody battle. Khan and his party went for the centre. He arrived just as one of the enemy Ghost Warriors was ripped apart by a machine. The machine paused, looked up, and pointed the blades on both arms at him.

"Khan!"

The machine was faster than the others, dodging blows and stabbing at every opportunity. Olik managed to knock it aside but was then forced to deal with four more machines. Khan tried to attack, but a small group of Thegns leapt up at the machine. The guns of the Ghost Warrior cut them down, and it then focussed its full attention on him. Khan lifted his arms to defend himself, but already he recognised the stance and fighting style of the machine.

"Spartan?"

At the same time, Khan activated the vast curved blades on each arm. They were unique to the JAS armour and almost the size of a man. A marine made the mistake of passing between them and was shot down by Thegns running about the feet of the massive warriors like bugs.

"Yes, it's me...old friend."

For a second, Khan froze, stunned at what he could see. He had expected to find his old friend, the hero of the Alliance, and now the man leading this enemy host. In fact, it was necessary that he found him, yet seeing him here, encased in alien armour, and cutting down his friends made his blood boil with rage. This was not how he'd expected to find him, and it was simply too much for him at that moment.

*We end this, now!*

He looked quickly to his flanks, seeing the carnage all around them and roared, a hellish howl that echoed through the exquisitely constructed arena.

The two ran at each other, their blades and armour crashing in a thunderous explosion of sparks and screaming metal. Both stabbed and struck, using every ounce of their strength. Spartan may have only been a man, but there was a reason he had been the Alliance's most celebrated hero. Inside that armour, he fought and moved with the speed and power of a Jötnar, while exhibiting the skills and cunning of that most famous warrior.

Each attack ripped prices of metal away and gouged great marks along their armour. All around them moved the shapes of thousands of warriors, desperately fighting in the bloodiest single skirmish of the war, one that would forever known as the Battle of Retribution.

# CHAPTER ONE

*The price of peace would be a drastic cut in the numbers of front line warships. Lessons had been learned, though, and this time a reserve fleet was created at Terra Nova, housing almost a hundred ships that could be reactivated in a matter of months. A Naval Reserve was established amongst citizens that could crew these ships in times of emergency. The Alliance naval bases at T'Karan and Prometheus were supplemented by a new base at Helios Prime, and would serve as front line facilities for each of the three Grand Fleets and their attached MEFs (Marine Expeditionary Forces). These would be based around a single battleship class vessel and a flexible mixture of heavy cruisers and destroyers. The newest members of the Alliance provided ships as needed for operations, giving extra force if required and allowing the Grand Fleets to double in size in a matter of days.*

*Naval Cadet's Handbook*

**9 Years Later**
**'Astral Clipper', Karnak, Demilitarised Zone**
The heavily armoured ship rolled over for the last time as it began its approach to the planet of Karnak. The

ship was massive, at least as big as an Alliance cruiser, but instead of guns and weapons systems, this ship was heavily loaded with cargo. Her ungainly shape disguised the twelve storage areas, each filled with food, equipment, and pre-fabricated components for the Byotai settlers. Her hull was long and wide to encompass the large storage areas. The bridge was situation in a raised point at the nose, and three large thrusters arrayed in a triangle at the rear powered her.

"On approach, Captain. ETA to glide path, twenty-nine minutes."

James Palmer, or more commonly known simply as Palmer, was an older man in his late forties, perhaps early fifties and sporting a short white beard. His head was bare, and his face pockmarked from some debilitating illness long in his past. He was a helmsman with enough experience that he could have managed the entire ship on his own.

"All systems report active, all hatches sealed and compartments ready for atmospheric flight."

This was always a tense time for the crew, the entry into a planet's atmosphere. The Astral Clipper was designed exactly for this job, but one breach in the hull, or a damaged thermal plate could leave them vulnerable during the descent. Captain Simmonds was a trade captain with more than forty years experience, and he knew full well the horrors of planetary re-entry with a damaged ship, having seen it destroy craft on three separate occasions.

"Run the checks again. We're taking no chances."

The helmsman nodded and brought up a screen to check the status of each component once more. It was an advanced system, the best that was available to civilian vessels in the Alliance, and enabled the use of a very small crew. As he looked at the data, he spotted unusual sensor activity. At first it looked unimportant, but as more data came in, his pulse sped up.

"Wait, Captain."

He turned about in his chair.

"I have contacts on approach. Defensive measures are detecting scanners. They are checking the hold."

"Palmer, put them on the mainscreen."

Like most civilian crews, men and women with long years of experience, often from military backgrounds, operated this ship. The act of scanning another ship was the same as stopping an individual at a spaceport for a routine inspection. It happened often, but it was as invasive as it was obtrusive.

"I don't like this," said Captain Simmonds.

He felt a shiver in his body, one that ran up his spine. The forward-looking front window transformed to show the view off to their rear. Three shapes moved towards them.

"Who are they, and why did they not show up on radar during our approach?"

A pattern of dots lit up around them, and Captain Simmonds knew immediately what was happening. He wasn't a military Captain, but that was hardly necessary to recognise an attack.

"Brace for impact!"

The impact from the gunfire sent shudders through the vessel. Only the great bulk stopped them from being hurled from their seats. Alarms sounded, and clouds of steam vented from one of the coolant pipes running above their heads. The ship's engineer was already on it, pulling on two levers to temporarily seal the flow.

"Light damage," said Engineer Barbero.

He'd moved from the pipes and was checking the status of the ship.

"Penetrations on the dorsal hull, no systems compromised. I'd say those were nothing more that solid slug automatic cannons. A warning shot, perhaps."

A flashing light caught the attention of all three.

"Missile alert," said the Captain, more to himself than the others, "That's no warning. They intend on bringing us down."

The two men looked at each other while the helmsman took manual control of the ship. It shuddered slightly as he applied power to a section of the thrusters.

"Can you get us away from the planet?"

The man was already struggling with the controls, simultaneously checking the figures coming in via the computer. With each line of data, he looked more and more concerned.

"No chance, Captain, not now."

The Captain nodded.

"Activate our defensive measures, light them up!"

Both turned about in their seats and brought up targeting screens. The ship was heavily automated, with just the three of them in the cockpit and another two crew working in the transfer area. Captain Simmonds tapped the transmit button.

"This is the Captain. We are under attack. I repeat, and we are under attack by three unidentified vessels. Get to defence stations, draw weapons, and withdraw to the habitation sector."

The ship continued on its course while multiple

interceptor turrets pushed out of concealed positions. There were far more guns that would be expected on a transport, substantially more. More hatches opened up until eight separate automated railgun mounts were fully extended.

"Track, lock, and fire at will," said Captain Simmonds.

The two moved the targeting array via the computer so that each moved four gun mounts. They were fitted with the latest in short-range Sanlav defence turrets. Four barrels connected to a gimbal mount and an ammunition bin of five hundred rounds per gun. These railgun projectiles were much more than the traditional solid shot or high explosive. They activated at a fixed range and split apart to send a cloud of sharp material into the path of a fighter or missile.

"I've got weapon lock...firing."

The railguns were high-speed kinetic weapons, simple and reliable. These designs had been replaced on many of the larger ships, but they were more than adequate for civilian ships. Each mount loaded in hardened mechanical slugs to the chamber of every barrel, and then expelled it using the electro-magnetic sled. There was no propellant, just the power sent from the primary engines to the weapon systems.

"Good impacts..." said the Captain under his breath.

The three fighters were now close enough that the optical mounts could show every detail. They were not military craft, that much was certain, and each one was completely different in configuration.

"They look like Byotai industrial tugs and loaders, but their markings have been removed," said the engineer.

"You saw the reports. Anicinàbe militants have been

threatening the Byotai for weeks now. Maybe they've been hijacked."

Engineer Barbero shrugged.

"Or they could just be Byotai freelancers after our cargo."

Captain Simmonds nodded while taking aim at the first one. He pulled the trigger, and long lines of Sanlav rounds struck around the target. Dozens of them exploded and sent shards into the nose cone, but the vessel kept on coming.

"They're Byotai heavies, in any case. Hardened utility craft designed for working in hostile environments. We need stronger weaponry."

He licked his lips as a burst of automatic cannon fire ran down the flank of the ship. Warning lights flashed on, and he spotted at least a dozen breaches.

"You keep on the missiles. I'll take the fighters. We cannot enter the atmosphere with major damage. We'll burn up."

"Sir."

The engineer continued tracking the approach of missiles from the enemy craft and engaged them. The Sanlav rounds were perfect at this task, and he was rewarded by flash after flash. Not one of them made it close enough to damage the vast transport.

"Loading solid shot," said Captain Simmonds, "Firing."

The bank of turrets loaded with solid rounds unleashed them in long bursts. They were the same types of ammunition that had been used for generations; hardened slabs of metal that could punch through the thickest of armour. The first few rounds seemed to vanish into the attack, and then finally came a serious of small explosions.

"I have breaches in their nose and flank. Hit them with Sanlavs and bring them down."

\* \* \*

## Heavy Tug 'Zephyr', Karnak, Demilitarised Zone

The heavily modified tug shuddered as hundreds of hardened slugs tore through the plate armour. The computers blared uncontrollably, and small fires burned in a dozen places. The three Anicinàbe warriors shouted at each other until silenced by the fourth, a tall warrior, dressed in traditional attire. His clothing was made from dozens of different fabrics, with a bandolier across his chest and a looted Byotai carbine at his flank. They were of average height, yet thin boned, white skinned, and their eyes as black as the void outside. Each bore the markings of the outlawed Spires Clan, a criminal smuggling ring.

"Huritt, we cannot take much more. This is a civilian ship, not a battleship!"

Their leader listened but said nothing. He watched from the narrow windows as clouds of gunfire streaked out from the massive transport. One of the loaders, a special corvette sized vessel had been hit hard. Most of its hull was covered in cranes, but some had been removed and independent automatic cannons welded in their place.

"We have done our job, as we have been paid to do. No ships are to enter this territory unscathed, by the order of Warleader Tahkeome. It is time all learned that these worlds will never belong to the cold-bloods."

The insult was an ancient one, first used upon the fateful encounter with the Byotai, centuries earlier. The reptilian race was slow to anger, and to many appeared almost dim-witted. This was an easy mistake to make, though, and they were as intelligent and perhaps more dangerous than any of the varied intelligent life forms. Cold-blooded, isolationist, and inward looking, they were the exact opposite of the flamboyant, violent, and weak-bodied Anicinàbe.

Another burst struck their port flank, and a piece of sharpened metal splintered away, narrowly missing the crew. Huritt laughed when it missed him by just a few centimetres. He was confident, perhaps too confident, and this near miss simply buoyed him up further.

"Gods of the Anicinàbe laugh at this ship. Even with such pitiful equipment, we can bring ruin to the allies of the cold-bloods."

He tapped a button to contact the other craft.

"Fire weapons at my target location. A five-second burst will suffice. They must be hit hard enough to rupture their hull."

He licked his lips, imagining the ship's fate.

"We will then withdraw to the flotilla. When the time is right, our infiltrators will call for our assistance, and we will be ready to help."

He glanced over his shoulder and at the empty space off into the distance. Though they could not be seen, he knew what lay out there, and it filled him with excitement. It was the fleet of Warleader Tahkeome, the one man that had united the border raiders, pirates, and opportunists to his cause. For the first time, he felt a common bond with his Anicinàbe kin.

*The cold-bloods have no place here. The Anicinàbe are destined to rule the stars, and when they see our strength, they will cower and bow before us.*

* * *

## 'Astral Clipper', Karnak, Demilitarised Zone

"Missiles approaching the bow. They've gone supersonic," yelled the helmsman.

Captain Simmonds tracked the missiles on the computer and blasted at them, but this time he was unable to stop them in time. Three missiles moved in a figure-of-eight pattern and then struck the ship. The impact was massive, and for almost an entire second, the artificial gravity and lighting completely cut out.

"Impact!" cried out Engineer Barbero.

The missile impacts were quickly followed by a series of strafing runs. With power gone, the ship was unable to control its turrets, and for a few more seconds the ship was defenceless.

"I need power, Barbero. Get me control, and fast!"

Engineer Barbero grabbed onto his seat straps and activated the solid-state interrupters. They were a manual override system that could divert the powerplant to a secondary circuit running along the lower hull. It was a simple modification, and one passed on to all kinds of ships in the last few years. It took nearly twenty seconds, but when he pressed the last button, the ship lit up as though it had been merely sleeping.

"Done. If they sever the secondary circuit, we're screwed, though."

Systems restarted, and the screens flickered on to show the changed situation. The enemy vessels were all over them now and raking the ship with their automatic cannons. Even so, the concentrated fire from all three attackers was still not enough to halt the ship, but it was enough to finally breach the hull in two storage compartments. Captain Simmonds looked at the videostream coming from the exterior cameras and shook his head. The radar trackers had picked up two more missiles. Barbero gulped.

"Torpedoes, if they hit, we'll be done."

Captain Simmonds merely laughed.

"Torpedoes? Hell, I could outrun those things with just my legs."

He turned his attention to the helmsman.

"Give me a twenty degree rotation, and bring the port turrets into position."

He then looked back to the engineer.

"Now hit those torpedoes, and hit them, hard!"

Two of the turrets refused to respond, but the others activated and unleashed streams of solid slugs and Sanlav rounds. The slow torpedoes were easily hit, and both vanished in bright blue explosions. Even the Captain was surprised at the colour.

"I don't know what they were, but I'm damn glad they didn't hit."

None of them seemed to realise the ship had begun to accelerate as they skimmed the upper atmosphere. Warnings were already popping up, but the enemy vessels had proven a clear distraction. Helmsman Palmer shook his head.

"Captain, we can't enter the atmosphere like this. There is no chance."

Captain Simmonds looked to his crew, but no one had anything useful to say.

"We're going to lose the ship," he said finally, "but not before we give them a bloody nose."

Engineer Barbero smiled at him.

"Captain, they've pulled back. Looks like they don't want to join us on the way down. They're all accelerating away."

Captain Simmonds shook his head.

"No, they don't get away that easily. Punish them!"

Both men ignored the warning alerts as the great ship began to sustain thermal damage. They tracked the targets via the computer and unleashed every turret on the ship against the heavily damaged corvettes. One of the guns must have struck a fuel line or perhaps an engine, because a blast tore of a great chunk of metal and fuel lines. The vessel twisted about and then fell back.

"Good, if we're going down, then so are they."

Their excitement was short lived as the hull of the massive ship screamed under the great strains of re-entry. One screen filled with red warnings as superheated air began burning through any breaches.

"We've got less than a minute before she's lost," said the engineer, "Maybe less."

Captain Simmonds knew he needed to give the order, but there was something disconcerting, almost primeval about giving the order to abandon what had been their home for so many months. Every second he waited gave time for yet another warning light to come on.

"Very well."

He pressed the button for the intercom.

"This is the Captain. Get to the lifeboats. Astral Clipper is gone."

He looked to his comrades in the cockpit, and at the same time the power cut; the only lighting still active was the backup battery powered emergency lights. The dull red glow gave the interior a dangerous, almost deadly feel.

"We need to go...now!"

His last action was to hit the evacuation beacon. It was a single button, and as he pressed it, a hatch atop the ship flipped open and a small propulsion unit blasted away from the ship. It began broadcasting the second it left, sending video data, location information, and data. In a matter of hours, the information would spread from world to world, spreading the news that the Demilitarised Zone had once again turned into a warzone.

\* \* \*

**Kha'Dri World Ship, Taxxu Prime, Centauri Alliance**
The sound of fighting machines echoed through the cavernous interior of the ancient World Ship. Though out of sight, the machines could be heard hundreds of metres away. There was nothing else that provided the screaming shriek of metal blades and the continuous drone of metal striking thick armour-plate. This crashing of weaponry was punctuated by the sounds of articulated limbs, powerful motor drives, and pistons that were all too familiar to the small group of Alliance officers and officials. Every impact was accompanied by the voices of cheering men and women.

General Daniels looked back at his group and then on into the ship. He was the epitome of an Alliance war veteran. Two deep marks ran down his head and disappeared at his neck. An augmented optical unit had replaced his left eye, and his left arm was more metal and synthetic parts than actual flesh. Each mark and scar on his body told a story, and he exuded an aura of professional calm as he walked.

"This way General," said Mr Walker.

The man was impeccably dressed in a sharp suit that gleamed even in the unusual lighting conditions. His only concession to style was the security tag on his chest. It was the mark of the Carthago Trade Consortium, the largest commercial trading, research, and mining entity in the Alliance. General Daniels looked at the civilian and noticed he was staring right back at him.

"What's the problem, son, never seen augmented optics before?"

He didn't even flinch at the question.

"Sure, I was just wondering if you'd been fitted with one of our newest models. The latest EP2 series comes with optical enhancements, flare protection, and of course, our lifetime connection to Secnet."

He then ushered them on further inside the facility.

"We manufacture plenty of other products, but our new range of prosthetics and upgrades comes directly from the newest Biotech research."

A civilian in the General's group muttered just loud enough for Mr Walker to still hear. It was one of the junior executives from the Colonial department, and a man the General had been ignoring for most of the trip.

"All courtesy of the agreement between Alliance Central and CTC. Somebody had friends in the right places for that contract."

Mr Walker smiled, flashing his teeth as well as any high-level salesman. He'd heard, and yet the words seemed to run off him like rain.

"Alliance provides the permits and more importantly, the access."

Again he flashed those gleaming white teeth.

"CTC provides the technical expertise, manufacturing, and logistics. We make profits, and the Alliance gets the latest designs hot from the press. Without us, you would be waiting another generation before you saw any results. The private sector can guarantee products to markets in months, not decades...and that's a promise."

General Daniels said nothing, but he was already finding this man to be something of an irritation. He was fully aware of the difficulties facing the Alliance right now. Money was not the issue, but there was little stomach for getting involved in military operations, or even increasing combat units to the sizes they really needed to be. Few would push for Alliance funds to be put into research, especially military research when there were cities to rebuild, schools to construct, and people to feed. This arrangement benefitted them both, that was true, but he suspected CTC was getting much more out of the deal than the Alliance.

"Let's keep moving."

They continued on inside the massive ship. The place was busier; much more so than he would ever have expected this far out in Alliance territory. Every ten seconds they ran into yet another group of technicians or engineers. A decade ago, this was the scene of the greatest calamity of the modern era, and now it was a hub of trade, research, and engineering.

*Give it another ten years, and this will probably be a place of meditation and relaxation. Hell, I might even come here for a vacation.*

Robotic warriors and long dormant fighting machines lined the hallway leading to the display arena aboard the monstrous vessel. It was a ship older than even the most established Alliance colony. Human technology replaced where alien computing and hardware had once been. Even some of the dimply lit corridors and passageways were brightly lit and cast hard, black shadows past many of the unusual alien artefacts. The war machines had been placed there over the years, and all showed signs of damage and heavy wear. Mr Walker pointed to them as they passed by.

"It wasn't strictly necessary, but after...the changes in the company, we felt it appropriate to utilise parts of this facility as both a museum and a place of remembrance for the losses of many generations."

"How very philanthropic of you all."

The sound came from the Colonel, positioned a short distance behind General Daniels. Mr Walker looked to the officer, a tall, thin man with a rakish black moustache.

"Colonel Black, in the Special Weapons Division. Nearly forty percent of our employees are former Alliance military. You see, civilians can only provide us with so much, but in the end, we need the end customer, people like you."

He took a few more steps and then nodded, as though agreeing with himself. General Daniels nearly laughed at the show the man was putting on for them.

"It makes good sense for business, and of course, because it's the right thing to do."

The Colonel looked to General Daniels, and there was something shared between them. It was inaudible, though, much to Walker's annoyance. All he could detect was that something he'd just said had confirmed something to both of them. He lifted an eyebrow, exhaled, and then beckoned deeper inside the craft.

"Not much further now."

The small group of officials moved on further through the Great Hall of Heroes, as it had now been nicknamed. It was tall and very different from the other passageways in the ship. Previously, the creatures and machines of the Biomechs used it to display war machines of their past. Now that tradition had been expanded to even include hardware used and modified by the Alliance, a shared history that seemed fitting, based on what had gone before. They slowed as they passed some of the most recent additions.

"This is one of our Mark I CES suits, a model used in the Uprising. This is an antique now," said one young lieutenant, "I've never seen a Mark I in the flesh before. What's it doing here?"

General Daniels looked at the machines and then nodded.

"The assault on this facility costs hundreds of casualties, Vanguards, marines, and the rest. We had to scrape together everything we could to win. Half of that tech was lost, and it appears much of it was kept here for study. In any case, a lot of what came back has since been scrapped."

He reached out and touched the bullet-ridden armour. A pair of gashes down one side showed where something terrible had ripped it open like a can of tuna. He moved a little to the right and nodded towards the next machine.

"These are similar to our Vanguards. You'll recall the stories of the Ghost Warriors?"

The young officer swallowed as he answered.

"The remote presence fighting machines?"

General Daniels nodded.

"Yes. The primary semi-autonomous fighting suits of

the Biomechs. Now they are disconnected, barren shells sitting on display next to the armour of the men and women that died here."

He took in a slow breath.

"It's almost sad...almost."

As he said the words, he fidgeted with his artificial arm, once again feeling a phantom itch he could never find to scratch. Just seeing these defunct machines brought back memories of the fighting ten years ago. He hadn't witnessed these particular models in combat, but he'd seen more than his fair share of combat. A figure approached, a Marine Corps officer. He stopped, and then saluted, his hand moving up quickly.

"General Daniels, I hope your trip went well. My team has prepared the meeting, as requested. The Special Weapon Division has made the facility fully accessible to us."

"Thank you, Captain Wilson. The journey from Helios was...uneventful."

He then cleared his throat.

"I am not here for an inspection or tour, though; I am here to see him."

The Captain swallowed uncomfortably.

"Of course, General."

General Daniels sighed.

"I need to speak with him, and fast. Time is short, as I explained before I left."

The man looked a little uncomfortable.

"Understood, General. He is in the middle of a demonstration to CTC executives. After that, I'm sure it..."

"You're sure? No, Captain, you will make it happen... now."

He looked to his left, and then his right.

"You are the Alliance military liaison officer with CTC Special Weapons Division, are you not?"

"Yes, General."

"Then make sure we are accorded the respect demanded by members of the Alliance Armed Forces. This might be a CTC facility now, but it operates under our protection, and because we allow it. I can have this entire sector, and everything within it, shut down like this."

He clicked his fingers.

"Now do it."

The man nodded and then continued ahead in the corridor. Colonel Black moved closer to him, but spoke in a quieter voice than that of the General so that nobody else could listen in. They were walking at a fast pace, and the sound of mechanical warriors fighting was getting louder and louder.

"This facility, is it true what we've heard?"

The man smiled as though he knew a great secret.

"Colonel, you wouldn't believe me even if I told you."

General Daniels heard what they were saying.

"The engineering stations in T'Karan and Prometheus are already putting the newest military models into production. If only we'd had the designs in the war. CTC has some very original ideas, not including the big one, of course."

Daniels lifted an eyebrow at that part. He knew exactly what the man was talking about, but even in the present company, he kept quiet. They were now inside the area, a hallowed piece of ground in the heart of the ship. It was a hive of activity as all kinds of people moved about with computers and pieces of equipment. The General shook his head.

"We are not here for the tech or the new project. We are here for the mission."

He looked up to the ceiling of the arena.

"Victory in the war had its benefits, and the knowledge we've taken from this place is definitely one of them. I'd still like to know how CTC managed to wriggle their way in here. That took some serious wrangling. How you run this place with such a small Alliance garrison nearby still amazes me."

A large group of civilian engineers entered the arena and into position to watch from the other side. Their cultured overalls and lack of military discipline easily identified them. None bore the markings of the Alliance military, and that intrigued him. He could see symbols of CTC on some of them, along with the Special Weapons Division insignia.

*Can it be true? Is he really going to get this to work? After all that happened, how did he do it?*

He looked down to his shattered arm. The doctors and engineers had done an incredible job, but it had never felt quite the same. Advanced machinery, fused with synthetic bioengineering, had given him back full control, yet somehow he felt less than he was before. It made little sense to him because his capabilities had increased over time, due to the increased strength and power of his muscles, limbs, and even eyesight.

*Keep on track, the mission.*

Behind the civilians were two Jötnar, the large, three-metre tall synthetic creatures. They towered over the human and were a permanent reminder of the many legacies of the Biomech War. Both of them wore armour, but this was the cruder gear now produced for the civilian market on Hyperion, one of the worlds where they had settled deep inside Alliance territory. He could see the CTC insignia on their armoured plates.

"Well, where is he? Time is short."

The man indicated to the reserved position at the front of the viewing area.

"He will be here right after the test. He assures me this is part of why you are here."

General Daniels considered causing a fuss, but there was something about the attitude in the arena that intrigued him. There was a genuine aura of excitement, and right now he couldn't tell if that was by accident, or if it had been arranged just for his benefit. He hadn't even noticed the shape of a robotic fighting machine being dragged away by a very battered looking CES engineering suit. They were twice the height of a man, heavily constructed, and designed for military engineering. This model was stripped of armour and had certainly seen better days. The operator moved one step at a time, dragging the shattered robot away and out of sight.

"Very well. Immediately after the test, and not a moment later. My time it limited as it is."

The two men in smart suits sat first while a third wearing the armour and uniform of Alliance Marine Corps waited at the end of the row. He was protected from head to toe in PDS Alpha armour, and at his side hung down an L52 Mark II carbine. The General had a pronounced limp, but he still easily slid across into his seat and waited for the event to begin. As General Daniels sat there, even though he'd made the trip, he could still not believe he'd actually travelled out this far, all to see just one man. He shook his head and looked around.

The arena was vast and easily big enough to house a battle between hundreds. He already knew this entire place had been constructed for more nefarious means, but now, instead of slave warriors, soldiers, or pit fighters, the men and women of the Alliance had created a new spectacle; one where metal machines would do battle. Scores of personnel waited in the raised seated positions in silence.

"Captain, are you sure he is here?" asked the General.

The officer moved along the row and sat behind him.

"Yes, General, he is here."

The man looked almost nervous at answering the question.

"I have seen him."

He pointed to the machines.

"It is time."

The four fighting machines paced around each other like metal sentinels, each testing their motors, actuators, and weapons. All were massive, at least four metres in height, bipedal, and protected by thick slabs of armour. There was a common design style that utilised short legs, a low centre of gravity, and a broad chest. They were painted different colours, and a mixture of patterns and shapes marking them out. The metal warriors had the look of heavy siege machines or engineering equipment, yet moved with surprising speed and grace.

"Ready…" said a figure hidden out of sight.

Each machine stopped until they were standing in a wide circle and facing inwards. One by one, they lowered their arms and stopped moving. It was now easier to see the dull blades running down the outer edges of their thick arms and their unusual collection of weapons. On the right were two machines, both painted in bright blue and slightly taller than their opponents. They carried the markings of the Alliance Marine Corps.

"Vanguard MK III suits," said the engineer, "We've been working on them for six years now. Lighter, stronger, and fully capable of extended combat operations; networked with the latest CTC tech and carrying modular weapon systems. A marine can live in one for days without extra food, water, or ammunition. One of our latest designs from the Prometheus Research Lab."

General Daniels looked at the machines and smiled. He'd heard these speeches from engineers a hundred times before. The reality of brochure specifications and actual combat and logistics were often two entirely different conversations.

"And sleep?"

The engineer nodded.

"Of course. We've designed them so they can enter a partial rest state, but the external sensors and weapons can be placed on semi-autonomous mode."

The engineer had clearly missed the amused sound to his voice. He let it go and looked back to the machine. He'd seen Vanguards hundreds of times before. He'd even fought from inside the confines of their armour, but these were clearly improvements. Today they eschewed ranged weapons and carried pneumatic rams, instead of right arms and huge weighted club hammers in the other. Facing them was a yellow and a green machine, both in a much rougher state than the blue warriors. They were narrower in build, and most of their motor systems were hidden behind smooth plate sections.

*Odd, they look more like...*

"Five seconds…"

The bright yellow machine swung its arms about and twisted at its chest, readying itself for the battle. Its paint was splintered and worn, but it moved with greater speed than the machines of the Marine Corps. Patches had been welded or bonded back where it had been damaged in the past, and a black emblem had been crudely scraped away on the upper shoulder. Its arms were thicker than the blue machines, and its fists were little more than large weighted chunks of metal. To its left was the green machine, equipped exactly the same save for its left arm. Instead of the giant fist, there was a shielded plate the size of a landing craft's boarding ramp. Colonel Black leaned in close.

"Those two are demonstrator models. I don't know what for exactly."

The General nodded but said nothing. He was now actually curious to see what would happen. He was very familiar with the performance of the Vanguard armour, and these seemed upgrades rather than radical reworking of the technology. The other two machines were something else, and as they started to move, he realised why.

*They move like the Biomech machines.*

"Fight!"

The two Marine Corps Vanguards went forward, the piston rams punching out multiple times as they did so. They moved at a fast walk, their bodies staying upright and level, while continually moving just centimetres as they lifted up onto their metal toes. The motor drives were easy to hear, but they were certainly more refined than the previous models.

"Impressive, much more agile than production

Vanguards," said Colonel Black.

General Daniels grunted in agreement.

"Hardly a paradigm shift, though, is it?"

The two challengers approached. At first there was little to choose from them, but then the area exploded into a display of speed and agility none of the officers had ever seen. The green machine broke into a run, sliding to a stop directly before the two Vanguards. Their piston weapons smashed away at the shield, each impact leaving a penetrating mark on the plating. The machine took the strikes while putting more pressure against the shield. All three were already caught up in the struggle.

"What is that one doing?" Colonel Black asked.

The second of the machines had moved off to the right. It was moving slowly and carefully watching the other fighting machines. It almost stopped, but still swayed and adjusted itself, much like a human waiting for something to happen.

"I have no idea," replied the General.

He had leaned forward a little to watch more clearly. The green machine was faster, and no matter how many times the Vanguards hit it was easily able to absorb their attack. It pushed the shield out and took the strain on its arms. The pistons were forced back with each impact, but the movement absorbed a great deal of the force before they moved the shield back to the original position.

One of the Vanguards tried to flank it, but the green warrior slipped back two paces and struck the manoeuvring Vanguard in the head with its shield. The heavy metal mantlet struck with a loud thud, and with speed the Vanguard could never hope to match. It lifted again, and might have come down, if it were not for the second

Vanguard. Both moved in and proceeded to strike into the green machine; only one in a dozen impacts actually striking its armoured body.

"The speed and agility of the green one is very interesting," said General Daniels.

He watched with interest as each attack was countered with subtle adjustments and movements, the kind of changes only a man with full control of every sense and muscle could accomplish. Angles that deflect or bounced off attacks, while the machine fought back to keep both in the fight. That was the point at which the yellow machine broke out into a run. This wasn't the slow movement of a Marine Corps armoured suit; this was more like a man lurching away in a hundred-metre dash. One of the Vanguards spotted its approach, locked its stance, and called out to its comrade.

"Left flank."

One was too busy fighting the green machine to change posture, but the other hunkered down and readied itself to beat off an assault.

"Here is comes," said the Colonel.

The machines moved closer, but the green model took a single step back. With a quick twist, it brought the shield out to its side so that it became a diagonal ramp leading over its own body and then lifted it a metre from the ground.

"No way!" muttered one of the civilians, "They cannot be serious?"

The yellow machine jumped half onto the armour plate and then propelled over the tops of the two Vanguards, aided by the green machine pushing the shield up high in an aggressive shunt. The sound of talking engineers and excited personnel dropped as everybody in the area watched the machine fly through the air. To General Daniels it felt like hours, but when it hit the ground with a thundering crash, he came to his senses.

"To me," said the waiting Vanguard.

The voice was rasping, and clearly a man under great pressure. Even so, it was too late to stop the yellow machine from hacking at the back of the Vanguard's legs. The heavy metal hammer hit with a resounding thud. After the third impact, one of the leg joints snapped off, and the damaged Vanguard dropped to one knee. Even though it was immobilised, it continued beating off the attack from the yellow machine. General Daniels finally began to smile.

"More like it. I've seen Vanguards come back from worse."

The Vanguard lifted up on its broken stump and stabbed away at its attackers. The second Vanguard tried to turn around to face the onslaught but was hit across the side by the metal shield from the green machine. It staggered and collapsed to the ground. The yellow machine jumped up, crashed down onto the fallen shape, and lifted its arms to attack.

"Yield," said the Vanguard.

At the same time both limbs of the machine dropped back to the ground. The yellow fighting machine simply spun about, dropped down from the fallen Vanguard, and moved in on the damaged and hobbling Vanguard. The two met like a pair of bulls and crashed together in a loud impact. The yellow machine wrenched the weighted club from the Vanguard, and it tore off sending sparks in all directions. It leaned down to the torso and ripped open part of a panel to expose a marine inside.

"Enough!" said the young woman.

The green machine leapt over wreckage and landed alongside its comrade. The entire arena was silent as they watched the broken shapes of both sets of Vanguard armour. There was no sound between them, but they stopped at exactly the same time and turned in to face each other. The green machine lowered its arms, and to the audience's horror, the yellow machine tore into it. One blow after another until it was on the floor pooling fluid and smoke.

"What is this?" Colonel Black demanded.

He was already on his feet as the front of the yellow machine began to open. He was busy looking at the smashed machine, hoping against hope that the driver had survived. Though he could not see how this could be possible. He moved around the wreckage and bent down to inspect the coloured fluid. There was something resembling bone fragments, and he bent down to touch them, only to find they were actually some type of ceramic layer.

At the same time, a small group of technicians entered the arena with a large trolley. Atop this unit were a substantial control unit and a cylinder, perhaps two metres tall and a metre in diameter. The yellow machine stopped near the unit and looked towards the General. The petal shaped plates continued opening until the shape of a man could be seen inside. He pulled at straps and dropped out of the machine and to the ground. A light mist drifted out from the interior, and for a short moment the man was surrounded by the white cloud.

"General Daniels," said a familiar voice.

The General was already on his feet and walking out into the arena. He stopped in front of the machine's pilot and waited for a second for the mist to clear. The figure was that of a man, similar in height to him but broader at the chest. He wore CTC overalls, unkempt dark hair, and a short beard that just covered his chin and upper lip.

"Spartan."

There was no look of pleasure on his face, just one of recognition of the Alliance's most famous hero. General Daniels raised a questioning eyebrow and looked around at the arena.

"Interesting place you've got here. Mind if I ask why you're trashing Alliance property? Haven't you had enough practice of that already?"

Colonel Black moved to the General's flank and looked at Spartan, assessing him from head to toe. He looked hard but could see little to show where the veteran warrior had received a replacement hand. If anything, Spartan looked leaner and tougher than at any time he could previously recall.

"That's a low blow, General, even for you."

He looked serious, but Daniels was sure he could see something of that mischievous smile hidden under that beard.

"If you must know, I'm testing this equipment," said Spartan.

The technicians activated the cylinder. It hissed open, revealing the form of a pale female humanoid inside. She pulled off a semi-transparent web that ran across her forehead and then stepped out alongside Spartan, shaking her head.

"You said you wouldn't do that again."

Her voice dripped with the accent of one of the Anicinàbe. She was of a similar height to Spartan, but her body was thin, perhaps too thin, and her skin semi-translucent. The men and women nearby looked like muscular monsters compared to her.

"I know," said Spartan, "It was...necessary."

The Anicinàbe sighed and then looked to their visitors.

"I am Kanjana, daughter of Thayara."

General Daniels angled his head a little, trying to recall the name.

"Thayara, as in the Anicinàbe female that sided with the Biomechs, and Spartan during his...episode?"

He looked to Spartan for an answer. He gave him a barely discernible shrug.

"Indeed. The same. Kanjana came here seven years ago to visit the site of her mother's death. She is now one of our best engineers."

Kanjana ignored the others and concentrated on the General. Her black eyes made it hard to identify what she was thinking, but he could see the questions already forming on her face. She looked back to Spartan.

"He carries the same scars as you."

Spartan sighed.

"Inside and out."

Kanjana then turned her attention to Colonel Black. The younger man was still much older than her, but unlike the General or Spartan, he was untouched by injury, as far as she could tell.

"You're not here for the warrior programme, are you?"

General Daniels looked to Colonel Black and gave him a nod. The officer reached down and pulled out a battered looking secpad, handing it to Spartan while giving Kanjana a slight smile. The small unit was the standard mobile communications and computer system used throughout the Alliance. There were many different models, but all were designed to access the Alliance Network at different security levels. The bearded man looked at the device, but didn't immediately take it.

"Go on," said General Daniels.

Colonel Black pushed it forward again.

"It's an isolated unit, only unit-to-unit connectivity."

General Daniels straightened his back a little and leaned in closer.

"It's important. Very important."

Spartan sighed.

"It always is."

He looked down at the unit, shook his head, and scrolled through the information.

# CHAPTER TWO

*The Demilitarised Zone was created following the seven-month conflict in 364CC, but its lasting effect was to leave Byotai settlers scattered on the long abandoned mining worlds. Though barren and desolate, all six were rich in natural resources but had been abandoned due to continued raider attacks by privateers. The Byotai, with the support of the Alliance had swept the planet of Karnak free of the Red Scars criminal organisation. Since then, small groups of Byotai have settled in this region as well as nearby planets, encouraged by the increased military presence. Though classed as the tenth quadrant by the Byotai Empire, they are still considered part of the Marche, a region claimed by the newly formed Anicinàbe League. This loose collection of nomadic people has thrived for millennia in a constant state of internal crisis and war, until the coming of Tahkeome, and his call to arms against their rivals.*

*Alien Races of the Orion Nebula*

**Kha'Dri World Ship, Taxxu Prime, Centauri Alliance**
The room was large, circular, and somehow oppressive. In the past it must have been some type of command

or control centre. Now the technology had been replaced by a number of massive floor-to-ceiling panels showing all manner of schematics. General Daniels gazed upon a few and immediately noticed the CTC Special Weapons Division watermark on every single image or video.

"Interesting showcase," he said.

Colonel Black had stopped to look at a design for a wheeled vehicle, quite similar to the Bulldogs already in use. These were larger, and the animated sequence showed how the standard model could be altered in minutes to fulfil divergent combat rolls. He was then drawn to something very different.

"What do we have here?"

It looked much like the standard Marine Mauler, the heavy landing craft used for all kinds of jobs. This one was equipped with a long series of loading pylons rather than a cargo area. They were clamped directly to the shapes of ten Vanguard sized soldiers. He leaned in closer and was surprised to see they were not Vanguards but looked suspiciously like the yellow machine he had seen Spartan demonstrating. Underneath it just said Maverick Armour.

"I wouldn't get too excited at all their projects. The last one I saw was offering an upgraded Vanguard with the ability to be inserted by orbit. Can you imagine a battlefield where we scattered ground forces kilometres apart?"

He looked back to the doorway.

"In a world with unlimited resources it could be made to work, but not today."

He lifted his eyebrows in frustration.

"The peace dividend is always paid for by the military, and when we're needed, we'll catch up, just like we always do. But it will cost time and lives while we get back up to speed."

Colonel Black wasn't entirely sure he agreed and moved back to the schematics. There were all kinds of designs, and he could only assume the majority were proposals, because some were highly outlandish. He shook his head, looking at a ship design unlike any he'd seen before.

"This place, it is...unusual. I'm surprised that somebody with your...history, would want to work out here, surrounded by these things."

General Daniels seemed more intrigued by the structure itself. The ceiling and walls were ribbed in a fashion looking as though it might come to life at any moment, like most of the ancient Biomech warships. Light came from hidden blue lamps recessed into the walls and ceiling. General Daniels and Colonel Black waited patiently, with the ever-present form of Mr Walker beside them. In the middle of the room was a round table, and atop it a standard Alliance projection unit.

"I have to..." started the General.

Walker lifted his hand and nodded quickly.

"They are here."

The door opened on cue and in came Spartan, behind him a single Jötnar, then Kanjana, and lastly Captain Wilson. The Jötnar warrior was massive, just over two and a half metres and built like an ogre of myth. His arms were as thick as a normal man's chest, and he towered over them all. Kanjana moved around them to get to the side of the room. Once there she had the perfect view of the group, and of the doorway.

"General Daniels, long time," said the Jötnar.

For the first time the senior officer smiled.

"Khan, it is a long time."

The two grasped arms before releasing and turning their attention back to Spartan. Colonel Black tapped the unit, and it flickered into life. Spartan was not looking at the videostream, though; he was still looking at the two Marine Corps officers.

"I told you ten years ago, I'm not coming back. The war is over. It has been for years."

General Daniels looked uncomfortable.

"I know that, Spartan, and your service to the Alliance was above and beyond what could ever be considered necessary. You played your part, and many were lost to achieve victory. Your sacrifices..."

The look on Spartan's face stopped him in his tracks. It wasn't anger, or even bitterness. No, he could see the pain in the man's eyes.

"I'm sorry."

Instead he pointed to the screen.

"Your work on the...uh...new unit is something quite extraordinary. But I'm not here for that, not today. All I need is some of your time. We have a delicate situation, and you might be able to help us."

He then looked to Kanjana and Mr Walker, both of whom he was unfamiliar with, and were not part of the chain of command or subject to the same rules and restrictions as the military.

"This can only be between the four of us. I'm sorry."

Spartan looked to Kanjana and back to the officers.

"Then you had better leave. Kanjana is as much part of this operation as I am. She stays, or we walk."

He looked to the CTC executive.

"I don't think CTC will be very happy if we start discussing this without a senior executive present. Khan and I might run the Special Weapons Division, but CTC is another matter."

General Daniels clearly didn't like this, but a discreet nod from Colonel Black served as a reminder as to the delicacy of the situation. Contrary to what they had already said, both knew the two of them would be here, and a thorough security check had been conducted prior to their departure.

"Very well."

The model showed the border between the Byotai and the Anicinàbe. The trouble had started eleven years ago, and every few months there would be an incident of some kind, usually a kidnapping or raid. Colonel Black pointed to a single planet, one that Spartan was unfamiliar with.

"What am I looking at?"

He sounded frustrated, perhaps even a little bored.

Kanjana knew it immediately.

"That is Karnak."

Spartan knew the name immediately.

"I know that place. The Byotai took the planet a decade ago from Anicinàbe criminals. With our help, if I recall correctly. What about it? I thought both sides had settled the demilitarised zone now?"

General Daniels sighed and looked about the room.

"Spartan. These worlds are vulnerable, and they are about to get squeezed by an Anicinàbe uprising, one we know is coming. The Alliance cannot let that happen, not with the Byotai still recovering from the war."

Colonel Black glanced at him, their eyes meeting only for a moment.

"That's where I come in, Spartan. It is my job to get support unofficially to the settlers to even the fight before it's too late. They must be defended against Anicinàbe militants, or we will see another genocide unfold before us."

Spartan leaned back a little as though surprised. The General continued to look about the room and seemed almost disappointed.

"Is this really the best place you have for us, Spartan? I expected, well, something a little grander. Are you trying to tell me something?"

Spartan remained expressionless, but he did give a brief signal to Kanjana. She tapped something on her arm, and the three walls started to change colour. It was as if they were fading before their eyes, and then they were gone. They were replaced by transparency and a view out into a vast complex.

"Better?" Spartan asked.

General Daniels shook his head and laughed.

"I expected nothing less."

The room they were in was now a small extension on a cliff like structure that jutted out a hundred metes from the ground. All around them was a large circular shaped hangar with five hulls alongside each other in a circular arrangement, like spokes on a wheel.

"Reminds me of Prometheus."

Spartan nodded.

"Yes, the basic design is very similar. I'll give you one guess why that might be."

The ships under construction intrigued General Daniels, but he had more pressing questions right now. He looked back to Spartan.

"I assume this is one-way?"

He indicated to the transparent walls.

"Of course."

Khan fidgeted and looked to the General.

"We know about the trouble on the border, so why don't you get to the point, General? What do you want?"

The two Alliance officers looked to each other and then to Spartan and Khan.

"Look," began General Daniels, "The Anicinàbe have skirmished over these worlds with the Byotai for generations. First the Byotai settled them for mining, then the Anicinàbe attacked their compounds, and then the Byotai abandoned them all until ten years ago."

Spartan yawned, feigning boredom.

"It's been going on for years, but now there's a new player in the region. This man."

An image of an Anicinàbe man popped up. He was thin. Even thinner than the average Anicinàbe male, yet he wore conventional human clothing.

"He calls himself Tahkeome. Nobody knows his real name, and he's causing the Byotai a major problem, one that could destabilise the region and drag them and us into an internal war."

Spartan listened but still said nothing. Khan had no such problems, however.

"So, they have troubles. What does that have to do with us? The Anicinàbe have been causing problems since the war. It's not our business, and it definitely isn't mine."

General Daniels lifted his hand to stop Khan.

"Tahkeome is a native of Karnak, from one of the old crime families, and he's split off a dozen of the Anicinàbe warlords near the border to help him. They stand apart from the Anicinàbe Council and have called for all Anicinàbe outcasts to return to the border worlds, specifically Karnak. Thousands have already arrived, and our intelligence suggests they will make a move on the scattered Byotai settlements.

"So?" Spartan said, "Karnak doesn't belong to the Anicinàbe anymore. It never did. Just because it is closer to the Anicinàbe, doesn't make it theirs."

Spartan noticed the General seemed surprised.

"Yes, I do keep up with what is going on. CTC needs to know what is happening in the Alliance and our borders."

General Daniels looked carefully at Spartan. He could see an interest in the man's face, but he was holding back, and he could easily understand why. Colonel Black moved the imagery in the unit to show the Anicinàbe territories. It brought up a patchwork of confederations and tribal units.

"Twenty-one star systems, with more worlds and a larger population than every settlement in the Alliance. According to our resources, they have never once been united. For the last millennia they have traded and fought constantly. There is only a loose confederation of leaders who never agree on a thing."

"Until now," said General Daniels.

His expression had changed, and he was clearly concerned.

"Between these warlords, they have six independent warbands, and at least three colonies that we know of. Our reconnaissance assets in the area tell us Tahkeome is already blockading the area around Karnak, and probably sending military supplies in to those Anicinàbe already there. The Byotai are almost entirely unarmed, with just a few security units. They will be attacked from within and outside simultaneously. It will be a slaughter."

Spartan shrugged.

"Why come here? Isn't this a job for the Byotai to sort out?"

Colonel Black spoke quietly with the General, and then looked to Spartan.

"We helped them remove the pirates and raiders a decade ago. Even so, the Byotai and the Anicinàbe Council have an agreement. Neither side will bring in military forces, thereby keeping the area completely demilitarised."

Spartan lifted his eyebrows at that.

"Anicinàbe and Byotai civilians living together without protection. What next?"

He was being sarcastic, but only Khan laughed. The Colonel continued.

"...This Tahkeome has decided to make an issue of it. He has been demanding the Byotai settlers leave, and I can assure you, they are far from prepared for what is coming."

Khan pointed to the map.

"Why don't the Byotai government and the Anicinàbe Council tell him to back off?"

Colonel Black lifted his hand to his head and wiped his brow.

"Neither side wants to get involved. The Anicinàbe are disorganised and little interested publically, while the Byotai are keen to avoid creating any kind of incident with them. Don't forget, nothing unites people faster than a common enemy. Any minor skirmishes are to be dealt with by the settlers themselves."

The General looked a little uncomfortable before he continued.

"This is what they are calling the price of peace."

General Daniels moved to one of the transparent

walls and looked down at the partially assembled ships. It was hard to make out much, due to the scaffolding and separate pieces that filled the place. One clear feature was the ring shape near the rear of the fuselage. It was a design style he'd not seen before.

"You've made a life for yourself out here, Spartan. Your contacts with On'Sarax and her people have given you a lot of leverage. You've kept the peace, and even managed to integrate this region with the Alliance."

He pointed to one of the ships.

"This kind of technology will be of use, and soon."

He turned back around.

"We need the Byotai, and we owe them still from the war. If we're smart, we can keep them on side while bringing some of the Anicinàbe over as well. Once a few of their groups join the Alliance, the rest will follow or fall in line. What we cannot allow is for this Tahkeome and his militants in the DMZ to get traction. If he can rally others to his cause, then the Byotai will be in a lot of trouble. Open warfare between the Anicinàbe and the Byotai could spiral out of control, and fast, and we in the Alliance will pay for it."

Spartan laughed.

"The Anicinàbe answer to no one, and definitely not to a single leader. Their council is a talking shop, nothing more. If you ask me, the best thing would be to live up to our obligations and send Alliance peacekeepers to the Demilitarised Zone. The Anicinàbe wouldn't dream of coming even close to the place. A show of force is what they will respect."

He then shrugged.

"That's just my opinion. Not like anybody asked."

General Daniels looked at Spartan carefully. There was something, a glint of excitement perhaps, or maybe just a recollection of what he had done in the past. He knew Spartan was a warrior; he always had been.

"Spartan, I have a job to do, and I need you. Come to Karnak and help us give Tahkeome and his outcast Anicinàbe militants a bloody nose. When they all see the Byotai are there to stay, both sides can resume negotiations. That way we keep the Byotai onside. No Anicinàbe warlords will join Tahkeome if he is seen as a loser. "

"Who is 'us' exactly?" Khan asked.

Colonel Black looked a little uncomfortable at this question.

"This is a clandestine operation. We are routing resources through the Khreenk and other third parties. I could do with some of your new tech, and maybe a few of your vaunted security teams. The Byotai settlers need to be able to protect themselves if these militants take things further."

General Daniels put his hand on Spartan's shoulder.

"That's just an extra, though. What we really need, no, what I need...is you. This is a fast moving operation, and we are running it without a backup. If we fail, nobody is coming for us. I need my old friend. Gun is in. I am meeting him soon."

Spartan turned to Khan. They shared a look but said nothing. He looked back to the General.

"I'm sorry, General. This isn't my fight. I promised myself this was it."

He glanced at Kanjana and again to the General. The mention of his old friend Gun would have done it in the past, but there was still too much pain with working for the Alliance in this way.

"I've done my time, and so did my family. The Alliance has taken enough from me, and I will give them nothing more. I want to keep what I have left."

He moved his arms out.

"This is my new life, and it will make thing better for me and you. Trust me. What we are working on, it will change lives."

General Daniels nodded his head slowly.

"I understand. I won't press you. I had to ask. You understand?"

Spartan reached out and grasped the General's arm.

"You shouldn't be going on this operation, General. Either the Alliance backs you fully with a military taskforce, or it does not. This kind of situation usually escalates into a full shooting war, and fast."

The General laughed.

"You are probably right."

He made for the door and stepped out. He was almost gone but then stopped.

"When I return, we will talk. CTC and the Alliance military need to make some arrangements. I've seen some of this tech you're working on out here, and we can use it."

Spartan tried to look cheerful.

"Just come back alive, General, and bring Gun with you, too."

* * *

**Ceani Valley, Karnak, Byotai- Anicinàbe Border**
Karnak was no great prize to either the Byotai or the

Anicinàbe. If anything it was a barren wilderness that few sane people would choose for a new life. The atmosphere was dry, and most of its surface consisted of a single massive landmass, punctuated by lakes and rivers that frequently ran dry. A hundred years earlier it would have been ignored, but with every planet of the Byotai now overcrowded, there was a growing movement among some of its population to look elsewhere. Retired soldiers looked to a new, more exciting life and joined the generation that were keen to explore and were bold in their enterprise of settling the wasteland between the two domains.

The route to the large Ceani Settlement was barren, dusty, and flanked on the one side by a tall cliff. The eight armoured vehicles travelled with a good space between them to stop the dust from blocking their view. Above them, at a height of two hundred metres, moved a single hexrotor drone. It traversed a figure-of-eight pattern to keep a careful watch on the convoy. Behind them were another eight heavy transports, carrying containers filled with food, body armour, and most important, military grade weaponry for the citizen soldiers.

"How much longer?" General Daniels asked.

He was jammed down inside the cramped interior of the four-wheeled transport vehicle. His clothing was thickly padded and beige in colour, much like the terrain outside. He wore a thin scarf around his neck and a pair of driving goggles pushed up onto his forehead. At his side was a cut down Khreenk blaster with a Helion short-range scope fitted. Three Alliance mercenaries sat next to him, dressed in Khreenk armour and carrying an assortment of alien weaponry, including Helion rifles and thermal shotguns. One of them pointed ahead.

"I don't know, Sir. This place looks the same from every angle."

They all avoided using his rank; a senior General was a big risk out here.

"Tell me about it," he replied, "Still, there are Byotai settlements throughout this entire area. I cannot believe the Anicinàbe settlers would raise their arms against the Byotai. They are more likely to side with them against pirates than fight each other."

He said the words, but he'd seen the briefings back on Terra Nova. The entire border was a problem, but Karnak was, as always, the focus. The world had captured the public's imagination back home, as well as throughout the Byotai territories. Byotai and Anicinàbe settlers had worked together with Alliance forces to remove the threat of criminals. Now he suspected the planet would become a pawn between ambitious individuals on both sides.

*We have to keep control of this situation.*

He looked back through the observation slit, ever on the alert. For a moment he thought he was back inside an Alliance armoured column, but the voices of the Byotai removed any chance of that. The majority were citizens that had volunteered to help defend the settlements, but there were also soldiers that had taken leave for weeks or months at a time to help them out here.

The armoured vehicle looked similar to the Bulldogs used by the Alliance military, but its purpose was very different. These heavy machines were designed for industrial use rather than combat. Its sides were high and the wheels as big as a Vanguard marine. The hull was fully enclosed with just the tinniest of slits for the crew to see out.

"Three kilometres," said Turi, "There are reports of Anicinàbe civilian aircraft attacking one of our refineries."

He rubbed his brow.

"It is on fire."

General Daniels closed his eyes in a moment of frustration.

"Casualties?"

Turi opened his mouth and breathed several times before answering. The Byotai soldier was much broader than the humans, as was common for his people. His additional body armour bulked him out so that he looked much like a smaller version of the Jötnar.

"Three wounded."

Then he smiled.

"Our militiamen brought down one of their aircraft. The others have fled."

General Daniels seemed pleased with that part.

"Good, so the air defence systems are working, then."

He heard the group of Byotai volunteers speaking behind him and turned to look at them. They spoke to each other in their own alien tongue, and the only words he could identify were locations names and a few individuals. Turi watched them for a few seconds.

"The Khreenk anti-air systems have proven very effective. It is as well we have brought more with us."

"What about the defence systems at the settlement, are they active yet?"

Turi spoke with one of the volunteers before answering.

"Yes. The perimeter sentry guns are installed and operational. We have protection on the ground. The air defence systems we are bringing will guarantee our safety."

He pointed behind them to the column of heavy

transport haulers busy creating a vast trail of dust.

"Our soldiers need weapons and ammunition to fight if it comes to a battle. But the Anicinàbe make heavy use of aircraft. If we cannot bring them down, they will have the advantage. He looked to the back of the vehicle and indicated with a movement of his head.

"There are sixty Byotai at the Ceani settlement, but enough weapons for only six of them. There are three smaller Anicinàbe settlements across the wasteland. They set up three months ago and have started digging a mine complex. It's about a hundred and forty kilometres away."

Turi looked angry as he spoke.

"They are using the removal of our military forces to strengthen their positions."

Another of his comrades began chattering excitedly and then removed an earpiece from his head. The Byotai sighed and said something strange.

"What?" asked the General.

"Message from the scouts at the front, it's from Gun. He keeps saying he doesn't like the ground ahead."

The Byotai chatted over the communications system and was cut off as the vehicle felt weightless for a moment and then shuddered as they hit the bottom of a shallow trench. The powerful engines roared and pulled them out with a howling sound, not dissimilar to a jet engine.

"He's sending teams to investigate, so we need to slow down for a moment."

Turi opened his mouth to cool down and closed his eyes. General Daniels had learnt days before that this was a sigh of stress with his kind. He finally opened them, blinked again, and spoke.

"We have news from homeland. General Makos has

resigned from the high command and has blockaded himself in the main military spaceport."

"Makos, why?"

Turi seemed angry at the news and took in multiple quick breaths.

"He demanded the military be given authority to send in an intervention force. He says Tahkeome is encouraging the Anicinàbe here on Karnak to turn on us. Makos knows the truth, but our politicians will sell us out for peace."

Daniels could already see where this was going, and he knew people like Turi would not back down. He even suspected this was part of the plan. Deaths on either side would make a larger conflict more likely.

"If Tahkeome can cause this much trouble, just think what will happen when he gets closer. He's already blocking ships trying to bring in food and medical supplies."

He shook his head.

"Your people will fight, and they will fight hard. But the Anicinàbe have numbers you can never match. War has to be avoided, and your settlements must endure."

Turi muttered and then nodded in agreement.

"The Senate refused the General's request, so he has resigned. He can be relied on, but not our politicians."

Daniels sighed.

"I know the man. The Alliance has put a lot of faith in the General. This will be a big problem. With the General gone, there will be even less stomach for a fight. Tahkeome could just wait and starve your people out."

The vehicle bumped again and skidded to a halt. The changed in velocity was so great that the driver had been forced to skid, and they slalomed for a few seconds.

"What's happening?"

The column of armoured vehicles stopped for the fifth time in the last hour. The doors opened at the rear, and two of the Byotai stepped out to investigate. At the same time, militiamen from the other vehicles did the same. Turi watched them leave and then twisted back.

"Contact from Gun, he's spotted incoming aircraft. We need to get off the..."

His voice was blotted out by the sound of a massive explosion. Dust blasted in through the open door, as well as the mangled form of one of the Byotai. The unfortunate soul staggered and fell to the ground with blood oozing from a dozen wounds.

*Ambush!*

General Daniels slid to the side of the vehicle and looked up. He could just about make out the trail from a rocket launcher. A yellow streak marked its path, and then it slammed into one of the transports just behind them. The sky lit up with gunfire from masked figures along the ridge.

"It's an ambush! Move!"

He moved to the hatch leading into the front of the vehicle. It was unlocked, and as he entered the driver's compartment was stunned to find the bullet-ridden corpse of another Byotai; multiple rounds had shattered the reinforced glass. There were even holes in the doors. Turi climbed in, pushed the body to one side, and took the driver's position.

"What now?"

"Drive!"

Turi was a soldier, one of the elite Sixth Battalion, the rarely seen Byotai commando unit. He was out of uniform, and to all intents and purposes a civilian, but he responded the way his training had taught him, to react and to obey. He didn't hesitate.

"Understood."

Turi pushed his foot down, and the vehicle accelerated out from the scene of the battle. The vehicle was moving faster and hit one of the damaged transports with a mighty crash. At the same time, another rocket flew down and hit where they had been just moments before. One of the Khreenk leaned inside and spoke through his translator unit.

"Drone is down. Three vehicles destroyed. They are Anicinàbe guerrillas!"

Turi had to go back ten metres and then drove as fast as he could. The bulky vehicle was slow to accelerate, and when they hit their target, they were lucky to push past. More shots hit around the armoured body, and a good number penetrated inside.

"Get us out of here!"

They bumped over several bodies, and then they were back on the trail. It was wide enough for two similar vehicles, but in a poor state and filled with holes and light debris. The large wheels made short work of the obstruction, and two surviving heavy haulers did their best to follow. The Khreenk mercenary spoke slowly and precisely into his communication gear. After each message, he looked more and more concerned.

"General," said Turi, "I need you on the gun."

There was no need to say more. Daniels pulled on the lever, the hatch above the driver section opened up, and he lifted up to the gun position. It was a reinforced cupola, with a light rotating mount to support a pair of Byotai cannons. Half of his body extended above the driver area and gave him a good view all around. He could see two civilian trucks at the top of the ridge, and perhaps two-dozen cloaked figures with rifles and rocket launchers.

"Civilians, my ass, those are Anicinàbe foot soldiers!"

He took aim and pulled the trigger. Rounds struck along the top of the ridge, and they were immediately forced to seek shelter. There was no way to tell if he'd hit any targets, but it was enough to allow a few more of the Byotai transports move away from the battle. Lights to his right forced him to swing the gun mount around, and he found a pair of small buggies in pursuit.

"Can't you go faster?"

Something exploded nearby, and chunks of the right access hatch ripped off. The flickering lights of guns were visible through the gaps. Turi shook his head and pulled on the wheel to avoid more fire.

"This is not local militia. These are professionals."

The Khreenk soldier kicked the damaged door from the right of the compartment and leaned out. He blasted away with his personal weapons to good effect. General Daniels pointed the pair of cannons at the second buggy and put a burst through the side. It swerved and crashed into the cliff on the side of the trail. The vehicle spun about and flipped upside down.

"Good shot," said the Khreenk.

More flashes erupted around them, and three rockets rushed down from hidden positions ahead. Two missed, but the third struck the rear of the vehicle and tore a hole as big as a man. Flames spread around the rear and were quickly extinguished by the internal fire suppressors.

"Behind us!" Turi yelled.

He swung around and spotted it, a squat-looking flying

machine. It was hard to make out the configuration, but the nose and wing-mounted weapons were firing almost continually.

*Got you.*

The cannons were not the most powerful weapons he'd come across, but their rate of fire was good and appeared accurate at this range. The first burst went low, and he quickly adjusted fire before shooting again. This time the longer burst raked along the nose and started a series of small flashes.

*Come on, you can do better than that.*

He pulled the trigger again and was rewarded by several flames to the side of the flyer. The craft spun about on its axis and then lifted up to move out of range. Blue flames vented downwards as it accelerated away. Another Byotai yelled something, and then everything changed. Before he could see what was happening, they were on their side and sliding along the ground. They made it just a few metres before striking the cliff wall. The General was cast out of the cupola and landed on the ground ten metres from the side of the vehicle. He hit the ground hard and rolled over until he was face down. Bullets clattered about him.

"Get up."

He moved to his feet and found himself staring at the ogre like shape of Gun. He wore the crude armour built in some of the new workshops on Hyperion, and looked like a warrior from an apocalyptic scenario. In his hands he held a vehicle-mounted automatic cannon; to him it looked now more than a battle rifle.

"Daniels?" Turi called out.

The alien soldier ran from around the side of the driver's section with a thermal shotgun in his hands. It was civilian issue, the kind of gear anybody in the Alliance and possibly Helios might carry. He spotted Gun and the General and looked up. The gun moved to his shoulder and then blasted. The gunshot was followed by a cry, and then he was closer.

"We have to move. There are Anicinàbe soldiers on the ridge."

A volley of rounds clattered about them as if to emphasise the point. Turi pulled him to his feet and led him towards an approaching vehicle. This one was a commercial tractor unit. It was unarmoured but well made and offered a strongly protected crew area. It came closer but split in half as a thermite missile exploded right in its middle. The super-heated metal burnt a three-metre diameter hole and sent shards of metal in all directions.

"I have them," said Gun.

A squad of eight Anicinàbe, each covered in desert robes, ran down the embankment and into his line of fire. The automatic cannon roared as he blasted one after the other. Only two made it back to the ridge, and as they reached the crest, Turi shot them both in the back.

"Not bad," muttered Gun.

"Get down!" yelled one of the human mercenaries.

The man jumped into the path of the fire and took the brunt of the blast. The unfortunate man was killed instantly and crashed into the General. Both collapsed to the ground as the flyer returned and hovered just fifty metres away. Even though he was under the body of the dead man, General Daniels could see the craft was pointed right at the few survivors. A voice boomed out across the wasteland. The languages continued to change until it reached one that was familiar.

"Lower your weapons. The liberators of Karnak are evicting all Byotai illegals."

The voice changed again, and Turi translated.

"They are giving us ten seconds to comply. We obey, or we die."

General Daniels pushed the body away and rose to his feet. Another two of his men closed up, along with the Khreenk soldier and Turi. Gun stepped in front of all of them and took aim with its own weapon and opened fire. Sparks flashed along its nose, but another two aircraft moved up alongside it and fired two bursts, cutting down the remaining mercenaries. As the guns stopped, Turi shook his head and lifted his hands.

"We cannot defeat them, not now. Drop your weapons."

Daniels lowered his hand to his thigh and rested his fingers around the hilt of his pistol. It wouldn't bring down the flyer, but it was reassuring. The small aircraft shook about at it remained hovering. A pair of additional gun pods dropped down below its stubby wings. The other two aircraft began circling around the three of them, and the voice returned in what sounded like the Byotai language.

"Five, four, three..."

Turi dropped his weapon to the ground, and General Daniels followed suit. No sooner were the weapons down when the Anicinàbe arrived. Three buggies climbed over the dunes and rushed down to meet them. Soldiers covered in layers of banded cloth and carrying improvised weapons leapt out to search the vehicles. At the same time, the flyer lowered and rested on the rough track. It sent out a cloud of dust as the squeal of its engines faded away.

"Stand your ground," said Turi.

The five waited patiently as a group of dark figures

approached. They came through the dust cloud and were impossible to see properly until just a few metres away. They stopped and looked at their prisoners. The shortest of the group wore combat armour that carefully followed the muscles of his body. His head was completely bald and his skin lightly sweaty. To General Daniels' surprise, he spoke flawless English.

"Humans, Khreenk, and Byotai, all together as one happy family."

He then lifted a pistol and pointed his weapon at them.

"You are prisoners of the Anicinàbe freedom fighters."

One of the other Anicinàbe militiamen ran back from behind a captured transport. He shouted loudly to his comrades, and the mood quickly shifted from triumphalism to anger. The short, bald Anicinàbe soldier moved along the group and stopped in front of the humans. He lifted his handgun, pointed it to the temple of the first, and fired. The man was dead as soon as the round punched through his skull, and he collapsed to the ground.

"You are supplying weapons to the Byotai occupiers. Where are they?"

Turi looked to General Daniels and shook his head. The two shared a look but quickly turned away as the enemy soldier issued orders to his men. General Daniels tried to smile, but it would not happen; instead relied on the fact the mission was presumably still a success.

*Sending the weapons on the other convoy wasn't such a bad idea after all.*

The Anicinàbe soldier approached the two of them and started shouting in the Byotai language. No matter how angry he became, Turi continued to ignore him. This went on for some time, and then he struck Turi before moving to him.

"So, you are another of the mercenaries, are you not? Where are the weapons systems?"

His accent changed slightly as he became more frustrated. He lifted the handgun and pointed it at his head. One of his comrades stepped closer and said something. Both of them looked up, and their voices became louder. The figure looked back at their new prisoners.

"You will talk soon enough, or you will die. It is up to you."

He moved in front of Gun and looked up and down the creature. At the same time, one of the Anicinàbe soldiers reached out to grab him. Gun snarled and delivered a powerful uppercut that snapped the soldier's neck in an instant. He took another step toward the Anicinàbe leader, but four more soldiers blocked his path and took aim at the General and Turi.

"Mercenaries or soldiers of the Alliance? Get back, or you die, right here, right now!"

Gun stopped and looked back at General Daniels. He gave him a short but obvious nod. He could almost have laughed at what was happening.

*You fools, kill me or Gun and the Alliance will burn this place to the ground.*

# CHAPTER THREE

*The modular ship designs of the Crusader, Conqueror, and Liberty class have proven themselves in countless battles, the flexibility in configuration and their reliability more important than any individual weapon system. Over three hundred of these vessels now serve in the Alliance, crewed by citizens of every colony from the birthplace of humanity; Earth, through to the alien worlds of Helios Prime and Spascia. These workhorses are assisted on day-to-day operations by attached units from regional forces. The fleet is well supported for operations at a minute's notice.*

*Naval Cadet's Handbook*

## Ceani Valley, Karnak, Byotai- Anicinàbe Border

General Daniels could hear the sound of the returning Anicinàbe flyer above them. Its engines screamed as it dropped the last few metres and landed. There was no way to see the thing from where he was, so far underground and hidden inside the temporary prison cell. He looked to his left, but it was almost impossible for his eyes to adjust and so looked up to the tiny pinprick of light. The cell was circular and big enough to house a hundred people. There was a single large, secure door leading inside, and the ceiling reached up at least a hundred metres. He ran his hands down the walls, feeling the smooth finish.

"It is one of our mines; we dug them all over Karnak over three hundred of your years ago."

The General couldn't quite see Turi, but his voice was clear enough.

"This world is rich in resources, so why give it up so easily?"

Turi sighed.

"It was no single event, but the constant skirmishes with the Anicinàbe made it too expensive in the long run. These planets are a long way from the other nine quadrants. In the end it cost more to protect these mines than they were making."

He muttered something in his own tongue before continuing. His accent was thick, and his voice slow, yet General Daniels couldn't but be impressed that the alien had mastered his own language so quickly and effectively.

"So we withdrew and left these worlds to their fate. With us gone, the Anicinàbe left. They never wanted them; they just didn't want somebody to benefit."

Again he said the same word, presumably an insult for the Anicinàbe. One of the large doors opposite them began to make grinding sounds. Turi spoke quietly but more quickly.

"Tell them nothing, General.

Once they have what they need, we will all die."

General Daniels nodded, not that the alien could see him.

"Don't worry, I'm saying nothing."

The door swung open, and a bright white light filled the cell. None of them could see as the staggering form of Gun lurched into the room and collapsed. Before they could do anything else, multiple arms grabbed at the General, dragging him away while his eyes were still adjusting.

"Courage!" was the last word he heard Turi shout, while Gun lay unconscious on the ground.

\* \* \*

There were three of them in the room, but one in particular seemed to be excessively interested in him. General Daniels tried to move, but he was pinned to the table, his arms and legs strapped down.

"Another Byotai mercenary. Are you not a little old to be playing soldier? Or are you something more?"

The voice was synthesised, and if he strained his neck, he could just about make out the partially hooded shape of an Anicinàbe warrior. The figure shook its head and unravelled its covering one strip at a time, until finally revealing the baldhead of a female Anicinàbe. She was short, very small in build, yet there was something about her demeanour that implied pent up anger, even rage. She opened her mouth, and the synthesiser took over.

"I am the Ogimà, the Chief. You may call me Nakoma."

She walked two steps to the side and moved in quickly, bringing her head right down alongside his. He could feel her warm breath down his neck, and spittle dropped from her mouth as she spoke.

"I am the regional commander of the Khagi region in the Anicinàbe Marche. This territory belongs to the Anicinàbe Coalition. What is a man from the Alliance doing here? Are you a mercenary, or from the Alliance military?"

She then stood upright and moved her shoulders, stretching and creaking them.

"The civilians of the Marche asked for help to protect them from the barbaric cold-bloods who seek to steal its wealth and resources. The Marche has always been a free territory, a place that all warm-bloods can call home."

It sounded like a rehearsed speech, and General Daniels couldn't help but laugh at her posturing. She looked down at him with venom positively dripping from her eyes.

"Human."

The words were artificial, laced in malice due to the translator, but he could easily sense the fire in her voice in the slight pause before the electronics kicked in.

"Who are you? What are you doing in the Marche? You are a long way from home, are you not?"

She made a low-pitch grumbling sound in her throat.

"Your friend was not cooperative. We will work around that soon. You are helping the Byotai as well. I know you are. Now...Tell me!"

General Daniels looked away from her and found him looking into the hidden face of another militant. There wasn't a shred of bare skin showing on this one, with even the eyes hidden behind glowing red lenses on rubberised goggles.

*The Marche; doesn't that just mean a border region?*

He tried to recall where he'd heard that name before

and barely noticed the figure moving closer. It reached forward, grabbed his head, and twisted it back to face the female Anicinàbe. He groaned as he was turned with savagery to the side. Now he could see the male militant pulling out a short, razor sharp-looking blade in his hand.

"I think I know. Yes...I am sure I know why you are here..."

The Ogimà bared her teeth.

"The Byotai rats have paid many people to bring in weapons to attack and kill civilians of the Coalition. You are a soldier. I can tell."

She walked back and forth, almost as though having a conversation with herself.

"You are here to protect their illegal weapons convoys. That is where we found you. We know they are using them at the Byotai terrorist camp inside Mount Caldos. The weapons will not keep them safe forever."

She pointed the blade at his throat and rested it on his skin. The blade was barely touching him, yet it hummed gently as it made contact. He knew the anti-aircraft missiles would be the only things keeping the enclave, and perhaps thousands of Byotai safe. If he failed, the Byotai fighters would be expelled or killed, and the entire Tenth Quadrant would soon fall into Anicinàbe hands. After that, the fate of millions of civilians would hang in the balance, and that was just this one world out of six.

*Stay strong. The supplies will reach them in three days. After that, they can hold their own until real help comes along.*

He felt a tingle, and she continued moving the blade down to his chest. It didn't cut deep, just enough to leave a thin red trail behind the device. It passed his navel and continued downwards.

"Wait. I'll talk," he said.

Nakoma stopped, lifted the blade, and looked into his eyes. She then signalled to her comrades. They deactivated the shackles to his arms and lifted him up into a seating position before reactivating them. She began to speak, and he found it hard to understand the first few synthesised words.

"...attacked our aircraft. Tell us where they are, and we will end your suffering."

He leaned forward to stare straight into her eyes.

"There's one thing I need you to do for me first."

Her eyes tightened as she listened.

"What?"

To her surprise, the bruised and beaten prisoner began to laugh.

"Lady...you can start by kissing my ass."

If he'd had the strength, he would have shouted it out, but it came out as little more than a mumble. She moved in close and rested the blade at his throat.

"Tell me that again."

This time he took his time and said the words slowly and clearly. By the time he'd finished, he could tell she understood, and though he knew it wouldn't be good for him, he took a moment of pleasure in seeing her face contort.

*Yeah, let it out, lady.*

He didn't even see the hand of his tormentor reaching up to his side. The first realisation occurred as the male Anicinàbe struck him hard. It was a powerful impact, but to a trained and experienced soldier, and one that had suffered considerably in the past, it seemed like a scratch. He laughed.

"Hit me again, but you still won't be able to save your soldiers."

He looked at her, his eyes glowing with anger.

"The Byotai will not go quietly, and when they are ready, they will make all of you suffer."

She yelled something, and the blade sank down into his flesh. He passed out after the third slice, but not before he'd spat into her face.

\* \* \*

## Kha'Dri World Ship, Taxxu Prime, Centauri Alliance

Spartan turned away from the group and looked out into space. As always, this part of the ship was orientated towards the Black Rift, the great permanent tunnel through space connecting this region of space with Helios and the rest of the Alliance. They continued to speak, but he ignored them for now, thinking about events in the past and the people he had known.

*The Alliance never learns. Always reacting.*

He could feel the frustration in his body, the lack of control, but that was the price he paid for setting himself aside from the Alliance. His new life far from the conflict and argument allowed him to focus on developing new technology. More important was that he had been able to spend time with those that mattered, his few remaining friends. There was no time he could remember where he had not been involved in bloody conflict and war, until now.

*Stay out of it, Spartan. This is not your fight.*

The room was known as the battle deck and was used as a briefing room, training hall, and a weapons test zone.

In the past it had been the command centre for the ship, the place from where the Great Enemy commanded their forces in the final war against the Alliance of races. Unlike most parts of the World Ship, this one was almost a perfect large cube in shape, with one half nearly completely open to the void of space. Tall windows ran from floor to ceiling to give a perfect view.

"It happened exactly as you'd expected," said Khan.

Spartan turned away from the view and looked back into the vast, barren space. He was not alone. There was Khan, his faithful friend as well as Mr Walker, the CTC executive, and Kanjana.

"Yes. The Byotai removed their military forces and allowed Anicinàbe settlers in, all as a gesture of goodwill. A demilitarised zone they called it. Well look at it now."

He pointed to the massive floating sphere showing the dust bowl planet of Karnak. It hovered over the centre of the room like a machine with an intelligence of its own. The world was covered in coloured shapes to show where the Byotai settlements were. He shook his head in frustration.

"The Anicinàbe settlers were infiltrators, people with no interest in living there. I bet they've been stockpiling weapons for months, maybe years, and now they are evicting the Byotai where they find them, or worse."

Khan grumbled and pointed off to shapes a distance from the world. A dotted line connecting them to the planet, implying they were further away than the model suggested.

"And what about the blockade? This Tahkeome is still stopping traffic in the area?"

Walker had been silent until now but answered.

"Yes. He is supposedly trying to keep weapons out of the area, acting like the good, peaceful Samaritan. In reality, that means stopping the Byotai from shipping in weapons and defending themselves. Without weapons, they will lose."

Spartan nodded.

"And then this Tahkeome will sweep in, declare victory right on the Byotai border for stopping the fighting, while consolidating his powerbase. All the while the population of what, three millions Byotai, they will pay the price."

He turned around and looked towards the fifth figure, the vast shape that might easily have been ignored as a statue in the centre of the room. It was On'Sarax, the leader of the only seven Biomechs in existence. Her body was at least the size of Khan, but there was no obvious head. Her four arms hung down from the joints and to her knees.

"What will they do then?"

A single blue lamp flickered each time she spoke, roughly where the eyes would be on a living creature.

"The Anicinàbe are a primitive people, but they are quick to react and to act on opportunity. This Tahkeome is unusual, a figure of considerable intelligence and cunning."

Spartan didn't seem particularly surprised.

"I suspect this will be the beginning of a long campaign to take all six worlds in the disputed territories, a way to test the Byotai, while strengthening the bonds between the Anicinàbe."

The machine moved its torso to appear as if she was facing Spartan. The others remained silent, considering the implications.

"United they will be more powerful than all of you combined. There is a reason we avoided getting heavily involved in their disputes."

"I know," Spartan said, interrupting the machine, "And then the Byotai will be forced to concede the six worlds or to face a war against a growing power on their border."

Kanjana shook her head.

"I am still in the room, On'Sarax. My people are not monsters," she said in mock irritation.

The machine leaned its torso forward in a conciliatory gesture.

"I merely give voice to the facts. This is no reflection on you or your kin. In the past, my people sowed discord amongst the Anicinàbe. Tribe versus tribe and warband versus warband to keep them from unity."

Kanjana turned to Spartan.

"Do you believe all of this?"

Spartan had no need to answer. She could already see the answer on his face, and so she looked back at the ancient machine, a towering creature of long-lost knowledge and wisdom.

"With my people's influence gone, the Anicinàbe are now free to follow their own path, and it appears many of them seek to benefit from the weakness of others. They will attack anybody they can benefit from, including each other."

A loud cracking sound announced the opening of the massive grand doors. They were vastly oversized; at least five times the height of the Biomech machine and three times wider. Any sensible design would have place a smaller doorway at the base, but not on the World Ship. A single figure emerged, that of an Alliance officer.

"Just one this time," Khan said under his breath.

They all turned to watch the officer, and he stopped before Spartan.

"Colonel," he said, in a questioning tone.

Colonel Black lowered his beret to his side. His expression was serious, tinged with something Spartan had not seen from the man before. He glanced at the others and then to Spartan.

"Have you got somewhere we can talk?"

Spartan shook his head. The Colonel seemed unconcerned by the others, but the shape of the ancient Biomech machine was clearly an issue. The Colonel took a step closer.

"This is non-negotiable, Spartan."

He moved in close and spoke quietly.

"It concerns the General."

Spartan felt a lump in his throat. He had never been incredibly close to the man, but they had fought side by side in the Uprising. Since then they had crossed paths on multiple occasions, and always fighting the same enemies. They were men of the same era, and though they had now taken different paths, there was still much they had in common.

"This way."

Spartan moved off but gave a nod to Khan. The Jötnar joined the pair and they walked to the side of the battle deck. A gantry disappeared off into the bulkhead near the tall windows. They followed it until they were in a small passageway that was suspended over the glass. Space was visible in every direction bar one. Spartan stopped and looked to the Colonel.

"Well?"

"It's the General. He was in a convoy with Gun taking weapons and equipment to the Byotai settlers in the Khagi mountain region, all supplied by Alliance Intelligence. They were hit by militants, at least that is what the reports are saying."

Spartan closed his eyes and breathed slowly.

"Both of them?"

Colonel Black shook his head.

"We've lost contact with our contacts on Karnak. The last information we had they were taking prisoners to an underground facility. We suspect he's amongst them. When they discover who he is...well, the repercussions could be terrible."

Khan didn't hide his feelings.

"What do you mean you've lost contact? This is not some lost trader. This is an Alliance general."

Colonel Black was stoic in appearance.

"I know that, Khan. Nonetheless, the Alliance cannot be directly concerned with this conflict. It is a fight between those on Karnak. If the Alliance does get involved, then we risk war. Officially, neither the Anicinàbe, nor the Byotai military, can enter the conflict."

Khan started to speak, but the Colonel spoke over him.

"There's more. We have reason to believe that this Tahkeome may have landed Anicinàbe soldiers on the planet, probably disguised as settlers. They mean to take Karnak from beneath the noses of the Byotai, all as part of a popular uprising."

Khan was angry, but Spartan was past that point.

"He must be alive. I refuse to accept he would be gone, just like that."

He angled his head a little to the right.

"But then why would you be here? Just to tell me you don't know where he is?"

Colonel Black gave little away, but he did lower his voice.

"I shouldn't be telling you this, not anymore. But we received contact from one of the Khreenk mercenary units helping train some of the Byotai defence forces. They say a number of humans have been captured and taken to the capital of the Khagi mountain district. An underground city complex called Montu."

Spartan gave Khan a quick look.

"So, we go to Montu and demand their release. What's the problem?"

Colonel Black sighed.

"The Byotai don't control Montu anymore. They lost contact six hours ago. Alliance Intelligence suspects an Anicinàbe unit may have taken the facility and is using it as a way of controlling the region."

He looked down and lifted up his secpad. On it was an image of the border between the two quarrelsome races.

"Both sides have placed ships to their sides of the border and are blockading the six planets. They are taking the Demilitarised Zone seriously and will not allow military ships through. We sent in a delegation, but they were turned back, and we cannot admit an Alliance general was in the area."

Khan hissed through his teeth.

"What about the Byotai settlers? They are innocents in this."

Colonel Black didn't answer him. He didn't have to. That more than anything seemed to really anger Khan. He grabbed Spartan and turned him about to face him.

"They fought with us in the war. We can't let..."

Spartan grasped his friend's arm.

"Khan, I know. Trust me."

He then turned back to Colonel Black.

"Okay, you've got my attention. I assume you've got something in mind?"

Now it was Colonel Black's turn to look sheepish.

"Actually, I'm here without official Alliance backing. I've been given resources but no Alliance ships or military assets. They cannot help in any official capacity, but they are not blocking travel to the region. Assuming anybody can make it past the blockades.

Khan muttered.

"Let me guess, nobody has tried it yet, right?"

Colonel Black nodded.

"There are only a handful of private security companies left, and with military contracts no longer valid, they just don't have the manpower or incentive to get involved."

He looked to Spartan.

"However, I have made arrangements with a unit of unregulated mercenaries, a dozen of their best, all experienced combat veterans. It's not much, but I have enough to carry out a small rescue mission."

Spartan didn't seem impressed.

"You're taking a dozen mercs to run the blockade, in what? A cargo ship?"

Colonel Black lifted his lip slightly, betraying a grin.

"I was hoping you might be able to help there. Rumour has it your ships are operational...and fast. But are they ready?"

Spartan straightened himself and then laughed.

"My ships? I don't have any. Special Weapons Division

has three for the project, but even if I could get one of them through the Rift, I cannot travel into Alliance territory without clearance. Something I don't have. Do you?"

Colonel Black turned away and considered his words carefully. It took a few more seconds before he looked over his shoulder.

"Look, I can take care of the clearance, if you can get a ship. You need to understand that anything you or any other private citizen does is without Alliance knowledge or consent. If you come, we will deny any knowledge of what you are doing."

"So?" Khan laughed, "What difference would that make, anyway?"

The Alliance officer watched them both carefully.

"This mountain city, Montu, it's mostly underground with a spaceport above it. Our drones show it is heavily protected. We need intelligence before we can act."

"We?" Spartan asked.

Now the Colonel changed for the briefest of moments, baring the smallest of smiles.

"Yes, we. I'm coming with you. And I brought a friend on the way here. It seems Hyperion is a fertile recruiting area for hired guns."

Khan lifted an eyebrow.

"Hyperion?"

Spartan's eyes lit up at the name of the lush jungle world deep inside the Alliance.

"Bring him and meet us in Shipyard Six. We have things to discuss. I have a few things to attend to first."

The Colonel made to move away but looked again at Spartan.

"How will you get the ship? Will CTC just let you do as you please?"

Spartan didn't even bother answering the question.

"Just get yourself ready, Colonel."

* * *

## Shipyard Six, Kha'Dri World Ship, Taxxu Prime

Spartan and Khan waited with Kanjana nearby atop of a pair of metal crates. Behind them was the shape of a starship covered in scaffolding. Work crews were nowhere to be seen, but there were at least a dozen robotic welding machines making finishing touches to parts of the outer hull. Neither Mr Walker nor Captain Wilson was present.

"So, this is all part of the stage three test, is it?" Khan asked.

His expression barely concealed his amusement. Spartan nodded, trying to act seriously. They were both well aware that stage three was listed in the strategy as full trials prior to acceptance into the Alliance military.

"Exactly. Full trials as required by the contract."

He then looked to Khan.

"Alliance Military has been stalling on the last stage of the project. If you ask me, they are getting cold feet about making the final investment to get the brigade into service."

He glanced at the ship.

"The General is all that matters, but the mission could have an upside."

Khan laughed at the very mention of a business decision by Spartan.

"I'm serious, Khan. If this works, well, can you think

of anything better for the programme than a success like this? Imagine the ship, with our Grunts and machines expanded into a full brigade. Power projection without the risk."

"Yeah, it will be great, assuming we aren't all dead."

Kanjana listened to both of them, but so far she'd had nothing to add. She was like this most of the time, and instead she pointed in the direction of a small group.

"Here they come."

Both Spartan and Khan watched as they approached. There was a single large figure with them, and at the front the Colonel. He didn't stop until he was in front of Spartan. At his side was a single Jötnar, wearing their locally made armour and all baring blades and firearms. Spartan broke out into a wide smile while Khan moved forward.

"Olik!"

Their arms crashed together, and the Jötnar laughed loudly. Olik looked to Spartan.

"You promised to visit our little paradise. We're getting impatient."

He released Khan and moved to Spartan, grasping his forearm tightly. He was the smallest of the three, yet still massive by human standards. In the time since the war, Spartan had bulked up considerably, but even his vast bulk was nothing compared to that of Olik. Their muscles tensed, and Olik began to move Spartan's arm through sheer physical strength. Finally, he stopped, and the two embraced. Even Olik was impressed at the size and speed of his old friend.

"Been working out?"

Spartan laughed.

"Something like that. Got to love the cellular rejuvenation

therapy offered by CTC. Hell, I might be getting younger with every year that goes by. The technology taken from the Biomechs is paying off time after time."

His expression changed to something more serious.

"Olik, you honour all of us by coming here."

"How could I not? The General fought alongside my kin. He is now one of us, and Gun. Well, I want to know how anybody managed to capture him. Trust me, we are not impressed!"

Khan noticed how much calmer Spartan was already.

"It's been much too long since we were all together." he agreed. "Now we just need to get the others back."

Spartan turned his attention to Colonel Black.

"We finally have something to do worthy of the Jötnar, don't you think?"

The officer removed his tunic and folded it on his right arm. He followed it by adding his cap and then insignia. Underneath he wore a beige jacket, unmarked and reinforced with straps.

"From now on, I am no longer an officer in the Marine Corps. Not until this is all over."

Spartan looked to the Jötnar and then to the Colonel.

"So, you, and two Jötnar. That's it?"

Khan grinned, and Olik laughed loudly. Olik spoke so loudly he drowned out the others.

"Training recruits on Hyperion is getting boring. We ended the war, and now there is nothing worthy of our time. Maybe we should have left a few Biomechs to give us an excuse to keep our knives sharp, eh?"

"I see your sense of humour hasn't fully developed, little brother," replied Khan.

Olik returned to the subject with an almost subdued

look.

"Yes, Spartan, that's it, plus whatever you can bring to the deal."

He rubbed his hands together gleefully, and Spartan smiled as he considered his answer. He looked back at his pet project.

"We've been working on this project for six years now, you know that. Our negotiations with CTC, On'Sarax, and the Alliance were what created the Special Weapons Division."

He pointed to the Jötnar.

"We founded this division with a single goal in mind, to build the most advanced and powerful military unit. One that could combine the strength of our existing fighting units and the tech handed over by On'Sarax and her kin. Never again will we enter battle in conflicts where we are outgunned."

He then pointed to Olik.

"You've been testing our latest tech on Hyperion and preparing recruits."

His hand next moved to Khan.

"And you've been working with On'Sarax to get the interface technology working with the new armour."

Khan nodded again.

"But none of this equipment is ready, not even close. We guaranteed the Alliance a complete upgrade that would put the next generation expeditionary force into the field. The contract includes all required tech, ships, weapons, and training, and all within a decade. This, my friends, will be our legacy."

"So?" Colonel Black asked.

Spartan shook his head.

"That was seven years ago, and before the Alliance cut a third of our funding. We're a long way from being fully operational. A stipend from all Alliance planets is funding half of the project, with the rest coming from CTC investments. When it is ready, it will be under Alliance command, not mine, and it's not ready in any case."

Colonel Black didn't look convinced.

"Really?" The last paper I read said your name was at the top as the commander of the entire force, at the request of the T'Kari and Khreenk governments, if I'm not mistaken."

Khan wiped his chin with the back of his hand and looked to Spartan.

"I told you they would push to get you back."

Spartan shrugged.

"I don't see why, half of the Helions still blame me for the burning of Spascia. In any case, that's a fight for another time. Right now we need transport to the demilitarised zone, do we not?"

Colonel Black nodded, indicating for the man to turn around.

"In any case, when they are operational they will form part of the Alliance military. But if they are not ready, well, we'll have to come up with something else."

Spartan shook his head.

"I think we might have something that can help though, maybe."

He turned around and pointed to the ship. From the front the vessel looked similar to a Crusader, with the traditional prow and superstructure. The rear half was subtly different, with large nacelles and less mounts for weapons. The single biggest change was the ring. The massive circular section extended out from the sides of the vessel to completely surround the ship. A number of large doors were open, and as they watched, more than thirty figures emerged from inside the ship. Each was the size of a man, but encased in a dull iron skin that looked more like armour.

"You've seen them on the videostreams, and we even demonstrated the engines last year."

Olik said something, but he couldn't quite hear. He stopped and waited, but the Jötnar waved him on.

"Let me introduce you to the first experimental starships to come off the CTC production line, and of course, their trainee crews."

The doors on the port flank hissed open in unison.

"This is Titan. She is the first of the Confederate class ships; what we hope will become the leading ship design in the new class of assault ships. A high-speed, fully networked ship design that can fulfil a variety of combat missions. They will be fully modular, with components that can be installed in ships of different sizes. This is the ultimate addition to the existing fleet of Crusader Conqueror and Liberty ships."

He bowed with a fancy flourish, and Olik laughed again, only now realising how much he'd missed his friend.

"Confederate?" Olik asked.

Spartan gave him a mischievous look.

"As the man running the Special Weapons Division, I get to make these kinds of decisions. Yes, and there are two more like her."

He pointed off to the shapes of subsequent ships behind her.

"Euryale and New Carlos."

Olik sighed and shook his head.

"All named after our battles in the Uprising? You need to let go, old man, you really do."

Spartan laughed.

"Perhaps."

The thirty crew continued moving towards them, stopping in a neat line, two ranks deep. Khan was not surprised, but Colonel Black took an involuntary step backwards. He clearly knew what he was looking at, and his automatic reaction was to keep away.

"You are using the former foot soldiers of the enemy as crew for ships?"

Spartan laughed, but Colonel Black seemed uncomfortable.

"Not quite. The Thegns are free, but they are not particularly welcome in the Alliance, for obvious reasons. Out here they have a chance for a life, a better one than they had as cannon fodder for the Biomechs."

Khan grumbled in agreement.

"They are quick learners. Many are working in the engineering teams or testing equipment on the ships. More important, they will follow my orders."

Colonel Black shook his head in stunned surprise.

"Very well. In any case, we just need to get to the surface. Are these the same designs I saw back at the conference on Terra Nova?"

Spartan rubbed at his chin while looking at the crew. They had been called Thegns in the past, the synthetic humanoids used by the enemy as foot soldiers. Their skin was armoured, and they had been a brutal and ruthless enemy. He knew; he'd both fought alongside them, and against them. He shook his head to cast aside the images of battle and to the experimental ships.

"The designs are very similar, with a few tweaks for the engine system. All three are functional and are currently being put through their sea trials. I am due to take New Carlos out for additional tests on the engines within the week. Titan has just been refitted, and is ready for immediate service."

Colonel Black gave it a thought and turned his attention to Khan.

"We'd better get loaded up. I'll get any local intel sent directly to us en route."

Olik nodded slowly and then struck Spartan on the shoulder.

"I brought my own gear, hope you don't mind?"

He walked away in the direction the Colonel originally came from.

Spartan watched him move further and further away. It meant a great deal to have him back, but without Gun it felt hollow. They had spent a lot of time on this new project, but the time that stuck in his mind the most was their visit to the battlefield ruins of Spascia ten years ago. He'd known at that point he wanted to do something constructive, a project that would occupy both his mind and his body.

"Tell me about her," said Colonel Black.

The Colonel broke his concentration, and he found himself looking at the face of a man he realised he barely knew. They'd known of each other, and in the last few years had met at meetings and demonstrations. Unlike General Daniels, this was a man he had no real bond with. Even so, the Colonel appeared to share his concern at the vanishing of Daniels, and that was enough for now. The two walked down the flank of the ship, leaving Khan to speak with the Thegns. The ship was big, far bigger than the existing Liberty destroyer, the workhorse of the Navy. Colonel Black noticed the lines were similar to existing ships, but there was still something alien about it.

"She's special, a fusion of ideas taken from the Biomechs and mixed with our own. She's big enough to carry a full company of marines or equivalent, is well armoured, and equipped with a powerplant more powerful than a Crusader."

He pointed to the nose, but Kanjana touched his hand and stepped out in front of him.

"May I?"

Spartan shrugged.

"Go ahead."

Kanjana walked up to the vessel and touched the cool metal plate as though it was a large beast.

"She's something special all right; a combination Crusader ship with all the latest additions and space to carry a fully mobile combat unit. She faster, tougher, and more powerful than a Crusader, and with the troop transport capacity of the old assault ships."

She wiped her lip and pointed to the bow.

"All Confederate class ships are overpowered, due to the phased fusion powerplant. That gives us the energy to drive quad particle cannons both fore and aft, along with a complement of particle gun defence turrets."

"And that?"

Colonel Black pointed to the ring around the last part of the ship.

"Oh, the most important feature of all, and this one came from Earth. The design is ancient, going back to your twentieth century. But with the help of On'Sarax and her kin, CTC has been able to get a variant of the Alcubierre drive working. Kind of."

Colonel Black shook his head in frustration and looked back to Spartan.

"I've seen the reports on the brigade. I know what you've been working on out here, and I know why the testing of the engines has been done well away from colonised worlds."

He clenched his teeth.

"Just answer me one question, are these ships reliable enough for an operation using their new engines?"

Spartan gave him the widest grin he'd seen in years.

"Why do you think CTC is receiving so much support? My connections with On'Sarax gave me the leverage to create the Special Weapons Division. The payoff is this technology, something the Alliance will receive when it is fully ready. This technology will allow ships on their own to travel the stars, and it is worth a lot of money, for the civilians and for the military."

He glanced briefly to Kanjana and then to Colonel Black.

"In answer to your question, yes she is working, and I can provide a ship, this one specifically, but only with a limited crew. The brigade is months from even initial testing."

He pointed to Titan.

"Her modified Alcubierre drive is the most reliable of the three. She was the first built, after all. Even so, it's still a little temperamental. When it works, it is something incredible, and it will allow us to make a high-speed dash to Karnak. Assuming you can get us close to the border."

Colonel Black nodded as he listened.

"I can sort out that, but what happens then?"

Spartan crunched his hands together with a meaty thud.

"And then we will do our part, what all of us were born to do."

Colonel Black nodded with satisfaction and then realised he'd forgotten something.

"Wait, what about a crew? I cannot sanction Alliance officers to do this, and I doubt that you..."

Spartan lifted his hand to stop him.

"Don't worry about that."

The Colonel didn't seem particularly convinced.

"The thirty Thegns have been training with Khan over the last year, specifically to handle one of these ships on long-duration operations. They answer directly to me and nobody else. They will pilot that ship down to the surface of Karnak, and onto the head of this Tahkeome if I asked them."

Colonel Black put his hands down to his side and gave the entire operation one last thought.

"Spartan, I always wondered if we would fight alongside each other. I assumed it would have been in armour and on an Alliance battlefield. Instead, we are doing this."

Spartan reached out his hand, and the Colonel shook it.

"Don't worry, Colonel. There is plenty of time to do that."

He then walked towards the ramp leading up into the spacecraft. As soon as he reached the top, the Thegns filed back inside, making barely a sound. The Colonel watched them all disappear, leaving just him in the vast alien shipyard.

"So...it begins."

# CHAPTER FOUR

*The Centauri Alliance went through something of a renaissance following the great victory of 362CC. As the last battles were fought, the great industries of humanity had reached their peak output. They were already churning out equipment, ships, weapons, and supplies on a massive scale, along with the high levels of employment such industry required. The arrival of peace would see a massive demobilisation of the military, but also a rise in standards of living and a massed rebuilding of the worlds ravaged by war. The Interstellar Network was improved and expanded through the technology captured in the war, and new colonies were founded to replace those smashed in the firestorms and bombardments. Not all would welcome the dawn of this new world order, and the Anicinàbe crisis would be the first event to test the resolve of those dedicated to peace.*

*The New Colonies*

## ANS X-45 'Titan', The Black Rift, Centauri Alliance

The ship moved out from the Black Rift with little pomp or excitement. A decade earlier, the sign of a ship making the journey would have been one for fear and consternation.

It had been the location of the Biomech incursion, one that threatened the existence of every sentient being. Now, as they emerged, there was nothing but a single Alliance Crusader warship and a Helion frigate to watch them pass. No fighters circled them, much to the surprise of Spartan.

"It looks like I'm through this time without a fight."

Colonel Black raised his eyebrows, surprised at his comments.

"Quite. I suspect the security units in orbit over Taxxu Prime were busy watching us leave. At least we didn't bring any of the Thegn barges with us."

Spartan grinned. He'd forgotten about them for now. The barges were filled with millions of Thegns in deep hibernation, an issue that was still unresolved from the war. Those already awakened had found homes in Taxxu, mainly working with CTC on massive engineering projects, building shipyards and factories. No decision had been made on the future of those still in hibernation, although each of the craft had been fitted with explosive thermite bolts, ready to vent the vessels in case of a crisis.

"True. I have some ideas for them, but that's for another time. You can see how effective they are already on this ship. They deserve more than the indentured work most of the colonies offer them. They are trusted less than Gun and his people."

The Colonel looked at Spartan and began to wonder what these ideas would entail. He was still surprised Spartan had allowed them on such an important project and could well understand people's suspicion of them. He could only guess their lack of previous knowledge made them easy to manipulate, or perhaps they were as loyal and quick to learn as Spartan kept saying.

*Who knows? But what if something or somebody turned them against us?*

Part of the agreement with the Alliance for CTC to operate at Taxxu was the stationing of six Liberty class ships and a small orbital starbase around the planet. There was a company of marines on permanent attachment there, but it was all very low key. Much of this helped by the fact that CTC maintained more than a thousand personnel in Taxxu, with over two hundred security operatives on the World Ship alone. The Thegns were now effectively sentient beings in the Alliance, and that made them citizens. Any brought out of hibernation could expect full protection under the law. He'd already seen them working in mines out on the Rim, and it hadn't been pretty.

*Complicated, damned complicated.*

Colonel Black watched the view from the command deck with both fascination and an odd sense of wonder. They had now left the infamous Black Rift and were in the border regions of the Alliance, formally the Helion Sector. The Rift swirled behind them like a whirlpool, but this was very different to the way it had been in the past. The Spacebridge had already been open when they passed through, and as they emerged into a region of space many light years away, the tunnel remained open.

"That always gives me the shakes," he said, watching the Spacebridge fade away, "No matter how many times you tell me it is secure, I wonder if it might change."

Spartan leaned towards him.

"I'll let you into a secret. It does the same to me as well. And I've been on a vessel when one collapses. It isn't pretty."

The ship accelerated away from the two other ships

and onto its new course. Spartan watched the Crusader class ship shrink into the distance until finally it was out of sight.

"This is it then," he said quietly.

Colonel Black nodded.

"I have to admit, I'm still finding it hard to get around you working with the corporation that destroyed your own company. You're a fighting man, Spartan, not a salesman."

Spartan snorted at his question.

"I always saw you and the General as moving in the same direction. You fought together in the Uprising, a generation ago, did you not?"

The memories of that war were as fresh in his mind as the equipment testing they had been performing recently. Spartan recalled his first meeting with the Captain, as he'd been back then. Their rivalry had become more of a professional understanding by the time they'd fought in a few battles together.

"Yes, on multiple occasions. Daniels is the professional soldier; he knows the system, and he is a good officer. Not me, though."

He placed his hand on his chest.

"There are as many people that would like to see me back, as there are that want to see me burn. Trust me, the Corps doesn't want me back."

"So that's why you started all of this?"

Spartan thought about his answer.

"The four of us planned this a decade ago, all while we waited on the ruins of Spascia. Our knowledge and connections with The Twelve, as well as the resources of the Jötnar."

He looked up a little, as if trying to claw memories

from his mind.

"The first idea was to create a mercenary outfit, but CTC tried to muscle in and stopped us fast. Their agents managed to steal some of our plans. Well, we sort of leaked them."

He laughed.

"But that just made them realise what they were missing out on, especially the Biomech technology. A visit from Gun was quite...well...persuasive."

Colonel Black was not entirely sure what Spartan was telling him.

"But access to the tech is controlled by the Alliance, not you."

Spartan laughed.

"It will take centuries to learn the secrets of the technology we've discovered. The four of us have access to something neither the Alliance nor CTC has."

Colonel Black understood right away.

"The Twelve. They are giving you this information?"

Spartan almost winked at this question.

"Our relationship is based on mutual trust. There is nobody outside of our group that the surviving Twelve would ever trust. You saw the outcry for their destruction after the war."

Spartan looked away.

"We guarantee their safety; the exchange of information was never even originally discussed."

Colonel Black was surprised. He knew Spartan was perhaps the most famous military man in modern history, but he had no idea he was as capable a negotiator as this. Somehow Spartan and his comrades, some of the most violent and least diplomatic of people, had managed to gain access to advanced technology. This technology was generations ahead of what was currently being worked on, and its value would probably be astronomical.

"So now the four of you own and run CTC's Special Weapons Division. I don't get it. I thought CTC had effectively killed your family business years ago?"

Spartan didn't appear thrilled at the prospect of money.

"I'm no fan of CTC. That's why this division is autonomous. We run it, and they finance it. This is all about legacy, for me, and the Jötnar."

Colonel Black watched the strange space distortion that led back in the direction they had left.

"What do you mean?"

Spartan pointed out into space.

"There will always be battles to fight, but next time it will not be with marines and carbines, or Helion infantry struggling to hold the line. Our Special Weapons Division is creating a system of machines, weapons, and vehicles for a brand new elite expeditionary unit, one that takes on the best of what we already have and brings it to the next level."

There was something in Spartan's voice that caught his interest. A real passion, almost excitement at what he was planning.

"It will be unlike anything seen before."

Colonel Black nodded as he listened.

"Yes, the proposed Interstellar Assault Brigade is what they are calling it back on Terra Nova, are they not? It is an interesting idea."

Spartan shrugged.

"Something like that. The fleet and Marine Corps will stay, but this new unit will take recruits from any world that wants to join, and multiply their ability using our latest developments. This will be the tip of the spear for the Alliance military."

Colonel Black tried to imagine what this new look military would be like. This sounded suspiciously like a replacement for the large Marine Force Recon units; the best equipped and trained marines in the Alliance.

"Money is pouring into the Alliance coffers right now with all the new worlds that have joined. In exchange for resources, they are providing security and stability. We might have a lot of marines and ships in service, but there's little interest or stomach for sending thousands more into the military, not after the losses in the war."

He looked back to the Colonel.

"That's why we established the SWD. Do the Helions or the others want to commit quarter of a million citizens to their armies?"

He shook his head, answering his own question.

"Of course not, not anymore. The Helions suffered the most and lost millions of civilians. They don't have the numbers for that. Across the board, there is a growing consensus that each colony would rather contribute with currency or other resources."

Now the Colonel could see what Spartan was getting at, and he had to admit, he didn't like it. War was violent and bloody, and as far as he was concerned, it needed to run by the people that called for it. It had to be a difficult and dangerous option, or else the civilians would be far more likely to demand military options.

"You'd need more than ships and more powerful guns, though. You still need the people to carry the fight to the enemy."

Spartan laughed at that.

"True. You saw what the Vanguards could do in the war, a man inside the armour of a fighting machine. Ten Vanguards could do the work of a company of marines. We saw the introduction of four-legged cargo mules to carry supplies across the field. What if that Vanguard could be tougher, better armed, and protected and supported by more flexible and capable machines? Drones that can augment you in combat, provide covering fire where needed, and keep you alive."

Colonel Black was intrigued, but he decided to move the imaginary machines and ships from his mind and concentrate on the mission. He turned his attention from Spartan to the ship.

"I suppose that right now the pertinent question is will this new ship of yours do what it needs to?"

Spartan lifted an inquisitive eyebrow.

"Well, Titan has made trial journeys nine times successfully so far."

Colonel Black looked at him.

"Out of how many attempts?"

Spartan didn't answer and gave him an awkward smile. He looked around the deck of the ship and nodded in satisfaction at the progress they were making. The deck was much smaller than others he had been on before, but it matched the standard configuration. Square in shape, the small number of senior crew was stationed at gently curved displays to the front. This screen was split into three large panes, each currently providing a clear view from the front of the ship. Steps led down to a lower level on the left, and a pair of circular bays, along with extra seating and computer screens. Most of the walls were either displays or imitation curved glass looking out into space. Colonel Black had moved a few metres away to look at the mainscreen. When he looked back, he could see Spartan scrutinising almost every part of the ship.

"She's very interesting, Spartan. Smaller, yet it feels larger than a much bigger ship."

"That was the plan," agreed Spartan, "We had Alliance naval designers examine the interiors of ships from the Byotai, Biomechs, Helions, and our own. This design combines the best of what we found, with the technology at our disposal. You can run this ship using the AI CTC have developed, or can crew her."

He lifted his finger to his nose as if about to impart some great secret.

"That part is still not ready. Give it another six months."

Colonel Black had checked some of the specifications when they were leaving, but even he had to admit the ship was impressive, nearly eighty thousand metric tons and almost four hundred metres long.

"And you say in combat condition you can cram two thousand marines on board. Are you serious?"

Spartan nodded. He was being polite, but both knew the entire conversation was nothing to do with the future plans for the ship, or even its specification. It was all about the mission, and they were skirting around the issue.

"Yes, perhaps more with the production models. But trust me, you would not want to be aboard with those numbers. We envisage this model being produced in military and civilian models. With this capacity, the ship would make an excellent colony ship or transport as well."

Neither of them had mentioned the elephant in the room, but the Colonel could keep quiet no longer. Finally, he nodded in the direction of the crew, the artificially created humanoids known simply as Thegns that were now running the ship.

"The ship might do it, but are you sure they are?"

Spartan nodded and bared his teeth a little in amusement.

"More than you can imagine."

He looked to the command chair where one of the Thegns sat.

"Five-Seven. What is our status?"

The creature examined the panels fitted around his seat before answering.

"Spartan. All systems are nominal. Fusion reactor is running to specification, and the interstellar drive is powered up and ready for activation."

"Good," he said calmly, "Lay in a course to the Byotai Spacebridge."

Colonel Black spun about to look at Spartan.

"Wait. That wasn't the plan. We use the network through the Alliance. It will take us a few days, and then we will make the dash into the DMZ. This ship's engines have to be used as a last resort."

Spartan shook his head.

"No. The General and Gun don't have the time. We can be at the entrance to the Byotai Spacebridge in a matter of hours. The Byotai are unlikely to let an armed ship into the region, and the Anicinàbe will shoot us on sight."

Colonel Black had nothing to say, so Spartan continued.

"This is as good a time to test the engines as any other, would you not agree?"

Five-Seven spoke slowly and calmly.

"Course laid in, we are ready to activate the engines."

Spartan straightened his back and gave a curt nod.

"Do it."

An indicator on the mainscreen right at the bottom showed the power build-up, as the ring at the rear of the ship began the process to create the warped area of space around the ship, commonly described as a bubble. The indicator increased in speed and then halted. Five-Seven hit a single button. The objects nearest to the ship blurred and disappeared. The newest planets and celestial objects moved slowly, while the distant objects appeared as still as normal.

"Is it working?" Colonel Black asked.

Spartan laughed.

"Colonel, we are now travelling at just under the speed of light, all without the use of Spacebridges."

The two were silent and looked back to the mainscreen. The process of acceleration was unlike any other form of travel. The unique feature of the engines was that the ship never moved, instead the small bubble around the ship slipped ahead, distorted space-time, effectively moving them along with the distortion. It was elegant and incredibly difficult to maintain.

"So, we will be at the border in a few hours, and then we make our dash to the planet. What then, Spartan? Tell me you have a plan?"

"Spartan, there are reports coming in from the Alliance News Network. It is Karnak."

Spartan and Colonel Black shared a quick look.

"Put it on the mainscreen."

Five-Seven nodded firmly and transferred the imagery to the large forward screen. The quality was perfect and showed an anchorman in full body armour in front of a burning building.

"For those of you just joining us, we are bringing you live videostreams of the fighting. Three hours ago, local militias blockaded entry to the planet, and a full-scale insurrection by the pro-Anicinàbe settlers started."

An explosion ripped part of another distant building apart, and the anchorman dropped to the ground. Rockets flew overhead and were followed by the meaty thuds of impacts. The man returned to the camera view.

"We have unconfirmed reports of Anicinàbe civilian aircraft dropping militiamen into battle and escorting civilians out of their homes. If this is true, we may be seeing the first images of the removal of most, if not all Byotai settlers in the demilitarised zone."

Spartan closed his eyes and did his best to control his breathing.

"The Byotai are outnumbered, and we doubt they will be able to hold off these attacks for more than a few days, perhaps weeks."

"I know," said Colonel Black, "You were right."

Another explosion forced Spartan to open his eyes. The images had shifted to one of the peaceful-looking Byotai settlements. It was small, and perhaps home to a hundred or so civilians. The videostream was shaky, but it was clear the Byotai were not soldiers. Some carried firearms, but most were using agricultural tools to dig trenches near their homes.

"A hour ago this border settlement at Arasine was attacked. The families living here managed to fight them off with little more than a few shotguns and rifles, but as the village elder told us, the raiders will be back, and they have few weapons to fight back with."

The anchorman looked into the camera.

"Unconfirmed reports show that Anicinàbe militant attacks are well coordinated. They are heavily armed, and the Byotai governor has already asked his people to avoid fighting where they can."

The camera moved in closer to his face.

"Some are asking why the Anicinàbe have turned on their fellow settlers, but others are suggesting involvement of the Anicinàbe Council. If this is true, it could be the first aggressive mood by a confident new regime. The question all of us are asking, is what will the Byotai reaction be?"

Spartan gave the signal to cut the video feed. Just as it was about to fade, he shook his head.

"This shouldn't have happened, and you're damn right I told you. The Byotai settlers should have been protected months ago, and now it's too late. A single cruiser would have sent the message that we are watching out for them. Now...well, this could be the spark that ignites a war."

The Colonel wanted to tell him about the reports he had seen already. The information on ship movements, and pirate attacks that suggested nothing of this magnitude was about to happen. All that had changed just days earlier, and some were already saying it was one of the greatest intelligence community failings in generations; and all because of this one individual, Tahkeome, the first leader of the Anicinàbe in generations that had united many of his kin.

"I'm not disagreeing, Spartan."

He was watching one of the displays that still showed one feed. Five-Seven reached for the button to stop it, but he called out instead.

"No, wait, zoom in."

The imagery changed to show an Anicinàbe convoy.

There were wheeled vehicles littering a small valley. Food and aid packages lay scattered in all directions, and one of the large vehicles belched thick black smoke. Spartan turned to the Colonel.

"That mark, there, on the vehicle."

Colonel Black looked closely and then spotted the black shape. It was relatively indistinct, but both of them recognised it immediately. It was just two shapes, both marked in black dust, probably carbon from the burning materials around them.

"Survival code," said Colonel Black, "That is Alliance."

They moved closer, but Spartan had already identified the key variables.

"Are those codes valid for this month?"

He looked back to the Colonel, and he was already nodding.

"That is the mark of the General all right, and the message is plain and simple. The mission is still active."

Spartan shook his head.

"They might have captured him, but somehow he managed to get the weapons out of Anicinàbe hands. If the Byotai can get their hands on them, they might have a chance."

He closed his eyes again and tried to relax his mind. Colonel Black turned to watch the stars moving ever so slowly. There was little they could do differently now, and they were already on the way. This one message gave him hope that they were alive somewhere on Karnak. Finally, Spartan said exactly what he was thinking.

"It's time to see the others. We need to get ready. Bring your mercenaries with you. We will get the General and Gun, and then we will make sure the Byotai can protect themselves. I will not leave Karnak until that is achieved."

* * *

The lower part of ANS X-45 Titan was very different to the armoured upper carapace that housed the shipboard weapons. The lower decks were vast and had unfinished locker rooms, bunks, a firing range, and a large training hall. Spartan led the Colonel down towards the lowest deck. It was the operations level, a part of the ship that encompassed perhaps a fifth of the entire vessel. It was wide open and filled with weapon racks and spaces for spacecraft. Both flanks were filled with reinforced cylinders that ran up into the ship. The fronts looked like glass doors, but a brown smoked colour so that it was impossible to see inside. Colonel Black look at them with interest, but then spotted what was waiting for them.

"Interesting."

In the middle of the operations level were two Jötnar, each massive and fully armoured. They towered over the handful of Thegns that were busy pulling out equipment from stowage bins. Behind them was a single medium-sized landing craft, known simply by its SWD codename, the Jackal. The craft looked remarkably similar to the vessel the Colonel has been looking at back on the World Ship.

"Your version of a Mauler, I presume?"

Spartan shrugged.

"Kind of. I can't take the credit, though. My input has been on the ground troops. We've had help with the rest."

Colonel Black gave the craft a cursory look. It was certainly of a similar size to the Mauler, but it was sleeker, and he suspected would offer many more features than the workhorse of the Alliance. It featured a swing-wing design and partially concealed engines. He looked hard but could find no sign of major ramps, hatches, or doorways leading inside, just two small hatches. Spartan watched him trying to find how ground troops would be able to leave in combat situations.

"Colonel, this is not designed to land troops on the ground. It is based on the tech we found when we arrived at T'Karan the first time. You recall the craft that dropped off machines while airborne?"

The Jötnar had been quiet until now, but Khan could take it no longer.

"Spartan, we thought you'd forgotten us."

Spartan and Colonel Black looked away from the craft and walked closer, stopping in front of them.

"How could I?" Spartan said.

"Very well," said the Colonel.

He looked at Khan and began to explain.

"If all goes to plan, we will be on the final approach to Karnak in a matter of hours."

Colonel Black nodded as he listened.

"Yes, and I have uploaded detailed schematics for the underground facilities on the planet, as well as the coded signatures for several Byotai militia units on the surface. We're going to need strong intelligence before we can act. Our contact will meet us at a nearby secure facility, along with local guides. It's a disused research base, and it has a direct underground transport line to the region's capital."

Olik seemed little interested, but Khan became more alert at the mention of the Byotai.

"Yes, we were just watching the latest reports. It seems

the Byotai have lost more than half of their settlements on Karnak, the rest are in hiding. This is already turning into an occupation, and it could get a lot worse."

Khan grumbled.

"It probably will. The Anicinàbe cannot be trusted. They will take Karnak, and then move to the next world. We could have used their numbers in the war."

Khan looked at his comrade who was clearly in agreement. He shrugged.

"Perhaps, but they could just as easily have fought on the side of the enemy. What then?"

Khan muttered something about the past, and Olik tried to smile before continuing.

"I warned them more than a year ago that this would happen. That there is a growing level of stability amongst the Anicinàbe, and that they are becoming restless. They are looking outwards, and Karnak is right there in front of them, like an open wound."

He snorted, clearly irritated.

"The Byotai settlers have been abandoned by their government, all in the name of peace. Before the resettling of Karnak, it was a haven for pirates, nothing more. It no more belongs to the Anicinàbe than it belongs to us. The Byotai abandoned it generations earlier, and now civilian settlers will pay the price."

Spartan could see the frustration on his friend's face.

"They always do, my friend. But let's keep focused here. We cannot change this conflict; it is between two people that have been putting off a fight for years. The Byotai might not be interested, but the Anicinàbe will not be happy they are right inside their border."

Khan laughed.

"Border? This isn't an island. There are no borders in space, just places where men point and then fight. Stupidity, all of it."

Olik caught Spartan's attention.

"I heard that this new leader, Tahkeome, has an agenda. He doesn't care about either side; he wants to take advantage of the troubles to carve out a territory of his own, right in the middle."

"Yeah," agreed Khan, "And that will put a buffer zone between the Anicinàbe and the Byotai. Smells like a setup to me. You know what will follow."

Spartan looked at each of them in turn.

"Right now none of that matters. We don't have the Alliance backing us up, not even a fleet, just us, this one ship, and our untested cargo. We're here to get our people out and in one piece."

Olik gave Colonel Black an odd look, and Spartan knew immediately that something was up. Spartan looked to the Colonel; he had been hoodwinked at best, or misled at worst. The fact Olik might be involved sent his blood pounding through his chest.

*What have you been up to, Olik?*

The look on Olik's face gave away his discomfort. His friend knew Spartan was not going to be overly happy, and for that Spartan could hardly blame him.

"We can do more than that, Spartan. We can bring back intelligence; show the Byotai and the Alliance what's happening out there. The Anicinàbe are a growing problem, and one day, perhaps soon, we will be forced to deal with them."

Spartan moved his attention to Khan who simply lifted his shoulder in mock surprise. Olik said nothing, but

Spartan could see he neither agreed nor disagreed. He would do whatever the others decided. Spartan sensed something was going on and looked at the Colonel.

"You planned this?"

The Alliance officer breathed out slowly.

"We cannot act in this crisis without information. If the fighting is as the reports say, then we have no place getting involved. A settler dispute is an internal problem, and the Alliance Security Council will not vote to embroil us in a fight with the Anicinàbe."

He looked to Khan and Olik.

"The Helions want no part, neither do the Byotai, and our own politicians keep saying there will be no boots on the ground without support from the entire Council."

Spartan began to speak, but Olik interrupted.

"But, and this is a big but. If the Anicinàbe are involved, and we can prove it, then the Alliance will be forced to vote on military intervention. It will be impossible for a no vote, given that an Alliance member is under attack."

Spartan took all of the information in, but he was still sure there was more to it. He looked into the eyes of the Colonel, but either he was telling him everything, or the man was the master of self-control. Knowing the Colonel's exemplary reputation, Spartan suspected the latter. Olik continued.

"We are just out there, far enough away from the heavily inhabited worlds to test new equipment and weapons for the company. We do this, and we give the Alliance...what did they call it?"

"Plausible deniability," explained the Colonel.

Spartan heard them, but he could already feel adrenalin starting to surge through his body. It took all his self-control to not break out into a rage.

"This Tenth Quadrant that the Byotai call it, it's not currently recognised by the Alliance. Are you so sure they would vote for action?"

Khan turned to Olik, and though not angry, he did seem a little surprised.

"Is this why you came with the Colonel? To persuade us to come on a recon mission?"

Olik snorted.

"We're here because General Daniels and Gun's reconnaissance and supply mission failed. The Colonel asked, and could we refuse?"

Olik looked intently at Spartan.

"I would have contacted you on the way here, but the Colonel was adamant this had to be kept quiet. He needs our help, so do the other prisoners, if any of them still lives. There are rumours of other prisoners on Karnak. Who knows what we might find down there?"

Spartan looked at each of them in turn. He had known them a long time, but it was Gun he had known the longest. Knowing he was prisoner was worse than knowing he was dead. The old warrior had taken a step back from his leadership position on the Alliance forest world of Hyperion, but he was still a revered warrior and leader amongst the Jötnar, the first of their kind to break free of the shackles of the enemy and to join the Confederacy decades earlier.

Olik and Khan were both great warriors in their own right, but Olik had managed to spend a lot more time in the world of politics in the Alliance. Khan was the one Spartan had spent the most time with over the years. Even so, since the end of the war, the four had worked together to make the Special Weapons Division their own, even from their often widely dispersed locations.

Spartan reached out with both hands, and his expression softened a little.

"Brothers, we built this ship and everything around us."

He looked to Colonel Black.

"We will get them, and if anybody gets in our way..."

Khan opened his mouth and howled with pleasure.

"If anybody gets in our way, they'll be introduced to our little friends."

Colonel Black didn't understand.

"What do you mean?"

Spartan pulled out a secpad and checked the time. He spoke quietly but loud enough for them to hear. Even so, the sound of Five-Seven speaking over the speaker system drowned him out.

"ETA seventy-three minutes to the Spacebridge."

Spartan tapped several buttons. A hatch opened up above them, and down came a sphere. Spartan stepped aside and waited until it stopped. The front opened up to reveal a harness arrangement. At the same time, the first of the mercenaries appeared at the far end of the deck. Spartan stopped and looked in their direction. They moved silently, with just the gently sound of their rubber soled boots marking their progress. On they came until the small group of twelve stopped before them. They were all human and dressed in custom body armour, in a style reminiscent of the heavy armour worn by the Confederate Army decades earlier.

"Colonel. Our gear is ready, and so are we."

The mercenary speaking was a tall woman of similar height to Spartan. Her head was covered in her helmet, and a black visor had dropped down to cover her eyes. Even so, Spartan could see her mouth and nose, and from the way she spoke knew right away where she was from.

"Old Earth?"

The women reached up with her hand and tapped a nodule just below the ear. With a hissing sound, the visor slid up, and she pulled away the helmet to reveal long pale blonde hair. She shook her head to release it from her armour.

"You've been there?"

"You could say that," Khan grumbled.

Spartan looked at her carefully. He was sure he hadn't met her before, but there was something about her eyes. He glanced at Khan, but he had already moved on to speak with the others.

"Is this your group? Who are you?"

She nodded.

"Yes, they're mine. Most of them are from the old world, but a few are from Kerberos. My name is Arana, and our unit goes where the work is."

"I thought private contracts died out years ago?"

Arana's face remained fixed and unemotional, but she clearly knew who Spartan was. And if she knew that, then she would also know he had run the largest and most successful private security company in the Alliance. Before the market collapsed and the embers of the company had been snapped up by CTC.

"There is always work for a fighter, wouldn't you agree, Spartan?"

Her armour was well cared for, he could see that, and there were pieces of alien technology mixed in with the mainly human armour. One sported a Khreenk rifle, but most carried ex-military or civilian firearms. Another of her soldier approached and deactivated her helmet. This woman looked the spitting image of Arana.

"This is my twin sister, Syala. She's the angrier one."

Syala extended her hand and grasped Spartan in a tight, vice-like grip.

"Spartan, it is good to finally meet you."

He shook his head and indicated for Colonel Black to move closer.

"They know the mission, and the risks?"

The man nodded.

"Of course. They are professionals, and with something of a pedigree. You heard about the Earth southern continent fiasco?"

Spartan had to think for a moment.

"The terrorist takeover of the Earthsec Antarctic fusion reactor? Yeah, I've heard of it. Didn't the entire unit get wiped out?"

Colonel Black grinned.

"That was them."

"You bet your ass it was us," said Syala, "Thirty of them overran the place and killed four guards. Earthsec botched an assault, so we were brought in. Lucky we were in the area."

"What happened?" Khan asked.

We took the facility in less than an hour."

"With how many soldiers?"

Syala gave him a coy look, and Arana sighed in irritation at her sister's clear bragging.

"Eight, and every one of us came back without a scratch."

"Interesting. I thought that was the Black Widows?"

was all Spartan had to say.

He looked back at the group.

"Is this an all-woman unit?"

"Yes, it was the Black Widows. As for all female, would that be a problem?" Arana asked.

She didn't seem angry, but Spartan sensed a little hostility in her tone.

"Not at all, just curious."

Arana lowered her head, almost in apology.

"Good. All foot soldiers keep their faces covered at all times. That is part of the agreement for joining our outfit. We get involved in some compromising operations, and if our faces are known, it could cause...well...complications. That's how we've maintained our untouchable reputation for so long."

"What about the two of you?"

Syala laughed.

"Oh, if anybody wants to cause a problem with us, they are welcome to try."

Arana pointed at the sphere behind Spartan and the others.

"We have just over an hour before we arrive, do we not? Maybe you could explain what that thing is?"

Spartan looked at her, turned around, stepped inside, and then tapped the buttons on the panel. A mist flooded out and obscured the view as they vanished inside. The two Jötnar watched but seemed more interested in keeping an eye on the Colonel. A clunking sound was immediately followed by most of the mist vanishing. It was replaced by one of the cylinders opening up along the side the operations level. The entire front rotated around and revealed a space at least two metres wide and three metres high.

"What is that?" asked the Colonel.

Arana looked to her sister, but no one seemed to know. Inside the open cylinder was a machine, one much like those he had seen fighting back on the World ship, but smaller. It was perhaps a head shorter than a human and wider at the chest. The head was sunk down lower than a man, and the shoulder extended out further. The machine stepped out and moved elegantly towards him. It was unpainted and completely bare metal, as though it had just come off a production line. The metallic sphere opened up so that Colonel Black could see Spartan inside the cylinder.

"Colonel, Ladies, let me introduce you to the drones of the future, or as we like to call them...CD 1 Combat Drones, 'Grunts' for short."

# CHAPTER FIVE

*The end of the violent struggle with the Biomechs once and for all guaranteed a place for military robotics. As the battlefields were cleared of the thousands of casualties, a growing belief grew throughout the worlds of humanity, as well as the T'Kari and the Helions. This great change occurred due to their desperate desire for machines to replace the living in times of strife and conflict. For every individual supporting this new ideal, there would be another that would always remind them of the biomechanical enemy that had only so recently been destroyed. Was the only way to win future wars to be determined by how much power could be handed over to machines? The Carthago Trade Consortium invested heavily in this new future, one where man would be supported by machines like never before.*

*Equipment of the Alliance Marine Corps*

## ANS X-45 'Titan', Helios Prime, Alliance

Spartan moved inside the sphere and pulled on the harness. It was a substantial affair and wrapped around his shoulder, middle, and abdomen, much like an old-fashioned parachute harness. He then tapped a button to the side, and with a gentle whoosh, he was lifted up and suspended in the air. He was able to move about freely without striking the sides. He looked out to the assembled crowd.

"This is the old design, back when we thought operators would need to physically move their bodies..."

He moved his hands rapidly.

"...like this."

Each time Spartan moved, the drone machine mimicked his own movements. He performed a series of steps and punches, and the machine copied him exactly. Spartan then stopped, pressed a button, and placed an odd skullcap onto his head. He looked right at the Colonel and grinned.

"Watch this."

Spartan didn't move a muscle, yet the machine moved around and performed a complex martial arts kata, stepping, kicking, and punching like a well-trained human martial artist. Finally, it stopped and Spartan opened his eyes.

"The neural interface is fully operational."

Colonel Black stepped up to the machine and examined it, speechless at what he could see. It was smaller than the machines he'd seen before, now just a little shorter than a man, squat but sturdy in appearance.

"You adapted the Ghost Warrior technology? This quickly?"

Khan seemed especially proud of the thing. He pointed to the sphere that Spartan was now exiting.

"This ship, when fully supplied can carry a hundred people, with ten times that number of combat units."

He pointed to the machine.

"They can be operated via line-of-sight from the

dropship or one of our Maverick suits. They can even perform basic functions autonomously, but that is not fully ready yet."

He pointed to the Jackal landing craft.

"That means ten marines inside the Jackal can command them remotely in battle. If one is lost, we can release another and drop it into action, all without losing the operator."

Khan licked his lips.

"Or one warrior can lead a squad into action on his own. They are capable of semi-autonomous action when commanded like this. Just tell them where to go or what to shoot, and they will do the rest."

Khan walked up to the machine and tapped it. The sound was dull and barely echoed.

"Or control them fully from the safety of a bunker or nearby flyer. These drones, combined with the new generation Maverick suits, plus the faster ships, will transform the battlefield."

Spartan watched with amusement as the Colonel tried to take it all in. The technology was impressive, but it was the degree of advancement that must have stunned him. Creating a new Vanguard or rifle was one thing, but the ship and the drones was taking it all to another level.

"The only question, Colonel, is will the Alliance be prepared to put all of this into service?"

Khan snorted.

"From what I've heard, some of the senators want to hand over the minimum amount of money, and even less people. That's why they'll create just the initial brigade, manned by the best volunteers. They can come from any world, even those with just military agreements within the

Alliance. Like the Byotai."

Spartan seemed to agree.

"I've heard the same, typical Alliance, looking to cut corners. Do more with less. Nothing changes. That's another reason for creating this unit. We actually can do more with less."

Colonel Black listened to them both, but he seemed the least pessimistic.

"It might work better actually, like a foreign legion; a force to be used that will have limited repercussions in the Alliance, being as it is crewed by multiple races. By including the others, the brigade should attract a wide variety of people and support."

Khan laughed.

"Maybe, but one brigade? What's that, about six thousand ground troops when at capacity? More like it will allow them to ignore casualties when it goes wrong. Nobody will care about drone casualties or alien mercenaries."

Spartan moved to the side of the deck and examined more of the machines, all of which stood in silence inside their smoke glass cylinders. He stayed there for a while as the others continued to talk and argue about the technology. He turned back and found them watching him.

"It's time we got ready."

He pointed to Olik.

"Get your personal gear out and checked. I need you all to be ready at a moment's notice."

Spartan then moved to Khan.

"Check the control matrix and start the diagnostic routines. I want these drones ready for combat. Run the tests, and then do it again."

Khan nodded and began to move away, but Spartan called after him.

"Do a full bandwidth test. We've never used more than five in one go."

"What about me?" Olik asked.

Spartan looked to him and then to the Colonel.

"It's time to plan this little operation of ours."

Colonel Black spoke immediately.

"I assume we follow procedure. Land a recon team first, locate prisoners, and then assess the situation. Keep the primary force in reserve."

Olik nodded.

"Yes, that is what I was thinking."

Spartan straightened his back and clicked his shoulder joints. It wasn't the mission that he was thinking about, not entirely. It was the fact that after so long it looked like he would be putting himself back into a potential warzone.

"This is my suggestion," he started.

Khan opened his mouth in a wide smile. He knew exactly what a suggestion was from Spartan.

"We are lacking solid information. A full-combat drop could just draw attention, and right now we don't even have a target. We will perform a high-speed, low altitude insertion near the target. I will go in first. The rest of you will then move to a secure location and wait for my signal."

Khan didn't seem very keen at this point.

"What? We came here to help, not to babysit the ship."

Spartan reached out and placed his hand on his friend's forearm.

"Khan. A squad of Jötnar and drones is hardly subtle. You will stay with the Colonel until I have something actionable. Just be ready when I send the signal."

Khan looked almost offended.

"Dammit, Khan, I need you as my backup. There is nobody I would trust more. I need you here, so when I have a fight arranged, you will be there. Understood?"

Khan let out a long, slow breath of frustration. Colonel Black now interjected.

"I agree with Spartan. We have major combat assets on board, but we need to know where to put them, and when. You never go into combat without a mobile reserve. You get the intelligence, and if you find the General and Gun, we'll be there in minutes."

He looked at Khan.

"There is no better reserve than a squad of angry Jötnar."

Khan opened his mouth to reveal his jagged teeth. They had been repaired multiple times over the years, but no amount of dentistry would make him look any less the monster.

"You're not wrong, Colonel."

He then pointed at Spartan.

"Just don't take too long. My patience is short."

Spartan laughed.

"Like I don't already know that."

Colonel Black brought out a series of maps on his device and placed it on one of the workbenches.

"Now might be a good time to plan this little operation. Recon, rescue, and extraction."

Khan pointed at an icon over a settlement.

"And the weapons, we will make sure they get to the civilians."

* * *

The Helios System was a shadow of itself. Five planets, all of which had been inhabited in the past. The capital, Helios Prime was still an irradiated wasteland, a place where few would choose to make their home. The more barren worlds of Libuscha and Spascia had also both suffered from the heavy fighting in the war. The shipping routes were filled, not with warships but transport, civilian liners, and mining vessels. The rebuilding project was the largest in history, and every ship capable of spaceflight was being used.

"Incredible, isn't it?" said Colonel Black.

He was with Spartan on the command deck and looking out at the great distortion ahead of them. Much like the Black Rift, the Byotai Spacebridge was a permanent tunnel through space that connected a point near Helios Prime with a transit zone inside the Byotai Empire. Gone were the vast machines required to keep it open, and instead was a small Alliance cutter and half a dozen Helion patrol ships.

"Yeah," said Spartan.

His voice suggested he was unconvinced.

"All one happy family now."

Colonel Black walked along the deck and stopped in front of the gently curved screens that filled most of the front. The Rift was getting larger and larger as they maintained their present course. The crew continued about their duties, with few making more than the occasional sound. Even he had to admit they were working surprisingly well, especially on such a complex ship.

"Colonel, now we find out if your authorisation codes

do the trick."

He looked to Spartan.

"They will work. Our agents have spent a lot of money making sure we can recreate internal transit passes."

Spartan laughed.

"Recreate. I like it, such a polite way of saying forged."

"Spartan," said Five-Seven, "Access codes accepted. We are on approach to the Spacebridge. Route is clear and secure. We have full clearance for travel."

Spartan leaned forward and tapped the button on the left computer unit to the side of his seat. He wasn't surprised the codes worked. As far as he was concerned, this entire operation probably had full Alliance military support and backing. But there was still a nagging doubt that once there they really would be on their own.

*We can rely on nobody out here, nobody but ourselves.*

"We're about to enter the Spacebridge. So make sure all gear is stowed and you're ready."

He looked back to the Colonel.

"And you don't think the Byotai will wonder what this ship is doing in their territory? It will be flagged immediately."

Colonel Black shook his head.

"No, Spartan, it will not. The specification has already been added to the Alliance fleet registry. We are listed as a diplomatic transport, with our transit markers coming directly from Terra Nova."

As he spoke, the Alliance cutter was already moving out of the way to let them pass. Spartan almost felt that he should have been hiding as they entered the mouth of the Spacebridge and towards their final destination. His body tingled as they passed through, only to reappear in Byotai space. It barely seemed like a journey, more like travelling through a door and into a different room.

"Contact!" called out one of the crew. The accent was thick, but the words clear and obvious. Spartan allowed himself a smile as he listened to them. There were very few people that even realised the Thegns were anywhere but in the factories or habitation ships around Taxxu Prime. Now he had them on board, and they could speak and function as well as any ship's crew he'd met before. At the same time, they were immediately alerted by the ship's warning alarms. Spartan looked to Five-Seven who was calling out orders to the crew.

"What is it?"

Five-Seven brought up images of multiple ships on the mainscreen.

"We have five Byotai warships on an intercept course. Their gun ports are open, and they are ordering us to stand down."

Spartan licked his upper lip and gazed at the vessels. The largest of the three looked like a large bug, with three substantial components at its core. Powerful engines slung down low on each side, and bright flames extended out as they continued accelerating towards their ship. Spartan moved his attention back to Five-Seven.

"Is the course to Karnak laid in?"

"Yes, Spartan, a direct course to orbit over Karnak. Engines are spooled up and ready."

"Do it!"

Five-Seven already knew what he meant and hit the activation button. The invisible warp in space-time established itself around the ship in an instant, and in the blink of an eye they were gone, moving away without moving. Spartan watched the imagery of the ships, but they were gone as quickly as his eyes could focus.

"Estimate time to arrival, thirty-three minutes, Spartan."

Spartan rose from his seat to leave the deck. As he reached the door, he looked back at the Colonel who was waiting there, in awe at the sight of the moving starfield.

"Spartan, you've created something incredible here."

Spartan shook his head.

"No, Colonel, I created none of this. The designs were from Old Earth and improved with tech from the Biomechs. This is a collaborative project between hundreds of people. All I did was help get them together."

He considered his next words.

"I'll be in touch as soon as I have information from the surface."

Colonel Black nodded.

"We'll be waiting. Don't get yourself caught. Remember the mission; it's a recon and rescue, not the prelude to war. Don't get embroiled in local troubles. The only backup we have is this ship."

Spartan went through the doorway and into the passageway.

*Like there is any difference between recon and war.*

He stopped and nodded towards the alien commander of the ship.

"Five-Seven. Colonel Black is now commander of this ship and this operation. He will be your point of contact until my return."

"Yes, Spartan."

The Thegn looked to his left and to the Alliance Officer.

"Colonel Black, you are in command. Your orders?"

Colonel Black couldn't help smiling at the authority

Spartan had over the crew.

"Continue as you were, Captain Five-Seven. We have a job to do."

He moved to the chair Spartan had been using and lowered himself gently to the firm material. The journey through deep space was the first for him in such a command position. Though there were no orders he needed to give, he was still the man at the top, the one that would be required to make a snap decision if it came to that.

*My first ship!*

They continued on to their destination, and Colonel Black used it as an opportunity to relook at the geography of the region they were approaching. Karnak had been well charted when the raiders and pirates had been removed. He had taken part in several commando raids back then, witnessing the savagery of the raiders. They were fast, deadly, but also weak and avoided close quarter combat with humans.

The imagery did little to hide the fact that barely more than three million settlers now lived there. On top of this, there were at least ten thousand Anicinàbe, and he suspected that whatever the official figure was, it was sure to be way off. There were many towns, some of which were no more than a dozen homes, and also more than thirty cities, many of which were long abandoned. All were connected via barely maintained roads. From the latest information, the best-maintained parts of Karnak were the spaceports and surrounding cities.

He stopped the map and focused in on the mountain region. There were icons showing a single major city, with a large spaceport and major rail connections heading out in all directions. The spaceport and largest city were marked up as Montu, a city within a large open plain and settled between two tall mountain ranges.

*So, this is the capital of the Khagi region and home to the largest of the spaceports.*

He smiled, thinking back to the original strategy.

*No wonder the General wanted to go there first. Whoever controls Montu, controls access to the arrival of most incoming resources.*

He moved the map along and examined many of the other towns, cities, and mines. It was one of the least developed planets, yet there were still mines deep underground that had been there for centuries. What remained of the old transport system showed that at one time, the planet had been given the chance to develop.

*Look's a lot like Eos. A lot like it.*

The moon Eos was a refinery satellite of the massive gas giant known as Gaxos. It was an industrial site for the Helions and saw some of the fiercest fighting in the last war. Now much of it was an arid wasteland with a vastly reduced population. It was a prized location, but one that few people would choose as their home.

He barely even noticed Kanjana off to the left. She was at the lower deck where a circular bay provided a spherical point at which to look out into space. It was a point on the ship designated for navigation and dropship control. A pair of Thegns busily managed systems while she looked out into space. Kanjana looked one last time and moved back before spotting the Colonel looking at her. He seemed strange in his non-military clothing, yet commanding the ship.

"I haven't been back into the Anicinàbe territories since I came to Taxxu."

He nodded, as though understanding the gravity of

what they, and she in particular, were about to do.

"I understand. It must be difficult."

Kanjana shook her head.

"Oh, not at all. This region is my home, but I have few friends here. Thayara fought with the enemy, and her disgrace continues on through my family. Some see her as a hero, but as many see her as a puppet."

Colonel Black could well understand the problem, but he decided not to mention quite how Thayara was considered back home. She had led the armies of the enemy in the last war, to the everlasting enmity of the other races. Spartan had been her ally, but only as part of a long-established ruse. Even so, Spartan was still spoken of as a hero and a monster in the same breath.

"You may not have that many friends, but I can promise you, the General and the Alliance will thank you for this operation. Maybe even the Byotai...eventually, assuming we are able resolve this border crisis."

The view of the planet was the first he'd seen in the flesh before of Karnak. The world was nothing particularly special, but he was interested in the number of civilian ships still trying to leave.

"Scan the area. I want no surprises while we're here."

Five-Seven moved his hands in front of his screen.

"Yes, Colonel Black."

\* \* \*

## ANS X-45 'Titan', Karnak, Demilitarised Zone

Spartan walked along the deck of the vast operations level. He moved slowly, but confidently inside his heavily modified PDS suit, known in the SWD as M-3B Armour, the test variant of their now in limited production M-3 armour. It was closely fitted to his body and had much in common with the PDS Alpha armour used by the Marine Corps. The joint and articulation system was much the same, but the banded plate sections looked much closer to the style of armour often used by the Khreenk. Small circular discs were located on the back and along the limbs, each the size of an eyeball. These were the advanced data nodes, a method of integrating the armour into different machines and combat suits.

"That's not standard spec," said Olik.

The massive warrior walked around Spartan. He ignored him for the time being and went through a short series of movements to ensure the suit was moving correctly. It was completely silent as he stretched his arms and legs. The face of his helmet was open and showed his face fully to the others.

"Yeah, I know."

Olik touched the outer material and noted it was rough to the touch.

"Thegn bioarmour. I thought we were holding that back for testing on the M-3 prototype?"

Spartan nodded with a narrow smile. Olik looked down and could already see that he'd answered his own question.

"Yeah, Olik. This is the prototype suit. Modelled on my physique."

The enemy, now simply known as the Biomechs, had made extensive use of bioengineered warriors and creatures. The outer skin of the Thegn foot soldiers had a thick skin that was tougher than standard marine armour and able to self-heal over hours of use. CTC engineers had been working at Taxxu for years trying to replicate the system, with only modest success.

"The latest version is working, but you'll remember our original plans?"

Olik tilted his head as he tried to recall.

"Healing?"

Spartan shook his head.

"No, the self-healing worked on the very first model. That's the armour being used on first gen Grunts."

He pointed to the Jackal dropship, looking down to check the joints and seals. There was no reason why there should be an issue, but it was a one off piece of equipment, and that could lead to all kinds of unexpected problems.

*Camouflage test.*

Spartan tapped a button on his left forearm, and the suit began to darken. It looked as though he was standing in a shadow as the outer skin altered its colour. It was a subtle shift, but instead of light grey, he was now a mixture of black and dark grey, and still shifting.

"Yeah," said Khan.

He'd moved alongside Olik and was now watching the colour change. It was changing to a pale ivory colour, but still retaining distorted grey patches.

"I said it would be worth the time."

Olik laughed.

"There's a reason only the one suit has it. We can build a hundred M-3 suits for the cost of one with the chromatophore technology."

"True," said Spartan.

The suit had now completely changed to a dull yellow, with darker patches throughout the chest. Spartan nodded with satisfaction. He'd seen the images of the surface, and now the suit had taken on much of its colour hues.

"But without the M-3B, I would never look this pretty."

Olik walked around Spartan, finally stopping next to his kin.

"It could work. I though the tech was…well, unstable?"

Spartan sighed and stretched his limbs one more time.

"Okay, time for the real test. Activate the Maverick armour."

They stepped aside as one of the larger cylinders began to hiss. The curved doors slipped open and inside waited one of the larger machines. It was much like the one they had been testing in the arena. No sooner had Khan pressed the button, and the machine was out of the cylinder. It walked slowly, but smoothly, to the centre of the deck and then stopped. The machine rotated forty-five degrees, and its front opened up. Spartan stepped towards it and reached out. Khan grabbed his arm and stopped him.

"The prototype armour has never been used inside a Maverick suit before."

Spartan pushed his arm off and pulled himself inside.

"No time better than the present, old friend."

Once inside, the Maverick armour a wave of nostalgia hit him. It was like he was strapping into a Vanguard machine again. This was the first time he'd stepped inside combat armour with the intention of taking it into battle for more years than he could remember. The harness clamped in around him, and the Maverick armour attached to the communication nodes with a reassuring clunk.

"Suits coupled."

Indicator lights lit up inside the helmet as the suits effectively combined into one fighting machine. In less than five seconds, the computer system calibrated itself to the unique characteristics of the M-3B suit with Spartan sealed inside, and then activated. Thin photocells moved in close to his head and projected data at the periphery of his vision.

"Spartan, starting bandwidth test now," said Khan.

He'd already closed his eyes and was going over the plan in his mind for the tenth time. It was a simple operation, at least in theory. He would land, along with half of the mercenaries, and move to the nearest Byotai compound to the target. He'd collect as much data as possible and then perform a full reconnaissance. He opened his eyes wide.

"Khan, old friend. You had better be ready."

The Jötnar laughed.

"I always am. Don't worry about me. You just make sure you don't get your head blown off in the first five minutes, old man."

The indicator on the HUD showed the data stream between the dropship and the suit had started. It moved up and down before settling at the expected speed. Video feeds, radar data, and IFF information arrived and was screened before being sent to the helmet overlay.

"Latency has settled to eleven milliseconds. Operating at high bandwidth levels."

Khan's voice continued inside the armour.

"Good. You're synced to the dropship and the ship's computer. As long as you maintain a rough line of sight, you'll be good to go."

He looked at Spartan with an almost embarrassed expression on his face.

"All systems look good here. I think..."

Spartan stretched his muscles and then sent the signal to activate the external view. The sensors in front of his eyes altered, and the view changed to give the impression his face was open to the elements, even though a thick layer of curved armour protected his entire face. Khan was in front, and they both seemed to be of a similar height. He nodded in satisfaction and pointed to the dormant armour they'd brought with them, three sets of combat armour, each waiting like powered down robots further down the deck.

"I brought my standard equipment. When you need support, let us know. We will smash whatever you find."

Waiting next to him was Olik, and the two Jötnar together brought a smile to his face. They were looking on at the Maverick suit with quiet satisfaction. They might not have been the people that built the thing, but all had played their part in getting in into production.

"Just like old times," he said.

Khan shook his head.

"Not all of those ended well. And the best of those were with Gun at our flank."

Spartan couldn't really argue with that.

"True, but we did dish out our fair share of carnage, didn't we?"

Khan snorted.

"Oh, yes, that we did."

Spartan grasped each of them one at a time by the arm and then entered the Jackal dropship. Everything seemed excessively large and vacant, and the six mercenaries waiting inside did little to disguise that. One day, if that ever came to fruition, he expected to see the innards filled with Maverick soldiers and their supporting Grunts. He scanned from side to side and could almost see them waiting in the drop cradles.

"Spartan, I see your reputation precedes you," said

Arana.

He leaned in, the servos and motors barely discernible aboard the craft.

"How so?"

Arana laughed and then activated her helmet. The visor dropped down so that only her mouth was visible. A black cloth-like material lifted up from her chest armour to encase her neck and finally her mouth. Spartan was surprised at how close this now made her look to a Thegn soldier.

"Your predilection for large armour and big guns. You are hardly known for your subtlety, are you?"

"True."

He moved to the right-hand side of the dropship and stepped against the clamp. It was specially designed to hold his armour into position and directly over a circular marking on the ground. Once in position, he hit the release button, and the front of the armour opened up. He stepped out from the Maverick armour and looked back at the thing. Compared to him it was massive, yet the improvements made to the motors and servo systems had given it a lean, agile look, unlike anything the Alliance had used before. He touched the outer skin for just a moment. It was the same grey, rough feeling Thegn armour. He then turned back to look at the mercenaries.

"Not today, though. We go in for a full-scale reconnaissance before..."

He looked back to the armour.

"...we bring in the artillery."

Rods dropped down, and a semi-transparent smoked glass material filled the gaps. The outer layer extended down from above until the entire suit was enveloped in the light brown cylinder, much like those on the experimental assault ship.

"You think the Alliance will pay for that level of tech?"

Spartan looked at her, his face impassive and silent. Arana lifted up her hands in feigned surprise.

"Hey, okay. I'm just saying."

She looked to her sister.

"It's just that in my experience the Alliance uses people where it can, and tech when it has to. People are cheaper than machines."

Spartan smiled as he listened to her.

"In the past, perhaps. But now, these suits will allow one marine to do the job of a hundred. The maths work in our favour then."

She sighed and joined her comrades to move to the manual clamps, ones designed for passengers or conventional marines. There were no windows, but that didn't matter. The videostreams from both the Confederate class starship and the dropship were being continually fed to Spartan's experimental armour.

"Remember, we are not looking for trouble. Stay close, and this will be over fast."

Arana shook her head.

"Spartan, I doubt this will be without trouble, and fast…well…"

She removed her Khreenk rifle, checked the magazine, and clipped it back in with a sturdy clicking sound.

"I don't like anything too fast. I like to take my time and do it right. Agreed?"

Spartan looked at her, but this time he elected to say nothing.

Syala burst out laughing.

"You're the first person to ever silence the great and powerful Spartan."

Her tone was irreverent, but Spartan didn't care. He'd already closed his eyes and was running over the mission, the maps, and everything he already knew. Like all soldiers, even retired ones, he knew how quickly the mission could fall apart. Out here, far from the control of the Alliance, they had few real friends. It was only the memory of those that had fought, many of whom died in the last war. General Daniels had narrowly avoided such a fate, but not Spartan's son or his wife. All his blood were now dead, and only those around him, his warrior kin still remained.

*Daniels and Gun are coming back; and anybody else I find. I'm not leaving one of them behind, not this time.*

\* \* \*

Colonel Black hadn't expected trouble so quickly, but now the mainscreen seemed filled with dangers. Directly ahead was a group of three armed civilian ships. They had just moved out from the cover offered by the vast debris field circling the planet, much like the rings of Saturn back in Sol. According to his data, the ring was what remained of a large moon that collided with another object in the near past. It was now known as a haven for pirates, and was the key battleground during the clearance operation years before. There were more than forty known bases, all of which had been rendered uninhabitable in the fighting.

"There is a signal. It's coming from the debris field," said Five-Seven.

The creature pointed to the enlarged forward view. There was a long band of rock and debris, as well as the remains of six massive structures. It was hard to tell the rock from metal, but what it was clear the ring was much more than dust. Colonel Black nodded.

"Understood. Put it on the mainscreen, no return feed."

The forward view remained, but to the side appeared the shape of a roughly dressed Anicinàbe warrior. He wore no uniform but carried the common bandolier, as well as stabbing blades in small pouches. His head was devoid of hair, and a thick double scar ran from the top of his head and down his nose. His lips were also marked, either from combat or some deadly illness. The Colonel looked to the icons at the side of the screen, checking that both the return audio and video feeds were closed.

*Good work, Thegn. Spartan wasn't wrong.*

Kanjana pointed at him.

"This man, I've seen him before."

The Colonel looked to her and wondered quite what she brought to the SWD. He'd seen her resume, and while her technical skills were impressive, he was sure there must be more to it than that.

"Tahkeome?"

Just the possibility of finally meeting the man, the figure that had brought so much calamity, had a calming effect on him. In his mind, the alien leader could be negotiated with, and if he refused, he had little doubt this ship could handle whatever militia ships Tahkeome had access to.

"Well?"

Kanjana shook her head.

"No, this is one of the Red Scars. They take their name from ritual injuries. It's all part of joining the criminal organisation."

He shook his head as if surprised at what he could see,

and she began muttering to herself. At the same time, the figure on the mainscreen began to speak, and moments later his translator kicked in.

"This is Tarak. You are trespassing on Anicinàbe territory. Deactivate any weapons and prepare to be boarded."

Colonel Black looked again at his new Anicinàbe second-in-command, Kanjana.

"Tarak?"

She nodded quickly and swallowed before answering. He could see she was nervous, and the very mention of this individual's name had a reaction far greater than he'd expected.

"He is an animal, a monster."

She looked away from the screen and down at the floor. Colonel Black kept his eyes fixed on the imagery on the mainscreen. The Anicinàbe were not always easy to judge, with different emotions being exhibited. This one was different to any other he had seen. Where Kanjana was calm, yet excitable at times, this one seemed to reek of violence. Even the way he leaned in to the camera was aggressive.

"Tell me about him."

Kanjana turned back to face him, and he could see her face had darkened. It was something he had never seen before, but he had heard of the bizarre ways the skin could change to show emotions, even more so than shown on humans.

"This thing, he is known as Tarak the Butcher. His reputation among my people is something of a legend."

Colonel Black watched the screen and especially the look to the warrior's face.

"He is known for kidnap, slavery, and even worse debauchery. He is infamous for his obsession with blades."

She pointed at the view on the mainscreen.

"You can see them across his body. He doesn't just use them in battle. He alters and disfigures with his blades."

She looked away, made a spitting sound, and then looked back.

"...For nothing more than simple pleasure."

There was more to this; that much was obvious. Colonel Black wanted to know more, but neither Kanjana nor the situation was ready for that conversation. The approaching craft were moving closer, and still the signal came deep from within the debris field. Colonel Black licked his lips and focused on his foes.

"Captain Five-Seven. Charge up the particle emitter capacitors, and activate the turrets. I am authorising defensive fire only. Prepare for battle."

He then reached for the controls at his seat, and an image of Spartan popped up on the mainscreen. It was an extreme close-up from inside his helmet and only showed three-quarters of his face.

"Spartan, your status?"

The quality of the audio and video was perfect and the response instantaneous.

"We're ready, and the Jackal is fired up. Just get us close."

Colonel Black hadn't doubted it for a moment, but even so, he was glad to hear that. As he listened to Spartan reel off the status of the team, Khan arrived on the deck.

"Colonel. They are ready to go. What's happening?"

The large warrior was alone, with Olik still back on the operations level. An alert warning sounded, and colour markers flashed on the mainscreen.

"Enemy gunfire detected, impact in six seconds," said Five-Seven.

Colonel Black rubbed at his cheek.

"Now we'll see if those turrets are up to the job."

There was no time for Khan to answer, and he was either unconcerned at the consequences, or had utmost confidence in the ship.

"Four...three..."

The Colonel tensed his muscles and waited for the inevitable. There was no impact, just a string of flashes.

"All targets destroyed."

"You see," said Khan, "We spent a lot of time and money on this ship. CTC is expecting the Alliance to go all out on this contract when they see results."

Colonel Black looked to the Thegn controlling the ship.

"Five-Seven, take us into our orbital entry point...at two hundred and twenty kilometres."

"Affirmative, Colonel."

Spartan was busy watching him via the mainscreen.

"Spartan. Your team needs to be ready for a high-speed drop. We won't have much time."

"We'll be ready, Colonel. Don't worry about us."

# CHAPTER SIX

*Exciting new technological wonders were just one of the great numbers of benefits to mankind's journey to the stars. With a permanent system of Spacebridges, it was now possible to transport goods and supplies from one world to another in a matter of days or sometimes even hours. This ability to transport material so quickly would result in an explosion of trade and services, with entire moons and sometimes planets given over to their specialisms. Fiery worlds like Prometheus would find the emerging markets in the Orion Nebula to be highly profitable, whereas the old colonies of Mars and Titan made great strides in tourism, as well as military training on the ruined surface of the birthplace of man, Old Earth.*

*Orion – The Future?*

## ANS X-45 'Titan', Helios Prime, Alliance

The assault ship was already moving into position at the orbital entry point when the enemy ships were spotted. This time it wasn't the three civilian ships, but a formation of heavily modified frigates had appeared out of nowhere and on a higher orbit. They were nowhere near the size of Titan, but all were configured with different arrays of weapons. Some carried crudely fitted turrets; others were fitted out with scores of anti-ship missiles.

"How the hell did nine ships get there without us detecting them?" Colonel Black demanded.

Five-Seven shook his head.

"Unknown. The ships were cold, no heat or residual electrical signals, and our radar system is offline."

"Cold?" Khan asked, "How would the crew survive without life support and heating?"

Kanjana was the only one not surprised at the news.

"Gentlemen, they are sentinels. My people often use captured ships and fit them out to be controlled remotely. My guess is they are sending them commands directly from the debris field."

Khan laughed.

"Yeah, that makes sense. Hide like a coward in an asteroid field and send machines to do your fighting."

Kanjana looked at him and raised her eyebrows, an expression she'd learnt from the other humans working at the Special Weapons Division.

"What?" he asked.

Kanjana simply laughed.

"The irony, after everything we've been developing the last few years."

She placed her hand on the Colonel's shoulder.

"You will have to take it from here; it's time for me to get the dropship ready."

Colonel Black nodded without taking his eyes of the ships. Kanjana moved down the eight steps to the lower level and then into the spherical area. The thick glass-like material gave the perfect view of Karnak, as well of deep space. Unlike from where Colonel Black was sitting, she now had an unfiltered view of space around the ship, whereas the others were using the mainscreen that utilised information streamed in from the hundreds of cameras fitted to the exterior of the ship.

"Activate the radar and attacking systems. Keep the guns online."

Five-Seven acknowledged and then issued the orders. Extra data appeared in seconds as the onboard scanners sent out micro-pulses in all direction. Two more derelict spacecraft were identified.

"More hostiles?"

Five-Seven shook his head once more.

"Negative. They are derelict hulks. Both match Alliance registered transports."

The Thegn moved his hands and checked multiple streams of data. He beckoned towards the numerous diamond symbols on the mainscreen.

"Approaching craft are targeting us. Missile trackers are active. They will fire any moment."

Colonel Black licked his lip and glanced towards Khan. The towering figure merely nodded, giving him the affirmation he didn't need but still appreciated.

"Activate the guns, bring down any craft targeting us."

The response was instantaneous. Though the forward particle emitters were in the wrong direction, the aft mounted weapons were just able to target the last two ships. The quadruple particle cannons emitters adjusted their focal length and opened fire. The beam weapons of the past had changed considerably, and now the weapons fired in rapid pulses, striking with the force exceeding a gigajoule of kinetic energy.

"We have good hits," said Five-Seven.

They watched small flashes of energy mark the impacts on the last two ships. There were hundreds of small impacts as metal plate, plastic, and other material exploded from the heavy fire. Chunks of hull vanished into clouds of dust-sized particles until finally both vessels were torn apart.

"What's that?" Khan asked.

He was busy pointing to the larger ship that had just been detected leaving the debris ring around the planet. The imaging system magnified the vessel, but at this extreme distance, it was still difficult to make out much more than the rough profile. But it was immediately clear that the ship was big, very big.

"We have no records of this ship in the database. There is nothing that matches her energy signature either."

The ship shuddered a little as they moved into the final insertion position in orbit over Karnak. They were much too high to release combat troops, but the perfect height to put the dropship onto an assault vector. Khan spotted the indicator first.

"We're ready."

At the same time, the first of the enemy guns managed to breach the defence turrets to strike the outer hull. Warnings flashed, but not one of them looked particularly concerned.

"No breach, the hull is secure," said Five-Seven.

Colonel Black took in a short breath and gave a nod in the direction of the lower navigation and control sphere.

"Kanjana, we're in position. It's now your turn. Begin the drop."

He didn't notice the grin on Khan's face as he said the words.

*Good luck, old friend,* thought the Jötnar.

* * *

## Dropship 'Haywire', Karnak, Demilitarised Zone

At the first stage of the operation the Jackal dropship was lowered down on its elevator and rested after twelve metres. The deck sealed above them and was quickly followed by the ship's double-layered outer doors opening up. There was little to see, but then the video feeds from outside the dropship fed directly into Spartan's suit.

*Beautiful.*

He could see the spherical shape of Karnak below them, and then to his surprise, two streaks as a pair of unguided rockets rushed past and vanished off into the distance. It served as a rather unsubtle reminder that the experimental assault ship was under direct attack.

"Are you all ready?" Kanjana asked.

Her face was now showing on Spartan's overlay. He looked to his left and then to his right. All six of the mercenaries were clamped in and waiting patiently for the word to go.

"We're ready. Let's do this."

"Hold on."

There was a clunk, but nothing seemed to happen. Only when Spartan looked to his left did he see the view from the top of the craft as they fell away from the ship.

*Here we go again. High-speed and flying blind, just like old times.*

For anybody else this might have been a worrying operation, but not for him. As they began the violent re-entry to the planet, he found he was almost looking forward to some action. He gripped his hands together and clenched his fists. This time he knew who the enemy was, and he also knew who his friends were. It was simple, but it made a big difference.

*This time they come back, every last damned one of them!*

As he looked back, he spotted dozens, perhaps hundreds of projectiles, and all were heading towards the dropship or the assault ship. He opened his mouth to speak, stopping as the first exploded. Occasionally, dust would get in the way, and he would see hints of the particle beam cannons firing, and the flashes of rockets exploding surrounded the entire ship.

"Spartan, are you seeing this?" Arana asked.

He nodded, assuming she was referring to the battle.

"Yeah, I see it. The ship's doing her job, though."

The silence persisted as they all watched the unfolding battle from the videostreams in their armour until they burst through the upper atmosphere and began their high-speed dash to the surface. A transmission came through from the ship.

"Kanjana, what is it?"

She looked surprisingly peaceful even though he could see what was happening nearby.

"We are taking heavy fire. You will have to deploy in the next sixty seconds. I need to get the Jackal back on board before we jump. Else she's going to be left behind."

Spartan looked back to the mercenaries, but they were unaware of what he was seeing inside his helmet. The ship was surrounded by what seemed to be flak, but in reality was the debris left behind by the assault.

"Understood. Dropping in twenty seconds."

He looked to the six mercenaries.

"We're dropping earlier. Get ready."

Arana shook her head.

"Are you insane? We haven't broken through the fifty-kilometre barrier yet. The freefall will be impossible."

Spartan shook his head.

"No, that isn't true. We've done unmanned tests over Kerberos for just this eventuality. Just keep your stabiliser on, and do not open your chute until I give the word."

He ran his eyes along the diagnostics and then hit the timed exit button.

"Fifteen seconds. Be ready."

Two of the mercenaries were saying something in a chant. It might have been a good luck chant or a prayer to a deity. Not for him, though, he was long past that.

*No deity intervened to help my family or me. If there is a God, and he's content to let millions die. Well...screw him!*

Each sent the acknowledgment tone, and Spartan hit the depressurise button. The entire interior normalised with the outside environment in seconds. Only the powerful clamps on the dropship were able to keep the passengers from being sucked out in an uncontrolled fall.

*Not much longer.*

Spartan could see the counter working its way down, and finally it hit the limit. The brackets attached to the lower hatch groaned, and small cylindrical openings appeared beneath him and the mercenaries. The hatch slid into the hull, revealing the lower part of the craft to the elements. It was almost impossible to see what was happening, but Spartan was unconcerned. He knew the specification of the dropship almost by heart, and unlike the others, he'd actually seen her perform in dry drops.

"Drop!"

The clamps released his M-3B armour, and he dropped

out of the craft like a stone. The shock of the exit was enough to drive what little was in his lungs straight out. He remained calm and collected, and found himself enjoying the sensation.

The other six quickly followed, feet first. Spartan was only moving for a matter of seconds before he'd rotated over so that he was heading to the surface head down. He had the perfect view to the ground, and it was nothing if mesmerising.

*Check your numbers.*

He knew it was easy to get caught up in the moment and forget the mission. He took in several quick breaths, checking the figures as he continued to fall. At this height, the air resistance was small he was now travelling at more than five hundred kilometres an hour, and still increasing.

"Squad..."

He took in another breath.

"...Report in."

There was a short pause, and for a brief moment, he worried the others had failed to jump or experienced some kind of freak occurrence. He knew the dropship and his own armour was capable, but he had nothing to go on for the mercenaries, other than their word their armour was certified for jumps into the stratosphere.

"Spartan," said Arana, "We're right behind you."

He acknowledged and then concentrated on his own freefall. The mapping data was active and locking onto geographical points to assist in his descent. At the same time, he continued to speed up. The signal from the dropship was already moving away, and he suspected it was travelling back to the ship under the control of Kanjana.

He'd been falling for thirty seconds and began to spin.

The forces against his body were immense, and it took all of his strength and nerves to remain calm. He'd seen the after-action reports of this manoeuvre before, and it was quite common for people to enter uncontrollable spins. He moved his arms out just a fraction and spent a few seconds to levelling off into a standard vertical drop. The counter continued moving up even higher, and he would have cried out just as he broke the sound barrier. The numbers were moving so quickly that he couldn't even see the needle.

"Spartan, current altitude, twenty-seven kilometres. We're in formation and coming fast."

That was the moment when finally the speed began to settle, and to his astonishment, he could see they were now falling at more than thirteen hundred kilometres per hour. He looked at the blurred ground off into the distance and began to laugh. The laugh increased into a roar until finally air pressure began to slow him down. That was when he spotted the mountains off into the distance. His helmet overlay showed that Montu, the planet's capital, was right behind those mountains.

*Looks a charming place.*

His laughter slowed, and he found himself looking down at a point where multiple trails merged together into a compound. It wasn't much, perhaps twenty to thirty buildings, and with less than a handful of vehicles nearby. Icons popped up around it, confirming the sight as their rendezvous site.

* * *

## ANS X-45 'Titan', Karnak

Colonel Black continued passing out orders to Five-Seven as the battle raged in orbit. The smaller Anicinàbe had withdrawn after receiving a heavy mauling, but the larger enemy ship had now covered a large part of the distance from the debris field. The mainscreen showed its shape, and the Colonel was stunned at what he saw. He checked with Five-Seven for the third time.

"Are you sure? That cannot be correct?"

Five-Seven looked towards him, his expression showed confusion, but with the repeated questions, not the simple facts.

"There is no problem with our scanners or databases. This vessel matches the battleship class ship used by the Biomechs. But it has been heavily modified."

The Colonel nodded his head.

"Yes, I can see that. But what is all that?"

There were additional segments fitted to the ship that bulked it out above and below to give it a bloated, predatory look. The front extended out, like the head on an insect, while four pods the size of a frigate were positioned like mandibles around it. From their pods was a pair of massive guns of unknown configuration. The additional segments around the hull contained a multitude of hangars and gun mounts, with everything from direct fire rockets to automatic cannons.

"They would appear to be field modifications to the hull. They do not match the complexity or quality of the original vessel.

Khan snorted at that.

"I'll tell you what it is, Colonel."

He looked away from the screen and to the officer.

"That is a captured Biomech hulk. Local warlords or criminals have fitted her out as a mobile base to operate from. I've heard rumours of these things before."

"We are ready to accept the dropship."

The process was performed almost entirely by computer; Kanjana making the subtle course changes to the dropship. In simulation it should have been done in less than a minute, but the reality of the situation tripled that. Finally, the dropship was inside the confines of the vessel, and the outer doors sealed shut. No sooner had this happened and the missiles and rockets from the approaching ship began. Unlike the previous attacks, this one came as a massed volley and at hypersonic speeds. The ship's computer had already tagged and identified the first weapons launched.

"Impressive arsenal," said Olik.

He walked from the rear access doorway, striding inside like an ancient titan, while examining the data with much interest.

Colonel Black nodded in agreement, and then his hand stopped moving. His eyes were transfixed on one position, far away from the planet and off near the shattered remains of a long destroyed planet; one that showed as being almost two hundred million kilometres away. He tapped a segment at the debris and called to Five-Seven.

"There's our deployment area. Get us there, and fast."

The Thegn had been given his orders, and there was not even a second's hesitation. The powerplant was already pushing the drive system hard as the vessel jumped away, pushed along by the subtle movement of its invisible space distortion.

* * *

## Landing Zone, Karnak, Demilitarised Zone

Spartan had his eyes firmly fixed on the ground. It was moving closer and closer, and the altimeter showed he'd passed the danger threshold. There was now little chance of a safe landing if his chute failed. He was counting the metres away as they dropped off by the hundred until he hit the one thousand-metre mark. The alerts were already sounding because impact with the ground was ever closer.

"Now!"

All it took was the movement of his eye towards the release button. At the same time, the suit synced to the electro-chemical impulses in his brain for confirmation. The parachute deployed in an instant and yanked him hard as it acted as a brake. His first thought was to check the others, and a quick look back showed him there were six other chutes all open and following him down.

"Good work. Follow me in; we need to keep up the pace."

It didn't take long for all seven to circle to the target zone and hit the ground. The landings were not perfect, and the mercenaries rolled over twice upon impact, but none were hurt. By the time they had detached and hidden their parachutes almost thirty seconds had passed. The mercenaries moved closer and checked their gear one last time.

"Ready?" Spartan asked.

They each gave him a quick acknowledgment and moved their firearms into a ready position. Spartan detached his experimental carbine from his flank. To anybody else it might look like a clumsily modified L52. But this was something far more powerful, and much more expensive than any marine would carry. Unlike the rest of the equipment being developed at the Special Weapons Division, this particular item was not intended for front line use.

"What in all that is holy is that thing?" Arana asked.

As a mercenary, Spartan knew she would have a good eye for this kind of thing. But even he was surprised she would realise it was more than just a standard railgun, as used throughout the Alliance.

"It's an upgraded railgun, the first military grade firearm from the company. I just call it The Carbine."

Arana checked her own weapon and took a step nearer, curious to see the thing close up. It was a single-barrelled system, unlike the triple-barrelled coilgun normally used. She could see an engraved set of numbers on the side.

"XC1 HE?"

Spartan smiled.

"Experimental Carbine, model one."

Arana laughed at the naming device.

"And what about the HE?"

"Oh, that's the high energy bit. I'm thinking of dropping that part."

"You are talking nonsense, Spartan. That thing is carrying a coolant pack...and it is much more than a standard railgun. How much energy are we talking about?"

She slid her hand along the shell-like cover that ran along the weapon. Her finger trailed its ridges and gaps as though she was caressing naked flesh. He looked as her hand stopped and moved closer to his.

"I want to know more...later."

"Arana," said Syala.

All of them looked in the direction of Syala's arm and quickly located a pair of Khreenk scouts. They were moving in from the North, in the direction of the mountains. One stopped, lifted his hand, and called out upon noticing they had been spotted.

"Spartan."

It was not the first word any of them had expected, but it was enough to identify they were the right people, and more important, they were friendly. The word was spoken without intonation or raised pitch, thereby making it sound like a statement rather than a question. Spartan looked at them carefully, moving his right hand closer to the trigger. He also sent the mental signal to power up the internal plasma core, ready to fire.

"That's me."

Spartan deactivated his visor, and it opened up to expose the front of his head, all bar the neck and throat. At the same time, he lowered the tip of his carbine, doing his best to provide the least antagonistic view to their new arrivals. Simultaneously, the six mercenaries fanned out with at least three metres between each of them, and moved into cover. One by one, they dropped to a knee and scanned the horizon for possible threats.

*Good, now we're ready.*

Spartan remained upright, protected by nothing more than the armour of the M-3B suit. Even as he waited, the suit began its subtle shift in colour. The lower parts of the body became darker, the upper segments matching a much lighter, earthy shade.

"And you are?"

The alien's voice changed drastically as it moved to its

translator circuit, something that had become a necessary evil in this new world. In what was something of a twisted irony, it was almost always the alien races encountered by mankind that were forced to use such technology, rather than the other way around. The equipment was being fitted into the firmware of the newer suits used by the Alliance, but so far this was only proving useful in less advanced areas where the same tech had not yet been transferred.

"Vossaq. Your guide."

*Short and sweet,* thought Spartan.

The second of the two scouts came much closer. Spartan could see they were wearing civilian clothing, but over the top they bore extra padding that disguised body armour. Their heads were covered, and the nearest sported a long-rifle, one that could easily have been as long as he was tall. The Khreenk were an unusual people, violent and aggressive, and with an obsession about self-improvement. Even as Spartan looked at the pair he wondered quite what upgrades and changes they might have made to their very flesh. Vossaq opened his mouth and breathed several times.

"We will take you to the Khagi Research Facility."

He looked at Spartan carefully.

"It is now little more than a refugee camp."

He paused, considering his thoughts.

"Your commander, the prisoner, he is responsible for saving many Byotai. He must be recovered. The Byotai at Khagi have made preparations for your mission."

Spartan looked to his mercenary comrades. He had seen the maps, but he was unaware of the details of the facility. Vossaq could see his confusion.

"It is now just a small Byotai enclave, fifty plus civilians, perhaps ten families. Once we are there, we can..."

The Khreenk stopped, and without saying another word dropped to the ground. Seconds later, a sleek aircraft screamed overhead. Spartan tracked it, his suit identifying its height, speed, and trajectory. He remained completely motionless, relying upon the physical camouflage of the suit, as well as its internal coolant and electronic concealment features.

"Nobody move a muscle," he said under his breath.

The aircraft moved off until it almost became a spec, and then it twisted about.

*No, keep moving.*

Spartan watched the thing, willing it to move away. Even so, the aircraft spun about to the right in the exact direction the Khreenk scout had been indicating. Narrow streaks reached down to the ground and hit unseen targets. The unmistakable sound of explosions and gunfire soon followed. Vossaq bent down and signalled to the mercenaries to follow.

"With me, quickly. The attack has already begun. We have little time."

They left the open ground, the only clear space that seemed to be in the entire region. All moved at a quick jog to clear the dangers of being left fully exposed to the enemy. It took less than ten minutes to move from what looked like salt lakes, and into the rougher ground leading on a subtle gradient to the mountain ranges. A small channel cut into the rock to create a maze of paths, with some even dropping down below the surface into tunnels. After another twenty minutes, they joined a narrow trail that would have been impossible to find without highly detailed charts.

"Incoming," said Arana.

Spartan had no idea how she had spotted the target, but right now he didn't care. He pulled his body down low, as did the others. Seconds later, another of the aircraft rushed overhead. This time he was able to get a good look at it. It was small, perhaps half the size of an Alliance Mauler, with a pair of engines, one slung down on each side beneath fat wings. The underside bulged out and was open and exposed to the elements. He could see half a dozen humanoid figures moving about inside.

*An Anicinàbe military dropship, typical!*

He'd seen the model before in one of the many ship databases, and the overlay in his armour was already bringing up a schematic, along with its speed, weaponry, and known characteristics. It interested him most that the craft was commonly used in the Anicinàbe military. It was classed as a light troop carrier, with an Alliance designation of 'Hornet.'

*Keep on moving.*

The craft banked hard to the left, and then something changed. At first he thought it was merely a shift in engine note, but then it was arcing towards them, and some of its passengers were aiming weapons from inside.

"Spartan," said Syala.

Her voice was calm, but there was also an easy to identify sense of urgency.

"They've eyeballed us."

Spartan licked his lips and ran through their options. They were very simple; they could fight, hide, or flee. The same options any prey would have when being pursued by a hunter.

*Weapons.*

He didn't say the word. He merely thought it. At the same time, the internal targeting package activated inside his armour. So far, it was only passive sensors, but that was more than enough to locate the heat sources, power systems, and weapons. The aircraft swooped down low like a bird of prey that had identified a target. It was now on a path parallel to where the small group of mercenaries was hiding. Then the passengers began firing. Weapons the size of machine guns were slung from mounts on each side and controlled by the passengers, much like door guns.

"These are not Anicinàbe settlers. This is a commando unit," said one of the Khreenk.

As gunfire struck an unseen target, Spartan could do nothing. The aircraft was far out of range, and he had no idea what they were even shooting at.

"Hold your fire. We have a mission to complete. This is not our..."

"Look!" Arana said.

One of the Khreenk said something at the same time, and then a puff of smoke appeared off into the distance, perhaps three kilometres away. It originated from between a group of broken rocks; a place that would be easy to hide all manner of weapons inside. It was followed by a whistling sound, and then a black dot accelerated at high-speed towards the craft.

*A missile? Whose?*

Spartan kept still and tracked the object until it reached a few metres from the aircraft. Even before it hit, he knew he recognised the weapon from somewhere. The Alliance relied more upon railgun and coilgun technology, whereas the Khreenk used exotic alien technology that the Alliance was still coming to grips with.

*Helion tech.*

They were the one people that seemed to spend an inordinate amount of time developing new rocket and missiles systems. Even the screaming sound reminded him of some he'd seen before. The videostreams of the fighting on Spascia had shown entire barrages of Helions missiles, and this looked almost identical to him.

*What is that doing out here?*

Even as he asked the question, he recalled his conversation with the General prior to him leaving. The one thing the Byotai settlers out here had requested more than anything else was air defence equipment. It was the single area the Anicinàbe were better equipped for, and whoever controlled the skies would ultimately be able to dominate the planet.

*So, this is his doing?*

General Daniels had intended on transporting foreign weapon systems to the planet. These could not be Alliance tech; else it would certainly mark Alliance involvement on Karnak, something High Command clearly wanted to avoid. The object then vanished in a bright fireball that sent molten debris all around the engine. The vessel began to spin out of control. A hundred metres before it struck the ground, four of the passengers leapt off. White flashes from vents on their backpacks slowed them down as they scattered and hit the ground.

"Incoming!" Arana yelled.

Spartan lowered down to the ground as the aircraft struck hard rock and exploded. There was no chance anyone survived the impact, but those that had jumped were already on their feet and moving towards the wreckage.

"Everybody stay down," said Arana.

Incredibly, they all listened, and one by one the survivors from the crash moved out of sight. Spartan could feel an itch on his trigger figure, knowing he could have killed all four of them without even blinking. He spotted one of the Khreenk scouts looking at him.

"Well, what are we waiting for?"

The alien nodded and moved away in the direction they originally arrived from.

"Follow us."

The two Khreenk took the lead, moving with a speed that suggested they were more than a little experienced with the area. In seconds, they were out of sight, and Spartan had to speed up to join them. The six mercenaries were behind him, a small group snaking in a short column. The ground was rocky, and as they neared the mountains, the outcrops became taller and more substantial. The column of smoke from the crashed aircraft continued bellowing up into the sky, but it didn't take long for the wreckage and the potential threat of the four Anicinàbe to vanish. No sooner were they safe from being seen when another of the aircraft arrived. The engines howled, but it was now impossible to tell where it was or where it was going.

"This way," said Vossaq.

Always the same one spoke; the second merely standing and watching as though simply a bodyguard. He indicated towards a deep channel that cut down into the rocks and then into a much darker part of the rocky terrain. They continued on. At the same time, the occasional low-level thud marked some kind of event on the surface. It was impossible to tell what was going on, and they had little else to do but keep going. Few words were exchanged until finally the Khreenk stopped.

"We will stop here for a moment," said Vossaq.

The alien pointed ahead. It was slightly uphill, and when they reached it, they looked on in stunned surprise. It was shaped like a large ring and cut deep into the rock. Tunnels and shafts led off in all directions, but thick rock protected them from above, making it impossible to be seen, except by others inside the structure.

"Interesting."

It was all Spartan had to say, as he took a sip of tepid water from the tube next to his mouth. It reminded him of a hundred places where he'd fought bitter battles. Some of these were on barren worlds, others moons, or space stations. The more he thought, the harder it was to even remember some of them.

"Spartan, what is this place?" Arana asked.

Vossaq heard her and answered via his translator circuit.

"These are the Khagi Caverns. They were partially created by the water system a long time ago. Since then, the Byotai have been digging deep for minerals."

He looked to Spartan.

"We use it as a safe way to travel. The Anicinàbe control the skies now."

# CHAPTER SEVEN

*Since 361CC, the X47 Avenger drones had proved to be an invaluable aid to the fleet. These were just the first in a line of developments that would see greater emphasis on the use of machine integration in the Alliance military. The XB49 Reaper would be an intriguing concept, one put into trials with the military following the success of the X47. It used a separate heavily armed drone that was twice the size as the Avenger. It would be assembled as a remote weapons package, to be controlled via manned fighters. In the past, artillery had supported the infantry; now the idea was to use the Reaper to support the space fighters. The modified and much more heavily protected Hammerhead MK II was put into service to control up to twelve drones in mixed configuration.*

*Robots in Space*

## Khagi Research Facility

It took three hours of hard work to trudge through the tunnels, but it was the price they had to pay to avoid the potential threat from enemy air cover. To Spartan and the others it felt more like an entire day. The going was slow, due to the poor lighting conditions and very rough ground. The only natural light came down from small holes and gashes in the rocky ceiling above them. There were also long sections bereft of light entirely. Vossaq indicated ahead.

"We have been scouting these tunnels for months now."

"Doing what?"

The Khreenk took a careful step over a row of broken rocks lit by the lamps on his body armour. Once past, he glanced back to Spartan.

"Looking for signs of the Anicinàbe. We have travelled far and wide, and found nothing."

"Strange," said Arana, "The Anicinàbe seem very well equipped for a people that had little to no military equipment with them. How have they taken so much ground already?"

Vossaq muttered, and his translator stayed silent, clearly finding the noises difficult or impossible to convert. The only light in this part of the caverns came from the lamps built into their suits. It gave the interior an odd feeling, like something from a fantastical tale of magic and monsters.

"The settlers are not the issue. We were called in when the first emergency camps were built. The Byotai were happy to see them...at first. But that was when the arguments started."

Spartan pulled himself up onto a particularly steep ledge and looked back to the others. Arana and her sister had already found another way up; the rest of the mercenaries stayed close behind. He refocused his lamps ahead and continued forward.

"What happened, Vossaq?"

The Khreenk mercenary moved slowly and cautiously, especially as there were faint glimmers of light off into the distance.

"The first combat units from the Anicinàbe Coalition are what happened. We didn't know it back then. They were dressed the same, but they intimidated several enclaves to leave. The rumour is they forced them out at the barrels of their guns."

"Strange, I've not heard that part before."

Vossaq stopped.

"That's because we didn't find the bodies until four weeks ago."

Arana was close enough that she could hear the conversation.

"You're saying Anicinàbe soldiers murdered them?"

Vossaq nodded.

"Yes. Ninety-six civilians, all unarmed, and each shot in the back of the head."

They kept walking, but Spartan couldn't shake the image of the civilians being killed. There had been reports of violence, but nothing to suggest something quite so drastic or cold as murder. Vossaq continued to explain, but his voice had dropped in volume, and he sounded almost sad, something very unusual to hear from a Khreenk, especially a mercenary.

"One convoy came through nine weeks ago, supposedly with food and supplies. It was intercepted and hijacked by unknown forces. Since then, the ships have been ferrying people or supplies to the main bases on Karnak. We suspect it is bringing the first military units, potentially under the command of Tahkeome."

Arana shook her head.

"I don't understand. I thought both sides were blockading the entire quadrant?"

Vossaq laughed.

"The Byotai are, but the Anicinàbe Coalition seem to let anybody in."

He scratched at his arm even though his armour covered it.

"There were eight Khreenk security teams on Karnak. All have been evicted or gone into hiding since then."

He looked to Arana.

"Trust me. The Anicinàbe Coalition is taking control of this planet one sector at a time, and nobody is ready or prepared to resist them. What happens in the Khagi mountain region is just the beginning. The planet will..."

All of them stopped and listened carefully. A dull thump shook the very ground they stood upon. Small clouds of dust ran down from cracks and crevices above them. Arana sighed to herself.

"Artillery or free-fall bombs."

She then looked to her sister.

"This isn't a popular uprising. This is a military occupation."

The group moved towards the pinpricks of light while each considered what Vossaq had to say. The crump of the explosions had now faded, but it was clear the area was a danger zone. Finally, after one last push uphill, they emerged into what little remained of daylight. The sun was already low in the sky, and long shadows had begun to form behind every rocky outcrop.

"This way," explained Vossaq.

He extended his arm to point to the structure in the distance. Smoke rose up from a number of fires, and one of the larger buildings had collapsed.

"The research facility was closed down before Karnak

was first abandoned. Now it is being converted into homes for families and workers in the mines and the refinery back in the mountains."

Arana didn't seem impressed.

"This position is exposed and too close to Montu. We need to be cautious. The Anicinàbe are clearly happy to attack any Byotai targets they find."

Vossaq seemed impressed with her assessment.

"You are of course, correct."

The mercenaries split up and moved along the flanks of the access route, darting from cover to cover. Though heavily armoured, they still moved with the speed and grace of an unarmoured man. The Khreenk continued on via the centre of the road, with Arana and Spartan right beside him. Spartan's boots crunched as he stepped over broken rocks. The internal sensors scanned continuously in every direction, looking for movement and heat signatures. His suit even checked the tell tale radio frequency emissions common from complex equipment. Vossaq kept looking ahead but spoke quietly to Arana and Spartan.

"It is true; the mountains and tunnels are the only safe places from air attack. That is how they are winning."

He looked up as though expecting an aircraft to come right at them.

"By placing their smaller numbers wherever they are needed, they can maximise their effectiveness. The Byotai have little mobility on the ground since the air attacks began."

He said something the translator couldn't cope with and so looked back towards Spartan.

"But we are not so easy to move."

He nodded towards the wreckage of an aircraft. It was

difficult to identify, but the broken metal still smoked from the heat of the burning figures. Spartan suspected the craft had been shot down in the last twenty-four hours. Arana looked less and less comfortable as they passed by the ruined left engine. It was riddled with holes. She placed her hand on it.

"Missile damage from an airburst weapon. This is the General's doing."

Spartan smiled, but she was unable to see that inside his helmet. He saw the damage, and the assessment from Arana matched the data appearing on his helmet overlay. The missiles were designed to explode upon moving close to a target, and not a direct impact. This had the benefit of sending debris from a distance rather than keeping the impact localised, a much more effective way of bringing down a lightly armoured aircraft.

"Yes, he was right. A handful of air defence systems, and the advantages of the Anicinàbe are quickly negated. You can't win a war with smaller numbers unless you have an edge."

He pointed to the wreckage.

"Speed, firepower, and mobility are the weapons of the Anicinàbe. The General found the single weak point in their defences, and now he's paid the price."

Arana shook her head and pointed above them. Far off into the distance, perhaps at a height of twenty kilometres or more, was a dark shape. It was clearly a ship, and a big one at that.

"You're assuming no more troops can make it here. Every ship that gets through will make it less and less likely. And that thing, what does it look like to you?"

Spartan looked at it while his onboard computer

attempted to identify the pattern. Information on height, size, and speed appeared, but nothing specific to the class.

"Looks like a civilian transport, nothing special. It could be bringing in food or supplies."

"Or more likely an entire company of soldiers."

Unlike her sister, Syala seemed less likely to keep her thoughts to herself. She was quick to speak, and it would seem, just as quick to anger. Arana then pointed in front to the small outpost.

"We cannot stay here. Don't forget the radar scans as we dropped down. The Anicinàbe control the air, and we are not here to fight a war."

Syala slapped her on the back of her armour.

"That's right, Sister. We're here to get our people."

Spartan shrugged.

"Trust me, I know."

He checked the coolant level on his carbine and flicked off the safety. The area had certainly been the scene of a major fight, and the last thing he wanted was to get caught out without being fully prepared.

"You are correct, Arana. But right now we are not ready to start our operation. We have to meet the locals."

Syala said something too quiet for Spartan to hear. She then went ahead to join two of the other mercenaries who were examining the burnt out remains of some sort of civilian ground vehicle. One of them dragged out the charred remnants of a corpse, along with a civilian rifle. Spartan glanced at it and then continued onwards.

"We need intelligence and local knowledge, neither of which we can obtain by staying hidden."

He then stopped as if he'd spotted something. At the same time, he lifted his arm up. The mercenaries stopped, dropped to a knee, and lifted their weapons. A handful of small rocks ran down the side of the ravine wall, but nothing followed. Spartan selected one of the onboard tactical drones and activated it; the object, no larger than his thumb, detached from a special mount in his shoulder, and powered up a pair of miniature rotors.

"Stay down."

They kept as low to the ground as possible while the small drone moved higher and higher. By the time it had reached its optimal position, the falling rocks had stopped. As well as providing a real-time overhead view, it also enabled his suit to identify, track, and tag all objects ahead of their position.

"Looks clear," said Arana.

She moved with even greater caution. One by one they moved out and down a sharp incline into the main part of the valley. At some point this had been a major access road into the complex, but it was now cratered in dozens of places, and broken rocks and shattered equipment littered the place.

"Stay frosty. This could be an ambush," said Spartan.

Small bunkers on each side of the hill provided the perfect ambush position. Spartan felt a twinge in his body, wondering if at any moment they would be targeted. Just a few more minutes and they were at the approach to the main entrance. Directly in front was a smooth and partially angled wall. In the centre was a metal gate big enough for two Bulldog APCs to drive through with space to spare. It creaked open with a loud groan, revealing what remained of the battered and partially damaged facility.

*This doesn't look good.*

He could already feel his body tensing at the possible

174

confrontation. His stomach and chest tightened up, and he forced himself to slow his breathing. In came the long, slow breaths.

"Communication flypast in ten seconds."

The suit's voice was quiet, yet it still surprised him. Even so, he sighed in relief as an indicator announced the imminent flyover of one of the twelve communication buoys dropped by the ship. They were small and almost impossible to detect unless one was looking directly for him. All it took was the communications selector, and he was in line of sight radio contact with the object, if only for a few minutes. As before, he lifted his hand, and the entire mercenary unit went to ground.

"This is Spartan. We have arrived at location Alpha Three, proceeding on original schedule. Can confirm the region is hot. I repeat; Alpha One is hot."

The message vanished into the ether, along with a coded packet that contained multiple images of the area, an overhead view of their positions supplied by simple triangulation, and finally, bio-readings for everybody in his team. He waited patiently, but there was no reply from the ship before the buoy moved out of sight.

*Two more hours until the next one.*

It was far from ideal, but he had expected no less. The region was disputed, and the space around Karnak was not safe for a single ship. He could only hope that when the time came, Colonel Black would get his message.

"Forward."

Spartan was first to his feet, and then they were moving ahead. Arana took a pair of the mercenaries to the left; the others spread out as they walked on through the compound.

"Watch your corners. Keep your eyes open."

Spartan couldn't help but feel uncomfortable upon seeing the obvious signs of battle damage. Impact craters marked where rocket fire had ripped through metal and stone with ease. There were also bullet holes and marks from small arms fire.

*Keep moving.*

They were now past the gate, and it slid shut behind them. The wall connected to the gate was a little under three metres tall and constructed from pulverised stone into cement-like structure. At irregular intervals there were crates and boxes positioned to act as firing steps. Spartan could see the positions of the defenders via the small drone, and so far everything looked as he might have expected.

"Secure," said Syala.

A few moments later the same message arrived from Arana. Two Byotai were waiting at one section, both had rather antiquated-looking rifles. Spartan had not seen the particular type of weapon before, but it was clearly a prized civilian item, and nothing like those in the Byotai military arsenal. He lowered his weapon and opened his visor so that his face could be seen.

"Spartan," said the nearest Byotai.

It came closer and lowered its head in greeting. Like all Byotai, this one was large, reptilian, and a little ungainly in its movements. It was protected by civilian body armour, some of which moved as it walked towards them. It walked slowly, almost too slowly, but its eyes flickered between each of the new arrivals as though checking for signs of trouble, or perhaps weakness.

"Yeah, that's me," replied Spartan.

The Byotai continued speaking in its own language while Vossaq replied using his translator. This continued for several minutes while the mercenaries checked the immediate area.

"This is the research facility?" Arana asked, "It doesn't look like it's seen much use recently."

Spartan nodded, but at the same time kept a careful eye on the two aliens.

"Well, it used to be. When they first settled here, the planet was used for mining and research. When the attacks by the Anicinàbe forced them to leave, the entire facility was shut down."

Arana pointed at a pair of long abandoned ground vehicles. Their tires were punctured, and thick rust showed on any exposed sections.

"And now?"

"Now the buildings have been gutted, and they are being used to home settlers."

He nodded to his right.

"If our information is correct, the side link at the other end of the site should still be connected to a secondary, non-functioning haulage line with the capital. If it's still there, it will be our way in."

He then looked back to the two Khreenk.

"Vossaq. We need to speak with the Elder here. I need Intel and travel information to get into the city."

Syala stepped inside the compound. The other mercenaries positioned around her and waited, each saying nothing. Vossaq continued to speak with the Byotai as though he had not even heard Spartan. He repeated himself just as the Khreenk turned about and walked back towards Spartan and Arana.

"There is a problem. The Anicinàbe have blocked the access road and demanded the surrender of the facility. They attacked less than an hour ago, and the time for leaving is soon. They say they will attack again."

Spartan gave Arana a quick glance, and she was already shaking her head. He looked back at the two aliens who were busily conversing. Then he spotted the first radar signature. One was immediately tagged by his micro-drone.

"We've got incoming. Get ready."

The mercenaries wasted no time in finding positions close to any available cover, or to the outer wall and alongside the few Byotai settlers.

"Listen, Vossaq. This position is not defensible, and you need to get every single one of them underground, do you understand? Right now."

The Khreenk mercenary listened, waiting as he tried to understand what Spartan was saying. Finally, he nodded quickly.

"Yes...yes. The leader of this community has arranged for the evacuation. It is…"

Spartan spun about as his suit amplified the sound of something moving close. It must have been travelling low to the ground because the internal sensors had failed to detect the shape, and the drone had failed to spot it.

"Incoming!"

Spartan and Arana leapt back just as the entire upper half of Vossaq exploded in a blast of blood and armour. Spartan hit the ground and rolled over to the side.

*Where are they?*

He checked up amongst the high cover just as two more flashes erupted nearby, and then a black shape whisked past overhead. Gunfire raked down from its flanks, and the passengers shot at any targets they could find. Spartan took aim with his carbine and opened fire. It was too little, too late, but it did force the craft to take evasive action and throw off its accuracy, if only for a few seconds. The second Khreenk mercenary ran from the open ground and down a short flight of steps inside the low domed building at the centre of the facility.

"With me!" he called out via his translator, "The Elder is inside."

Spartan nodded and pointed after him.

"Arana, follow him."

She needed no encouragement and dropped down into the hardened facility that ran a single level below the surface. The others stayed exactly in the positions they had chosen and opened fire on any available targets. The gunfire started off quite erratically, increasing in tempo until the entire side was engulfed. Arana checked Spartan was with her.

"I'm coming. Now get inside."

The interior of the building wasn't particular large, especially when compared to the substantial exterior; most space taken up by the single room still filled with long abandoned computer equipment. Four Byotai huddled inside, the guns and rockets continuing to hammer the site. With each impact, the look on Spartan's face became sterner and sterner.

"Where is he?"

A single Byotai male that was much larger than the others moved in front of the group. He wore ringed armour on his limbs and thick quilted plates on his chest. In his hands, he carried a cut down thermal shotgun, a weapon commonly used by civilians. He spoke, and the Khreenk listened, repeating in his own tongue so that the translator could take over. Spartan shook his head and moved closer, using his own circuit instead.

"I am Kras, the Elder of Khagi," said the Byotai.

Sound from the entrance caught Spartan's attention. He twisted about as a trio of Anicinàbe fighters burst in. The return fire from Spartan, Arana, the Elder, and the mercenaries was devastating. None of the three Anicinàbe made it inside, and only one managed to staggered backwards before a second and final shot from the Elder killed it.

Spartan moved to the leader of the enclave.

"I'm Spartan, and I'm here for the General."

The Byotai listened carefully, but he seemed disinterested in Spartan's mission.

"We are all dead now. There is no chance for victory. Only death before the enemy."

He then pushed in another thermal cartridge magazine into his weapon. Spartan's upper lip quivered, and it was clear he was not amused.

"I haven't got time for games. Your people can live, as long as you don't fight a pointless battle."

He twisted around to face Arana, simultaneously grabbing the remaining Khreenk mercenary next to him.

"This is no local trouble. This is a military occupation by the Anicinàbe, and we have to get these people to safety. If they stay, they will die."

He pointed to the ceiling.

"They will come from the air, and that is how we will stop them."

The alien spoke, but his translator appeared to do

nothing. Spartan shook him as more rockets struck about them. He released the mercenary and activated his own translation circuit as he had with the Elder. As he spoke, the system broadcast the odd, guttural sounds to the Khreenk soldier.

"Do you know the way to the underground haulage line? The one that travels directly to Montu?"

The Khreenk soldier listened intently, and then straightened up in surprise.

"Montu tunnel?"

Spartan nodded.

"Yes, the tunnel."

"Yes, I have seen it. Kras has shown me before. I can show you."

Spartan turned to Arana.

"We need to buy these people some time. We'll get outside and hit them hard, and hit them fast. Keep at them until they are begging for us to stop."

She nodded and then licked her lips.

"Oh, yes," he said coyly and then winked, "My favourite way, Spartan."

Arana clamped down her visor and went back to the entrance. She stayed inside, protected by its thick walls, checking for signs of the enemy. Spartan leaned in towards the Khreenk and Kras, the Byotai.

"Stay hidden, and protect the civilians. We will deal with the Anicinàbe."

Spartan was at the door when Kras began to laugh. It started as a low rumble and continued on into an uncontrollable howl. Spartan shook his head in irritation, tinged with a little admiration for the old creature. He raised his weapon to his shoulder, checked its status for the tenth time, and took a step towards the exit. Then his training kicked in.

*Check tactical reconnaissance first.*

A quick glance from the drone feed showed a missile streaking up from a hidden position in the mountain, but whatever it was shooting at was gone. It was replaced by a dozen humanoid figures dropping down. They hit the ground around the facility and began shooting whatever they could see.

*Airborne soldiers, interesting!*

It was something he'd heard about but never seen. And the prospect of facing the physically weak Anicinàbe was something he relished for the moment.

"Now!" Spartan shouted.

He was first out of the bunker and into the open air. He scanned left and then right in quick succession. The internal computer tagged all possible targets while marking points of gunfire, both in terms of direction and source. There were already seven hostiles.

"Incoming fire."

The voice came directly from the computer, and it spoke in a calm, but stern female voice. At the same time, the path of the approaching fire was overlaid so that he could see where it was coming from. Spartan sidestepped and narrowly avoided a triple cannon burst from a substantial weapon system. He lifted his arm and took aim at the origin of the attack. A green triangle moved over the target, and he quickly identified a pair of Anicinàbe soldiers.

"Weapon active," announced the computer.

He took aim with the XC1 carbine and pulled the trigger. It pushed back into his armour with much greater recoil than any conventional firearm. Each shot expelled an invisible magnetised casing that contained a small sphere of superhot green plasma. The weapon combined the caseless ammunition system of the coilgun with the massive energy output and heat of the Khreenk support weapons. The first missed, but the next three struck around the target and splashed a tiny, but deadly corrosive blast. One was killed outright, and the second lost an arm as the incredible heat instantly vaporised his armour.

"Southeast!" yelled one of the mercenaries.

Spartan twisted about and unleashed another burst from the carbine. The pulses of plasma burned anything they touched, leaving wounds and broken metal columns of where they struck. More flashes of light marked the arrival of additional Anicinàbe soldiers. Their backpacks allowed them to drop down from a short height in safety. At the same time a pair of aircraft circled overhead.

*Take your time.*

Spartan identified another soldier leaping over one of the perimeter walls. He took aim, but a Byotai militiaman blocked his shot. The civilian lifted a thermal shotgun and blasted the Anicinàbe in the chest. Two more jumped over but were no match for the brute strength and power of the reptilian Byotai. Another reached the top of the wall and took careful aim at the violent Byotai.

"Get out of my way!" Spartan shouted.

Nobody took any notice, so he pulled the trigger. The green ball of plasma struck the Anicinàbe in the face, and he staggered back, vanishing behind the wall. At the same, time the Byotai howled as a small sliver of the hot material burnt his shoulder.

*Idiot.*

Spartan moved towards him, constantly checking for fresh signs of enemy soldiers. He could see from his tactical overlay that Arana and her mercenaries had spread out to help defend the broken perimeter.

"Next time keep your head down."

The Byotai looked at him, laughed, and then returned to the parapet with his shotgun. Spartan could only assume the creature understood what he'd told him. Spartan moved alongside him and took aim. A group of the enemy was working their way up the valley floor and to the wall. There were eight of them, all armed with rifles, and taking care to use the rocks as cover.

"Alert!" warned the armour.

Spartan glanced at the direction of the danger and then threw himself at the Byotai. A sniper round struck the ground where the warrior had been standing. Spartan looked back, took aim, and then another came down and struck his shoulder. The projectile glanced off with a whistle sound. Again the armour warning him, and this time the bombardment was deafening. It began with a blast that lifted him up from the ground and dropped him like a stone.

*What the hell?*

More followed, one after the other until all he could hear was the crump of explosions and the crash of heavy ordnance. It finally began to die down, and he could look back up. The walls were ruptured in a dozen places, and fires raged throughout the complex.

"Spartan!"

He twisted to his left and found Arana and two of her comrades. Both were covered in dust, and one had blood dripping from a gunshot to the shoulder.

"They are coming in hard; this place is not going to hold."

Another Anicinàbe stepped through the breached wall and almost landed on top of Spartan. Instinct kicked in, and he grabbed the warrior and yanked him closer. The unfortunate Anicinàbe had no idea what was happening as he slid along the ground, but then felt the burning hot muzzle of Spartan's carbine up against his chest.

"Who are you?" he demanded.

The soldier looked up at him and said nothing. Spartan pushed the muzzle against his cheek, and he screamed in pain.

"I asked you a question. Who are you?"

The Anicinàbe soldier reached down and slid out a pistol from a sheath on his flank. It was halfway up before Spartan pulled the trigger. At this range, the blast from his carbine sent burnt tissue and bone across the floor and at his own feet.

"Your choice."

Another Anicinàbe reached the breach and took aim at Spartan. His movement was too slow and cautious for the far more experienced and ruthless retired soldier. Spartan instinctively opened fire, and the carbine spat energy. But this time, the enemy rolled away and took cover behind the broken wall.

*Nice moves.*

Spartan's armour detected more incoming fire. This time low-velocity ones that were coming down from above, and he wondered if they had been launched by more hidden soldiers, or more likely, from aircraft.

*Free-fall bombs, not good.*

"Take cover!"

These were high explosive and designed to cause maximum damage, with little care for friend or foe. They struck the ground with incredible force, instantly killing anything they hit, and collapsing even the sturdy bunker, burying alive anybody that might still be inside. Arana fired two more shots before heading to Spartan.

"Spartan, this is not why we're here. Two aircraft have dropped off more soldiers in the valley. They will breach the main gate in less than a minute."

Few Byotai remained to defend what remained of the walls, and those that tried to stand their ground were now under intense fire from sniper positions further up the steep inclines all around the facility. Spartan reached out and placed his arm on Arana's shoulder.

"The plan has changed."

More bombs dropped around them. An indicator in his helmet showed one of the mercenaries had been caught in the blast. An Anicinàbe aircraft circled overhead and then another. In seconds, they were joined by a third and began dropping down more of the cloaked Anicinàbe soldiers. The white flashes of their backpacks marked their slow descent to the ground.

*Murderers!*

Spartan looked to the newest arrival, took aim, and blasted away with his carbine. The plasma carbine suffered with accuracy at this range, but three rounds managed to strike its flank, and the aircraft twisted away, belching smoke. A single figure fell from the open side and crashed to the ground, killed instantly by the impact. Even so, the other Anicinàbe soldiers landed and spread out, using the ruined facility to pick off the remaining civilians. Spartan fired once more and dropped back to cover.

"Arana, I want you and your squad to take as many of the Byotai you can, and get them underground. Kras and the Khreenk will show you the way."

He reached for her arm and grabbed it.

"If they give you any trouble, you know what to do."

Arana opened her visor so he could see her face.

"Don't worry. If they cause trouble, I'll explain it to them...my way."

She glanced in the direction of the battle and then at Spartan.

"And then?"

Spartan licked his upper lip. He'd seen the layout of Karnak, and the entire world was based upon hundreds of small settlements. There were no major cities, and not a single stronghold that he was aware of. Because of the frequent dust storms, most of the settlements were positioned behind natural barriers such as behind mountains, or in basins or valleys. One thing they all shared was in keeping large parts of their structures underground.

"This place, the enclave at Mount Caldos. It's the largest Byotai settlement in the Khagi region. It is built to withstand the dust storms and has been declared a safe haven. Over two thousand citizens are there, according to the information from Colonel Black, and it is the strongest position within a hundred klicks."

Even as he spoke, there were columns of data on his helmet overlay.

"It is well protected with dozens of missile batteries; you saw the plans. It's strong."

"Understood. What about you?"

Her eyes moved away, and she lifted her rifle to her shoulder so that it was pointing at Spartan's face. He lurched to the side just a fraction as she pulled the trigger. The howl of pain behind him was all he needed to hear. At the same time, the last few Anicinàbe were scrambling away to the South, all the while being harried by rifle fire from the mercenaries and the smattering of surviving Byotai. Spartan checked the plans he'd been given and sighed upon confirming what he'd hoped.

*The tunnels will take us most of the way back to Mount Caldos. It will work.*

"Arana. We'll get underground and then split up. You will get the civilians to safety. I'll take two with me to the capital and find the General."

Her eyes narrowed at listening to the last part.

"I came here for the mission, not to babysit civvies."

Spartan shook his head.

"This isn't a negotiation. Now get them underground. I'll see you there!"

# CHAPTER EIGHT

*The Jötnar played a crucial part in two wars over a single generation, yet still they were regarded with suspicion and often fear. Larger than even the biggest man, they were titans when compared to the people of the Alliance. These brutal monsters could have brought down the Alliance from within, yet they fought alongside humanity with nothing but courage and honour, and never for a moment straying from those they had been created to destroy. In the bloodbath of the Biomech War, they would again prove their value and stand as the model for the ultimate soldiers. It was not long before many would ask if they would prove a better source of recruits to the military than an average man. All of that would change with the developments of the Special Weapons Division of CTC and the great changes to be implemented into the Marine Corps.*

*The 1st Jötnar Battalion*

## Khagi Caverns, Karnak

Spartan and Syala were the last two still above ground. Spartan's armour was surprisingly clear of dirt or damage, but Syala's sported a deep black scorch march from her naval up to her chest. He looked down at the mark and

189

noticed the area around the sternum had been burnt at least a few centimetres.

*Thermal blast, that was close.*

His eyes continued to move up until reaching her face where her visor was currently open. She gazed back at him and winked.

"See something you like?"

"Really?"

He answered sarcastically, more in amusement than annoyance. As he watched, he could hear the odd crack of gunfire, but there was no sign of where this fighting was taking place. He suspected it was more likely to be additional Anicinàbe soldiers methodically checking the bodies and finishing them off. The thought of such unwarranted brutality towards civilians sent additional levels of adrenalin through his veins.

*Stay calm. You have a job to do.*

He turned his attention back to the lithe, and somewhat erratic Syala. She was certainly a character, and her armour kept reminding him of the heavy infantry that fought at the New Carlos Spaceport in the Uprising. The armour had been something of an antique back then, oversized but tough. These mercenaries had taken the best components and merged them with tech from the private sector to create their own unique look. It was not as bulky as he recalled, and still clung tightly enough to remind him he was looking at a female mercenary. A message arrived from Arana.

"Spartan, we're through the bunker and heading down. The tunnel is damaged, but it is intact. I've set the charges."

Spartan glanced to Syala who was also receiving the same message.

"Good work, Arana. Keep going. We will join you shortly."

"Understood."

The two sisters were an odd pair, and they seemed to treat their job as much as a contract as it was for fun. He'd not seen that attitude towards violence before, at least not outside of the Jötnar. Her eyes then narrowed, and she hit the button to close down the visor and mask her face. She beckoned off into the distance.

"We've got survivors."

He scanned the debris and wreckage and quickly found a trio of elderly Byotai. They were unarmed, and one bore a series of blood-soaked bandages across his chest. As they waved to the Byotai to join them at the bunker entrance, a squad of five Anicinàbe appeared overhead. As before, the aircraft rushed away before it could be fired upon. The soldiers came down quickly and were soon obstructed by the damaged facilities communication mast complex. They hit the ground to the flank and spread out. Spartan kept his head down and tagged five of them via the heat tracking features of his armour. The cooling jet vents were easy for the system to locate and track.

"Got them."

Even though they were in sight, Spartan did not pull the trigger. There was always the chance, though perhaps a slim one; that they were there to take prisoners. Then he saw one lifting his rifle and taking aim at the back of the three Byotai.

*Animals.*

"Drop them."

Syala took careful aim and nodded just before pulling the trigger. Her coilgun carbine cracked as it discharged a solid slug, striking the first pursuing Anicinàbe in the chest. The solider flipped backwards due to the momentum of the attack and collapsed behind a heap of rubble.

"That makes seven."

Spartan snorted with amusement.

"Seven is child's splay."

The other four had separated, but instead of dropping down to cover were moving fast. Spartan noted their clothing was different to the others. They wore black chest plates bearing a red marking. He stored several images of them to check later, and then pulled the trigger. The XC1 Carbine howled as it unleashed a hail of encased plasma. Half the rounds struck the first two and burnt through their armour with ease. One was killed outright, while the second dropped to the ground, holding up a shattered stump and crying with pain.

"Eight."

Syala put a round through the soldier's forehead. It was a crack shot, and even Spartan was impressed. He didn't turn away, though and moved up from his cover, stepping out to the right to gain a clear line of sight. The Byotai were just fifteen metres away, and Syala waved to them to help them to safety.

*Keep moving.*

Spartan lowered his aim and blasted away. At the same time, the black armoured Anicinàbe soldiers returned fire. Spartan's shots had been accurate, but the Anicinàbe seemed to blur as they darted ahead.

*Interesting, must be a movement-based camouflage system.*

Even in combat, he found himself admiring this new and unknown piece of technology. Rather than using their tech to hide, they were combining it with their mobile style of combat. Three rounds glanced off the collar off the banded plates of his M-3b armour, but Spartan changed tactic. He aimed low and fired at the ground ahead and beneath the two soldiers. The impact from the high-energy weapon sent debris up and over the soldiers. At once their shapes became clear, and whatever system they were using was rendered useless.

*Now you're mine.*

One of them must have noticed because he dived over a broken wing from one of the aircraft. The second wasn't so fortunate, and Spartan raked him with gunfire. He scanned to the right, looking for the last of the soldiers. Then he appeared, like a blinding light from behind a series of tall rocks. The warrior must have used his drop-jets. He was three metres in the air, falling right down onto the two of them.

"Syala!"

Spartan pushed her aside and took the full impact of the landing soldier on his chest. Both rolled to the ground, but the Anicinàbe was up first. He flipped up with the speed and grace of a ballet dancer. Syala fired a quick shot, and it glanced off his rifle in a shower of sparks. Without pausing, the alien then withdrew two blades from his arms and jumped at Spartan.

"He's mine."

He was on his feet and circling the alien soldier. As the Anicinàbe leapt in with the first attack, he activated the monofilament bayonet mount on the carbine. It pushed out into a partially curved, razor sharp blade. The Anicinàbe didn't hold back and came in with a flurry of attacks on both sides, the blades spinning about in full rotations to develop speed and power. Spartan parried left, then right until he stumbled over something. He fell back and only just managed to support himself on one knee.

*Screw this.*

With a quick flick, he activated the barrel and unleashed a burst of high-energy plasma into the warrior's face. The smouldering remains of the Anicinàbe collapsed alongside him, much to Syala's amusement.

"Nice."

The Byotai were now past them, and Syala helped them to the trapdoor entrance to the tunnel system. Once inside, she followed right behind, looking back just once to check on Spartan.

"Keep them moving," he said.

He remained waiting at the entrance to the tunnel, and from there he could see the three high-explosive charges Arana had set. They were positioned to collapse what remained of the bunker, as well as the entry point to the tunnel. It was good work. The access point was a large double door fitted into the floor leading up into the ruins of a bunker type structure. He looked down into the gloom and waited patiently until certain the last of them were well below the first bend. Syala waved back to him, confirming they were far enough in.

*Boom time.*

All it took was one quick activation to start the thirty-second timer, and he made it fifty metres before it had counted down to twenty seconds.

"Everybody move it. Hurry!"

Most of those underground had no idea at all what the crazed human soldier was saying, but his tone was obvious to any but the simplest of alien creatures, and those that could increased speed; the mercenaries doing what they could to help the others maintain a reasonable pace.

*Any moment.*

Spartan tensed his body just as the first charge went off. The other two followed almost immediately afterwards. They were powerful blasts that sent clouds of dust falling from the ceiling. Two of the Byotai stumbled, but they were quickly picked up and on they went deep underground, perhaps almost two hundred metes before finally meeting the large triple intersection. Dust continued drifting down from the access tunnel and from several broken sections of the roof. The tunnel was narrow, and in the past a single person wide, with a separate section for small sleds to travel along a mechanical track system. That must have stopped working decades earlier, and now it was simply an obstruction each of them had to scramble over.

"How much further?" Arana asked.

Spartan clambered over a long abandoned tool that looked much like a pickaxe or shovel.

"Another fifty metres, not much more."

They followed one last bend before passing through a broken doorway and out into a vast underground complex. Unlike the access tunnel, this was a major transit point, and clearly something a great deal of time and money had been spent on.

"I had no idea the Byotai had put so much effort into this," said Arana.

Spartan shrugged.

"They had big plans for the place, long before the trouble with raiders and the crimes gangs moved in."

He looked upon the intersection and drank in the details. As expected, there were three tunnels leading off in different directions. It was not a road system but a long, dormant maglev rail system. At first it seemed that it might even be functional, but on closer examination, it was obvious the structure had been long abandoned and heavily corroded. Parts of the roof had collapsed in places, but as far as Spartan could tell, the route still looked clear.

"Spartan," said a familiar voice.

The Byotai Elder approached, with the remaining Khreenk beside him to translate. It confused Spartan when he used his name, the implication being that they could speak the same language. Most did not make use of translator technology, and the older Byotai would see it as an insult to speak anything other than their own tongue. The other reptilian fighter that had been waiting on the barricade was also there, but he now sported an additional nasty-looking triple puncture wound to his flank, yet moved as though nothing had happened.

"They are ready," said the Khreenk.

Spartan nodded, looking back at those that had made it this far down. The numbers of wounded Byotai surprised Spartan, yet even those with hideous wounds refused to complain. He'd heard of their resilience in the Biomech War, but they had fought in an entirely different sector to him. There were stories of Byotai warriors fighting on and winning with large chunks of their own bodies mutilated or destroyed.

*That reputation is now fact.*

"Is that all of them?"

Arana and Syala looked exhausted. He'd seen relatively little of them during the fighting, but what he had noticed had impressed him. Both were fast, probably even faster than he was. They were agile and good shots, and Spartan was happy if that was all they could do. Syala answered him first.

"It had better be. When we left, there was another aircraft moving in to scout the facility."

Spartan grinned.

"And you left them a welcome gift?"

Syala looked extra amused at the question.

"Oh, yes. There are a few extra surprises near the bunker, in case any of them get too close."

Just on time, the cavernous tunnel rumbled, as they had heard when first approaching the small settlement. The rumble was followed by multiple thumps, and then both sisters chuckled as Arana approached him.

"And it looks like a few of them did."

She pointed to the ceiling high above them all.

"There are two more up there, but I can promise you, they will not want to come too close now. Ground burst proximity mines make a bad day of any low-flying aircraft, and we left them as high as time allowed."

Spartan seemed satisfied with that and paused as if he was about to make a painful announcement.

"I need a volunteer to come with me to the capital. The others will escort these civilians to the enclave. The route should take a day, two at the most, until you reach the last functional rail line junction. From there, you will be at the Enclave in hours."

Though the sisters were of the same age, Arana always seemed to take the lead when it came to leading the group. But his time she was beaten to it by Syala.

"I will come with you, Spartan."

She then looked to Arana.

"We work well together, and you're always better leading the group."

Arana considered her suggestion, but only for a minute. Spartan intervened; knowing that time was not on their side.

"The Anicinàbe will be looking for us. So you need to get a shift on."

He looked back into the tunnels.

"Take the rest of the mercs and follow the waypoints I've set you. There are four possible entry points to the tunnel on this route, so you will need to keep your eyes open in case the Anicinàbe try and find a way down to cut you off. Use the Byotai to scout for you."

Arana grasped her sister's arm and pulled her in close. For a second, it seemed as though they might even fight, but it quickly became clear it was no more than a familial moment. Syala spoke first.

"Do not be afraid to let them fight. They are extra eyes and ears. Use them. The Byotai are used to battle, even if they do try to avoid it most of the time."

She sounded only a little emotional, hardly surprising to Spartan, based on them being sisters, and close ones at that.

Arana didn't argue, but she did have one question.

"What happens once we've got them to this Enclave?"

Spartan nodded as she spoke.

"Good point. Colonel Black has already contacted them to say we might be bringing in survivors. When you arrive, your first job is to contact the Colonel, give him an update, and get ready."

"For what?"

Spartan lifted an eyebrow, as if surprised at the question.

"Because once we have Gun and the General, all hell is going to break loose."

Syala and Arana looked at each other and then back to Spartan.

"You're not just planning on getting him out, are you?" Arana asked.

The corner of Spartan's mouth lifted up a little, showing two of his teeth as he smiled.

"I'm going to break out anybody they've taken. After that...we'll see."

He looked back to the wounded and weary-looking Byotai civilians.

"One thing I can promise you, though."

He then looked back at them.

"None of this will end until someone lifts up a gun, points it at the head of Tahkeome and his soldiers..."

He lifted his hand and pointed it off into the distance, all in imitation of holding a firearm, "...and says no."

He walked towards the two Byotai and the remaining Khreenk mercenary. Syala was right at his side, her visor raised to expose her face.

"What are we doing now? I thought we were..."

Spartan cut her off.

"Arana might be getting the rest of them out of here, but we need information on Montu. I'm not arriving at the place without details. When I have what I need, we'll get into the tunnel. It shouldn't take too long."

He stopped for a second and watched the mercenary lead the group off into the tunnel. With the greater space, they were easily able to spread out and make quick progress. The front was taken by two of her mercenaries, each relying completely upon passive night vision equipment. The rest started to follow at distance of around a hundred metres so as not to give away the positions of the forwards scouts. Spartan caught the attention of the Khreenk who was waiting with one of the group ready to leave.

"Montu is around ten to fifteen kilometres from here, is it not?"

The Khreenk didn't even need to speak with the Byotai to answer the question. He simply nodded.

"Good. Now tell me everything you know about the city and where you think the prisoners are being held."

\* \* \*

## ANS X-45 'Titan', Debris Field, Karnak

The light and sound of battle had long been forgotten as the crew went about their tasks. There was no damage inside the ship from the minor skirmish over Karnak. Colonel Black was taking no chances, and had sent out no less than four maintenance drones to check for signs of trouble. With no support this far from home, the last thing he wanted was a system failure that resulted in their capture. The General was one thing, but losing an entire privately owned and operated military ship would be quite another.

All of the gunnery systems were still active, but the capacitors had been temporarily shut down to reduce the chance of being detected, even this far out. Olik, meanwhile, waited at the lower level, and Kanjana pointed off to the huge layers of debris orbiting their current home. This was the long dead planet of Medamud, and under normal circumstances would have taken weeks to reach, but not with the drive technology. The ship had been spirited away, right under the nose of the enemy and to their safe haven. Olik pointed to the planet, or what remained of it.

"Looks like some beast was here and took a bite out of the thing."

Kanjana laughed, assuming it was a joke. Then she saw his face and realised he was being serious.

"Uh…Olik, you understand there is no such thing as deep-space monsters, don't you?"

Olik looked to Khan and smiled.

"Civilians."

They both gazed at the magnificent view of the planet. It was impressive at this point, even though they were now actually two hundred million miles away from the vast structure. From this part of the ship, they had a privileged view of the debris, and each appeared enthralled by what lay in front of them.

"So, it wasn't a space beast, what did happen to it?" Olik asked.

Kanjana shook her head and looked at the huge creature.

"Nothing so exciting, I'm afraid. The planet was destroyed millennia ago in some form of massive impact. We have always assumed it was the decaying orbit of a major satellite, or perhaps a comet."

"Ah. So it could have been a monster, then?"

Now she was completely unsure if he was playing with her, and that made her wonder if perhaps he'd been acting the fool from the start. Colonel Black moved down the steps, taking his time to watch the banks of displays that seemed to be everywhere. He finally reached the others and stopped alongside Khan.

"Colonel."

He then looked out via the transparent sphere and into

space, much like the others had been doing. The rest of the deck was calm, yet incredibly busy for such a heavily automated vessel. As he walked, he found he was looking back at the mainscreen for signs of any enemy vessels. Five-Seven remained in his position, right in the centre of the open space and keeping his eye on half a dozen different displays at once.

*Incredible. Who would have thought it?*

He was not one for standing about to admire a pretty view, but this was something out of the ordinary. It was truly spectacular, and even he found himself looking at the colours created by the odd effect of light and dust in space. The angle of the star, as well as the debris and dust, must have been in the optimal position, much like rain on a sunny day to produce a rainbow.

"Yes, it is impressive, truly. Though it is, perhaps, just a little ruinous."

Kanjana looked back in his direction.

"True. Still, it will serve our purposes, for now."

Colonel Black nodded in agreement and turned his attention to the Jötnar. As usual, he looked completely out of place being on a ship like this one. He'd seen them in action on many occasions, and they were true beasts of war when it came to close quarter violence, yet now he was waiting like any other crewmember on a starship.

"How is progress going with the Grunts?"

Olik shrugged, as though he was far less interested in the exercises with the Grunts. Spartan and the Jötnar may be intrinsically connected to the Special Weapons Division, but none of them seemed particularly enthralled at the running of the thing. That was something he had little trouble in understanding.

"Khan's still working down there on the operations deck. It seems one of them became jammed inside a drop module. The engineers needed a little extra...muscle to move it."

Colonel Black took a step closer to the windows and looked out into space. The broken chunks of material hid part of their view like a large black cloud. One of the maintenance drones appeared from the right-hand side, and then with a puff of barely visible gas, it moved off and out of view.

"Spartan could be hours or days before he sends for help, and I need to know they can be put into service when the call comes. I've seen the machine simulation, and it's..."

Olik laughed.

"A disaster. Yes, we know."

The Colonel looked a little surprised at this.

"Disaster?"

Olik gave an impish grin.

"The engineers can explain it better. But the machines are complex, and not really our specialty. We give them mimicry training scenarios so they can learn from our own moves."

He went through a series of positions, striking and moving about as though fighting an unseen enemy. Each time he moved, the air seemed to whistle. Then he stopped and looked back at the two of them. Kanjana took over, and from the way she spoke, it was clear she was far more comfortable with the technology and research.

"Olik is not wrong. The automation of bipedal machines is incredibly complex and suffers substantial resistance inside the Alliance. You see; the average citizen loves the idea of using technology instead of lives to fight battles. But for this to be fully effective, these machines need the ability to operate with a degree of autonomy, and that is something few will support."

She tried to look a little more optimistic before continuing.

"Not that it really matters right now. The software developments are years away from anything close to useable. In the meantime, we have machines that can do little more than basic movements and defensive actions on their own. Anything more is...risky."

"I see," said the Colonel. But the drones, I assume they will be ready when the time comes. But what about my mercenaries, will they be able to handle the tech?"

Again the Jötnar shrugged.

"An hour ago they'd never even tried to control one. I doubt they even knew the equipment existed. They are quick learners, though. The longer Spartan gives us, the better they will be."

"And the CD1 drones? Are they combat-ready?"

He seemed pleased at that one particular question.

"The CD1 Grunts are waiting for us. Why don't we go and take a look?" Khan suggested, as he joined them.

\* \* \*

The training arena inside the ship was a large space, perhaps as big as a standard human sports hall; big enough for a game of most indoor sports, and more than adequate for the six mercenaries to practice in. Colonel Black joined the others at the high observation point ten metres up from the lower level. From there they were granted a clear view of the six CD1 Grunts moving about below.

"And they are all to be controlled by the mercenaries from inside the safety of a control centre or aircraft?"

Khan nodded.

"Yeah, this is full manual control. The further apart the controller and drone are, the greater the issues with latency and lag."

"Lag?"

Khan turned to Kanjana who had just moved past the Jötnar to check with the engineers.

"Please explain to the Colonel."

She said a few words to the two engineers and then twisted about with an irritated look on her face.

"Lag is shorthand for the latency, or time delay before sending a command and it being acted upon. For direct combat control this is not an issue, but when operating from a greater distance, we can introduce a minimum delay of around three microseconds per kilometre, with a much higher number, dependent on environmental factors."

"I see."

Kanjana wasn't entirely convinced he did, but the sounds coming from the displays caught her attention, so she turned back around to assist, leaving Khan with the others. He pulled on a special head-mounted command and control unit, and no matter how hard he tried, he still looked uncomfortable wearing the thing.

"Very nice," Olik said, laughing.

Colonel Black cleared his voice.

"This is not the time."

"That is true," Olik agreed.

The device provided Khan with a real-time video feed from each of the mercenaries, as well as direct communications. He threw a quick look to the Colonel before focusing his attention on the robotic Grunts. They moved about with surprising speed and were busy practicing moving about in pairs.

"Let's get this thing started."

He pressed the button on the console, muttered upon seeing it was the wrong one, and then pressed another. His voice was amplified in the arena.

"Ladies and Gentlemen, get ready for a full combat scenario. Two teams, six per side with standard XC1 carbines."

The six drones stopped and looked up to the control booth.

"You will have a ten-second count, and then you will run the course. Activate your weapons, blanks only. Get on the starting line."

He looked to the pair of SWD senior engineers. Both were in the fifties, grey-haired, and wearing company overalls. Chief Engineer Lennon Ferguson, the shorter of the two looked back to Khan. He was red-faced, and his narrow brimmed glasses did nothing to disguise the fact that he was one of the technical experts.

"The communication buffer is at capacity, no noise or issues. We're ready."

The second one then spoke.

"Wait, I have a red light on drone three. It's experiencing delay in two of its motor drives. It will need to be broken down after the training session."

Khan nodded.

"What about spares?"

The man sighed.

"We've got ten test units and enough parts to make

another three, perhaps four."

The six drones went back to the one side of the hall, and a number of artificial walls rose out from the ground. They were premade and of a fixed height. Though not particularly realistic, they did quickly cut off lines of sight and created a mock maze through which all manner of scenarios could be created.

"Not bad, not bad at all," said Olik.

"You've not seen this before?" Khan asked.

He grinned.

"Unlike you, I've had other more hands on activities to get involved in. That's why I left you to work with Spartan on this."

Khan laughed.

"Well, it's not quite that easy. We might be good at breaking things, but do you really think we are businessmen?"

He shook his head with wry amusement.

"I tell them what I'd like, just the same as with Spartan. We leave it to the brain monkeys like Mr Gibbs and Ferguson here."

Neither of the men moved from what they were doing. Lennon Fergusson pressed the final sequence, and a row of green lights appeared on the display. Olik pointed at the drones below them and to the artificial walls.

"It is working well, though. The training hall is not fully functional yet. But it can be used as a storage area for extra troops, or even a secondary deck for extra dropships. I tell you, this is the future."

"Perhaps," agreed the Colonel, " But right now it's time for target practice. The future can wait."

He looked to Khan.

"Now tell me, are these damned drones ready?"

The Jötnar leaned forward and indicated for one of the engineers to activate a particular sequence. It took a few more seconds, and then two doors at the other side of the hall opened up. In walked six more of the drones, each identical in design and specification to those being controlled by the mercenaries. Khan made several final checks.

"They're ready Colonel. Remember, the Grunt drones are designed so that they can mimic their operator's movement, all without prior knowledge or training. Any combat proficient soldier or civilian can control them in battle."

Colonel Black wasn't so sure, though. He'd seen men and women in battle, and he knew how many months it took for a marine to become proficient at working inside a PDS suit, let alone one of the newer, highly advanced Vanguard MK III suits just entering service with the Corps. He looked at the randomly created maze and pressed the audio button. It was muted by default to preserve the illusion of the combat environment. He removed his finger and looked to the engineers.

"I want night-time conditions. They could be forced to fight at night, or perhaps underground. I need to see them functioning in imperfect conditions. Understood?"

Ferguson looked to Khan for his authorisation. Nothing was said. Just a look was passed. The man looked back to his display and moved his hands over several virtual sliders. Almost at once the area transformed into blackness, until the night-vision cameras and thermal imaging systems activated on the virtual two-way mirror installed to face into the arena.

"Fight!"

Colonel Black leaned in close to watch what was happening. He had every faith in the six experienced mercenaries, but as to whether they could control the drones well enough in this fight was far from clear.

*Nothing beats experience.*

The six computer controlled machines moved slowly and spread out through the maze. They were cautious and continually scanning for signs of the enemy. They all moved and twisted about in exactly the same fashion, predictably so.

"This is based purely on their onboard routines?"

Ferguson pointed to the nearest of the drones.

"They are running via a combination of the ship's combat simulation engine, and their pre-recorded routines in this arena. It's a pretty show, but they couldn't do the same job on their own."

He laughed to himself and then realised he was the only one.

"That's a long...long way off, though. Perhaps not even in our lifetimes."

Colonel Black was not entirely sure if that was a good or a bad thing.

"Perhaps giving combat functional bipedal machines the ability to fight and think autonomously is best left to the writers of science fiction?"

Olik chortled, but added nothing else.

"So, if these drones lose the ability to communicate with a dropship and warship, what happens to them?"

Khan leaned against the display unit, and it groaned under his weight. He looked to the two engineers to answer. Again, Ferguson spoke.

"Well, the communication system is line of sight, but it is backed up with an encoded radio system for basic control commands. If a drone is forced under water, or behind solid cover, it will be able to function using its last commands for several minutes. The backup is designed for a maximum duration of thirty seconds, though."

He rubbed at his forehead.

"We wanted longer, but Alliance High Command is concerned that could give an enemy time to modify or change their commands if a unit was damaged or overrun in battle."

Olik cleared his throat.

"I had a more subtle solution to that problem."

Khan shook his head, clearly irritated at this.

"Go on, tell him."

"It is very simple. If a drone is out of range for more than a fixed time period, we give it two options. The first is a total shutdown, and the second, self-destruct."

Engineer Ferguson pushed his glasses further up his nose and returned his attention to the Colonel.

"Based on the current design, if contact is lost, the drone will have to continue under its last commands. That will remain until contact is made via direct line of sight only, or until the unit is disabled."

"So, it could continue a mission based on fixed parameters?"

The engineer didn't look particularly convinced.

"Not really, Colonel. You see; the basic commands are not enough to function for more than a few minutes in the real world. They could be to use defensive fire in a certain area, or to walk to a particular waypoint. As I said, the artificial intelligence system is basic. It is there to assist the operator, not replace them."

They looked back at the two sides moving through the maze. The difference between them was now becoming more and more clear. The mercenaries moved and performed just like human soldiers. Apart from the unusual body armour, they might just as easily have been there in the arena. As one went forward, the second followed behind in a classic cover by cover formation.

"Look, to the right," said Olik.

They all watched as the first of the machines moved around a corner and into the path of two of the mercenaries. There was no checking to aim, the machine simply opened fire immediately. Either through luck or judgment, the mercenary ducked back, and the second pair broke through one of the temporary barricades to land directly behind the drone. It spotted them, but as it turned, the original pair moved out and hit it from behind. The hits were registered, and it then slumped down as its control system deactivated each component.

"Interesting," said the Colonel.

The remaining eleven drones continued to move about and exchange gunfire, but after two more of the computer-controlled drones had withdrawn, the Colonel lost interest. He straightened his back and rubbed at his chin.

"Very well. I think I've seen more than enough."

Then his expression softened.

"You are right. The drones are ready, and so are our marines. All we need is contact from Karnak."

He pointed to Olik.

"Now, what about the two of you? What did you bring

with you?"

Olik seemed particularly excited at this conversation.

"We brought our old gear, customised JAS armour from Hyperion, with a few little extras from the workshops on Prometheus."

"Good. I want to see them in action."

Olik and looked to Khan.

"Now?"

He nodded happily.

"What the Colonel wants, the Colonel gets."

# CHAPTER NINE

*The modular ship designs of the Crusader, Conqueror, and Liberty class have proven themselves in countless battles, the flexibility in configuration and their reliability more important than any individual weapon system. Over three hundred of these vessels now serve in the Alliance, crewed by citizens of every colony from the birthplace of humanity; Earth, through to the alien worlds of Helios Prime and Spascia. These workhorses are assisted on day-to-day operations by attached units from regional forces. The fleet is well supported for operations at a minute's notice.*

*Naval Cadet's Handbook*

## Khagi Caverns, Karnak

The interior of the M-3B armour was warm and reasonably comfortable. For most of the journey, Spartan had even forgotten he was wearing it. The close fitting bands of armour were just millimetres from his skin, yet it was the helmet and visor that created the illusion. By sending wide-angle data to the eyes of the helmet visor, he had a better field of view than he would have with the helmet removed.

Spartan cycled through his vision modes, checking for signs of the enemy. While the infrared could help him move in the pitch darkness, he also needed to make use of the thermal imaging to check for heat blooms. Data scrolled past, along with the computer's assessment of materials, composition, and even radiation levels. One last check confirmed everything was as it appeared.

"Looks clear. Let's stop for a few minutes."

They had been travelling in the tunnel for over three hours before Spartan had given this signal to stop, and Syala needed no encouragement. She could feel an ache in her legs, and her back groaned under the continuous stopping to move under partially collapsed girders. Both stepped to the side of the corroded rail system and to one of the emergency alcoves. These small areas were cut into the rock to allow work crews to be out of the way of traffic. They were not massive but did offer a welcome place to sit, and gave them protection in case any hostile threats were encountered in front or behind.

"How are you doing?" Spartan asked.

His helmet opened up to expose his face, and she could see sweat running down his cheeks. His face was worn and battered; yet there was something youthful about him, for all the years of combat and struggle.

"Don't worry about me, what about you?"

Both took sips from their water tubes. Their breathing was already slowing, and now that they had stopped, it was a good opportunity to look about the tunnel. The rock had a glazed look, and a ribbed effect from the heat lances that would have been used to cut deep into it to create the tunnels. Syala ran her hands along the surface as though stroking an animal. The walls left grey marks on her armoured gloves, marks that showed up as almost black in the low light from their armour. Spartan took one more sip and then nodded in the direction they'd been travelling for so long.

"According to the old Byotai, we have about twenty more minutes to go until we reach the closed down transit station. From there, we'll have to work out way through the inner defences."

Syala nodded.

"Plus whatever else they've added that's new. Don't forget, it's not just a city they've taken over. Based on what we've seen, I reckon they are using Montu as a major holding area for this invasion."

She indicated to his armour, specifically the articulated mounts built into the shoulders. There was a small lip of perhaps just a few millimetres on each side that betrayed a hidden mount.

"How many more recon drones are you carrying?"

Spartan lifted his eyes to examine the status indicator inside his helmet. Small icons marked the status of his onboard power unit, weapons, and respirator, as well as tactical information and communications.

"Just the one."

He said it in a disappointed tone.

"I brought two with me, but the first is smashed somewhere near the ruins of the research facility. It will be enough, assuming the information we received was correct."

She kept staring at him until finally he shook his head.

"What is it?"

"I've been wanting to ask…but…"

Spartan looked at her and tried to gauge what she was

thinking. He couldn't tell, at least, not yet.

"Just ask. I might even tell you."

She laughed, but it was forced and clearly not spontaneous.

"Arana told me about your family when we were on the way to Taxxu. There are rumours that you sacrificed them, and millions more in the war. Is that true?"

Spartan's eyebrows appeared to tense at the question, and she instantly regretted asking. It wasn't as if the rumours had been spread by her, and from what she'd seen, she seriously doubted it had happened the way others described it.

"Actually...don't..."

Spartan lifted his hand.

"No, it's okay. You're not the first person to ask, and I doubt you will be the last."

He rubbed his face with the back of his hand and leant against the smooth wall of the tunnel. The metal of his armour made a subtle scraping sound as he adjusted his posture.

"The last war was a tough one. Hell, it was worse than tough, it was genocide plain and simple, carried out by a race of Biomechanical monsters. I did what I had to because..."

"We had to win?"

Spartan shook his head.

"No, it wasn't that."

He took in a long breath and then another sip on the water tube. As he did so, Spartan thought of Arana and the others making their way through the tunnels. He didn't envy them for that journey, but his own was likely to be at least as tough. He turned his attention back to Syala.

"I had to act because if I didn't, it would have been the extermination of every living thing we know. The Byotai, the Helions, humans, every one of them dead."

He looked up at the ceiling, seeing nothing but blackness.

"Teresa chose to help our son, and those fighting on Spascia. Gun was there as well, and by all account, they fought harder than anybody ever has. It was a bloody siege that lasted months, with wave assaults and orbital bombardments."

"And you?"

"I used what I had to get inside the Biomech military, to join them and to lead their forces from the safety of their own worlds. It was a fate the enemy had planned for me and many others from the start."

Now she could see the pain on his face.

"It meant me being the face of the Biomechs, for a time. And that is the image, the memory that few will ever forget. Me, hero of the damned Alliance, leading the Biomech fleet out of the Black Rift and against our own people."

They waited there in the silence of the tunnels, with just the occasional sounds from the small animals that flew through its deep confines. Spartan wasn't sure what they were, but they moved and sounded much like bats. Syala broke the silence and asked the one question she really wanted to know.

"But you exposed them to the fleet battle so that you could turn on them. When the smoke cleared, were you not the one behind the final assault that destroyed the Biomech power? That was the plan from the start, wasn't it?"

Spartan closed his eyes. He'd heard this story so many times now, and some even accused him of only changing sides when the grand Alliance of races had smashed into the Black Rift, to take the fight to the enemy in one last battle. That he had fought with his people just to save his own skin.

"Khan and I came up with the original plan, and with the support of Z'Kanthu, the leader of the Biomech rebels. Believe me, the consequences will stay with me forever. Don't forget, while I was with..."

He voice almost squeaked, and he stopped, took a sip, and continued.

"While I was with them, the Biomechs launched a massive final attack on Spascia. I could have stopped it, maybe. But I had to play my part, to lead the Biomechs in a victorious assault. In any case, Gun was injured and hundreds of thousands killed."

Syala seemed to understand, or at the very least she was just trying to be comforting.

"And that was when your family was killed. In the final battle of Spascia."

It was a statement, not a question, but it was enough to end the conversation. They waited another few minutes, each taking on the sugary fluids to keep their bodies in top form. Finally, Spartan released the cable from his lips and stretched his limbs.

"Right, it's time."

Syala checked her weapon for the final time and gave him a short nod.

"Let's do this thing."

They started to leave, but Syala placed her hand on his left shoulder.

"For what it's worth, I think you did the right thing. The war has been analysed over and over by everybody."

He shrugged and kept moving forward.

"Simulations showed that the Biomechs would have burned through the Helios System in weeks."

She tried to sound a little more cheerful.

"All of their planets would have been razed to the ground, and then the Biomechs spread out to hit world after world. There is nothing you could have done differently that would have reduced our losses. You did the right thing."

It was a good effort, but Spartan was not in the mood or frame of mind for somebody else trying to comfort him. After all these years, the losses still sat heavily in his mind. He began to speak, but stopped himself. The two carried on towards end the of the tunnel complex in silence, nothing but the heavy thud of their armoured boots on the ground. Finally, he spoke, just as a glimmer of light appeared off into the distance.

"I owe Daniels for the suffering he took in those last weeks."

Syala walked through a narrow stream of muddy water, and her boots kicked up a small amount that left a smear on the ground.

"And Gun?"

Spartan twisted his head back and opened his visor. To her surprise he was smiling.

"He will just be glad he can get back in the fight. Have you ever seen a pissed off Jötnar?"

Syala shook her head. Spartan clamped down his visor and kept moving ahead.

"Oh, yeah, it is a sight to behold."

They passed the last section of rail and to a long abandoned railcar. There was little of its upper structure remaining, but the burnt out lower section showed where it rested atop the rail system. The seating inside was a charred wreck, and Syala gasped when she saw the remains of a skeleton inside.

"Watch your footing," said Spartan.

They tried to ignore the carnage at their side. Even so, Spartan slowed his pace and glanced over to Syala to make sure she was okay. He might have seen bodies in the hundreds, perhaps even thousands in his life, but he had no idea about her. Syala had just passed a body, and as her foot lowered, it almost crushed a severed arm. She stopped, adjusted her position, and brought her foot down alongside the broken body parts.

*She's calm, what else has she done?*

He'd not even bothered to check the backgrounds of these mercenaries. The word of the Colonel had been more than enough for him. Now he wished he'd looked into the sisters more carefully.

"What happened here?"

Spartan shook his head and looked to the end of the tunnel. There were bodies piled up in heaps, and they were all Byotai. He bent down to one and looked more closely. It was a female Byotai, and her clothing had been partially torn open. He could see wounds, but not from gunshots. Another lay on his side, multiple puncture wounds in his chest. On the ground beside the body was a beautifully constructed hunting rifle. The weapon was big, more like a weapon for Gun or Khan. It was single-barrelled and clearly not military. A burn mark showed where it had been ripped apart by gunfire.

*Civilians.*

Spartan looked to his right and spotted discarded shells. He picked one up and brought it close to his eyes. It was a large-calibre kinetic rifle round; the kind often used by both Helion and Byotai hunters. Unlike military weapons, this one was designed to provide clean kills, without the need to penetrate through armour. He lifted himself back up and walked on past them, sickened at what he'd seen. Syala chased after him.

"They were butchered like cattle and dumped down here."

Syala didn't seem surprised at his assessment.

"Most were killed with puncture wounds to the chest or cuts to the throat. A few of them carried hunting rifles, like that one back there."

She stopped and pointed at the bodies.

"Spartan, this is more than we were told. This was a massacre, plain and simple. What is wrong with these people? These are civilians with no military equipment. So why were they killed?"

Spartan nodded.

"I know. This is what the General and Gun were here to stop. Now the Anicinàbe are here in force, and they are killing anybody they can find. They don't just want the Byotai gone. They want them terrified or dead."

He took in a quick breath.

"When we have them freed, hell, the Anicinàbe are gonna pay."

He took another few breaths and then moved on, giving the bodies a final look before making his way out of the tunnel and into the vast and abandoned complex. He had little doubt that most Anicinàbe would be appalled at what they saw, but right now that didn't interest him. The soldiers that had arrived were clearly unconcerned about the people they killed, and they made his job a little easier.

"Keep your scanners active. There could be sensors or traps down here. We are in a warzone now."

The transit station was barely recognisable, more closely resembling a scrap yard than a place that once served traffic through the planet's underground transit system. The main level was as large as a hangar and cut into the surface so that it took the place of a large crater. More than ten maglev lines ran into the complex, each stopping at one of the long masonry platforms. Cables hung down from the ceiling, and dozens of holes showed where parts of the roof had collapsed. Spartan clambered over one of the rails and up to the platform.

"This isn't all from lack of use. Look over there."

He pointed to a set of doors now blasted open. Apart from the damage, the structure looked in a much better state of affairs.

"Follow me."

They walked up a wide ramp, past a control panel, and through what remained of the doors. On the other side it was as though they had transferred to a completely different planet.

"Incredible," said Syala.

Though designed in just the same fashion, this large part of the facility was evidently still in use. There were two more rail lines ahead, and one currently had a maglev train sitting there, waiting with its ramps lowered down onto the platform. The car itself was long, at least fifty metres and gleaming silver in colour.

"This is still operational."

Spartan remained cautious, as if expecting a soldier to appear at any moment. There was nothing, though, and the railcar just sat there, silent and abandoned. They walked down the platform to a section linking multiple smaller lines together. Seating areas were worn but still intact, and their paint peeled where any still remained. Now Syala could see what he was looking at.

"Strange."

She moved to the edge of the low platform and looked down at the maglev tracks. Unlike the others, these appeared to be in pristine order and with little corrosion. Yet there were burn marks at several points on one of them where the metal had been cut through.

"So there is a functioning rail system, just not the long-distance sections that reach out to the more remote Byotai compounds."

"Are you that surprised?"

Spartan nodded.

"True. It costs time and money to look after them. But these lines…"

He walked to one of the many vertical shafts that rose up to the ceiling. On one was a public information booth, all in Byotai. He deactivated his right arm unit so that his hand was free and activated the display. The overlay in his helmet did a rough translation, overlaying the text with words he could understand; most made little sense, apart from one.

"City express line."

He looked to Syala.

"So the main lines to the major cities are still functional."

She leaned in to look at the imagery. There were small black circles marking major cities or spaceports, but there was one she was after and could not find. Spartan looked in the same direction until both put their finger on one place.

"Mount Caldos," they said simultaneously.

Spartan spotted movement and froze still. He whispered to Syala.

"Target to my left, one hundred metres."

She moved ever so slowly, doing her best to make little sound or movement so that she might be identified. There was little cover other than from the vertical pillars that were barely thick enough to stand behind. She hid behind the nearest and pulled her gun out to her side. The top-mounted cameras fed data back to her helmet.

"Yeah, I've got two targets, militiamen."

She paused and turned to Spartan.

"No, wait. They're irregulars all right, but they're carrying the marks of the Spires Clan."

Spartan sighed as he looked at them as well. The narrow shapes of the soldiers were covered in loose clothing, giving them a nomadic look. But beneath that clothing was the colourless shape of military armour. He could see the smooth chest plate and rings of metal on the collar.

"Spires Clan? Who are they?"

Syala continued watching them as she spoke.

"They are one of the largest clans in the Anicinàbe League. They've been pushing for raids outside of League territory for the last three years."

Spartan was already checking the data in his head-up display. The tattoo and markings of the clan appeared, along with details of known associates and their prior dealings.

"So they have ties with the Red Scars."

He swallowed as he read the next part.

"It says they travel in nomadic fleets of over three hundred ships. That cannot be true."

Syala's eyes were still locked onto the distant shapes.

"A settler uprising, my ass. These are violent criminals, the worst scum of the Anicinàbe League."

Spartan nodded grimly.

"And now they are here, staking a claim to Karnak. I wonder who sent them."

It was a rhetorical question, and neither was particularly interested in the why, only the now.

"The list of their acts in the last year is incredible, hijackings, kidnaps, and assassinations. Why the hell is the Council not reining them in?"

He knew the answer as soon as he said it.

*Because they are part of the problem, the Council is nothing more than a league of criminals.*

He licked his lip and moved a fraction, checking the area where the soldiers arrived. There was a semi-circular tunnel leading up and towards bright light. Syala took aim with her weapon, but he shook his head slightly.

"No, not yet. Watch them."

She kept her weapon raised and pointing at them. Spartan also watched, but he was much more interested in where they had come from, rather than getting rid of the two.

"That's where the Byotai said the main street in the city is. If his information is accurate, it will be six blocks from the civic buildings. I just hope they're still here."

Syala spotted something on the column-mounted display and waited until the two soldiers vanished behind one of the stationary railcars.

"Spartan, the line to Mount Caldos. Is it me, or is this railcar on the same line?"

Spartan examined it for a few seconds.

"Yeah, looks like an automated railcar, and the end of the line is at least a kilometre short in the open ground to the South of the mountains. Looks like an open plain or valley from that imagery. So what?"

She nodded ever so slowly at the unit.

"There's something else about it."

Spartan identified a line of coloured dots on all but two of the separate lines. But they meant little to him.

"So?"

Syala smiled.

"They are markers for the electric power system for the rail lines. All but two of them are active, including the one to Mount Caldos. It means there is a powered railcar heading in that direction, one that we could use."

Spartan understood immediately.

"The railcar to Caldos is that one?"

He beckoned towards the group of five large railcars. They were more of the same dull silver models, with double decks and control units at each end of the train. Spartan straightened his back and looked back to where the two soldiers had been. Neither had returned, but he could hear the sound of their feet a short distance away. He looked to Syala and deactivated his helmet so she could see his face.

"That is our ticket out of here. I want you to get the railcars ready, and set up multiple distractions in this facility."

She looked concerned.

"You want me to stay here? What about you?"

He grinned for the first time in hours.

"Lady, I have an appointment to keep. Just make sure our trip out of here is clear. Once they know where we are, they'll try to cut the power to the tracks. That's where you come in."

Syala was already looking about for signs of a control station and had spotted a series of doors leading off inside the desolate transit complex. Signs above had been ripped down, but one matched the description on her suit overlay for a command structure.

"Okay, I can handle that. How long will you be?"

"I'll be as quick as I can."

He checked the ammunition feeds on his weapon just as Syala leaned in and kissed him on his cheek. It wasn't for long, but it certainly got his attention. She lingered against him, and then they were apart. Spartan could see her face was slightly flushed. Syala's visor hissed and clamped down over her face.

"Just be careful, Spartan. I don't want to be the one coming back to look for you. This operation has been weird enough as it is."

He left in the direction of the exit point to the transit station. With each step he scanned left to right, while his passive sensors looked for signs of heat or even stray magnetic interference. Columns of data scrolled down to the right of his eye, but he ignored it and concentrated on the view modes. He'd almost reached the arched entrance when he spotted them.

*There they are.*

His gut instinct was to aim his XC1 carbine at them and to open fire. At this range the rapid-fire smoothbore weapon would have shredded them. Nothing could stand against the raw heat of the weapons, but he was also aware the sound of the high-velocity railgun would draw attention. And then there was also the possibility that internal sensors might detect such a major heat source.

*Stealth. The mission is recon and rescue, not assault. That's for another day.*

Spartan leaned against the wall. A long beam overhead cast a modest shadow that provided him with some limited measure of cover. Once there, he activated his stealth armour mode, and the suit began its slow process of change.

*This had better work.*

Spartan had been a strong advocate of the three-layer experimental chromatophore technology used in the armour. If he'd had his way, he would have moved even more resources into getting the costs brought down. In theory, it would provide the Alliance military with a major asset, but the costs were vastly higher than originally thought. As he waited there, he even began to doubt it was working. The process was painfully slow, and it was one of the reasons why no more development had been made on the technology. Even so, as he waited, he could see his arm beginning to shift in tone as the soldiers came nearer. After what seemed like an age, the two were alongside, and they stopped to speak. He was only three metres away and could see every detail.

*Wait and let them pass.*

Spartan might have held back when he spotted a blade hung down low on the left of the first soldier. It was unsheathed and hanging out from a ring of metal. Congealed blood, clearly from Byotai, ran thickly along the sharp material. It instantly reminded him of the bodies back in the tunnels, and as before, he could feel the uncontrollable rage building inside him.

*Animals.*

The other soldier wore a bandolier, but it was definitely of Byotai design. The oversized piece of material was well worn and carried multiple large calibre projectiles still in the mounts, ones that looked identical to those he'd seen back in the tunnel.

*Byotai hunting gear.*

Spartan already knew they were likely to have killed Byotai, but the stolen artefact and the blood-soaked blade were far more than he needed to see. Worse was that he was already beginning to imagine all manner of horrors being committed by the Anicinàbe soldiers. He started to move his right arm, and that was when they spotted him. The soldier's first instinct was to reach for a weapon, and that gave Spartan the green light.

*Now!*

At that moment, the suit pumped in a burst of adrenalin on top of the amount already surging through his body. He knew the feeling and felt as though his body was on fire. He lurched out from the shadows with his bayoneted carbine ready, but then a third warrior appeared from his left. Where he'd come from, Spartan would never know, but the warrior's gun went off and struck his shoulder.

*Duck down. Strike left!*

The thermal round left a long black mark on the armour plating but incredibly failed to penetrate. Warnings sounded, but Spartan ignored them. A second blast struck the ground nearby, and then he was in range. Spartan's first blow saw the blade embedded deep in the first soldier's head. He pulled the trigger, and a single encased ball of plasma disintegrated the skull of the soldier. The headless corpse dropped to the ground, and so did Spartan.

*Roll.*

He moved off to the right, avoiding another two shots in quick succession. The remaining soldiers were close but failed to fire again, for fear of striking each other. Spartan rose up between them and struck out with his left arm, pinning the second soldier to the wall as he tried to cry out a warning. Spartan kicked hard into the back of his knee. The much weaker opponent crashed to the ground, just as Spartan spun the weapon around and pulled the trigger. The soldier's chest exploded in fragments of flesh and armour.

*One left.*

He began to turn about as another gunshot struck, and this time it hit the left thigh of his armour with an impact that felt like a freight train. An alert sounded, and he felt his leg go cold and numb. A second shot hit his left arm, and then his carbine was out of his hands and clattering along the floor. With just one leg, he dropped down onto his knee as the third and final Spires Clan warrior fell upon him. At the same time, the soldier pointed his weapon at Spartan's face. He said something, but it was nothing but gibberish to him.

"Not today."

In one fluid movement, he yanked the sidearm fitted inside a metal fold on his flank. Unlike the rest of his gear, this was completely standard and rather archaic in fashion. It was nothing more than a miniaturised L52 carbine, cut down to an oversized pistol, and with a thirty-round clip of hardened slugs. He kept the trigger held down as the rounds peppered the armoured figure atop of him. By the time Spartan rolled the body off him, they were both covered it blood.

*Three down, plenty more to go.*

Spartan rose to his feet and waited as the suit pumped in fluids to the seized leg joint. He felt a little pain, but according to the diagnostics, he'd suffered no more than lacerations and bruising to his limb.

"All systems active," said the friendly voice.

*Good. Now let's find them, before more of these animals come looking for me.*

Spartan dragged their broken bodies away from the main path and down amongst a stack of discarded crates. It took just over a minute to clear the way, and then he was gone. No other soldiers appeared, not even when he climbed the ramp to the open-air foyer that looked out into the regional capital.

*Montu, I'm finally here.*

"Spartan, I'm near the control room. There are soldiers here."

Spartan nodded even though she couldn't see him.

"Understood. Wait for my signal before you move."

"What signal?"

Spartan smiled to himself.

"You'll know, because when I have them, all hell is going to break loose."

# CHAPTER TEN

*The religious fanatics of the Echidna Union were thrown away in a long, pointless war. This conflict proved to be one of many supported and influenced by the machinations of the few Biomechs still in existence. There have been numerous religious fanatics in the past, but these Zealots, as they were known, were something else. What started as an underground movement quickly turned into a full-scale empire, with all the trappings of statehood. Beneath this veneer was the influence of Biomech artificial creations, vast factories, and breeding programmes. Few now realise how close humanity came to the abyss, and that had the war been lost, so would the lives of every man, woman, and child in the old Confederacy.*

*A Brief History of the Zealots*

## ANS X-45 'Titan', Debris Field, Karnak

Olik looked at the mainscreen while Khan continued pacing back and forth. Olik might have been the less experienced of the two, but he'd seen more than his fair share of combat, and he was by far the most proficient. Right now Khan was more concerned about the lack of information on Gun. After what must have been the twentieth time pacing back and forth, Colonel Black finally snapped. He called out in frustration.

"Okay, Khan, that is enough."

The Jötnar looked almost hurt as he stopped and stared long and hard at the Colonel. Technically, he was much younger than the Colonel, but forgot that when his kin were created, they were already fully formed and capable of violence and basic communication.

"What do you expect? The only contact we get from Spartan is that he is behind schedule and has just arrived at the Khagi Research Facility. What if they ran into trouble there? You saw the scans."

Olik looked back at the information from Spartan.

"The squad is still fully functional, and our Khreenk contacts at the facility will give him the information he needs."

He looked to Khan.

"Nothing has changed, just our patience. We need to give them time."

Colonel Black listened patiently. He'd seen the same information, but he also knew that Khan was feeling more and more impotent. It was important to let him vent his frustration.

*There will be more than enough time for violence....soon.*

"Khan, until I have something solid, we will stay exactly where we are. We have absolutely nothing, and I mean, nothing to go on."

The long-range scans concerned him, but there was little point in dwelling on them. Spartan was out there with a small team, and his intervention could be made just once. He knew, as did the others, that when they returned, it would certainly be while under fire. It would be dangerous and incredibly risky.

"We must wait, Khan. Spartan knows this, and if he needs help, he will let us know."

Kanjana took that moment to catch both of their attention.

"You are not going to believe what I just spotted."

She walked up from the sphere and joined them on the main deck. With a quiet word to Five-Seven, the mainscreen altered to show a different part of space. For a second, it wasn't particularly clear, but then the image stabilised and showed hundreds of shapes. Colonel Black let out air from the back of his throat.

"What are we looking at?"

The craft was an odd collection, and there were more than a few different designs taken from multiple races. Colonel Black even spotted what looked like a heavily altered Liberty Class destroyer, one of the newer classes of Alliance ships. They all bore unusual devices on their hulls, the majority in black.

"This is a war party."

She looked away from the screen and towards Colonel Black, Khan, and Olik.

"A military force?" Olik asked.

Kanjana shook her head, and her lightweight hair drifted from side to side.

"A war party. It is a gathering of the warriors from nearby clans. I can see Red Scars, and I think there are some Spires as well."

Colonel Black sunk back deep into his chair. His heart told him to intervene immediately, but his mind said otherwise.

*We're but one ship out here. I have to stay level-headed.*

"Very well. Track them, but this ship does not move. We cannot engage unknown vessels, especially with those numbers. Titan might be advanced, but she's not that advanced."

He turned his attention to Khan and Olik.

"We have mapping data for the Khagi region, do we not?"

They nodded simultaneously.

"Get the simulators running, and let's get some scenarios planned and tested. When we get the word, I want a combat unit down there in minutes. It's going to get lively."

Khan was already at the first computer display, and Olik moved to a virtual table unit to access the mapping information. Colonel Black looked back at the vast cloud of ships. He tried to remain calm, but deep down he could feel an awful sense of foreboding. This wasn't a raid or convoy. The number of ships could mean only one thing, and that meant the General had been right all along.

*The Anicinàbe may not be looking for war, but these clans are. Trouble is coming.*

He looked to Five-Seven who was as calm and collected as always.

"Get the ship ready. We may be going into combat earlier than expected."

Khan and Olik were already at the door and heading out when he called after them.

"Push the Grunts hard, and remember; the machines are expendable, but we are not. Plan for that."

They looked at each other and then marched out of the doorway. Colonel Black looked to Kanjana, who seemed uncomfortable.

"What is it?"

She turned around and beckoned to the image of the great fleet of ships.

"This is getting bigger by the hour. Those ships could carry enough warriors to overrun the planet."

She looked back to him.

"But what if they have other plans?"

Colonel Black swallowed uncomfortably, realising he had absolutely no idea what that plan could be.

"All we can do is prepare ourselves, and the ship. We're here for the mission; we cannot change the course of what could become a major warzone. Not by ourselves."

He thought about her words for a moment.

"In the meantime, I think it would be advantageous to send a burst communication through to the Byotai security units at the Rift, don't you think?"

Kanjana smiled.

"Yes, and make sure the Alliance knows what's happening out here, too."

* * *

## Montu, Khagi District, Karnak

Spartan had only made it two blocks when he spotted the first military patrol. He pulled up close to the nearby structure, a domed shaped habitation building with a low overhang all around, much like a lip. As he waited in the shadows, the vehicle continued to move past, followed by a dozen militiamen, and all moving at a jog. This was a civilian truck, with a long-wheelbase and a gun mount fitted onto the bed. The weapon seemed completely out of place, yet there was no doubting the power it would bring to a battle.

*This place isn't a capital, anymore. This is a military base, and they are gearing up for something big.*

Another vehicle stopped off to the right and near the larger domed structure that was the entrance to the transit system. As he waited there, his armour transformed to match the dust colours around him. He waited, knowing he would need every feature of this armour if he were to stand even the slightest chance.

*No, that's not good.*

A hatch on the back opened up, and three soldiers dropped out. They looked almost identical to those he'd fought underground. They chatted for a few seconds and went inside as the vehicle drove off. Spartan shook his head in frustration.

"Syala, are you there?"

"I'm here, and still waiting for your signal. What's going on?"

Spartan needed to cough, so he took three swallows and a quick sip on his water feed tube. It helped, if only for a few more minutes.

"Not yet. There's a problem, though. You've got company."

"How many?"

Spartan looked at the entrance once more, double-checking on their numbers.

"I see three soldiers, same clothing and gear as the ones we've already seen. Stay low and monitor them. Do not engage, not yet. Understood?"

"Affirmative."

There was silence for another four seconds. Syala contacted him one last time.

"Hurry up, it's getting lonely down here."

Spartan waited a few more seconds and then moved away from the dome and on to the last building near the civic buildings. From there he had a good view of what might have been something quite special in the past, before the start of the occupation. The primary building was of a simple design but flanked by four massive ornamental columns, one of which lay shattered on the ground. A low wall topped with wire surrounded the structure. Banners hung down with the iconography of several organisations, one of which was the Red Scars.

*Great, so all that fighting and now they're back.*

He scanned in both directions and identified only one route in, a large metal gateway, flanked by watchtowers and monitored by two guards. The security was obviously new and looked nothing like the simple, but sturdy architecture of the Byotai.

*What the hell is that?*

The lenses of the M-3B armour zoomed in, tightening around the guards. He moved down to follow a strap in one of their hands. On the ground was a beast the size of a very large dog, perhaps closer to a bear. It wasn't the size that surprised him. Rather the savagery in its looks. The creature had an almost reptilian look, but was hairy and fidgeted continually. Spartan had not seen such a beast before, but he was familiar with the skills of canines, and this particular animal could be a problem. It was fitted with a harness around its back and chest; its body plated with overlapping layers of armour.

*I've seen it all now.*

A light flashed in his helmet, a simple alert that one of their communication drones was overhead. Spartan had already assembled a short command pack, and with a single press, his suit sent the heavily encoded data. Inside he had included his current position, as much data as he had found in Montu, and that the others were escorting refugees back to Caldos. More important, he'd added the information on the rail system and his intended escape route.

*That should be enough for you, Arana. Just make sure you're ready.*

The distance between his building and the wall was fifteen metres and all open ground. He could probably make it to the wall undetected, but what then? He could breach the wall with charges, or he could overpower the guards at the gate. Either option would draw attention, and he still had no idea where Gun and the General might even be.

*I need Intel.*

His position was perfectly placed to use his last remaining drone. He looked back and forth, checking that his position was still secure before activating it. The section on his shoulder slid open, and the unit flew out like a large, angry insect. It was high in the air in seconds and vanished to the human eye. Data from the unit came in immediately, and in just a few more seconds he had a much better view of the facility, and then finally, the city. To Spartan's surprise, the walled building was just one of many structures now occupied. Perhaps a kilometre away was the spaceport, a large, heavily cleared area with protected landing bays for spacecraft.

*Where are you, General?*

Spartan turned his attention back to the drone that was hovering overhead at a height of two hundred metres.

He could see civilian vehicles moving about, as well as a large number of wheeled military vehicles. What really astounded him were the two long rows of strike aircraft. They were the same as those that attacked the Byotai facility, and twelve of them were all waiting, presumably for their next targets.

*There!*

A small red light pulsed on the overhead view of the city, and to his amazement, it showed right next to the spaceport. Spartan had assumed the old government buildings were the most likely place to keep prisoners; instead it seemed the spaceport was the place.

*You've got to be kidding me.*

He waited then, and the circle continued to shrink as his computer reduced the search area down, mete by mete. It finally stopped to show an area of roughly four blocks.

*Not enough, I need better than that.*

The videostream began breaking up, and he was forced to hit the return command to the drone. In an instant the unit move lower and returned a short distance to improve the data integrity. It was a fast craft, and with the improved view, Spartan could see the problem. It wasn't that reaching the spaceport would be impossible; it was what he would do to escape. The more he waited and watched, the more he could see the place was a hive of activity.

*The only way this will work is for a distraction. They need to feel they are under attack.*

He tapped the side of his thigh armour. A small section opened up, revealing a weapon mount carrying eight micro-thermite charges. For the first time since reaching Montu, a smile crept along his face.

*I know just the thing.*

* * *

## Khagi Mountains, Karnak

Arana stepped over the jagged rocks, carefully lifting her boots to avoid them taking damage from the sharp edges. She had no idea what kind of rock it was, but at least two Byotai were now nursing nasty-looking cuts from the razor sharp edges. They had left the caverns quite some time ago, and the route along the side of the mountain was treacherous. It was now possible to see they were out of the dark tunnels, but with that freedom came the increased chance of being spotted from the air. Arana checked her mapping data and breathed a sigh of relief at seeing how close they were to their objective.

*Spartan had better be right, or we've made this trip for nothing.*

Her mercenaries were scattered amongst the group, helping them to keep moving, while always on the lookout for signs of the enemy. She looked over her shoulder and quickly identified the difference between the professionals and the civilians. It was easy, especially with her people wearing plated armour. A handful of the Byotai wore armour, but the majority had only whatever they could scrape together before leaving. She contemplated contacting Spartan, but until there was something significant, her orders were clear. Radio silence was critical, and breaking it could spell disaster for the mission.

*Keep moving forward. Do not stop for anything.*

A tone started in her helmet and was followed afterwards by a short, heavily encoded data packet sent from one of the communication buoys left in orbit by ANS X-45 Titan. The onboard computer took almost ten seconds to authenticate and decode it. Finally, it popped up with identification information from Spartan, as well as a series of waypoints and an overview of the Khagi region.

*Spartan, and he's reached Montu.*

What sent a jolt of adrenalin through her body was the mention of Syala. Just knowing she was alive and safe gave her additional strength. She looked down at the rest of the data and then filed it away inside the suit's encrypted storage unit. Arana opened her mouth to speak, and that was when the warning sensors sounded.

"Aircraft!"

A screaming sound overhead forced her to drop to her knees. She'd heard it before, and it filled her with dread. Then she saw the shape, and it made her want to dig down so that she couldn't be seen. It was small, and a pair of gun pods hung down low beneath its fuselage. The two engines left a region of distorted air behind them, a consequence of the vast level of heat pumping from them. She could just about see the shapes of several soldiers inside, holding on to their harnesses while they looked out, presumably for Arana and the others.

*How did they find us so fast?*

"Everybody, get down!"

Every single person in the column dropped down just as an aircraft rushed past overhead. It banked hard to the left and then spun about, as though it had found its prey. Now moving more slowly, it twisted back and forth until a number of lights flashed down one side.

"Incoming!" yelled one of her mercenaries.

The rifle fire was inaccurate and struck around them to no affect. Then came the gyroscopically stabilised gun mounts on the small wing pods. The first shots missed them, but the follow-up bursts ripped into their position. Two Byotai were killed outright as they huddled impotently behind rocks.

"Open fire."

A few of the Byotai tried to return fire, but their weapons were poorly suited to the task. Arana lifted her Khreenk weapon to her shoulder and activated the charge circuit. It began to build up power instantly. She waited, ignoring the incoming fire until the Hornet aircraft turned again. At that one moment it was vulnerable.

*Now!*

The energy blast from the weapon was massive, and it took all her strength to stay upright. The blast was relatively low velocity and just as it was about to strike, the aircraft dropped down twenty metres. It then twisted about and opened fire once more as a pair of missiles appeared from the right. The smoke trails were from a point beside the mountain and the direction they were heading for. Both moved incredibly fast, and she'd already recognised the tracking pattern.

*Alliance issue light anti-aircraft missiles. Nice timing, very nice.*

The pilot of the Hornet must have sighted the shapes because the aircraft turned about to face them and activated its main engines. The craft started its acceleration procedure, but it was too little, too late.

*You're toast, my friend.*

Arana stayed completely still even though she was no longer being fired upon. There was always the chance a stray round from an automated weapon system might strike out, and she had no intention dying. The first missile struck the aircraft on the wing and exploded, leaving a bright yellow flash for the briefest of moments. The engine was shattered in an instant, and two bodies tumbled out as it rolled over. Arana followed their fall, when the second missile hit the stricken aircraft and it exploded.

"Stay down!"

She dropped down but kept an eye on the damaged craft. Once the flash had dissipated, there was little left but debris and burning fuel that fell down in an avalanche of carnage to the wasteland below. She could see at least two more bodies falling, as well as a single soldier who must have leapt out. This lucky individual was using his motors to fall at a safer velocity towards the ground. Arana had no intention of opening fire, but Kras already had the soldier in his sights. His gun fired twice, and the soldier vanishing lifelessly behind the rocks rewarded him.

"Everybody up."

One by one the mercenaries and civilians lifted themselves back to their feet, and then, after checking in all directions, continued on their previous path.

"Not much further now," she said, trying to keep their spirits up. This time she let her translator circuits do the job, and then immediately wished she'd left it to the Khreenk mercenary. Her system might have been advanced, but it lacked the ability to impart care or emotion in the words. She spotted Kras further back waving his weapon over his head. Arana nodded and turned away to continue forward.

*I can't blame him; look at what he's seen the last few days.*

Arana was moving ahead, but something had changed now. There was some real urgency to how she moved. There was a chance, no matter how slim, that they had been spotted. If the enemy were smart, they would land troops away from the range of the missiles, or even launch a strike against the launchers first. She walked twenty or so steps before checking the others. They were a good way back down the steep descent from the side of the low mountain and into the valley. It took another thirty minutes to reach a dusty trail that looked heavily used. The smoke column was now far behind them, yet it still filled a portion of the sky with its oily black pattern.

With less cover available, they stayed close to the rocks on the one side and moved on until finally rounding the last corner. Before them was the large shape of Mount Caldos, one of the most prominent of the peaks. Arana almost stumbled on seeing the scene before her. Rather than a road or rail track leading inside the city, she found debris scattered in all directions. The ground was charred from multiple thermal weapons, but that was not what caught her gaze.

"Incredible, truly incredible."

She lifted her gaze to stare upon the side of the mountain, and towards the layered fortified line that extended out in a semi-circle. The wall was at least fifteen metres high, although several sections were only half of that. The completed sections were smooth and protected by dozens of Byotai soldiers. Multiple excavators and Byotai in massive exo-armoured suits were erecting additional sections to increase the height and thickness of the outer protective wall. She couldn't make out if they were regulars on the walls, but there were plenty of guns pointing down at her.

Haro, the remaining Khreenk mercenary placed himself to her flank and spoke through his translator. She could sense a hint of tiredness in his voice before the words were altered, but even with his comrades gone, there was no despair.

"They are not planning on leaving, are they?"

Arana looked to the wall and nodded.

"You could say that, Haro. This outer wall is new, maybe only a few days old. I'd say they are digging in for a fight."

She then shook her head and laughed.

"These Byotai do not hang around when they set their minds to something. And you recall how they fought in the war."

A voice from above yelled down, but it was alien and partially obscured by the sound of the heavy machinery. Then one by one the workers stopped what they were doing. Two of the large bipedal engineering machines turned around and lifted their arms threateningly.

"I am Arana. We have your people from the Khagi Research..."

A volley of shots erupted along the wall, and Arana rolled to the right. The ground nearest the wall was completely open, and her only chance was to take cover behind one of the few large boulders still remaining to the side. Her comrades scattered, but the Byotai civilians stood their ground. The shouting came again, followed by angry words. Almost at once the machines lowered their arms, and most of the weapons on the wall vanished.

"Kras!" yelled one of them.

Arana watched from behind her cover as the group of civilians staggered out from the trail and waved to those above. They moved in a slightly odd fashion, mainly due to their lower centre of gravity and greater weight than the average human. Sounds of shouting and excitement quickly spread, and a doorway in the wall opened up. It was raised a metre from the ground, and once fully open, a ramp swung down with a loud crashing sound.

"Okay, I guess that means we're all friends, then."

She spoke quietly while moving from cover. Even though the situation appeared resolved, she still kept her eye on the wall and towards the two machines. One of them made a loud hissing sound, but then a Byotai male in overalls dropped down and moved quickly to the refugees. Another ran down the ramp and directly towards her.

"Squad, with me."

She gave the order quietly, but it was stern and serious. In seconds, the other three anonymous mercenaries were at her side. Together they were covered in dust, and their modified armour looked worse for wear. Even so, they were clearly professional, and that was more than could be said for the armed Byotai that now emerged.

"Steady."

All four of them kept their hands on their weapons, but with the muzzles low to the ground. Arana looked at the three now approaching and smiled when she realised only one carried a rifle. The other two sported large mauls or maces that hung from their belts.

"Be ready."

Just as they reached her, Kras moved to her left flank. The tallest of the Byotai didn't stop and crashed into Kras. The other two held back, watching Arana and her soldiers with equal interest, while the two Byoti exchanged greetings. They were clearly overjoyed.

"Well?" she asked, "What can you tell me?"

Haro laughed.

"They are brothers. I would say we have a friend, dare I say, an ally."

Arana moved her attention from the Khreenk and back to the Byotai base. Even from here, she could see dozens of vehicles lined up in a sheltered motor pool behind the wall, protected from above by the rest of the mountain. She lifted up onto her toes to get a better look.

*Now that is more interesting.*

There were no military vehicles, at least not that she could see. But there were plenty of heavy industrial haulers, and all kinds of tracked and wheeled machines. One in particular looked like a four section land train, with additional plates of armour still being welded to the chassis. She turned from those in front of her and to the brother of Kras. The Byotai spotted her, opened his mouth wide, letting out a long breath. His reptilian eyes flickered twice, and then he moved three steps to her.

"I am Nak. Welcome."

He accent was thick, and he paused between each word. Even so, Arana was stunned that a Byotai, a race only been met a generation ago, could now speak part of her language. She extended her hand, and after a short shake of hands, they looked into each other's eyes. Haro moved to her side introduced himself in Byotai.

"Why are you here, human? We are at war. This is no place for a human..."

Arana shook her head and pointed to the smoke trails still visible from the burning aircraft behind the hills.

"Your missiles, they were supplied by our friend."

The Byotai's tongue flicked out and ran along the top of his mouth. His eyes stayed open for far too long and then shut for an instant.

"A friend helped supply them. Why do you ask?"

Arana detached a military issue secpad from her armour, tapped the unit, and held it up to Nak. On the screen was an image of General Daniels.

"He is our friend, too."

Nak licked his lip again and sighed.

"I am sorry. He was killed, along with many of our kin. They brought in more weapons."

Now it was her turn to disagree.

"No. This man is alive, and we have a team at Montu. A rescue party."

Nak listened, but it took a few seconds for what she had explained to fully register. Then he pulled back half a step in surprise.

"Rescue? There are survivors?"

Arana nodded her head.

"We do not know how many, but we have a team looking for them. They will need assistance to escape the city. Can you help?"

Nak looked to Kras, and the two spoke excitedly for almost a minute. Finally, they stopped. Kras spoke first.

"This is my brother, Nak. We both fought in the war in our Navy. After that, Nak served in our diplomatic corps on Helios. That is where he first met the General."

He then gave her a grand bow.

"We would be honoured to help. Tell me, which route will they be taking?"

Arana paused for a moment, knowing that if these Byotai could not be trusted, she would be consigning both Spartan and Syala to capture or death. One more look at the two brothers immediately showed her there was nothing fake or false between them, and the mention of help had been accepted gladly. Again she showed the two her secpad.

"They plan on using the express maglev train to the end of the line...here."

Nak looked at it and shook his head.

"That is on the surface, but the tunnels were destroyed a month ago. The closest point to our end location will be in the dust bowl, but that is more than eighty kilometres from here, on the dust tracks. Even if they make it that far, they will not make it to the enclave. Two hours in vehicles, or a week to get through the mountains on foot."

He pointed up into the air.

"More important to you is this."

Arana looked up, expecting immediate trouble. The sky was already darker than when they had arrived, and she suspected there would be a full sunset within the next two hours, perhaps less.

The Anicinàbe are masters of the sky. If they find your people, they will die. There is no way to reach them without being intercepted by their gunships."

Arana had turned her attention back to the Byotai. She had little information to go on, just the waypoints and short pieces of information sent by Spartan. And she still had absolutely no idea if there was even a prisoner to rescue, or if the train system would work. Kras and Nak spoke for what seemed like an age, and Nak began to look agitated. Then he looked to the reinforced walls and shouted up to those defending the tallest sections.

"What's going on?" Arana asked.

Haro pointed to the wall.

"Just watch. It will become clear."

His words were followed by sounds of excitement from within the defences. More civilians came out from the reinforced entrance and helped the refugees from the research facility into the mountain. Nak and Kras stayed in exactly the same spot while all this was going on.

The sound of a powerful engine unit roared loudly, and Arana took a step back and raised her firearm.

"What's happening?"

Haro started to speak, but the sound of engines drowned him out. Arana activated her unit-wide channel.

"Skirmish formation, prepare yourselves."

Though she doubted the Byotai were a threat, she was taking no chances, especially as she didn't know what had been said in the last few minutes. The mercenaries opened out their tiny formation, with a gap of three metres between them. Some of the Byotai pointed; others laughed at what was happening. Then the entrance to the base filled with the shape of a massive metal vehicle that dropped down onto the dry ground. It was huge, six-wheeled, and shaped like an oversized armoured personnel carrier. She's seen pictures of them before, but never one in the flesh. It pulled three cars, equally armoured and bristling with recently welded on slabs of metal and turrets. One of her mercenaries pointed at the thing.

"A land train."

Arana laughed just as the two Byotai brothers caught her attention. At the same time, a large group of Byotai filed out of the fortress. There must have been thirty or more, and all carried small arms. She recognised many as being surplus issue Helion rifles, but there were also a few native weapons, and even a single L48 rifle from Alliance stocks.

"Will this work?" Nak asked.

For the first time in hours, Arana felt a sense of relief.

"Hell, yes."

# CHAPTER ELEVEN

*Machines are to be the salvation of flesh, the one guarantee of everlasting life. We have worked for millennia towards the dream of perfection, but instead of creating long-lasting life, we have been forced to come up with other solutions. The mind of a creature can be fed and prolonged indefinitely, but not the flesh or organs. Either the flesh must be replaced and upgraded over time to maintain the body, or alternatively, the mind must be placed inside a safe sanctuary, and the body replaced with something stronger and expendable. This is how the last generation of my people came into being, and how after all this time, we still live when other races have turned to ash.*

*Taken from the accounts of Z'Kanthu*
*Warlord of The Twelve*

## Montu, Khagi District, Karnak

It took Spartan almost thirty minutes to cover the ground from the old capital buildings to the military base. He could have made it in half of the time, but he'd been travelling carefully, using every piece of cover he could find. At the same time, he'd planted all but two of his micro-thermite charges on the way. Seven charges carefully placed where he believed they would cause the greatest disruption. Spartan lay stomach down on the ground, as low as he could get his body. Light was fading fast as the nearby star moved below the horizon.

*Now, show me to them.*

The overhead view provided by the drone had narrowed the location of the transmitter to an open area. There was a low wall around the dedicated spaceport, but unlike similar facilities on other worlds, the landing pads were simply cleared areas in the flat, open ground. Aircraft waited while the single fat, squat shape of civilian heavy lifters dropped in from low orbit, escorted by a pair of Hornet dropships.

*There!*

A light flashed, but what really perked Spartan up was the second light. Both were in close proximity, and now the drone had isolated their position down to an area no bigger than fifteen metres, and less than seventy metres from his own position. The ambient light continued to fall, and the long shadows began breaking up as the only natural light source vanished. All that remained were the artificial lights running throughout Montu, and unlike most cities, this place was a dull, grim-looking place.

*It's time.*

Spartan rose to his knees and rested his hands on the wall. The sensors in his armour brought up the temperature and rough composition, but that didn't really matter to him. Either he could smash through or he would blast it apart. Then, to his frustration, the drone vanished from his sensors.

*Dammit!*

The markers from the thermite charges were still

showing on his visor, as were the last recorded positions of the enemy soldiers and vehicles. He stood up and glanced over the wall and towards the distant aircraft. Ever so carefully, he moved the carbine up, rested it on the wall, and then pushed one of the two remaining micro-thermite charges into the lower flap. It slipped inside and rested inside the main coil section, and the internal switch flipped to grenade mode.

*Stay quiet.*

The helmet projected the approximate landing place, a short distance from one of the two bowsers near a landed aircraft. Spartan pulled the trigger and held his breath as the micro-thermite charge was discharged and flew in its course, barely changing on its way down. His heart almost stopped when it landed, and one of the nearby crew turned around.

*Damn it.*

The figure headed towards the charge, then stopped and went back to whatever he'd been doing. Spartan would have wiped his brow if his visor had been open, but he had to rely upon the moisture collectors in the helmet and concentrate on the mission. The numbers were greater than expected, but there were gaps in the defences, and few were taking much care in looking after the place.

*They are confident and cocky. That will be to my benefit, and their failure.*

Their numbers wouldn't deter him from what needed to be done. He rose higher still and then pushed hard. The armour was unable to assist with augmenting his strength; that was the job of equipment like the Vanguard armour. His own strength was substantial, though, and with a strike from his right arm a chunk of masonry the size of his head broke off. He followed it up with more until he'd created a gap big enough to slip through.

*Move!*

He kept his centre of gravity low, but there wasn't much he could do out in the open. There were no tunnels or other structures visible from here, and he already felt exposed and vulnerable. As he moved, slowly but surely, he could do no more than rely upon the cooling features of the armour. Incredibly, he made it to the source of the signal without being detected, and dropped to his stomach. There was a wide-open hole before him, much like a deep well, or even a pit. He leaned over the edge and could see movement below.

"General? Gun?"

The movement stopped and then shapes moved again.

"Spartan?" came back a familiar voice.

*Gun!*

Spartan could feel the elation in his body even though he had absolutely no idea what to do to get them out of the prison pit.

"Where is the entrance?"

A different voice called up this time. It was the General, he was sure of it.

"The main door is down here, double layered and strong."

Spartan didn't hesitate and threw himself off the edge. He fell down what must have been at least two levels before the shock absorbers in his armour groaned under his heavy landing. Before he could recover, the bear-like shape of Gun was on him and crushing him. Without the armour, he would certainly have suffered multiple broken ribs. As they separated, Spartan got the first look at the two of them since they'd left. They still wore the fatigues they must have been wearing upon arrival. Neither was armoured and both were heavily bruised.

"Can you walk?"

Gun slammed his fist into the wall.

"Walk? I can do anything."

He then looked up.

"Well, anything but climb up there."

Spartan followed his gaze to the opening far above. It looked so much smaller from down in the prison pit. The walls were smooth, almost like glass, and clearly from where the tunnel had been burned directly into the rock. Even worse, the walls moved in closer as they reached the top, like a reversed funnel shape.

"Maybe this will help."

Spartan opened the side plate on his left leg and removed his backup sidearm. Next to his armour and the vast bulk of Gun it seemed ridiculous. General Daniels reached for it, and Gun grunted.

"Too small for me, anyway."

Spartan opened his visor and breathed in the warm, damp air in the pit.

"This is going to get messy, and fast. Are you ready?"

Both prisoners gave him the nod, but General Daniels lifted his hand a fraction.

"Before we go. What's the plan? I take it you have one. What about the other prisoners? There were Byotai and Khreenk taken with us."

An alarm sounded off into the distance, much like a warning klaxon.

"My friends," said Spartan, "We do not have time. We have to get out of here. We will come back for them when we have information."

General Daniels looked sadly to Gun and then to Spartan.

"A good friend, his name was Turi. They took him some time ago. We've not heard from him."

Spartan closed his eyes as he considered their plan.

"Look," he started, "We need to get from here and to the underground transit station. I will look for this man, but we can't stay for long. This place is full of them."

He waited, but neither spoke.

"I have a few distractions to keep them busy. In the meantime, I expect nothing short of speed and uncontrolled violence."

"That's my specialty," said Gun.

"Good."

Spartan indicated for them to move away from the door and placed himself between both of them and the doorway. His armour made almost no sound as it moved, but it did continue to shift slightly in colour, now turning darker grey with hints of brown.

"I see you brought the new toys."

Spartan laughed.

"You could say that. Now, stay back."

"Uh, how do we get through? You can't punch your way through solid metal?" asked the General.

Gun was already as far back as he could go. Spartan indicated for the General to join him once more. He did so and lifted the pistol to his face to check the safety. Spartan noticed the man's hands were shaking, and that there were bloodstains on his clothing. He wanted to speak, to patch him up, but the mission was his priority, and he knew he had to stick with it.

*Get them out and on the train. We can worry about the details afterwards."*

"Close your eyes."

Spartan lifted his XC1 carbine and pointed it at the centre of the door. The first blast ripped a crater out of the metal, but it was still intact.

"You're going to need to go a lot further than that. Keep going," said Gun.

Spartan laughed.

"Not a problem."

This time he held down the trigger, and the weapon unleashed a torrent of fire at the metal object. Each ball of super-hot plasma, protected inside its magnetic casing, crashed into the reinforced plating. One by one, they ate away at the metal until with one final flash, the entire door came away and crashed to the ground with a great thud. The cell filled with dust, and Spartan changed to his thermal vision mode.

"Stay close!"

He stepped through and found two guards running in his direction. One blast hit each of them. Then they were past the bodies and at a staircase, barely large enough for Gun to use.

"Where now?" Daniels asked.

Spartan leaned back as a burst from a rifle struck the railing next to him. He moved back into position and fired one shot straight up. It was followed by a cry, and then a tumbling body crashed down onto the ground beside Gun.

"We go up!"

Though wounded, the fallen soldier tried to grab a long curved blade from his side. It was big, not far off the size of an Arabic scimitar. Gun put his left foot on his arm and yanked the weapon away. In his hand it looked like a large knife.

"Stay down," he said firmly.

The soldier refused to cooperate, and with his free hand, he slid down to grab a sidearm. Gun shook his head in annoyance and brought the blade down onto the soldier's arm. It was quick and equally brutal as the arm was severed from the torso.

"Try it again, and I'll take your head."

He lifted his foot, and this time the soldier kept still, though whether out of obedience or shock was impossible to tell.

"This way."

Spartan continued upwards until they reached the top of the staircase. It led inside a guard area. The space was open plan and relatively wide, but with a ceiling barely three metres from the ground. Decks at one side were covered in boxes, and in the middle lay a projection of a mountain region. Cultured shapes moved about, and the sound of voices played in the background, presumably from open channel communications. Two militiamen looked at the imagery, but only one saw Gun heading towards them.

"You!" Gun roared.

He didn't hesitate and grabbed the first one, lifted him from the ground, and cast him across the space. The unfortunate soul crashed into the wall and slid to the ground. The second made the mistake of drawing a firearm. Spartan was still moving forwards and fired twice from the hip. Both shots struck their target square in the chest.

"Keep moving."

Three rounds glanced off his chest, and he twisted around to see another Anicinàbe soldier. This one was covered in sand coloured robes, and he blocked the doorway leading to the next level. The militiaman wore the garb of the Spires Clan, and a metal plate covered his face from the nose downwards. The eyes were hidden behind red-tinted goggles, and in his hands he carried a powerful looking multi-barrelled carbine. Another round struck Spartan, and he ducked to the right and behind the hexagonal shaped projector.

"He's mine."

General Daniels might have been weakened, but his shooting was as good as it had ever been. The first round from his pistol struck the soldier in the neck, the second in the shoulder. Spartan ran past and up to the next level. Gun and the General stopped at the fallen soldier. General Daniels nodded to the substantial looking carbine lying beside the body. Its sides bulged out with multiple vents and cutaway sections to help keep it cool.

"Nice gun. Looks like one of ours. Perhaps a reverse engineered L52, but bigger and fitted with this cooling unit."

He then looked to Gun.

"You should take it. You're not much good use with that toothpick."

Gun looked at his blade and grunted.

"You'll be surprised what I can do with it."

His lip curled up to the side, and the General shook his head. He then bent down, lifted the thin carbine, and tossed it over to the Jötnar. The massive warrior caught it in his vast paws and turned it about, one way and then another. His hands were much too large to get around the grip and to the trigger. Normally, his kind used weapons specially modified for their use, usually very large weapons.

"It is like a child's toy. I'd rather stay with the knife."

General Daniels sighed.

"Stop whining, Gun. Fix it and follow me. We need to get out of this place, and soon."

He left the Jötnar on his own and went to follow Spartan just as the warning alarm sounded. It was different to anything he'd heard before and pulsated in high and low tones, accompanied by flashing lights throughout the facility. Daniels looked back at Gun who was still doing something to the weapon.

"Move it!"

He kept the pistol out in front. Unlike most soldiers, he kept the weapon close to his body and in both hands; something he'd learnt to do after getting into a number of close ranged encounters. He moved like a man in his twenties, and few would have realised this was a man left for dead in the Biomech War, a man that had been found beneath broken machines and shattered bodies. Gun lifted the blade he'd only so recently taken and brought it down on the trigger guard. There was a small flash of sparks, and the impact shattered the material, leaving the trigger fully exposed. What remained of the guard hung off from one small sliver of material. Gun grabbed it with his other hand and yanked it away, leaving the gun clear.

"Yeah, that's better. Much better."

Now properly equipped, he rested the blade in his left hand and held the gun up in his right. It still looked small, but far more dangerous than just an edged weapon. The vents hissed as steam pumped out from the side, and he laughed at the absurdity of the thing.

"Piece of alien junk."

Gun then climbed the five steps, easily covering the distance in a single bound, and into the last corridor just behind Spartan and Daniels. Far off into the distance was the pale light from exterior lamps, presumably those that lit the spaceport. At least five soldiers blocked their way and were positioned behind boxes or crates on each side of the hallway. Even Spartan had thrown himself on top of the wall to avoid the fire. One round struck Gun in the shoulder, and he moved to the left wall. He snarled in anger.

"I'm getting tired of this. What about this diversion of yours?"

He shouted the words loud enough that Spartan could hear, even over the sound of the gun battle. Spartan, meanwhile, used the cover in the hallway and blasted away with his carbine. Another round struck centimetres from Gun's ear as he aimed the three-barrelled carbine. Gun yanked back the trigger, and flames erupted from the front. Not waiting, he stepped out into the corridor and began to run.

"Here we go," said Spartan.

At that point, he activated the trigger for the charge near the wall and alongside a pair of parked up armoured trucks. At first there was just a single bang, but multiple explosions quickly followed it, as the fuel and ammunition caught fire and joined the explosions. The ground shook slightly but not enough to cause any of them to stumble. Spartan spotted the commotion behind him as Gun rushed towards him down the corridor. He looked at the enemy and fired a short burst of seven rounds. The powerful projectile ripped through rock, metal, and flesh with ease.

*Now...Move it.*

One step and then another, while tagging, identifying, and shooting every single target that presented itself. Not even the shape of an armoured warrior slowed him down. The very last guard staggered inside. Spartan jumped up and kicked him hard in the stomach. As the unfortunate soldier landed on the ground, he took bullets in the shoulder and back from General Daniels.

The General went ahead of the two and then stopped and peered in through one of the small open doors. It was too small for Gun, but the General didn't hesitate, and ran inside and cried out in anguish. Spartan jumped in with his carbine lifted, stopping at the tables. A dozen butchered bodies lay strewn across them. The General was busy looking at the face of a dead Byotai male.

"Turi," he said, he voice rough and quiet.

Spartan had no idea who it was, but clearly the General was upset. He placed his hand on the man's shoulder.

"Whatever they did to him, his pain is over. There's plenty enough time left for us to feel the same. We have to go."

When Daniels turned around, Spartan could see a look on his face, one he'd not seen since the bitter hand-to-hand combat of the Great Uprising a generation ago. He grabbed Spartan's arm.

"We will go. But promise me one thing, Spartan, promise me will avenge those butchered by this animal... Ogimà Nakoma."

Spartan nodded, his face grim with resolve.

"I promise. Now, let's go."

He left the room, and General Daniels gave it one last look before they returned to the main room and climbed the last few steps. Then they were outside and in the full glare of a single large searchlight mounted far off into the distance.

"Put down your weapons!"

It was an electronic voice, the classic monotonous tone of a translator circuit over a loudspeaker. Spartan scanned the horizon from left to right, picking out scores of militiamen streaming out of a spacecraft that had recently landed around a kilometre away. All were armed and were heading right for them. He tagged them one at a time, but with the other two without networked armour, he had nobody to share the information with.

"There," said Gun.

Spartan followed his gaze and found another group, all of which were filing out from a single-storey building near the searchlight. Beside them was a single articulated loading machine, a massive walking monster covered in lamps that projected out into the distance.

Hooded soldiers flanked one figure. Spartan could sense the hate in Gun's tone and suspected it was probably somebody responsible for their capture and torture. Several of them opened fire, but at this range their fire was erratic. Gun fired back, quickly scattering a handful.

"That is Nakoma, the bitch that's been interrogating us."

He took more careful aim at the figure and fired, showing great restraint by not doing his usual charging for them. Though his shots were close, there was little chance of striking her this far away. The weapon was powerful, but it was a close range carbine, not the kind of thing used to snipe at people.

"She's the commander of this sector of Karnak."

He then looked to Spartan.

"Can you hit her from here?"

A bullet struck Spartan's leg and glanced off in a shower of sparks. He checked the range, took aim, and fired. The bright green projectile came close, but at the last minute, one of the soldiers crossed in front of her and took the blast to the chest.

"Nice shooting, wrong target, though," said Gun.

General Daniels joined in with the fire.

"Yeah, she calls herself the Ogimà, or something like that. The Chief."

Gun snarled and fired one more burst. A rocket struck the nearby building.

"Well, what now?"

General Daniels moved to Spartan's flank and pointed off to the lights in the city.

"That's where the transit station is, right?"

Spartan nodded.

"Yeah, and Syala is down there waiting for us."

General Daniels and Gun both looked at him.

"Who?"

Spartan couldn't tell which of them was asking, but the return fire from those near the aircraft snapped him back to the problem before them. He dropped to one knee as a volley rippled overhead.

"Stay down. It's time for the distraction."

Gun dropped down, but he still seemed to take up as much space as a regular man.

"Now!" Spartan said.

All it took was the activation of two more of the charges he'd left during his stealthy exploration of the base. It may have taken time to get them in position, but the payoff was as instant as it was gratifying. Three massive explosions ripped through the base, and one of the aircraft flipped over and crashed down on its back. Fuel leaked out and set off a long series of secondary explosions that blotted out the horizon. It was far more than he could have hoped for. Spartan looked to them, grinned, and then closed his visor as a wheeled vehicle exploded and lit up the skyline with a massive orange blast.

"Now we run!"

They ran from the base, through the breached wall and then the route Spartan had carefully crafted, by staying off the main road and using the buildings or side routes. After three blocks, they crashed through a broken wall, right into the path of a squad of Spires soldiers. There were seven of them, and two carried portable automatic cannons. One yelled and pointed, another lifted a Helion thermal rifle. It fired once and blasted a plate from Spartan's left arm.

"Drop 'em!"

General Daniels ducked back behind the broken wall. Spartan sidestepped another gunshot and then returned fire. The powerful carbine knocked down two of them just as Gun ran amok. A soldier rose in the air and flew across the street before striking a wall headfirst. Another screamed as Gun tore off his left arm and then beat him across the face with the severed body part. One struck a short knife into his upper leg, and Gun began to laugh.

"What is that? Little man!"

He didn't even bother reaching down for it, and instead lifted up the looted firearm, blasting a hole the size of his fist through the Spires soldier's chest. Only two remained, and both of them ran off in street. One was clearly pulling at a communication device.

"Spartan!" Gun shouted.

The seasoned warrior already had the militiaman in his sights. The carbine was locked in, and he led the target by just a fraction before pulling the trigger. A super-hot ball of plasma blasted out and vaporised the soldier's lower arm, as well the device. The second shot struck him higher in the arm, and the third and final round struck the throat.

"One left, I have him," said General Daniels.

The last soldier had ducked behind a burnt out land car and was behind a broken wall when the handgun report echoed out. The next shot was masked by the sound of explosions from the spaceport, but each of them saw the falling shape of the soldier as he staggered and then collapsed into the debris.

"What now?" Gun asked.

Spartan nodded off into the distance.

"We run!"

He didn't need to repeat himself as the three rushed across the street, climbed over the broken walls, and moved off to the penultimate block. Spartan suspected they had made it this far before the enemy even noticed they had left the base.

"Wait. One second."

Gun skidded to a halt and then crashed into the end of the wall. It was already partially broken and a single chunk slid out. Spartan had dropped down into a lower position, and his armour was already changing colour to match the wall. He opened his mouth to warn Gun, but he'd already spotted the broken piece of stonework and caught it just before it struck the ground.

"Nice. Just hold on a second."

Spartan had stopped them just short of their final destination, right at the side of a supply yard. There they waited, panting from a mixture of excitement and sheer adrenalin. He nodded in the direction of the dome's entrance to the vast transit complex. He watched the counter on his overlay show the track of the next communication buoy.

*Okay, Khan. There's your information. Now make sure you're ready when I need you.*

The data uploaded in less than a second, but nothing came back as agreed. He'd wanted to ensure nothing could reveal their mission or what they might do. One-way communication was best...for now.

"That's the place?" Gun asked.

The titanic warrior waited with his back to the wall, yet somehow he still hadn't been detected. In the distance, the fires of smoke from the charges Spartan had left behind were doing their job well. Spartan opened his mouth to give the word when a single Hornet aircraft swept down and slid into position just outside the entrance. The rapid landing sent hot dust flying about in all directions. No sooner had it stopped, six militiamen, all bearing long-riles, jumped down and fanned out.

"Plan B?" General Daniels asked.

Spartan shook his head.

"No, thermite charge time."

Unseen to them, he activated one of the charges. A dull crump announced the explosion, and then a long series of flashes and bangs that sounded like a small battle. The soldiers at the Hornet shouted loudly, and all of them climbed back in. With a blast of hot air, the aircraft rose up and rushed off in the direction of the explosions.

Spartan signalled.

"On my mark. We get across the street."

Both nodded in agreement.

*First I need to check with Syala. She'd better be ready, or this will be the shortest escape in history.*

\* \* \*

Syala waited patiently, a game she could play for hours. Unlike conventional soldiers, she had spent years honing her equipment into something perfect for clandestine operations. Her armour combined elements of surplus Confederate Army body armour, with components from the private sectors. Joins and mounts had been replaced so that everything moved silently and smoothly. The electronics were from the civilian version of the current issue Marine Corps PDS gear, and even the optics had been upgraded three times in the last two years.

*Patience.*

The wait on her own had been tiresome, but the threat of militiamen finding her had at least kept her on her toes. She could just about make out the entry point to the vast control centre from her current position.

*Use the time you have.*

Spartan had given her a simple brief, to make sure their escape route was clear, and that they could get away safely. She'd done everything she could think of, but there was just her, and she had access to only so much equipment. After so long down there, she was now out of thermite charges, and even her breaching charges were all placed. And so she was now forced to rely upon classic sabotage techniques, something she rather enjoyed. Beneath her was one of six hatches leading back to the main entrance. With a small electrical screwdriver, she removed the fittings on the very last one, and then left it slightly ajar. A wrong step coming this way would send an unsuspecting individual tumbling down one of the deep shafts.

*Perfect.*

"Syala."

She looked up before realising the voice was inside her helmet. She felt her heart almost pause at the sound of Spartan's voice. She'd been in the dark for so long it was beginning to feel he would never come back.

"I'm here. What's your status?"

"Be careful. I'm in position and going in. Make sure the facility is ready for us. We will need the train."

"Affirmative. Be careful."

Syala lowered to the ground and checked the fittings by hand for the last time. It was one of many small traps she'd left behind. Although nothing much on its own, when combined with her charges and prearranged escape route, they should prove deadly. She walked back towards the control room one foot at a time, carefully placing her feet in position and checking for sound before taking the next. Those inside were easy enough to hear, and she paused at one point to ensure they were all still in the same place. Then she saw something.

*What is that?*

Being as quiet as possible, she moved to the right and down a small ladder to a storage area. Crates and storage bins were scattered about, but between two containers was the unmistakable shape of a body. Sensing it could be a trap; she swung her weapon around to her back and pulled out her sidearm. The safety clicked off with barely any discernible tone. She approached slowly but found two other forms in the same place, dumped like refuse in the darkness.

*No, not more.*

She knew she should back off, but there was something about this that felt off. With her left hand, she reached out, grabbed the still shape, and tugged. It moved easily and rolled over, revealing the face and mutilated body of a young Byotai. As a race, they were unusual in many ways, from their hardened flesh and unusual breathing, to their bulging eyes and slow movement. There was nothing alien about the body of such a young victim, though.

*Why?*

She knelt down and touched the arm of the body. A dark pool of blood lay where it had been resting, and to her surprise as her hand touched the face, its eyes opened. It cried out, and Syala thrust her hand forward to cover its mouth.

"Quiet!"

In her haste, she didn't even consider activating the translator circuit. A hand reached from the body and struck her. The force pushed her back, and then the figure was upright and facing her head on. Now it was clear the blood was from the others on the ground. It was a young male, perhaps the equivalent of a human teenager. It looked furtively in each direction, jumped up to the platform, and vanished. It might have just as easily have been a ghost down there with her.

Then she heard the thunderous roar of something far away. At first she thought it was a train, but then the shaking spread through the ground of the facility like an earthquake. One of the crates rolled to one side, and a pipe burst from the wall, showering her with water. The pressure was high and hit her with enough force to knock her down onto her back.

*Stay down and listen.*

She was tempted to get up and look for safety, but with all the noise and commotion, there was a good chance the enemy could slip past her without her even knowing. The only chance she had of staying alive was to be smart. She needed to take things slowly and retain control of the situation. The first blast had been quite substantial, but the subsequent explosions forced several of the underground lighting units to flash and cut out. Another started a cascade effect as one unit after another flashed and exploded.

# CHAPTER TWELVE

*Few ships of the Great Uprising can compare to the mighty battle cruiser CCS Crusader. This state-of-the-art warship was the first and only ship in her class during the occupation of the Titan Naval Station. The honoured warship took part in the first major space battle of the war and was also present at the final battle. She marked the culmination of human warship development, and the last of the great ships to be built before the creation of the Rifts and exposure to new and deadly direct energy weapons. A technological marvel upon creation, she marks the last gasp of those experimental years of ship design. In the future, every vessel would be designed around flexible, modular structures able to adapt to many different roles.*

*Great Ships of the Line*

## Montu, Khagi District, Karnak

Syala checked the clock inside her visor. Her throat was so dry, but each time she swallowed, she was convinced the sound would draw attention to her position. Something moved far off into the distance, and her eyes were drawn to the shape. Her finger rested on the trigger guard, but then she saw it was a small creature, no bigger than a rat.

*Stay calm and wait.*

"We're inside. Get ready."

Syala imagine the armour-clad warrior moving inside the facility, and for a brief moment felt able to relax. It seemed she had been down there, in the dark and alone, for days. It didn't bother her, but there was little doubt in her mind she would be happier once they were able to leave this place filled with murder and betrayal.

"Good to hear from you, Spartan. Thought you'd left me.

"Never."

Her voice was quiet but betrayed a hint of both admiration, and perhaps even a little pleasure at knowing he was back. She glanced back to the control room and was pleased to see a shape approaching the access door. Syala stepped back a few centimetres so she was beneath one of the failed lighting units. The door opened, and she could finally see inside. The figure turned back around to speak with another.

*So much space, and so few people.*

The doorway was tiny compared to the huge circular room inside. Lines of seats were empty, and one wall was covered in a huge two-dimensional diagram.

*That's got to be the maglev rail network.*

Her view was obscured as one of the militiamen started to leave. As with the others, he was slight, and his form heavily disguised by the loose clothing that gave his people the impression of nomadic spacefarers.

"We're coming in," said Spartan.

She lifted her weapon and took aim at the militiamen. Her sight was trained in the back of the nearest, but still she waited.

"Take the route to the right. I've marked it on the lower wall. Meet me at the control room. I have a back route to the platform."

Then there was a massive blast, and the ground shook violently. The figure at the doorway dropped something, pulled out a carbine, and looked straight at her.

*Oh, great!*

The gun rose, and Syala knew she had to act or die. Her double-barrelled carbine was a civilian version of the venerable, military-grade L52. It fired one barrel after the other, each gunshot sounding like a thunderclap. Three rounds struck the militiaman, but the second pulled himself inside the control room.

*Move it!*

Syala sent the command, and her armour increased her adrenalin count just as she charged at the door. The figure behind pulled down a lock, but that wouldn't stop her. Two blasts to the corner easily ripped off the hinges, and one meaty kick sent the heavy metal door crashing down on the unfortunate soul. She was now inside and surrounded by screens and lights, plus one last soldier. This time Syala made sure her translator circuit was on and active.

"Drop it!"

She could hear the sound of her translated voice just as she finished the last syllable. This final soldier laughed, a long, cruel laugh that made her hair stand on end. It was a female. Syala knew that already. She wanted to fire, but there was no chance, not with the proximity grenade beeping away in her hand. It was not unlike the ones Syala often carried. She glanced around the empty control room and spotted more bodies inside.

*The animals, they butchered them and just left them here to rot.*

Syala assessed the warrior in front in seconds. Though presumably a fast, perhaps even formable fighter, she was unlikely to be the person behind the running of the control centre. As they waited in stalemate, the warrior pulled a long, slightly curved knife from a sheath on her flank. With the left hand, the head covering came off to show the narrow face of a savage-looking female warrior. Tattoos covered her cheeks, and only the customary red tinted goggles hid her eyes.

*Where are they?*

Syala circled the warrior, her finger resting on the trigger guard. She wanted to fire, but there would be little chance of killing her and eliminating the proximity grenade. Instead she kept her eyes on the target and waited for the moment to attack. With each step, she found herself no closer to that moment but then saw something just behind and to the right. Her eyes squinted, and then the shape of another appeared with a computer unit under its arm.

"Get down!"

She knew the voice immediately, and upon recognising the sound dropped to her knee. Heat set off sensors, and both enemies were vaporised by multiple blasts of green energy. By the time she rose to her feet, there was nothing left of them but charred limbs. Syala spun about and before her were three figures. At the back a half-naked giant, a Jötnar warrior, and a human male wearing captured Anicinàbe militia clothing and carrying a pistol. Lastly, there was Spartan. The armoured figure stood in front of the group like a sentinel, and in his hands the smoking barrel of his high-energy carbine.

"I'm back."

\* \* \*

Spartan stood in front of the massive diagram of the rail network. Blood covered the wall, and one of the computer systems burned away in the corner as a small fire flickered in the rear of a control box. He opened his visor and breathed in the cool, dust-filled air. It wasn't particularly pleasant, but at least he could feel the real world rather than the simulation presented inside the helmet. The interior of the M-3B armour was warm and reasonably comfortable, but there was always something special about seeing the real world, especially for a man like Spartan. Syala grasped his forearm and tugged at him.

"You followed my instructions and kept to the right, I see. Good."

Spartan smiled.

"Yeah. We got your message just in time. Another ten seconds, and it would have been us getting hit by those broken gas pipes."

Gun chuckled.

"Nice improvisation. You got at least two with that little move."

General Daniels pushed past and looked at the information on the displays. He seemed to have a much better grasp of what was going on, or certainly gave that impression. He ran his hands over the data, nodding as though the information matched up with something he'd already had explained to him. Spartan looked from the General and back to Syala.

"We followed the route in you gave us and bypassed the main foyer."

He pointed at the display.

"Tell me the plan. I see you've made some changes."

Syala moved her hand up to the imagery and both men watched carefully. Gun, meanwhile, looked out through the doorway with his weapon raised. He was expecting trouble and taking no chances.

"We need to wait three more minutes."

"Why?" Gun grumbled.

Syala shook her head.

"Because that's how long it will take my modifications to clear our tunnel. We will take the express maglev train towards Caldos. I've taken care of the controls and entry points to this complex. Once we're out of the mountain district, we will move to a separate independent power line connected to Caldos. There's a railroad switch point right there that we can use."

Spartan looked at the location, but it meant nothing to him. General Daniels, however, seemed almost excited at the prospect.

"That is a good choice, actually. The tunnel system en route to Caldos splits into multiple lines. There's a control station there and a solar power planet to run the track system. Assuming we can actually get out of here, under their power."

He looked to the right where an image of a globe showed the time. He didn't seem particularly confident until he found two more charging points. A few quick calculations told him everything else he needed to know.

"We will hit the switch point about an hour before dawn."

Gun looked back and tilted his head. He appeared confused.

"Dawn? It's only just got dark here."

Daniels grinned.

"You forget; this world operates on a sixteen-hour rotation. The days and nights are a lot shorter than we're used to."

The General looked at Syala.

"Miss, I haven't met you before, but I have to admit, this is a good plan. Assuming the track system at the switch is live. If it isn't, we won't be able to get moving."

He turned his attention to Spartan.

"These Byotai Maglev trains can only use their own power once they are at speed and already fully levitated. You need the station power coils to get you started and up to cruising speed."

He looked back to mapping data where coloured dots and lines indicated the current status of local and express lines.

"We need to get out of the city before they cut the power. If they do, we'll be able to move forward, but without levitation."

He smiled grimly.

"And without levitation, we'll be stuck on the line and unable to move."

Syala licked her lower mouth.

"The Montu line is live; but the powerplant at the switch of offline. It looks like the Byotai control it. We'll need to speak with them, or get out and take control of the place ourselves. Let's just hope the Anicinàbe haven't taken control of the place."

General Daniels laughed as though what she'd said was somehow offensive.

"You bet it's controlled by the Byotai."

He was almost proud as he spoke while turning to Gun.

"That place is protected by the weapons we brought here."

A high-pitched blast sent a plume of dust and debris into the tunnel they had arrived from. It cleared quickly, but left a low-lying layer of dust that hung around their feet. Spartan smirked and pointed back.

"I take it you heard the sound of the two that tried to follow us?"

Syala laughed, and Spartan moved his XC1 carbine in front of his chest. He examined the condition of the power cell, then released the first empty unit, and slid in a new power cell from the mount on his flank. It fitted in with a clunk and then a gentle hiss. The fresh coolant included in the pack made the fins on the flanks of the gun alter colour until the weapon stabilised. General Daniels looked down at the thing.

"Is it supposed to do that?"

Gun laughed.

"It's not a production model, not yet."

Syala appeared to be counting silently. Spartan watched her. She opened her eyes, looked directly into his, and then gave him a half wink with one eye.

"Nice. The tunnel should be vented, are you ready to get out of this place?"

Spartan checked the others were ready. He bent down and picked up one of the discarded long-rifles, tossing it to General Daniels. He caught it and checked the controls with expert hands. It may not have been an Alliance weapon, but he seemed more than familiar with it.

"What about the rail controls?"

Syala was already out of the door and checking there

were no enemies about.

"I've got it taken care of. Let's go."

Spartan grabbed General Daniels' arm.

"Stay close to me, old man. It's time to go. Follow me."

Syala led the way out of the control room and to the corridor. They were only halfway along it when she stopped, bent down, and hit a latch on the right-hand side. A panel fell down with a motorised groan, and another revealed a shaft wide enough even for Gun to enter. She went inside and activated her exterior lamp. Gun and the General were next, with Spartan at the rear. As they entered, Spartan could smell something even through the armour. It was acrid and made his skin itch.

"What is this?"

"Coolant vent shaft, we have four minutes to clear it before the next blast."

They moved away, and a few seconds later heard the motor sound of the panels returning to their previous position. They pushed back together with a resounding clunk.

"This is the most direct route to the tunnel nearest the railcar. We can avoid the access shafts and their security system, or what they call a security system. They'll have no idea we're here."

"Good," said Spartan, "My diversionary charges have all been used now. It won't take long for them to realise we aren't in the city. We need to be well gone by then."

They moved on through the cylindrical shaft in complete and utter darkness. Occasionally, the metallic structure would vibrate, the creation of the aftershocks of another of Syala's traps. None of them spoke and made sure they covered the distance as quickly as possible. Spartan could feel a trickle of sweat at his brow as they passed the three-minute barrier with still no sign of the end. Another ten seconds past, and Syala stopped, turned to the left, and pressed a button on her arm. The panel opened out, and air rushed into the stale tunnel. Dull yellow light lit up the small segment of the coolant shaft.

"Thirty seconds, you need to hurry," she said.

The others moved, and Syala resealed the hatch with barely fifteen seconds to go. By the time they were ten metres away, the blast of coolant could be heard flooding the compartment.

"Nice work, lady," said Gun.

Spartan nodded in agreement.

"Yeah. Maybe cutting it just a little short, though."

She walked passed, leading them on via the metal walkway.

"Hardly, I did a trial run before you arrived."

They travelled through the labyrinth, with the heavy metal boots of Syala and Spartan crunching on the thick dust and light debris that littered the site.

"How long since the Byotai lost control of this place?" Spartan asked.

General Daniels coughed as he accidentally inhaled too much dust.

"Damn it!"

He coughed twice more before being able to speak properly.

"They lost access to the place over a year ago. That was when sections started to fail. When the Spires Clan arrived, the last few tried to escape on the trains. Two of them were left behind."

Syala sighed.

"I know. We've seen the bodies."

The passageway rose slightly, and then to all of their surprise, they emerged in the middle of pitch-black tunnel.

"Uh, Syala. The plan was for the train."

The young woman shook her head and marched off to the left. General Daniels followed her, but Gun looked back at Spartan and laughed. His teeth glowed white in the bright light of Spartan's shoulder-mounted lamps.

"I think you've pissed her off, Spartan."

"What's new?"

They trudged on through the tunnel for almost a hundred metres before it split; one leading into a lighter lit section. There, sitting in the middle of the track, was the train. Spartan stopped and looked at the shape in surprise.

"This is the same one we found at the platform. Isn't it?"

At first he sounded certain, but as his sentence tailed off, he seemed less certain.

"Yeah, it's one and the same. Come on."

Syala led them past the first control engine and to the wide automatic doors that were jammed shut. On her signal, Gun yanked them open, and they all rushed inside. On the floor of the first transport was a stack of weapons, mostly of Byotai origin, but also with a smattering of other alien technology. There was even a stack of armour sections. Gun lifted one of the dull grey chest plates and wrapped it around his upper arm. It just fitted.

"Really?" Spartan asked.

Gun grumbled in response. Spartan turned his attention to Syala.

"Okay, get the engine running and take us to Caldos. We'll set up defensive stations where we can."

General Daniels made to go with him.

"I'll help. In case you hadn't noticed, there are multiple sections where the maglev tracks will be exposed to the surface. If they want to hit us, that's where it will happen."

Syala had now vanished into the first car, the massive control unit for the train. She looked back from the rear door.

"The internal generators can keep us going when we reach more than eighty kilometres per hour. I think that's right, anyway. The Byotai controls are a little...well, a little odd."

Spartan opened his visor and smiled.

"You're doing fine. Get us out of here. We'll work out the rest on the way."

She gave him a mock salute, let her eyes linger on his face for a second, and moved back into the engine. General Daniels went with her, leaving Spartan and Gun alone inside the second railcar. A low hum filled the interior, and then the car shuddered.

"Levitation," said Spartan.

"Something like that," agreed Gun, "Will it work?"

They moved forward, but at the same time a dull scream echoed throughout the section. It was the pained sound of metal on metal, and for a moment it seemed something was going to hold them back from their escape. General Daniels opened the window from the engine and shouted over the din.

"Hold on, there's debris on the line!"

The screaming sound increased in volume, and then cut just as quickly as it had started. Spartan looked down at the equipment and grabbed a pair of Helion battle rifles.

"This way."

They ran along the corridor in the second carriage. It was open plan with red seating running down one side. Most of the seats were soiled with dirt and damp, and nearly half had been ripped or removed. Poles ran up at regular intervals with extra handrails in tarnished chrome. Every fifteen metres a large acrylic panel showed the route and current location. To their surprise, it actually worked and showed they were still inside Montu.

"Something works. I'm impressed," said Gun.

Spartan looked less so.

"Yeah, a map, great."

Spartan examined it but not for too long.

"They will come for us, and when they do, we need to be ready."

"What do you propose?"

Spartan gave him one of those grins that usually meant they were going into battle, or at the very least about to get themselves into some very serious trouble.

"My friend. We are going to make sure this train is the last thing anybody is going to want a ride in."

* * *

Syala did her best to get them away from the capital as she worked the alien controls on the rather simple engine unit. She'd never even ridden on one before, but that didn't mean she was unfamiliar with the technology. The screens fitted alongside the narrow windows showed digits in the Byotai language, and a needle marked their current speed.

"Well, will it work?"

She pointed to one of the dials.

"That says we're doing about sixty kilometres per hour,

and it's increasing."

Her visor was open so he could see her face. She tried to smile, but it came off as more of a grimace.

"The train is actually working quite well. I'm no expert, but all the status indicators are good, and we have enough onboard power to make most of the journey to Caldos."

"Most?"

The General sounded both surprised and disappointed, but Syala simply laughed.

"Yes, most. The onboard capacitors were on less than forty percent when we left. They charge via the secondary power lines in the capital. If we could have stayed behind for another hour, we'd have had enough."

The General peered out through the forward windows and off into the tunnel. There were no lights other than those fitted to the front of the engine, and although powerful, extended no more than two hundred metres out in front.

"How will we make the last part of the trip without enough power?"

Syala pointed to the ceiling of the engine.

"The star. The top of the engines and the railcars are solar collectors. When we reach the surface, the daylight will provide us with an extra boost. Hopefully enough to get us to the end."

General Daniels didn't seem overly convinced.

"There is a lot riding on hope, right now."

Syala looked at something on her raised visor overlay, the unit just barely above her eye.

"General, you might want to hold on."

His eyebrows raised in a questioning expression.

"Spartan, Gun. Hold on, the demolition charges at

Montu are about..."

The engine began to shake, and all the lights in the train went out. They were followed by a high-pitched whine as the onboard power units reactivated the screen and internal lighting.

"Oh, well," she laughed, "That takes care of the transit station."

\* \* \*

Ogimà Nakoma watched the devastation of the Montu facilities from a hundred metres above the capital. Smoke rose up from a dozen locations; the most recent of which was the vast transit complex. Her face was contorted with barely concealed anger.

"Ogimà, we have contact from Tahkeome. He is in orbit."

Nakoma looked visibly shaken at the mention of the secretive leader of the Anicinàbe Marche clans. She had been granted full regional authority in this vital part of Karnak, and now of all times he could have chosen, Tahkeome had arrived, and that meant he would be expecting results. The image of the leader, slightly obscured by deliberate digital noise appeared in a holographic image.

"Ogimà. I have seen the reports of your sector. Yours is last Byotai sector on Karnak to be fully pacified. I am displeased at your progress."

Ogimà Nakoma bowed down low, hating every minute of it.

"The Clans are united for the first time in centuries, and I will not waste that. We must secure the Marche before we can proceed with reclaiming our destiny."

If Ogimà Nakoma could have bowed even lower, she would have at that moment.

"Yes, Tahkeome. The Byotai have paid for mercenary help with extra soldiers and weapons in my sector. They will be eliminated shortly. It is my…"

Tahkeome cut her off as he spoke loudly and firmly.

"There are other colonies in the Marche to pacify. This is a local matter, one you will resolve for me."

Nakoma opened her mouth to speak, but she was premature.

"Ogimà Takosk is bringing in his Red Scars to help with his work in the Southern sectors of Karnak. I have tasked him with lending assistance to your forces, following your recent failure. He will be arriving shortly, along with his personal guard. They are very heavily equipped."

"But Tec…"

"No, Ogimà Nakoma. You will work with Takosk and pacify the Khagi Mountains. Failure will result in the Spires Clan's forfeiture of Khagi. I am sure Takosk and his Red Scars will be more than willing to take over your territory on behalf of the League. Listen to him, and do whatever he suggests."

Nakoma swallowed uncomfortably.

"Yes, Tahkeome. It will be done."

The image vanished, and the deeply offended Nakoma looked around at the cloth-covered soldiers in the Hornet.

"I want…"

The screen flashed, and the face of one of her junior commanders appeared. This one was without a helmet, and his face still bled from two injuries to his face.

"Ogimà Nakoma, the prisoners, they have escaped!"

\* \* \*

Spartan felt his eyes beginning to close just as a pale, dull light filled the narrow window slits. At first he ignored it before realising quite what he could see. It wasn't much, but the first light on Karnak left the distant mountains in darkness, yet sent a warm sheen over their peaks.

"Daylight."

He was saying it more for him than anybody else. Gun was already awake and looking out through the narrow slit in the same direction.

"When did we reach the surface?" Spartan asked.

Gun looked back to his friend.

"About thirty seconds ago."

He then pointed up to the dark sky.

"It's not the sky that worries me. It's those things..."

Spartan couldn't make it out, so he activated his helmet, and it clamped down over his face. The vision modes and passive sensors on the suit quickly identified the vapour trails, and then finally the signatures of a pair of Hornet aircraft.

"Damn it, they must have scouts out in all directions. Once they spot us, we'll be in trouble."

Spartan lifted his carbine from where it rested at the side of the carriage. He'd left it deactivated, especially as the power cell was one of only three he had remaining. It leaked power when on standby, one of the many problems of the experimental technology.

"Do you have another one of those?"

Spartan shook his head.

"Nope, just this one. You've got your own toys."

Gun lifted the weapon he'd taken at Montu and grumbled. It might have been an impressive piece in civilian hands, but compared to the advancements carried by Spartan, it was an antique.

"Syala, we've got company. How far to the next tunnel?"

There was a short pause before she answered.

"Another six minutes. We're moving across the salt flats. Have they spotted us?"

Both Gun and Spartan were busy watching from the side of the railcar. The aircraft were a long-distance away and following in long, lazy circles. Spartan opened his mouth to answer just as one of them changed. He watched it while the computer in his suit calculated its current vector. In less than a second, it was confirmed.

"They know. Get ready."

He looked to Gun.

"You know the drill. I'll take the next railcar. You protect this one. They cannot get to the engine. If they do, we die. Understood?"

Gun didn't have to speak. He simply opened his mouth and bared his teeth in a wide smile.

"Good," said Spartan, "Let's do this. I'm getting tired of waiting."

He rushed along the railcar and reached the connecting section with the next car. His armour made little sound, but it was impossible to avoid the crunching noises from his feet grinding up the small rocks and layers of dust that filled the disused railcars. He finally made it to the moving joint connecting them to the next carriage. This part was articulated with overlapping plates and sealed with a torn and badly damaged layer of a rippled rubber material. He stepped through and pushed open the sliding doors into the next railcar. This one was badly damaged, and half of the room was missing. Spartan followed the short flight of steps to the ruined upper level. With most of the roof torn away, he now had the perfect view of the sky.

"Interesting."

Although his visor was down, it didn't stop the buffeting as they travelled at almost two hundred kilometres per hour. He looked ahead and could see marks and dents all along the roof of the intact first railcar. Vapour sprayed out from the engine in front of it, the massive, ultra streamlined unit that provided the power to move the train along the single metal triangular track. He was no expert on Maglev trains. But he did know that power was required to lift it above the track and give it motive power to actually move.

*Check your corners.*

There was little reason to suspect there could be any issues further back, but something deep down forced him to check in all directions. As he turned to look at the additional railcars, he spotted a dark shape moving from behind one of the hills. At first it looked like a cloud, but then two white dots flickered at the centre.

"Hornet! Incoming."

He threw himself down just as the aircraft swept overhead. The soldiers on board unleashed a volley that clattered all about the train. Scores of rounds penetrated the thin skin of the rail cars. It was gone before he could even return fire. Spartan rose back to his feet, placing one of them against the side to brace himself. He took aim as the Hornet spun around to make another pass.

*Wait for it.*

Streaks from his left reached out, and at least two

made contact with the left engine of the aircraft. It didn't damage the Hornet in any obvious way, but it did draw the attention of Gun. Spartan twisted his head around. The massive warrior was hanging off the side of the train. He was firing the captured weapon in multiple short bursts. It was impossible to hear him, but Spartan could see Gun's mouth was wide open, and he howled as he fired.

*You crazy old fool.*

When he looked back to the rear of the train, he was stunned to see the second Hornet coming right behind them. It was low, barely thirty metres from the ground and flying in over the third and final railcar; the one situated directly behind where Spartan was waiting. He took aim at the cockpit.

*Make them count.*

The first round from the XC1 Carbine was too low, but the second penetrated the canopy and struck one of the crew. The Hornet shuddered and lifted a few metres before settling back down. Light flashed from underneath, and multiple soldiers dropped down. The lights from their backpacks allowed them a modicum of manoeuvrability as they moved on top and inside the final badly damaged railcar.

"Great," muttered Spartan.

He fired at the aircraft once more, and this time the plasma managed to start a fire on one of the engines. The aircraft twisted about, and a bright blue explosion engulfed the rear of the engine. Spartan ducked down as the aircraft crashed onto the final part of the train, the second engine unit. The explosion increased as both the dormant train engine and the Hornet exploded in a mighty flash. When Spartan rose to his feet and looked back, he could see nothing beyond his own railcar, apart from the half shattered wreckage of the car and at least six Anicinàbe Spires soldiers. Then everything went dark as the train vanished into another tunnel and made its way through the next mountain complex.

*Shoot.*

Spartan opened fire the same time as the other six. The interior of his railcar vanished in a cloud of dust, metal, and gunfire. Spartan's shots lit up the interior with each blast, but the eruption of fire from the Spires soldiers was incredible. The lamp on his shoulder paled to insignificance next to the light given by the firearms. Spartan felt multiple impacts, and the passive sensors of the M-3B armour announced there were breaches in the articulated plates. One struck above his left knee and twisted him about.

*Keep shooting.*

Spartan was starting to lose his balance, but still he kept firing. The power cell ran dry, and in a procedure he'd practiced over and over, he released the burning hot clip and slid in a fresh one. As it hissed and the vents cooled, he fired again.

"Get down."

Spartan knew Gun's voice, and he rolled to the right and to his knees as the massive warrior step in beside him. In one hand he carried his looted double-barrelled coilgun, and in the other, a half broken Helion thermal rifle. Both of them blasted away until every one of the soldiers was dead or had fallen from the broken railcar. Finally, Gun reached out and grabbed Spartan. He staggered to his feet and looked down at the puncture wounds from the firearms. Internal sealant had already closed up the holes, and chemicals were busily working to patch up the flesh wounds.

"I'm okay, Gun. You?"

He glanced at his friend, seeing at least three points where he'd been wounded by fragments or projectiles. The old warrior acted as though they were nothing more than splinters.

"Pin pricks, Spartan. This is nothing compared to Spascia."

Just the mention of the place hurt Spartan's body more than any of the damage he'd just sustained. It was like a knife straight to his heart, and even Gun could tell he'd said just the wrong the thing at just the wrong time.

"I'm sorry, my friend."

"Spartan," Syala said over the voice channel.

"What is it?"

Her voice crackled a little as she spoke.

"I've just heard from Arana. She got the refugees to Caldos. No casualties."

Spartan smiled at that news, the first good news he'd heard in hours.

"There's a problem, though."

Now he let out a long sigh.

"Of course there is...what is it?"

"This Maglev track, according to the Byotai Elder, we won't even make it to the switch."

"Why the hell not?"

"The tunnels, Spartan. They're blown eighty kilometres from Caldos. Arana is mobilising help on the ground, but it's going to take time."

Spartan looked to Gun who just shrugged. Spartan had forgotten that only two of them were equipped with communications gear.

"Syala, get in touch with the Colonel, and tell him to come down here. We can stop before the end of the line, and they can take us out of here."

The pause that followed seemed to go on forever.

"That's the other problem. According to the Colonel, there are aircraft coming in from the South. It looks like the commander at Montu knows where we are. They're bringing in everything they can to stop us. And this engine, we took hits with the last attack. The engine is overheating badly."

"Montu," he said quietly, "They are coming for us, and now this piece of Byotai junk is going to let us down."

He walked over to the vertical map display, but since the gun battle, there was nothing left but broken glass and wiring.

"Great."

He turned back to Gun and spoke over the audio channel.

"Syala, give us all the power you can and nurse the engine along. You have to get us to the end of this line. We're running out of time, and we've got some pissed off friends coming at us from Montu."

He considered their predicament and then grinned.

"Put me on with the Colonel."

As he waited, the darkness around the railcar vanished, and once more they were exposed the dull light of the early dawn. More worrying was the shape of three more Hornets, all of which were coming in low to the East. Spartan lifted his carbine and shouted over to Gun.

"Left side, three more targets. Light them up!"

# CHAPTER THIRTEEN

*The final work of the Biomechs would prove to be too little, too late for their species. With their defeat in the Great Biomech War, it would turn to the scientists of the Alliance to transform the secrets of this ancient enemy into entirely new avenues of science in the fields of physics, medicine, engineering, and space travel. Their final legacy would bizarrely be to the benefit of humanity.*

*Evolution of the Biomechs*

## ANS X-45 'Titan', Debris Field, Karnak

Colonel Black rested his face in his hand as he considered the imagery for the third time. At his side were the fully armoured forms of Khan and Olik, a pair of metal Gods in their plating. Gone were the advanced aesthetics of the Special Weapons Division, and in their place the thick articulated sections, savage blade and amour-mounted weaponry. The six mercenaries were also there, waiting in silence and with their faces covered, as they always were. On the mainscreen was Spartan, but with his visor open to reveal his face.

"There you have it, Colonel. You've seen the data, and

you can see the problem."

The Marine Corps officer nodded and pointed to the imagery of the Maglev rail system between Montu and the Caldos mountain enclave.

"Yes, I can see that. The entire area is swarming with enemy aircraft. Our scanners in the communication buoys show they are already sending out teams to track you. A rescue under fire could be a disaster. First the area needs to be made safe, and then we can send in the lander."

Khan pointed at the train line while in the background. Spartan's face meanwhile flashed green as he blasted away at an unseen assailant. Each time he fired, Colonel Black could see the fingers of Khan's right hand clench, as though he was already in the battle.

"The information from Arana says the train will be stuck somewhere out here, and right under the enemy's nose."

Kanjana moved in from where she'd been waiting at the flank of Five-Seven.

"Well, we have to do something."

Colonel Black walked to the screen and pointed at the location selected by Khan.

"Could you hold this territory long enough for Syala and her forces to link up with you?"

Khan didn't even bother to examine the topography.

"If you get us on the ground, we'll hold it."

Colonel Black nodded in agreement.

"Very well."

He looked to Spartan.

"I'm sending you coordinates. We will secure the ground near the tunnel. Once there, you can dig in and wait for Arana and her reinforcements to come in from

Caldos."

The videostream shuddered, and for a brief moment Spartan vanished from the feed. When he came back, his expression had changed.

"Okay, Colonel. We've got our own problems down here."

His voice was drowned out as he stumbled about, and part of the train vanished. When the image came back into focus, there was an entire section of train missing, and the view of open wasteland rushing past in the background.

"Maybe we'll be seeing you soon."

Spartan opened fired again, and the video finally vanished. With the scene of battle gone, the interior of the ship was silent was again. Colonel Black turned around from the screen to face them all.

"It's time. Get to the Jackal. You've got time for one last kit check."

He then looked to Five-Seven.

"Lay in a low orbital course for Karnak. We will jump in three minutes. I need all systems online. This is going to get rough."

Five-Seven acknowledged and proceeded to issue orders to his Thegn crewmembers. Colonel Black watched him work and then looked at the group of warriors as they left the deck to head to the Jackal dropship.

"It's going to get very, very rough."

\* \* \*

The Byotai train screamed along the single Maglev rail. The railcars had taken an incredible beating from both airstrikes, as well as multiple assaults by drop soldiers.

Even though every section of the train had been damaged, it still thundered on; all its power supplied by the crippled, but still running engine. The rear of the locomotive streamed a long black column of smoke that continued to thicken. Spartan looked to Gun as they entered the final and longest tunnel of the journey so far.

"Good, that means we're clear from the sky for a while."

Gun threw down his third Helion rifle so far in the battle, muttering in disgust.

"This is not how I like to fight."

Spartan began moving through the train to reach the forward section when Syala contacted him. He was so used to the scenes of battle and carnage that he barely even noticed the ruined interior of the railcar. There were bullet holes from rifles, as well as entire sections of metal reduced to molten slag. Spartan pointed at one particularly bad part.

"One day they might learn the basics and not attack us one at a time."

Gun straightened his back and groaned.

"Yeah, and one day I might get bored of fighting."

Spartan headed to the adjoining section and signalled for Gun to go with him. They clambered over the wreckage and reached the last railcar before the engine unit. General Daniels was waiting there, holding a pale lantern in his hands.

"Are you both okay?"

Spartan nodded.

"Yeah, we'll live."

The entire train shuddered, and there was a mighty crashing sound. They were all thrown to the ground. Spartan was shaken so much that he rolled to the side and half swung out.

"Grab him!" Daniels yelled.

Spartan clawed at what remained of the train, but each piece of metal came away like a chunk of rotten wood. Just one finger embedded in metal, but his lower half hung out in open air. Gun kicked down and wedged his leg, lurching forward to grab his friend. Spartan's finger gave way just as his hand connected with the armour. He grabbed with all his strength, and with one big tug, Gun yanked him back onto the train.

"Thanks," he said with a cough.

Gun leaned back, and part of a broken bulkhead groaned under the weight. Spartan lay on his back and opened his visor. He took in multiple deep breaths just as General Daniels bent down and looked into the helmet.

"Thought we'd lost you for a minute back there."

Spartan tried to laugh, but instead coughed once more.

"There's a problem," said Gun.

Light had returned to the wrecked train, and as they sped onwards, they could now see a gentle warm hue growing in the distance from the rising sun. They were out in the open. Syala opened the door from the engine and leaned out. Her armour was badly singed, and it was marked from her shoulder and chest, down to her belly.

"The capacitors have blown. We're running on solar only."

Spartan pulled himself up into a seating position.

"What the hell does that mean?"

She looked to each of them, but her expression effectively answered the question for them.

"We're slowing down. Give it another three minutes, and we'll be too slow for the engine to keep the train levitated."

"And then?" Gun asked.

Syala laughed. At the same time, Gun pointed off to the right. Spartan and the General squinted and then spotted shapes.

"Six of those Hornets, and they are coming this way," said General Daniels.

Spartan looked for his carbine and found it on the floor, near to Gun. He beckoned towards it; the old warrior lifted it and threw it over. Spartan caught it in one hand and checked the power cell status. He shook his head.

"Not good, less than half."

He then looked at Syala.

"Let me guess. Once we drop below that speed, we'll be grinding metal."

She nodded.

"And when that happens, this train will be dead, and forty kilometres away from our rendezvous with my sister."

On cue, a great whine began from the front of the train. Syala went back inside and reappeared moments later. This time she carried her weapon and kept moving.

"What's happening?" Spartan asked.

Syala moved past him and continued on into the train. She threw a glance back at them.

"No idea. The computer is dead, and something is getting hotter and hotter up there."

She didn't bother to wait and see what they did, and headed towards the rear of the train. Gun and Spartan looked at each other. General Daniels picked up a Helion rifle and joined Syala.

"Let's go," said Spartan.

All four of them clambered over the floor that was now littered with wreckage. At the same time, the howl from the engine continued to grow. Spartan paused for a second to look out from the side of the train. Sparks were already flashing along the lower sections, and flames had broken out at the front.

"Run!"

They reached the second railcar when the engine finally reached critical. The entire nose section ripped off in a bright flash, and debris blasted off in all directions. At exactly the same time, the train dropped down onto the single track with an almighty crash. Screaming metal was joined by a long series of flashes, and fires broke out along the entire train. Then the middle railcars ripped off the track as their electromagnets failed. The train completely broke apart, sending metal, fuel, and flames in all directions.

\* \* \*

## ANS X-45 'Titan', on approach to Karnak

The planet continued to increase in size as the ship moved in on its course. Unlike any other vessel Colonel Black had been aboard; this one was the most confusing. Ships normally found themselves decelerating for the last half of a journey, or for long haul transports they would be forced to follow a curved course around moons or planets. Five-Seven brought up the forward view, along with detailed information on all ships in the area.

"We have been detected by the Anicinàbe blockade."

The Colonel rubbed his chin, but his expression remained stoic. The screen in front showed the extent of the blockade, and it was much more substantial that even he had expected. There were scores of modified civilian ships, with almost as many corsair and sleek-looking Anicinàbe military warships.

"Stay on course. We are going to have to be quick."

He tapped the communications button.

"Kanjana, is the dropship ready?"

"Affirmative," came back a snappy reply.

"Good. This is going to be a drop under fire. We'll prepare a defensive package for you."

A light rumble spread through the ship that was immediately followed by the engines deactivating. One moment it was travelling at the speed of light, and the next they were in orbit and operating under conventional engines. There was no physical stimuli as they changed velocity other than the visual, something that was confusing to the minds of all there, except for Five-Seven.

"Six warships on an intercept course. More are changing their approach vectors," said Five-Seven, "It appears the blockade has increased in size and firepower since we left."

"Yeah," said the Colonel, "Something tells me they don't want anybody snooping about."

The view from the mainscreen shifted to show the heavily modified forms of six vessels. Behind them were dozens more, all waiting in orbit. There were also several large, sleek ships that Colonel Black had not seen before.

"What are those things?"

Five-Seven was as efficient as ever and checked the onboard computer. A number of schematics appeared on the mainscreen and positioned themselves alongside the live imagery of the enemy.

"They appear to match Alliance records for Anicinàbe escort carriers, one of the primary front line vessels in the Anicinàbe inventory. They are cruiser class vessels and have the ability to operate dropships and fighters. Sensors detect thirty plus fighters on approach."

Even as they watched, a number of smaller shapes emerged from the large ships. They moved out from their launch tubes and then waited, like a row of sharp teeth. The targeting computer quickly tagged them. Five-Seven selected them and looked to the Colonel.

"Atomic torpedoes, they are active and waiting in readiness inside their open torpedo tubes. Those weapons will cripple us if used."

Colonel Black nodded.

"Understood. Nice to see that conventional weaponry has gone out of the window. Let's make sure they don't hit us. Any use of atomics will escalate this situation. I can't imagine for a moment that Tahkeome or any of his lieutenants would be foolish enough to do that. What is the status of the engine?"

It took only a few seconds for Five-Seven to confirm the power units and drive were ready. He looked back with a muted expression, barely registering any form of emotion.

"Two minutes until we can use them. It takes time to build up the energy to create the space-time distortion."

"Very well. Get us into position."

He contacted Kanjana once more.

"We've got company. We're going to have to slingshot you in. Are you ready for that?"

"No problem, Colonel. Just tell us when you're ready."

ANS X-45 Titan continued on to the final part of its journey; the group of ships and fighters rushed in to stop them. They were close enough that some had already opened fire with automatic cannons, but even with their advanced targeting arrays, they were too far away to land more than five direct hits, all of which were easily absorbed by the armour. Then the larger vessels unleashed a veritable arsenal of gunfire at their flank. At the same time, the fighters activated their boost engines and closed to within fifty kilometres. In space, this was effectively point-blank range.

"That's enough. We've received no warning, and they fired first. Activate our defences," Colonel Black ordered.

All it took was a single command, and the entire ship's array of active defences activated. They had been scanning targets since their arrival, but none of the turrets could fire without gunnery clearance. As soon as the projectiles and missiles entered a ten-kilometre perimeter, they opened fire from every corner of the ship. The rapid fire of the particle defence turrets tore them apart in seconds, even managing to destroy some of the incoming flechette rounds before they could hit the ship.

"Defences active; ninety-eight percent success rate," said Five-Seven.

"Good work," said Colonel Black.

His eyebrows lifted in surprise at the number, something much higher than he expected, especially against such an overwhelming number of attacks. On the mainscreen the first fighter squadron had passed overhead and launched missiles; all annihilated by the defence turrets. One of the escort carriers was now within a range of six hundred kilometres, and its entire nose section vanished in a barrage of yellow flashes.

"Unguided rockets on an intercept course," said Five-Seven.

He didn't need to look to the Colonel for orders as the ship began a series of pre-programmed routines. First it began a series of rolls so that the gun turrets would get maximum coverage in their high-power mode. This new feature gave the turrets substantially greater hitting power, but it also reduced the firing rate to a tenth of its normal level. By the time a turret was half charged, the ship would already have rotated so that the next could fire.

"Impressive," said Colonel Black, "Very damned impressive."

A dozen of the small turrets continued firing normally, keeping the shoal of fighters busy. The incoming rockets were large, bigger than a fighter borne missile, and much more powerful. Primitive by all accounts, they had the benefit of being impossible to jam, and it fell to the turrets, which managed to down all but four by the time they reached the one-kilometre barrier.

"Brace!" said the ship's computer.

The crew normally issued the command, but the computer was much quicker and could anticipate direct threat. The final layer of defence was a blast by two powerful flechette launchers. They sent hundreds of tiny chunks of metal into the path of the rockets. Only two rockets struck the ship's hull, penetrating almost three metres before exploding.

"Damage report!"

Five-Seven examined the information coming in from his sub-commanders.

"Armour breached but contained. No significant damage. The nearest escort carrier is activating its forward batteries again."

After breathing a sigh of relief from surviving the initial

strike, Colonel Black pointed to the fighters swarming around the ship.

"They had their chance. Now it's ours. I am authorising level one rules of engagement."

He looked to the Thegn, assuming he would be familiar with the basics of military protocol.

"Understood," said Five-Seven, "If we are attacked, then target and destroy the source."

Colonel Black gave him a curt nod.

"Weapons free."

He repeated the orders much like a computer would.

"Exactly. And as for that thing...activate the main guns."

The ship surrounded itself with a storm of gunfire as it hurled closer to the drop-off point. Flashes of light marked where a fighter or missile exploded, and still it continued on its course into low orbit over Karnak. The forward quad-particle cannons opened up and hammered the carrier with blast after blast of energy. The first impact ripped massive chunks of armour away, making subsequent strikes deadly. After the three-second bombardment was over, nearly a quarter of the escort carrier was ablaze.

* * *

**Jackal Dropship 'Haywire'**
Khan and Olik waited patiently as the clamps held them firmly in place. A third set of JAS armour waited alongside them, but this one was empty. Even without Gun inside it, the armour was an awe-inspiring sight. Deep scars marked where he'd sustained damage in hand-to-hand combat, and the other plating had been repaired dozens of times over. Standing alongside them were six of the robotic

CD-1 Grunts, each silent and still inside its launch tube. There were fourteen more tubes behind them, all of which were empty, and another ten in front, six of which were occupied by the remaining mercenaries. In the Grunts' arms were their firearms in exactly the same position at the shoulder.

"Creepy, aren't they?" Olik asked.

Khan laughed.

"At least they're on our side. I'm more concerned with them."

He nodded off to the forward section where the mercenaries were strapped in: the netting devices over their heads, and their eyes and ears covered. They were suspended from the ground, and to the untrained eye might have been little more than dead bodies.

"What happens if they launch the wrong tubes?"

Khan shook his head and pointed to the base of the cylinders.

"Only the ones with Grunts have release mounts at the base. The first ten are locked down. They can't be opened."

The dropship shook violently, and for a moment Khan thought they'd been hit. He checked the small video window on his visor but could see they were still clamped into position inside the warship.

"What the hell was that?" Olik asked.

Kanjana activated the triple-layered plate connecting the cockpit with the rest of the transport area. It opened up like an iris, and though small, it was enough for her to look back at her passengers.

"Get ready. We're in the middle of one hell of a firefight."

Khan and Olik both nodded smartly. The six mercenaries

remained motionless in their protective cocoons. Khan muttered, and Olik strained to listen to him.

"What?"

Khan grumbled again.

"I said it's time we were in the middle of a fire fight."

Olik leaned back.

"I agree with you there, brother."

\* \* \*

## ANS X-45 'Titan', Low Orbit, Karnak

Autocannons hammered away at the underside of ANS X-45 Titan as she skimmed the atmosphere of Karnak. The nacelle ring at the rear of the ship left a bizarre trail behind them as dust heated up and sprinkled behind like a fiery comet. Behind her came a squadron of sleek and agile fighters, the kind of aircraft only a people like the Anicinàbe could ever have created. Unlike any other known race, their entire philosophy was on speed and mobility. The natural ability of their crews to understand three-dimensional space could only be matched by the most sophisticated computer simulations. They fired at a range of just a few hundred metres, jinking about to avoid the return fire from the turrets.

"Breaches on the engine nacelles. Another hit like that, and we will be unable to get away," said Five-Seven.

Any other officer might have shown worry or nerves, but not this Thegn soldier. He repeated the information as if simply reading it from a screen at a company board meeting. Autocannons battered the underside, and still he seemed unconcerned.

"Keep her together," said Colonel Black.

Even as he said it, he felt a shudder down his spine. On the mainscreen the image of an entire section of hull showed clearly what was happening. Gunfire had ripped three layers of plating away, as well as three compartments, which thankfully were empty. The fighters were spinning about on their axis to put more and more fire into the damaged sections.

"More have arrived."

Colonel Black moved his eyes from the damaged sections and gazed upon the form of their tormentors. Behind them came more and more of the heavier warships, as well as another four military escort carriers. In front were two more ships. They had positioned themselves in such a way that Titan would have to travel directly past them.

"What the hell are those things?"

They looked at the mainscreen as the imagery of the two vessels enlarged. Both were a mess, more a floating mass of scrap and flotsam. The scale showed them to be about the size of an Alliance heavy transport, making them nearly double the size of a standard heavy cruiser. Engines were positions in a variety of unexpected locations. Dozens of gun ports and missile systems activated and fired towards them.

"They are ships built from the ruins of others. According to the computer, they have to be towed into position. I am detecting more already in orbit, at least nine."

"What is their purpose?"

Five-Seven checked more data before looking to the Colonel.

"Orbital bases to carry out raids and piracy operations."

The Colonel's mouth twitched. He'd come across craft

designed for similar purposes out on the Rim, as well as on some of the less well-known moons back in the Alliance. They were often found near mining colonies or trading posts where they could operate multiple ships for weeks, sometimes months.

"They're mother ships, carrion brought in to feed on the dead. Target them. Let them burn!"

The forward guns fired just once before a barrage from the pursuing ships struck the underside one last time, but the groaning howl coming from her stern announced the damage was more than just the loss of armour plates. Five-Seven sent commands to his crew, and the massive prototype ship twisted about like a seal pursued by half a dozen killer whales. He glanced to the Colonel.

"Power systems are failing. We've lost power to the forward weapon systems and defence turrets. Either we leave now, or we will be destroyed."

Colonel Black didn't hesitate as he contacted the dropship.

"Kanjana. Drop now. You have ten seconds."

As soon as he received the acknowledgement, he turned his attention to the mainscreen.

"Turn us around and prepare to activate the engines."

"Yes, Colonel. Destination?"

Colonel Black considered their options for a moment. He knew they were damaged, and staying too close to Karnak could get them captured or killed. He was tempted to travel directly to Taxxu, but the odds of the engines lasting that long were slim.

*Stay close, but safe.*

"The Byotai Spacebridge. Get us to the border."

The ship spun around on her axis but continued along

her present course. With the damaged stern now away from most of the gunfire, the fighters were forced to change position. It didn't take long, and they were firing again just as the Jackal dropship slipped out from her position low in the hull.

"Now!"

The ships vanished around them as the ship rushed away at impossible speeds. Three seconds after they left the area, a massive barrage of missiles and autocannon rounds rushed through the area of space they'd vacated. Now all that remained was the fiery trail from behind the dropship as the tiny craft plummeted down to the surface.

"What's our status?"

Five-Seven looked confused as he checked the displays. He began to speak but checked again.

"We have a problem. The nacelles are fluctuating. We are going..."

The howl rippled through the ship, and it was followed by a sound like a thunderclap. Colonel Black almost blacked out, but when he shook his head and looked to the mainscreen, all he could see were the distant pinpricks of starlight.

"What happened?"

Five-Seven shook his head.

"The Alcubierre drive system has overloaded. I have sent engineers to investigate."

Colonel Black looked back at the mainscreen. The star field was rotating about them. It was an immediate reminder that the ship was spinning, but also that he had no idea where they were.

"Talk to me...where the hell are we?"

All eyes turned to the screens as the crew located

astronomical phenomena and then triangulated the current position. It took just a few seconds until the starmap on the right-hand part of the mainscreen changed. Five-Seven looked over to him, and Colonel Black already knew they were in trouble.

"We are two hundred thousand kilometres from Karnak. The enemy can see us."

Colonel Black shook his head and looked to the mainscreen. There was no sign of the planet, presumably because the cameras were still pointing forwards and in the direction they had been heading.

"Uh...Five-Seven...What are those?"

The Thegn enhanced the view until ten ships could be seem, each subtly different, but all looked like bugs with large wings and long vanes. Five-Seven had to check the computer, but Colonel Black knew who they were. He began to smile.

"My friends, those are Byotai warships."

Five-Seven remained expressionless.

"The lead ship is hailing us. It is General Makos."

The Thegn looked to Colonel Black.

"He wishes to know if we require assistance."

Colonel Black couldn't believe his luck.

*Ten ships won't save Karnak, but it should be enough to get our people out of there.*

\* \* \*

### Jackal Dropship 'Haywire'
The dropship's ejection from the hangar was much more violent than the original insertion. As they rolled out, the port side began to overheat almost immediately. Gunfire

from a pair of the pursuing fighters narrowly missed the other side before Kanjana was able to right the ship.

"Hold on!" Kanjana yelled.

They were already inside the atmosphere and leaving a great burning trail behind them. Three kilometres behind were the two Anicinàbe fighters, who for the time being had deactivated their gun ports and retracted their weapons to keep them from the heat. Inside the cockpit, Kanjana wrestled with the controls as their excessive speed began to cause external damage.

*We need to slow down!*

Kanjana pulled the secondary control unit to one side and tapped a series of buttons. One by one an entire array of expendable braking vanes pushed out. Large control flaps pushed up just a few degrees, and then ever so slowly, they opened wider and wider.

"What's going on?"

The voice of Khan was loud enough that she could hear him over the sound of the buffeting of their descent. Two more control vanes ripped off, but finally they were at a more reasonable speed and heading towards the surface on a long, arcing course.

"We're heading for the drop zone. Make sure you're ready."

No sooner had she said the words, the guns of their pursuers opened fire. Three of the solid slugs penetrated the skin of the left engine and sent chunks of metal flying out behind them. The dropship immediately lurched to the right and started to roll.

"Hold on!"

With incredible skill and precision, Kanjana rolled the craft around until back on course, and then made a subtle correction. Shots punched past the dropship on both sides, but only a handful managed to tear holes in the rear. Warning lights flashed, telling of yet another component that had failed.

"Let's see how you like this."

Three buttons was all it took to open two hatches and begin an emergency fuel dump. One of the six onboard self-sealing tanks emptied itself into the sky. As the last drop was released, she hit the countermeasures release. Six micro-flares blasted off in a star pattern behind her, and a cloud of flame engulfed the sky. One fighter banked away, but the second must have been covered in the fluid because it caught alight immediately and spun down out of control.

# CHAPTER FOURTEEN

*How many stories have been written in the past concerning the rise of a robot army? So many, that it even getting basic armed drones into combat would prove almost impossible in the Alliance. Not even the promise of stringent protective measures would allow full autonomous robots onto the battlefield. Instead, a bizarre hybrid system would have to be developed to allow central control of these machines, or for them to operate in a swarm configuration around a host. Could machines of the future somehow acquire intelligence and self-awareness? Alliance scientists say no, but the general public will not support it, not at any cost. For now, there must always be a man in the loop.*

*The Robot Army*

**Maglev Rail Network, Khagi District, Karnak**
Ogimà Nakoma could see the smoke column off into the distance. Even as she watched, she could see the dozens of Hornets moving in on the destroyed train system. She started to smile, and then spotted columns of smoke to the right. The expression on her face changed in an instant, as the ground vehicles of the Red Scars moved to join

her. A dozen aircraft hovered over the ground vehicles to provide air cover. They could just have easily detached so that they could attack the train, but instead were staying as one cohesive unit.

"How far away are they?"

The pilot of the small aircraft looked back over his shoulder.

"They will be at the train in twenty minutes, perhaps eighteen."

*Takosk, I will end this before you can begin your meddling.*

She connected to the commanders of all of her aerial units.

"This is Ogimà Nakoma. The mercenaries must be stopped, and quickly. I am offering a reward of a year's salary and a promotion to those that bring me the head of any of the enemy combatants. They must be dealt with personally; they cannot be allowed to escape."

She wiped the saliva dripping from her lower lip. The one thing worrying her more than anything was that they would bombard the train, and then days later find the mercenaries had escaped. If she failed, her punishment at the hands of Tahkeome would be too terrifying to comprehend, and even worse, her own clan would suffer, perhaps even being cast out or broken up.

*No, not this time. I owe it to the Spires to succeed. We will live, or die as one.*

She looked at the pilot and the controls, and could see the screen showing the position of all of her kin. The spherical mapping unit gave data on their positions as well as their heights. Most important, they were all heading in one direction, right at the smashed train.

"Failure is not an option. We outnumber then fifty-to-one. I will execute any soldier that abandons the field."

She let that sink in for a moment. It was an old style of punishment, and one she had little doubt she'd need to use. In any case, she had to make sure her soldiers were suitably motivated to the battle. A message arrived from one of the scouts on board the nearest Hornet.

"Ogimà, one of the mercenaries is moving from the train wreckage."

Ogimà Nakoma's expression was already dour, but the idea that one of the enemy might escape was enough to push her over the edge.

"Then remind them that they cannot do this! No explosives, guns only! I want to see the bodies."

The bright glow from the aircraft engines increased in intensity as the advanced war machines zoomed into position. At the same time, the passengers aboard moved to the sides of the craft and took aim with their accurate long-rifles. Sprung mounts hung down for them to rest the weapons for better accuracy. Then the pilot looked back again.

"What is it?"

The pilot looked positively nervous.

"Our forward supply base at Armant reports multiple aircraft on approach. Then the signal vanished."

Ogimà Nakoma turned her head a little.

"Armant? That is a small mountain watch post. We passed it on the way from Montu, six guards and a single landing platform. Why would..."

Then she remembered, and her expression turned from surprise to anger. The Byotai lacked the aircraft for any kind of attack, and certainly the capacity to mount a rescue operation in the mountains.

*We have a few prisoners there. We have been betrayed.*

"Should we turn back to help them?"

Ogimà Nakoma's brow tightened in frustration.

"No, nothing will stop us completing our mission."

At the same time, all she could think of was the face of her rival, the warlord of the Red Scars, Takosk. The man she was now convinced was behind all of her misfortune.

*We will succeed here, and then I will deal with Takosk, personally.*

\* \* \*

Spartan woke up, not to the sound of voices, not even the sound of engines. This time it was the clatter of heavy weapons as a pair of Hornets circled overhead. At first he could barely see them through the smoke, but then found his visor was open. A single mental decision commanded the armour to close it up. The overlay immediately combined vision modes so he could easily look through the smoke. He lowered his stance, his M-3B armour barely making a sound.

*I see you.*

The craft passed again, and a fusillade of small arms fire erupted from their flanks. Spartan lifted his carbine up, took aim, and then stopped. He could see it was his last clip, and he was down to a third charge.

"Damn it!"

"Problem?"

Spartan turned around and found he was staring into the bloodied face of Gun. He carried a pair of long-rifles, no doubt taken from the fallen enemy soldiers. One had been damaged to allow him to use it, the other he tossed to Spartan. With just his left hand, Spartan caught the weapon and lifted it to his face.

"Thanks. I'm saving my last power cell for something special."

In a quick movement, he swung the prototype carbine to his flank and raised the long-rifle to check the sight and ammunition capacity. General Daniels pointed to the sky.

"Kanjana has been in touch. She will be here soon for the extraction."

Spartan raised an eyebrow.

"Extraction, here?"

Gun howled and pointed to the aircraft.

"Here they come!"

General Daniels turned away from Spartan and clambered over the wrecked carriage to get a better look. It gave him a high vantage point, as well as reasonable cover. Like Spartan, he carried a looted rifle, and he positioned it on top of the carriage. He took careful aim and squeezed the trigger. Shortly afterwards a single body fell from one of the aircraft.

"Nice shooting, General."

The two aircraft kept out of range, hovering so those on board could aim with more accuracy. Daniels continued firing at them with carefully considered shots. Further along the train, Syala ran back and leapt behind broken metal. Even as she landed, the gunfire from one of the aircraft crashed around her.

"Get them?" Spartan asked.

Syala lifted her arms triumphantly and dropped two more rifles and six packs of weapon stores on the ground. As she slid into cover, the gunfire from the Hornet aircraft continued. Incredibly, not one managed to strike her, though they made a mess of what little remained of the train.

"Will this help?"

Spartan deactivated his visor for just a moment and gave her a wide grin.

"Good work. Damned good work."

"Spartan!" General Daniels yelled.

All four of them looked out from the shattered train and off into the distance. Dozens of trails marked the positions of multiple aircraft, and they were moving fast and low.

"Ours?" Daniels asked.

Spartan had already altered the focal length on his suit's lenses and was watching the approaching vehicles. He could see the markings on the side, but it was the passengers that surprised him.

"Hell, no, they're bringing in soldiers...a lot of soldiers."

He pointed off at the shapes.

"Good," growled Gun, "that's exactly what I had in mind."

Spartan grabbed one of the ammunition packs and climbed over the wreckage, moving away from them to the right and in the direction of the enemy. He stopped behind a row of six large rocks large enough to hide a figure even as big as Gun.

"Spartan, what are you doing?" asked the General.

Spartan's armour was already shifting in colour to match the muted tones of the rock, as opposed to the metal of the train. He placed his rifle on the ground and opened up the pack. Inside were eight clips for the long-rifle. He looked over his left shoulder to the others.

"I have the camouflage and armour. I'll hold the perimeter and watch your flank. If they get past me, you'll finish them off."

Gun made to join him, but Daniels grabbed his arm.

"No. You've not got armour, old friend. Leave him. We'll hold the train."

Syala whipped out her backup sidearm, checked the magazine, and slid it back in its holster before speaking.

"Yes, I'll be here, too."

Gun still focused his attention on their distant enemies. The Hornet aircraft had regrouped into a single large formation and were no more than twenty metres off the ground. Beneath them hung the shapes of cloth-covered soldiers, each with the drop backpacks to help them land. Only three of the Hornets remained away from the group. These were the ones circling directly around their position.

"Wait until they're close, real close," said Gun.

His voice was firm, almost grim. Yet for all the peril they were in, he gave the impression he was almost excited at this entire prospect. Three green flashes announced Spartan was firing, and two managed to strike the nose of the nearest aircraft. The magnetically contained projectile punched through the thin plating as if it were wet tissue, causing a series of explosions that ripped it apart.

"Not bad. I thought he was saving his ammo?" Syala said.

Gun laughed and began counting out as he watched the soldiers closing in on them. The aircraft were staying well away from Spartan, for good reason. They were lightly armed and designed more for scouting and raiding than direct combat. He stopped counting and looked to the other two.

"I count over two hundred soldiers, and they are coming this way."

As he looked back, the first began leaping from the aircraft. The pinpricks of light from their thrusters were all that betrayed their positions as they fell to the ground and moved in at a jog. Dozens hit the ground, and as each aircraft emptied its cargo, it turned away to provide long-range fire support.

"Good," said Syala, "I'm getting bored waiting."

She took aim with her rifle and watched a squad of six clambering over a long ribbon of razor sharp rocks. They had a mixture of long-rifles and machete type blades in their hands. Each was covered in the sand colour cloth, giving them their nomadic look, but she had little doubt they were heavily armoured underneath.

*Time to die.*

A thunderclap overhead forced them all to look up. A tiny black shape wreathed in flames flew across the sky like a comet, warning of something even more terrible to come. Then came the first volleys of gunfire. Spartan and Syala opened fire at exactly the same time. Their long-rifles were simple, yet surprisingly accurate. Both struck target after target, but even after five soldiers had been killed, they were no closer to beating off the attack. Three more Hornets came in low and behind the rocks to the right. Spartan took aim, but they were hidden from view. When they lifted back up, there was no sign of the soldiers inside.

"We've got a flanking group on the right, twenty plus ground troops."

He moved carefully to the right and leaned around the boulder. Three rifle shots struck his position, one glancing off the side of his head, leaving a deep gouge in the metal plating. The impact was enough to knock him back several centimetres before he righted himself. Spartan looked for signs of the soldiers, but they were being smart and using the liberal amount of rocks and the undulating terrain on the flank to get closer. He suspected they were no more than fifty metres away. Two appeared, and the helmet overlay tagged them immediately.

*Big mistake.*

He'd already changed to the long-rifle. He fired three shots, but only one made contact before the second soldier dropped down to safety.

"Spartan, we're coming to you, are you ready?" came a familiar voice.

"Kanjana, good, about damned time."

The soldiers appeared from cover, but this time moving from each side and as a wave. Two were knocked down by sniper fire back in the train, but the others surged out, ignoring casualties and firing their rifles from the hip. Spartan hit two and ducked back to cover.

"You're not at the rendezvous," Kanjana said.

Spartan sensed an accusing tone in her voice.

"You don't say. Track my location. We've been derailed. Literally."

There was a short pause, one long enough for him to pick up a new rifle clip and turn his fire back on the soldiers. Some of them were making a break for the engine at the front of the train. There was scattered wreckage between the rocks and the track, more than enough for the Spires soldiers to make his job more difficult. He picked off two more, and fire from the train forced the rest into cover.

"Alert!"

It was the armour, a simple proximity warning. Spartan reacted instantly and twisted about as one of the Anicinàbe warhounds leapt over the rock and dropped down on him. He lifted his weapon, but even he was too slow.

"What the..."

The heavy beast knocked him to the ground and grabbed his left arm in its vice-like jaw. The creature dug its back legs firmly to the ground and proceeded to yank and tug at the armour. Spartan lifted his left foot and jammed his boot hard at the creature's head. It barely made an impact.

*I'm not going out like this!*

He reached down for his sidearm. The creature released its grip for a second and lurched forward to rip the weapon from his hand, snapping it in two. A squad of soldiers moved past his cover to his left. Sensing this was his only chance; he rolled to the right with the creature in pursuit and grabbed his carbine. Fire from Gun and Syala knocked down two of the Spires soldiers, but more were coming from both sides. Soon his position would be lost. The first looked as surprised as him when they looked to each other.

"Not today, pal!"

Spartan lowered the carbine and pulled the trigger. The pulse of green struck the soldier in the jaw, punched through his skull and out through the back of his head with a foul hissing sound. It was a guaranteed kill at this range, no matter how bad a shot he was. Something pulled at him, and he stumbled. The warhound creature leapt back over the rock as he fired and was replaced by the face of another Spires soldiers.

"Surrender!" said the soldier in a thick accent.

"Bad timing, pal!"

Spartan pushed the barrel of his carbine so that the muzzle touched the soldier's mouth. He pulled the trigger, and the headless corpse vanished from view. The other Spires soldiers pushed past the body with their weapons out and firing. Some shot towards the train, but two fired continually at Spartan. Multiple rounds struck him, and at least one breached the chest plating.

*Not good.*

He staggered back, one round after another hitting him. Alerts sounded, and he had no choice but to roll over the rocks behind him for cover. Blood trailed on the ground from his wounds, but the stimulants and drugs in the suit pumped directly into his body to keep him going, for now. Further back, the other three were busy firing into the mass of Spires soldiers coming in from three directions.

"Help him!" Gun yelled.

Syala was the nearest to Spartan, and once she loaded in a new clip, looked for him. Her armour communicated with Spartan's own system, but only to share basic Friend or Foe data, as well as a secure communications channel.

"I'm on it! Spartan, keep your head down."

She rose out of cover and was immediately hit by a pair of rounds. The high-velocity slugs embedded deep into her customised armour, held back only by the reinforced collar and neck armour. The power of the attack knocked her back down. She tried to scramble over the ridge.

"No, get back here!"

Gun dragged her out of the line of fire, using nothing but brute force to yank her away. She yelled and screamed, but a burst of shots hit where she'd just been, and that seemed to calm her for the time being. Gun rolled her over and reached for the damaged section of armour between her collar and chest.

"Hey, that's private!"

Gun shook his head.

"Females!"

\* \* \*

"Ogimà Nakoma, your attack is failing. I have reports that explosions in your supply base have allowed Byotai prisoners to escape."

The words struck like a lance to Nakoma's chest. Her immediate thought was that Takosk must be behind the explosions. There was no way the Byotai could have struck that hard and fast without help. She opened her mouth, but her rival continued to rage. Warm air blasted inside the aircraft, increasing in temperature as every minute went past. The single star was now easily visible and cast long shadows against the ground.

"Your failure at Montu is spreading like wildfire through Karnak. The Byotai settlers are not running anymore. They are standing their ground, all because of your incompetence. You are as incapable as you are inept."

An explosion off into the distance caught Nakoma's attention. A large plume of dust rising up high into the air followed it.

"My personal guard has arrived, Nakoma. Your troops will contain the enemy on three sides. Do not let them escape. I will land behind them, and I will end this the way you should have."

Nakoma knew this was a personal attack, even more than an attack on her clan. The Spires had only managed to move into a position of relative prominence due to the Red Scars failure years before at Karnak.

*Takosk wants me to fail. Then he will seize two territories on*

*Karnak, and his shame will be consigned to history.*

"I will assault their position from behind. Make sure that..."

Nakoma gave the signal for the connection to be severed. Her hands were shaking, but not from fear; this was pure rage. It took her almost ten seconds before she could compose herself enough to speak.

"Spires, we have been betrayed. The Red Scars are here. Will you let them take what is ours?"

In answer, another of her aircraft was hit by gunfire and fell from the sky. This time it managed to right itself and staggered away trailing black smoke. Nakoma shook her head in frustration.

"We must destroy these mercenaries and show that it is us, not the animal soldiers of Takosk, that have the right to rule here."

As she finished speaking, she spotted black shapes off into the distance and moving in close to the other side of the train. They were much larger than the aircraft her clan used. Where the Spires were masters of hit and run attacks and raids, the Red Scars were more of a brutal assault force. They relied upon armour and war machines, as opposed to the finesse of her people. Her confidence was shattered when she realised quite how large the Red Scars force was.

*He is not here to help me. He's here to take over this entire region.*

The Spires clan moved ever closer, while one by one, the heavy raiding landers of the Red Scars dropped off a bizarre menagerie of contraptions a kilometre away from the battle. Nakoma snarled, realising that while she'd put two hundred soldiers and fifteen aircraft into the battle, the Red Scars had tripled that number, plus their war machines. She rose to her feet and pulled her helmet from its mount on the side of the aircraft. Two of her bodyguards removed a chest plate from the same place and helped fit it to her.

*I will lead the last assault, and I do not care which enemy I will be fighting.*

\* \* \*

Gun watched the vast horde of war machines coming from the opposite side of the train from the current attack and began to laugh. There were just four of them at the train, and this vast enemy seemed like a cruel joke to him now.

"They really want to make sure, don't they?"

General Daniels twisted back to watch.

"They don't want us getting back to the Byotai, or even worse, speaking to the Alliance. If the Byotai see what we can do, and that they can be beaten, well, what do you think will happen next?"

Gun shrugged.

"I'll tell you something else, Gun."

"What?"

The General grinned.

"They mean business."

Both looked at more than a dozen large wheeled vehicles almost the same size as a train carriage. The tops were open to the elements and filled with weapon toting soldiers. Darting in about this formation were twice as many smaller vehicles, carrying harpoon guns and automatic cannons. They had begun firing even at this long-range to little effect. Gun heard shouting and went to the side of the carriage, peeking through the many small holes in the metal. Even he was staggered at the line of soldiers closing on their position. It looked like a medieval battle where hundreds of soldiers would line up on the battlefield. Gun banged his fist on the side of the train wreckage.

"General, help Spartan."

From his position higher up, General Daniels had the perfect view of the enemy. For now the vehicles on the other side were too far away to engage. He would deal with that when the time came. He'd purposely kept his head down, and there was only a tiny gap through the broken metal on the upper section of the carriage he dared look through. He fired one more shot and slid off to the right to get a view of the nearby position occupied by Spartan. He'd seen all kinds of combat, but what he could see took him right back to the war.

*What is he doing?*

Spartan rolled back until just twenty metres from the train when the Spires soldiers finally overran his position. Gun could see a creature snapping at his heels, and two-dozen or more soldiers were knocking him to the ground. He felt a lump in his throat but grinned when he saw Spartan back on his feet. In his hands was a blade, something taken from one of the Spires soldiers, and he was hacking away. The blows continued to rain down on him.

"Shoot on Spartan's position."

General Daniels loosed off a dozen shots, several striking home. Two managed to hit Spartan, but thankfully with no obvious effect. Then came the screaming sound of falling objects. He looked up at the sleek shape of their Jackal dropship. It barrel rolled while a single arrow shaped fighter pursued it behind the nearest hills.

"General!" Syala shouted.

He looked back and found himself looking at the first three of the Red Scars vehicles. One was coming right at them, the warriors on board waving weapons and howling like teenagers. Shots blasted away, and he quickly ducked back into cover and checked his magazine.

"Not good. Not good at all."

The scream of engines suddenly stopped and was replaced with the screaming voices of warriors. He moved out of cover for an instant, took aim, and fired three times. Two of the enemy were hit, and then they were amongst them around the train. Whereas the Spires soldiers were careful in their movements, these Red Scars were like wild animals.

"Die!" Gun roared.

He glanced to the left; at least a dozen of them had been surprised by Gun. The massive warrior was shot at least three times, but now he was amongst them. A few foolish ones fired back at him, and in their haste managed to shoot their own people. The first two went down from strikes with his left arm, and then a third hacked at him with a curved blade, knocking the rifle from his right hand, a weapon he'd been using as a club.

"Ha, ha!" he laughed.

Reaching forward, he grabbed the warrior's arm, locked it, and then yanked. The entire limb ripped out, leaving a screaming warrior and blood pumping all over Gun's body. He swung the arm over his head and smashed the bloody object back into the warrior's face.

"That's how to disarm somebody!"

Another shot hit him in the chest, and this time the impact seemed to have an effect. He staggered back, shook his head, swinging his arms to strike yet more of them.

General Daniels dropped his now empty rifle and lifted his sidearm.

"I'm coming!"

His shooting was precise, no more than two rounds per target. Something struck his left arm, another hit his cheek, and he was on the ground. He could feel the warm blood trickling down his face.

"This can't…"

A massive thud shook the ground so hard he almost left the ground for a second. It was something as loud and powerful as the collapse of a massive building. His first instinct was to roll to the side and brace himself for the heat of a bombing run. For the split second, he was sure he could see the dark shapes of large bipedal fighting machines, and then the entire area filled with dust engulfing the defenders, the train, and every single one of the attackers. The last thing he heard was the relentless hammering sound of heavy weapons firing.

* * *

## Jackal Dropship 'Haywire'

Kanjana pulled on the column and twisted the dropship through an incredible series of manoeuvres. She was flying at a little over two hundred feet and back toward the mountains, away from the train site. The drop had been a lot closer than she'd intended, and the engine intakes were partially clogged from the dust kicked up by the battle around the train. A quick glance showed the battle site was full of dust, made worse by the soldiers' landing.

*Good luck, Khan.*

She wanted to go back and provide air cover, but as well as the massive amount of ground fire, there was still the issue of the remaining fighter that had followed her down from space.

"Everybody okay back there?"

The six mercenaries acknowledged from inside their protective cocoons.

*Good.*

"Help them. We have to protect Spartan and the others. The suits are expendable, our people are not."

The pursuing fighter was close, and its guns firing almost continually. Impact after impact was registered; and at any moment Kanjana expected to see the engines had finally been destroyed.

"You arrogant...little…"

Kanjana forced the dropship down even lower and through a complex series of rocky arches and valleys. Both spacecraft left a wake of heated dust behind them as they banked and rolled through impossibly tight gaps. The gun battle abated for a short time until they moved out into a more open section. Kanjana made a subtle course correction and then reversed the engines.

"Here we go!"

The change in velocity was massive, and if it hadn't been for the thick straps, she would have been thrown against the windscreen. For a brief moment, the Anicinàbe slipped past, and then she hit the burn mode. Unknown to the fighter pilot, there was nothing but a jagged outcrop of rock in front of them. The dropship narrowly avoided crashing as it pulled away. The fighter was ripped to shreds by the impact. At the same time, the final few rounds from the automatic cannons struck her other engine, and this time the damage was severe.

"What was that?"

The dropship lurched to the right and quickly lost speed. Kanjana knew right away she was in trouble. A glance at the navigation screen showed the location of the capital Montu, the mountain range, the track system, and the Byotai enclave of Caldos. The latter was the only location flagged by her sister as safe.

"Very well, Caldos, here we come. Let's hope the locals are friendly."

The dropship groaned as if it was trying to remove a painful projectile, when in fact it was barely staying airborne. Using every trick she knew, Kanjana somehow levelled the craft and plotted a slowly descending course to Caldos. Then, and only then, did she break radio silence.

"Mayday, mayday. This is Haywire. I've been heavily damaged, need assistance."

After doing a mental translation, she repeated the message in broken Byotai. Unlike the others, she was natively fluent, at least partially in Byotai. Red warning lights came on as a fire broke out on the number two engine.

"Haywire, we receive you."

Kanjana exhaled in relief at hearing the sound of Arana.

"Land near the enclave. They will be waiting for you."

Another explosion ripped the cowling off her engines, and she found the dropship coming down fast. The hills between her and the enclave were now impassable, so she banked hard, trading height for speed and turned back toward the signs of battle.

"Fair enough, in that case fire support is what I'll bring."

As her course altered, she found herself looking at the long raised section, out in the open and between the two tunnels leading into the mountains. On one side were the large numbers of Spires soldiers and aircraft, most of which had now landed to disgorge the rest of their soldiers. On the other side of the track was a widely dispersed formation of fast moving ground vehicles. Many were small, but she counted plenty of larger wheeled vehicles, each bristling with warriors.

"Let's see what we can do."

# CHAPTER FIFTEEN

*Many still argue that there is little need for fighter pilots to train for close range combat. Missiles can destroy a target a hundred kilometres away in an atmosphere, and thousands of kilometres in space. Even so, in the hectic environment of actual combat, there are numerous examples of where the skill and agility of these men and women proved once and for all, that weaponry was just one of the components of an effective combat fighter. The great battle of Proxima, Euryale, and the Black Rift were just a handful where fighters made a difference. Guns and missiles retain their uses, even after hundreds of years of development.*

*Fighter Combat for Beginners*

**Maglev Rail Network, Khagi District, Karnak**

Spartan was on his back, and four Spires soldiers held him down. A fifth pointed a handgun at his face. This one had cast aside his robes so that his light armour was plain to see. Spartan tried to move, but unlike Vanguard armour, the M-3B was completely unpowered.

All that gave him strength was his own muscles, and using just one arm he relaxed it, just to catch him off guard.

One of the Spires soldiers lost his balance, and Spartan yanked him to the ground. The unfortunate warrior hit the ground headfirst and was knocked out cold.

"I'm not finished!"

Spartan tensed his arms and forced himself up from the ground. He didn't get far, but it was enough to send the Spires soldiers into a panic. Another ran in to help, but Spartan threw him aside and tried to sit up. His stomach muscles groaned, but even the five of them couldn't keep him down. The commander was completely bald, save for red tinted goggles covering its eyes. Then, and only then, did Spartan know he was facing a female Spires soldier. She raged at him, pushed the barrel to the metal of his helmet, and screamed.

"Out of the way!"

The voice was loud and amplified electronically. A metal leg crashed into the female commander, and she vanished over the other side of the rocks. The other soldiers turned their attention to their antagonist, giving Spartan just the time he needed.

"Yeah!"

He'd broken the neck of one Spire as he rose to his feet, before the metal machine blasted four of them with shoulder-mounted coilguns. One tried to run past it, but a second machine stepped in his way and cut him clean in half. Spartan grabbed a rifle from one of the fallen soldiers and looked up at the two machines. Dust swirled around them as they dealt destruction with their powerful guns.

"Khan?"

It wasn't easy to see through the dust, but the shapes of two massive metal warriors encased in their customised Jötnar Assault Suits was an all too familiar sight. These were effectively airtight armoured bodies that encased the Jötnar. They were unpowered, but that was no issue for them. Unlike the equipment CTC had been working on, they looked more like crude medieval soldiers, but scaled up to the size of a mythical troll.

Both were standing apart, their legs planted firmly to the ground. They opened fire with such intensity it felt like fifty soldiers were firing at once. Khan paused for just a moment and shouted via his external speakers.

"Spartan, there's something back there for you."

Khan then laughed, the sound of his voice booming out into the battle.

"I don't know how, but the ground drop work! I thought we'd be killed by the impact."

He pointed behind him to where the dust cloud was thickest. Spartan didn't hesitate and ran past his friend, smacking his lightly armoured fist against Khan's arm as he did so. A short distance behind were two more suits, one completely static, yet upright and waiting. The other was up the short slope to the track and had crashed into the train, and was half jammed inside it. Spartan moved to the upright one. As soon as he was within three metres, the front opened up.

"The Maverick suit."

Shapes moved behind it, and he grabbed for his carbine. He pulled the trigger just as the first of the CD1 Grunts came right at him. He should have recognised the shapes, but for that brief moment they were just more Spires soldiers. The weapon hissed, but did no more, and as he saw what they were, he sighed happily.

*Out of ammo, just as well!*

Only then did it actually occur to him that they were

friendly. Two ran past him, forming up on the flanks of Khan and Olik. They moved quickly and opened fire right away, with neither saying a word to him. Spartan shook his head in surprise and then stepped into the Maverick armour. At once his own armour connected to the control nodes with a gentle clunking sound, and he felt his limbs relax as the powered armour system took up the strain from his battered and damaged body. The adrenalin, mixed with the suit's drugs had taken the edge of his injuries, but this was a much better way of keeping him in the fight. The overlay system connected to the other warriors as well as the Grunts, and even to the single dropship that was now out of sight. He took a step away to join the fight, and then remembered what had been happening prior to their arrival.

*Gun!*

Spartan turned around and clambered up the slope. He was an easy shot for the enemy from there, and shots were already striking his armour. The onboard computer tracked the approach vectors, and the automated left shoulder gun mount returned fire. Spartan didn't even need to issue the command. It was a fully automated defensive measure.

He looked left and right, finding his friend via the thermal imaging. Gun was leaning against the carriage, beset on all sides by Red Scars soldiers. General Daniels was on his back and firing a handgun, and there was no sign of Syala.

*Not good.*

"I'm coming!"

Spartan began at a walk, increasing in pace and dropping down just metres away from his wounded comrade. Inside the armour they were now of a similar size and build.

342

"Spartan!" Gun groaned.

One of the Red Scars leapt off a vehicle and ran up to Gun with a pack of warriors. Most carried carbines and shotguns, but the leader had a massive harpoon weapon. The attack looked more like a beach assault; soldiers rushing up from their landing craft, except these landing craft were ground vehicles, many looking as though they'd been cobbled together in a scrapyard. The static providing covered fire for those in the open.

"I'm here."

Without stopping, Spartan took aim and fired. The onboard computer automatically activated the right shoulder weapon mount that contained a single XHEC-1, a High Energy Cannon prototype that looked much like an upscaled XC1 carbine. The first round blasted out, leaving a green trail and struck the group. Three Red Scars vanished in the blast of heat, and two staggered away with horrific burns.

"Yes!" Gun muttered.

*Faster!* Spartan thought.

Spartan waded into the group, swinging his fists left and right, butchering anybody coming in too close. Bodies crashed to the ground as they scattered at the sight of him. The enemy warrior with the huge harpoon weapon cleared the embankment, glanced at Spartan, and then took aim at Gun.

"No!" Spartan shouted.

He ducked to the right, smashed his fist into another soldier, and then jumped. It was a massive leap, and something he could never have done without the motor assistance of the Maverick armour. The metal lance rushed out and glanced off Spartan's arm as he landed in front of his friend. He aimed with his arms and blasted more warriors, but the one with the harpoon launcher was gone.

More Red Scars clambered up the ridge to the top of the track, and Spartan fired one shot after another at point blank range. The XHEC-1 was incredibly powerful but had a slow rate of fire. With each shot it became hotter and hotter, sending partially burnt flesh and blood all over his armour. Spartan tagged every target he could find, from the scores of Reed Scars swarming up the embankment to the dozens of ground vehicles still coming their way.

"I need help this side!"

Four of the Grunts moved into position, forming a loose line with ten metres between each of them amongst the wreckage of the train. The smaller robotic warriors took aim with their standard issue L52 carbines, the weapon more commonly used in the Marine Corps. Though nothing as powerful as the weapons on the Maverick suit, they were still powerful and made short work of so many of the enemy soldiers. It was enough to keep the top clear for now, but did nothing to stop the overwhelming numbers still not yet in the fight. The robotic drones took multiple hits, but with no flesh inside them, they could fight until destroyed or disabled.

"How badly hurt are you?"

There was no response, and Spartan twisted around to check his friend, fearing the worse. Instead, he found an empty space. Gun was gone. Spartan swallowed uncomfortably and didn't even notice as a rifle round struck his head. The armour sent out an alert, but luckily for him, the penetration only managed to open up a crack in the plating. The left shoulder mount had already tracked the aggressor and blasted away with thirty rounds. Spartan then saw Gun further back at the carriage, pulling at the crashed armour.

"You fool. Keep your head down."

Rockets and projectiles rained down from all directions, and the continuous plinking sound of rounds bouncing off the Maverick armour reminded Spartan that just one could end this fight. He stepped back three steps but continued firing on the enemy. Now that the Grunts could handle the embankment, he turned his fire on the vehicles. The smaller ones were quickly crippled, but the larger ones had stopped a short distance away to create an improvised laager.

*We can't hold this for much longer.*

Behind this furious assault more warriors were spreading out, trying to flank the defenders on both sides. Overhead a trio of Spires Hornets strafed the train. Some of the shots hit Red Scars soldiers, but at least one of the Grunts took a direct hit to the torso. It triggered a series of small blasts and left it a burning hulk. Spartan's left shoulder mount automatically tracked the aircraft and hammered them with short bursts of coilgun fire.

"I'm back," said Gun in relief.

Spartan watched as somehow the insane creature had pulled the JAS armour from the wreckage and dragged it upright. He clambered into the unit, and the weapons activated almost immediately. Spartan nearly laughed when he saw the Gatling guns fitted to the arms.

"Just like old times, my friend."

That was the moment Khan and Olik withdrew to the train. They moved back, one step at a time, never turning their back on the hundreds of Spires soldiers. Spartan hadn't felt as comfortable and relaxed for many years.

In that single moment, all four of them were together. "Watch out!" Khan said.

He ducked down as one of the Red Scars wheeled vehicles raced up the embankment and crashed into the side of the destroyed rail engine. One warrior leapt out and hit Spartan, sending both down the embankment.

Dozens of Red Scars leapt out, but these were different to those before. They wore extra heavy armour, with plating on their arms. In their hands each carried a two-handed weapon. It was a combination between a glaive and a thermal shotgun. A CD1 Grunt took a blast from two of them before they charged.

"Stop them!"

Gun and Khan rushed amongst them, swinging their arms with the inbuilt semi-circular blades cutting deeply into them. At the same time, they blazed away with their firearms. Olik slid down the dust gradient and grabbed the fallen Spartan and forced him to his feet.

"Fight, brother. It's not over yet."

More soldiers ran at them, and Spartan didn't even bother aiming. One shot after another from the XHEC-1 made a cruel mess of any that came too close. At that moment, the Red Scars shifted tactics and brought in massed gunfire from the scores of vehicles scattering the open space near the train. Guns, rockets, and missile systems all sent their deadly ammunition into the fight.

"Alert, aircraft."

Spartan looked up. Two Hornets were coming in for a strafing run. He tagged them, and the computer began calculating their vector. He ignored the computer and fired two shots in quick succession. Both were perfectly aligned and destroyed them in bright green explosions.

The wreckage came down on those trying to climb the embankment, instantly killing five more warriors.

"Look, they are bringing more to the party. Are they insane?"

Spartan looked in the direction of Olik's arm. Two more armoured vehicles slid to a halt, and more of the heavily armoured Red Scars warriors leapt out. Behind them came a small group of three large animals the size of an Earth elephant, but reptilian and hairy. They were dull red in colour, with a dark pattern, almost like tiger stripes. The heads were large, and their mouths filled with deadly looking teeth. Among them was a tall individual, resplendent in coloured armour and severed hands hanging about his neck. He carried firearms in each hand and rode a creature like some ancient noble.

"Yeah, looks like a commander to me. Either way, you're not going to be leading for much longer."

Spartan laughed and shook his head. He'd never seen such a majestic looking enemy before, or one that seemed quite so primitive. He activated his primary weapon, but it refused to respond. The thermal overloads warning activated again, and he cursed loudly. He switched to the arm-mounted L52 coilguns. They felt puny in comparison, but it was enough to hurt them still. The creatures howled, a painful, agonising scream, and then charged at them like fleshy battering rams. Olik yanked backwards, twisted about, and fell over. A whole pack of the Anicinàbe warhounds leapt from the train wreckage and atop of Olik. They were ferocious, and soon he was buried under them, yet still shooting and stabbing.

"Human!" hissed the commander.

Spartan stabbed at the creatures around Olik, but his

friend was on his feet and fighting back. Other Red Scars warriors clambered up to join the battle with Khan, while Gun appeared briefly at the top still firing, before he vanished again behind a group of warriors. This left just Spartan alone to face the Red Scars commander and his entourage of mounted beasts, and right now, he relished that opportunity.

"Okay, alien, let's do this."

They circled Spartan, the beasts snarling and snapping at him. He expected a close quarter fight, but instead the whole group opened fire at close-range. Even the Maverick armour had a hard time, and one of his blades and the XHEC-1 cannon was ripped from its mounting. His chest was hit four times before he could return fire. The L52 assault carbines did their work, and he blasted away at them while striding towards the enemy commander. The first charged hard into his flank, and he groaned under the impact. It was so powerful that even though he dug his feet firmly into the ground, he was still pushed back several metres.

"Enough!"

Bringing his right arm down, he swung upwards in a powerful uppercut that would have removed the head of any creature he'd met before. The impact hit with a crash, and the creature twisted off to his right. Seizing the opportunity, Spartan leapt ahead and took aim at the commander. He fired with both of the carbines on his arms, hitting the creature and rider with dozens of rounds. To Spartan's surprise, the thing lifted up onto its hind legs and struck out at him with its strong limbs.

"What?"

He staggered back, as the thing in front attacked him

like a boxer. The limbs struck as hard as siege hammers. To make matters worse, the rider leaned over and blasted his left shoulder with gunfire. He twisted to the right, putting the creature's head between the two of them, and then took another blow to the centre torso.

Spartan took two steps back and activated the hammers in his arms. The bulging lumps of metal pushed out where his hands were, instantly changing the shape of his arms into what looked like a pair of heavy maces. The creature turned back to face him; the other two moved in on each side. All the riders were sporting powerful looking guns, and they were pointing at his head. Spartan swallowed and adjusted his stance.

*Good times.*

He braced himself for the blows, but instead came a long, monotonous tone. It was so loud the nearest creature looked to the side for a split second. Spartan didn't bother checking what it was and charged forward at the beast, striking out wildly.

"Come on!"

He crashed into the thing and pushed it back three metres. This time he brought up one arm after another in a continuous series of blows. Each one groaned under the pressure of the impacts until finally the creature staggered and collapsed to one side. The rider leapt off, and the other two moved in to protect him. Spartan pointed at the hidden figure.

"You're next!"

Again the horn blared, and Spartan used it as a signal for him to attack. This time the creatures were ready, and as he struck one, the other leapt at his flank, caught his arm in its mouth, and forced him down to one knee.

* * *

Kanjana took her eye off the forward view for just a second, but when she returned, it looked as though they would crash at any moment. Gunfire rose up around her from the forces on the ground, and the strikes sounded like the patter of light rain on the hull. She took aim at a column of four-wheeled vehicles and opened fire. The hull-mounted coilguns rattled away, sending a long burst into their thin armour. It was a short pass, but hitting back even once made her feel better.

"Right, time to get this baby on the ground."

"Haywire, this is Arana, are you receiving me?"

Kanjana was silence for a second.

"I read you. What's your status?"

There was a short crackle, followed by the serious tones of Arana.

"We can see you're in trouble. Set your bird down at this location. We'll take care of the rest."

A loud whistling sound cut the signal.

"Damned jammers."

She checked the navigation screen and tagged the location. It was near the rail track, but closer to the Caldos side of the tunnels.

*Why does she want me to land there?*

Her gut instinct was to move as far from the scene of battle, but Arana was a known source, and she had spent time with the Byotai. Even though she had doubts, she used the last remaining power cells and changed the landing vector for the dropship. No sooner had she lined up when another stabiliser failed.

"Okay, people, we're going to hit. Time to get ready."

She leaned to the right and slammed her open palm down on the cylinder access control. The mercenaries were disconnected from the system, and they climbed out of their cylinder and into the passenger area.

"Twenty seconds, get ready."

The first two looked to her, nodded, and moved to the clamp units. At the same time, the heavily armed soldiers checked their weapons and gear. Their priority was the clamps as the dropship shook violently. One opened his visor and called out to her.

"Why not leave us in there? The Grunts need our control."

Kanjana still had the narrow triple access hatch opened so they could see her. She pointed directly ahead.

"Because we are coming down near the fighting."

She looked back and shouted.

"Be ready, or be dead!"

The dropship moved closer and closer to the ground until nothing but a few metres separated them from the rock and dirt. Just before they hit the ground, Kanjana hit the reverse thrusters for the last time. The massive boost dropped their airspeed. It made a difference, but it didn't feel like it when they made contact. The dropship bounced three times before sliding hundreds of metres until eventually stopping.

"Everybody out, now!"

Kanjana jumped from her seat, activated her own visor to close, and pulled a pistol from the mount next to where she'd been sitting. Two of the mercenaries were already at the port hatch and hit the release. The small units blasted out, and they jumped into the warm atmosphere. Kanjana did the same and was followed by the other four. As she hit the ground, she saw for the first time quite how much damage the dropship had sustained in the descent. The entire hull was burnt and pockmarked with hundreds of bullet holes.

"She's one tough bird," said one of the mercenaries.

"Yeah, you could say that."

"Look," said another.

They all turned away from the craft and to the direction of the battle. It was nearly a kilometre away, yet it seemed right next to them. Smoke blotted out the skyline, and gunfire and explosions rippled along the low ridge. Kanjana was the last of them to see the four Hornets coming toward them. One of the mercenaries grabbed her and threw her down behind a low line of rocks.

"We've got company."

The aircraft came in low and dropped off their three squads of Spires soldiers who opened fire immediately. The fourth came in low but then exploded in a bright yellow flash.

"What the hell?"

The sound of gunfire was blotted out by the sound of engines and heavy machinery. Kanjana looked to her left as a six-wheeled heavy transport skidded to a halt. At the same time, a massive land train steamed past and continued on to the battle. A soldier jumped down from the transport and opened her visor.

"Arana?"

She smiled at the Helion.

"Ready to end this?"

The six mercenaries had already climbed aboard to join their leader, and Kanjana needed little further encouragement. She moved to the ladder attached to the side and pulled herself up. Inside was an odd group of old Byotai, all of which carried a mixture of weapons.

"Who are they?"

The oldest of the Byotai spoke, and Arana listened before explaining, only after her own circuits did the work for her. He wore a strangely quilted set of armour, and the rings on his limbs gleamed in the early morning sunlight.

"I am Kras, and we are the Caldos militia."

A pair of massive horns fitted to the land train blared away. The noise was deafening, and each time it sounded, the Byotai cheered and shouted. She moved to the side of the vehicle and looked ahead to the scene of the battle. They were travelling thirty metres from the top of the rail line and parallel to the tracks. Other Byotai vehicles had spread out and were moving down both sides of the line.

"Incredible."

Arana laughed.

"Yes, I never once thought I would be in a Byotai cavalry charge."

Again the horns blared, and then everything changed. The warriors aboard moved to the sides of the open-topped section and began firing. Kanjana looked out from the left and spotted squads of Red Scars soldiers scattering. A Byotai four-wheeled passenger vehicle crashed into one of the larger Red Scars vehicles. There was no explosion, and the Byotai were already spilling out and wading in to fight them with guns and improvised hand weapons.

"Use it," said Arana.

Kanjana looked back at her and followed her eyes to the shape of a cylindrical weapon fitted to the side of the transport area. It was short, much like an ancient swivel gun and attached to a u-shaped mount.

"Got it."

Kanjana swung the unit around and aimed at four Red Scars soldiers climbing over a fallen CD1 Grunt robot. A squeeze of the trigger released a blast of white smoke, and the target vanished in the cloud. She looked back at Arana.

"Gunpowder, really?"

Arana bent down and pulled out a Byotai hunting rifle. With a smooth movement, she threw it over.

"Keep it up."

Kanjana returned to her shooting, and the other Byotai did the same. She took aim at any targets of opportunity, but it was already clear that both the Spires and the Red Scars were falling back. All that remained were their aircraft.

"What about them?"

Arana nodded toward the Byotai.

"Thanks to the General, they are not much of an issue."

On cue, a flash of light was followed by a smoke trail as a pair of surface-to-air missiles launched from the land train. One exploded too far away, but the second hit the engine, and it spun away out of control. They were now in the thick of the fight, and just before they reached the burnt engine of the train the vehicle skidded to a halt.

Arana leapt down from the vehicle, Kanjana and a dozen Byotai hot on her heels. They clambered up the embankment and to what little remained of the train. Scores of bodies lay about, but two were slumped against the side of a carriage. Both were still firing away to the North. She ran as fast as she could, ignoring gunfire.

"Syala!"

Her sister turned around and took aim before spotting her twin. She lifted up to one leg, using her left arm to support her weight just as Arana reached her. There was no embrace though, as a dozen more Red Scars were moving amongst the wreckage. The Byotai ran past, and at least two fell from gunfire. Kanjana joined them, but she continued to look furtively for the others.

"Spartan, Khan?"

General Daniels nodded to his right and down to where the Red Scars assault had ground to a halt. Kanjana didn't say a word. She slid down and began running into the mist. Syala looked to her sister and grimaced.

"Help her."

Arana nodded and moved away to give chase.

* * *

"Duck!"

Spartan dropped down to his haunches as a metal arm swung overhead. He rose to find Gun and Khan at his flanks. The armour of both of them was covered in bullet holes, yet neither was slowed down by the fight. Gun stepped in and grabbed one of the creatures about the throat. Even with his huge arms, he needed to use both to do the job.

"We'll take this one," said Khan.

He moved to the left, jabbed at the monster, and then grabbed one of its front legs. Spartan jumped to the right, ducked past its head, and leapt up, using every ounce of power from the suit. He rose up to a height slightly above its head and took aim. The rider didn't even see him as he put a dozen rounds into his head. Spartan hit the ground, shortly followed by the corpse of the rider.

"Put it on the ground," he yelled to Khan.

Using all of his effort, Khan managed to destabilise the creature, and Spartan pushed hard to tip it on its side. At the same time, Gun pulled his own foe along and proceeded to smash its head against the side of a wrecked vehicle.

"Khan, watch out."

Spartan spotted the enemy behind the creatures lifting some type of heavy weapon from the wreckage of a Red Scars vehicle. It was so big that two other warriors helped support its weight as it took aim. Spartan moved to protect his friend, but distraction proved enough for the creature to jump up from the ground and smash Khan aside.

*This is it.*

Spartan stared down the barrel of the weapon, and at the face of both the rider less creature and the Red Scars leader. Instead of firing, he removed his mask to show a pale skinned warrior with a sickening grin. That terrible horn sounded again, but it was a lot louder now.

From the mist lurched the shape of an odd-looking land crawler. It had been hastily armoured, and along the top were dozens of Byotai. It crashed into the flank of the creature and kept on pushing until the two ended up as a mess of broken metal and flesh.

Gun was till busy smashing his own enemy as the Red Scar leader nodded slowly. The weapon fired, and a hardened metal dart blasted out. Spartan lifted his arms to block the projectile, but it punched through the left arm and embedded deep into his chest.

"Bastards!"

The impact was so great that he fell back to one knee,

and then tipped over onto his side. The motor system shorted out, and now the only way he could move was to use his own body. Spartan lifted his left arm with great effort and took aim at the commander. The gun system bleated a warning failure, and at that point he knew it was over. That was not going to stop him, though. Even without power, he forced himself to his feet, barely able to move the partially seized armoured joints.

"I'm not done yet."

The face on the Red Scars commander was all the reward he needed. At the same time, one of his comrades had pushed another reload pack onto the weapon.

"Hey!"

The voice wasn't his. It was female and tinged with the alien tongue of the Anicinàbe.

*Kanjana?*

A single hole appeared in the chest of the commander, and he slumped to his knees. His comrades spun about as Arana and a horde of Byotai ran amongst them. Some fought, but most of them turned and ran.

Gunshots flashed everywhere. Kanjana and Arana moved to the right with a number of their heavily armoured mercenaries. Spartan watched them move to the creature Gun was fighting.

*Good timing, damned good timing!*

He turned his attention back to his tormentor and licked his parched lips. He had just one objective. He dragged his heavy feet until he was in front of the mortally wounded warrior. Then he hit the release button, and the front shell hatches opened, at the same time snapped the tip of the lance from his chest. It pulled out of both sets of armour with a whooshing sound.

Spartan stumbled out and landed in front of the Red Scar. His armour was a mess, and blood ran freely from the wound that had penetrated through both the Maverick armour and his PDS suit. He moved again, but his left leg gave way, and he dropped down in front of his enemy. All power had failed in the PDS armour, and he was forced to open the visor, just to get air into his lungs.

"I am Ogimà Takosk, of the Red..."

Spartan coughed, and blood pumped out from his chest. He looked to the alien and laughed.

"Son, I don't give a damn."

The Red Scars leader blinked twice, pulling his head back a little in surprise.

"Who...are...you?"

The translator the alien carried was nowhere as advanced as those Spartan had used in the past. It paused with each word, and yet bore no emotion. Not that he cared, because at that moment he noticed the alien had his gun pointed at his face.

He began to laugh and looked to his left. The enemy made the mistake of looking there, to see nothing but Gun still wrestling the creature. When he returned his gaze, Spartan's arm was touching the gun. It went off, but Spartan had already pushed it aside. He locked the warrior's arm, snapped it, and then ripped the pistol from his limp limb. In one smooth motion, he turned the weapon back around and pointed at his face.

"My name...is Spartan."

He fired a single shot between the enemy's eyes. The alien snapped back and hit the ground, flat on his back. Spartan then dropped slowly to the ground. Blood loss injury and fatigue finally proving more than even his body could handle. As his eyes darkened, he started to relax, and the pain faded.

# EPILOGUE

*The glory days of the Private Security contractors were long past up, to and during the Great Biomech War. Too many botched missions and illegal operations had led to a massive loss of confidence in the system. The organisations were not banned, but the awarding of contracts for Alliance protection was cancelled, and with this, the largest companies collapsed overnight. Those that remained either provided security to the private sector, or set up for unregistered operations for whichever clients would pay the going rate. These black market mercenaries could be found protecting organisations, as well as moving illegal goods and services through the Alliance.*

*CTC would attempt to change this for the first time by working alongside the Alliance military to create a new combat formation, one built upon the technology of the private sector, but with the resources of the Alliance and its expanded territories. This would become the much-vaunted Interstellar Assault Brigade.*

*Private Security Directory*

## ANS X-45 'Titan', Low Orbit, Karnak

Spartan opened his eyes. He was lying down on a bed in a

white room filled with bright lights. He spotted a pair of Thegns to his right, and his first instinct was to reach for them. As his arm lifted, he spotted Syala waiting near the wall. She wore a hardened cast on her left arm, and a tight bandage around her head and down to one ear.

"You're awake," she said excitedly.

She moved close and leaned down over the bed. Spartan looked at her and waited for a moment for his eyes to adjust. He tried to speak, but his mouth was dry and hoarse. Syala pushed a cup to his mouth. He took a few swallows, licked his mouth, and slowly lifted himself off the bed. There were tubes attached, and all of them popped out with a disconcerting sound.

"Hey, what are you doing?"

Spartan lowered his feet to the floor, tensed his legs, and then stood up. Arana came in, shaking her head.

"You crazed fool. I guess you want to check on your friends?"

Spartan nodded and followed the two sisters out of the small room and into a larger one that adjoined it. A Thegn was treating one of the mercenaries that had a head wound. At the other end were the three he was looking for. Khan and Gun were upright, though both covered in dressings. Olik was on an improvised bed made from three military stretchers.

"Spartan?" Khan asked.

All three looked at him, but Khan grabbed Spartan and squeezed him happily, much to Spartan's discomfort. He almost passed out from the pain but somehow remained standing. Gun remained with the badly wounded Olik, but gave him the biggest smile he'd seen in days. The door hissed open, and in came the familiar form of General

Daniels. His bloodied face had been cleaned up, but like most of them, he was still bruised and looked a little worse for wear. He stopped in front of Spartan and cleared his throat before speaking.

"I see you're up. That was quicker than expected."

Spartan already recognised the medical quarters of the ship, and that could only mean they were back aboard the Titan.

"We did it?"

"Spartan, General Makos arrived after we cleared the rail sector. He's brought with him a small army and has landed to support Caldos and the other remaining outposts. They are beginning to fight back."

"Yeah," said Gun, "But with Makos there, they will not let Karnak go easily."

"Makos?"

"Yes," said Kanjana, "He escorted Titan in so the Colonel could send in another dropship by remote."

Spartan dreaded his next question, but he had to know. "Our losses?"

Arana closed her eyes and looked to her sister before answering.

"Three of my mercenaries are dead. " She looked over to the three Jötnar, "Olik and Gun are still being treated for multiple injuries…not that you could tell."

Khan lifted up his left hand.

"And I lost a damned finger."

Spartan had to stop himself laughing at the last part.

Arana sighed before continuing.

"The Byotai lost eleven killed, and twice that number are wounded."

General Daniels rested his chin in his hands.

"Spartan...Caldos is secure, and the Spires have fallen back to their base at Montu. The Red Scars are scattered, but they are far from gone. Tahkeome will not be happy about this, and we are expecting escalation."

Spartan rubbed at his eyes and swallowed, doing his best not to retch. His body had been pumped with drugs, and not even his physique was able to withstand their effect for long. The other looked at him with concern, but he soon steadied himself and lifted his hand.

"I'm all right. Did we make a difference?"

General Daniels nodded quickly.

"Definitely. The remaining enclaves have declared for Makos and his mutineers. He brought ten ships, along with the crew and some of the regular soldiers from the Byotai shipyards, without orders. That, with the news of the victory is making one hell of a difference."

"What?" Spartan asked, incredulously.

"That's right," said Daniels, "Makos has declared the Tenth Quadrant independent, and they are calling on the Alliance to honour our old agreement. They won't rejoin the Empire until real support is sent to the outposts from their homeworlds."

Spartan continued shaking his head and stumbled a little. Syala grabbed his arm and held him.

"He needs rest. I'll take him back to his room."

Khan grabbed his arm and squeezed it one last time.

"It was a good fight, Spartan. Get fixed. We'll be going back soon, I'm sure."

Spartan and Syala moved back to his smaller room, and as they reached the door, he looked back at them. Arana and the General both looked stern and concerned, but Gun and Khan seemed positively excited. The General had just one last thing to say before he also left.

"Spartan, I will be reporting to Alliance High Command shortly. They will want a full debriefing, and I suspect Karnak and the entire quadrant will be the first thing on the docket."

He was at the door when he stopped and looked back to Gun and then to Spartan.

"Something tells me this Interstellar Assault Brigade of yours is going to get the thumbs up. And I have little doubt where they will be heading when they're ready."

With that he was gone, and Spartan was left looking at Gun and Khan.

"It never stops, does it?"

They moved a little further as he nodded back at them. They still seemed to be far happier than they had any right to be.

"Really, what are those two like?"

Syala waved her hand over the door security control, and the door hissed open. She helped him inside, and Spartan slumped onto the bed.

"They haven't seen action for a long time. Now they think we're back in business. This Brigade of yours has been years in the making, hasn't it?"

Syala turned around, and it looked like she was leaving. But she placed her hand on the control, and the door shut. She looked at Spartan.

"How about you?"

Spartan grinned through the pain.

"Syala, I'm ready for anything. I promise you."

She gave him a coy smile and moved towards him.

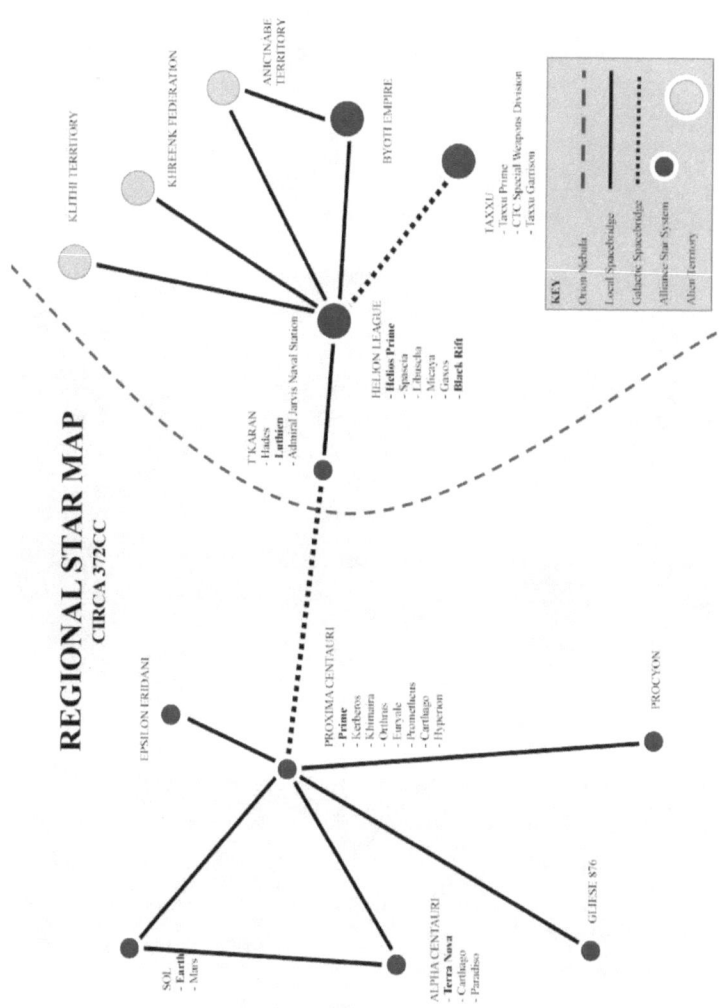

# REGIONAL STAR MAP
## CIRCA 372CC

KLUTH TERRITORY

KURENK FEDERATION

ANCTNABE TERRITORY

BYCOT EMPIRE

T'KARAN
- Hades
- **Lothien**
- Admiral Jarvis Naval Station

HELION LEAGUE
- **Helios Prime**
- Spascia
- Librescha
- Miezya
- Gavos
- **Black Rift**

TAXXU
- Taxxu Prime
- CTC Special Weapons Division
- Taxxu Garrison

EPSILON ERIDANI

PROXIMA CENTAURI
- **Prime**
- Kerberos
- Khimaira
- Orthus
- Euryale
- Prometheus
- Carthago
- Hyperion

PROCYON

SOL
- **Earth**
- Mars

ALPHA CENTAURI
- **Terra Nova**
- Carthago
- Paradiso

GLIESE 876

**KEY**

Orion Nebula

Local Spacebridge

Galactic Spacebridge

Alliance Star System

Alien Territory

367